MATTHEW DOBBS, ESQUIRE

BY

JOHN M. BREWER

∞ INFINITY
PUBLISHING

Copyright © 2011 by John M. Brewer
Cover Illustration by Colin Campbell, www.colincampbellstudios.com

ISBN 0-7414-6569-8
Library of Congress Control Number: 2011925723

Printed in the United States of America

Published August 2011

∞

INFINITY PUBLISHING
1094 New DeHaven Street, Suite 100
West Conshohocken, PA 19428-2713
Toll-free (877) BUY BOOK
Local Phone (610) 941-9999
Fax (610) 941-9959
Info@buybooksontheweb.com
www.buybooksontheweb.com

To Mary Sue: music, laughter and love

CONTENTS

I. NORFOLK

The train was not moving, but despite the quiet, I was having a hard time getting to sleep, lying on one of the seats of our compartment. I would doze off and either Mother or Father would say something. Doze again, and the other would reply. If anyone else had been present, I wouldn't have been able to lie down at all but I resented being constantly wakened in this way.

The train began to move and now the noise and motion of our carriage was added. Still, I must have fallen asleep, for suddenly everything turned on its side, there was a great noise, and I was pinned by an enormous weight. I couldn't move anything and began to scream, not very loudly, for it was very hard to breathe, but I became frantic, for I could not move at all.

This went on and on. I didn't understand what was happening, but now it was very hot and I could smell burning. Now glass was breaking and there were voices and I began crying for my mother and father. The great weight was shifted and I heard a man say, "This one's alive" and another voice said to get him out, fast, as the fire was spreading. Finally a hand grabbed my jacket and began pulling me up. As my arms came free, I began swinging them, and finally my legs were free though one shoe came off. I was grabbed by another pair of hands, and set out in some grass. There was fire in the carriage, and I saw one of the men shake his head for some reason.

Now people were asking me if I was all right, and I said I suppose so but I began looking for Mother and Daddy. I did not see them, and when I asked about them, everyone looked away.

* * *

It was two days later, and I was standing, still wearing only one shoe, with people I didn't know watching two boxes, coffins,

1

being set in holes in the ground, and Mother and Father were locked in those and couldn't get out and I began crying again, thinking how awful it would be to be locked in a box so I could not move at all or do anything to free myself.

* * *

I was in a house with more people I didn't know. The man, who seemed short and slight even to my four year old eyes, said he was the Reverend Paston. A lady who was even shorter and slighter, whom I took to be Reverend Paston's wife, asked me my name. I said, "Matthew Dobbs, ma'am." She then asked how old I was, and I said, "Four, ma'am." There was also a larger, motherly-like lady, who said she was Mrs Christianson, and would I like something to eat. I said yes and was led to the kitchen, and given some soup and toast. I ate some and then asked Mrs Christianson where Mother and Father and my little brother or sister that was to be born were, and she said I would not be seeing them again in this life, but would rejoin them in the next. At this moment, I realized they were dead and I was alone and my tears began again.

Mrs Christianson gave me a pair of shoes, worn and too large, but she said I would "grow into 'em." My remaining one disappeared. My hosts showed me where I was to sleep: a very small room with a narrow cot and a very large wardrobe – somehow I knew this was its name – nearly filling the floor space.

The room I was to sleep in seemed very cold. I had the feeling I had come from a place that was sunny and warm, a feeling I associated with my mother and father, and here it was cold, windy and rainy. I was to wear a nightshirt, the man told me, but since it was so cold I didn't want to. So at nightfall I kept my clothes on, crept out as soon as I dared and searched the house until I found a room used for storing things, furniture and boxes and chests.

One part of me wanted to hide in a small, concealed space but another very much wanted me to have as free a use of my arms and legs as possible. The best spot seemed to be on top of another large wardrobe much like the one in my room, only here there was much more room on top, so once I climbed on top I could stretch out and try to sleep. It was very dusty and dirty, as was everything in that room, so I lay on my back to avoid, as much as possible, getting anything in my throat that would cause me to cough or sneeze. I wanted to be as quiet as possible. Sometimes I could hear voices, calling me or the man, but I paid no attention.

* * *

By day I would go outside and wander. My sleeping place made me dusty and dirty, which prompted concern from the cook and disgust from Mr Paston, who I was told was the vicar. However, since my wanderings also made me dusty and dirty, no one seemed to realize where I was sleeping.

* * *

I liked going outside. When clear of the house, I could walk and walk. Sometimes I ran, as hard as I could, thinking that perhaps if I ran fast enough, I would catch up with Mother and Daddy and my unborn brother or sister. Once, I fancied I could see them, shining white and holding their arms open for me. But the ground was hard, even when it was sandy and I grew out of breath and had to stop and the vision faded.

* * *

I was always hungry. I stayed in the kitchen, when I wasn't outside, as much as possible, sitting in a chair in the corner with a box nearby. The cook frequently baked something called "pasties", which she informed me was the national dish of Cornwall, where she came from. I wasn't aware Cornwall was a nation, but the meagre amounts of food allowed me prompted her to make extra pasties and give me two or three. Also, since I wanted to be useful, I would go outside to the garden to pick some carrots and potatoes for the cook's use. Naturally, I began to pick considerably more than were strictly required, but the cook, Mrs Christianson, good-naturedly would wash the extra carrots and potatoes and I would sit in the corner eating these.

* * *

I was sitting on a chair in the kitchen while Mrs Christianson was preparing a meal. I had only the clothes I had on when the

3

carriage had overturned – everything else, apparently, had burned – and was very conscious of being dirty and sooty and smelly. I had made a habit of leaving the tiny room I was supposed to sleep in, and creeping to the room with the wardrobe and sleeping on its top. It had become less dirty and spider-webby and dusty over time – I realized eventually that was because I was cleaning the dirt and dust off with my clothes – and I could sleep on my crossed arms without worrying much about coughing. That left the bad dreams, which would awaken me. I hoped I wasn't making any noise, for I did not want to be discovered.

* * *

We were near the coast, in Norfolk, and Mrs Christianson said the North Sea was nigh. When the weather was fine, or rather less bad than usual, I went outside and turned inland. The ground was sandy and lumpy with big tufts of tall grasses, and I could easily hide but I did not know from whom or what. I came back for meals, of course.

* * *

I had begun to look through books, at first to find *a*'s and *the*'s, not a difficult task. When I asked to look at some of the books in the library in the house, Mrs Christianson insisted I wash my hands first, so I wouldn't mark the pages. It seemed there was a great deal of dust on the books, but I would open a volume and look for the only words I knew. Soon, however, I began to recognize other words, with Mrs Christianson's help, for she knew many (though not all) of them. After a while I could pronounce unfamiliar words, or make some venture at it, and began to read.

* * *

There were quite a few books, series by Dickens, Scott, Twain, and Austen (Mrs Christianson told me how the names on the ends were said). The first book I read, beginning to end, was *Great Expectations*. It took a very long time to get through it, and though I was disappointed at the ending, I went on to others.

* * *

I became aware that my presence was causing some disputes between Mr and Mrs Paston. He seemed to be looking for me often, especially at night, and this caused sharp words from his wife. I felt he was trying to shut me in something, confine me somehow, and I didn't want that. For these reasons, I began hiding from him more determinedly, even going outside, if the nights were dry, to sleep. I felt if I were not about, things would be easier, and I did not want to be the reason for any arguments. Mrs Christianson fed me – I was not allowed to eat with the Pastons, as I was so dirty – and asked me to weed the garden and of course bring in the vegetables required.

* * *

When spring came, the garden had to be planted and I was delighted to discover that I could plant as many carrots and potatoes as I wanted, and I realized for the first time that I could help relieve my hunger by my own efforts. I went into the chicken coop with Mrs Christianson to help collect eggs, though the roosters frightened me, and was given the task of removing the dung with a trowel and bucket. Eventually I discovered I could frighten the roosters off and that the dung, if turned into the sandy soil, resulted in bigger, better crops.

* * *

I had turned five, as nearly as I could judge, when Mr Paston told me a friend of his was to visit. He gave me the name of his friend but I forgot it right away. I was to have new clothes for the occasion, and Mr Paston said I was to be very, very nice to his friend. I had no idea what he meant, but was unenthusiastic, suspicious actually.

The clothes consisted of trousers and a shirt, both quite new, quite bright and when I tried them on in the room I was supposed to sleep in, very tight. It was hard to move in them, and I did not like that at all. So I resumed my normal clothes, dirty and worn but loose and managed to leave the house without being seen. I wandered and, as always, got rather grimy.

On my return, Mr Paston's friend, who was rather short and slight like Mr Paston himself, appeared very put out by my absence and even more annoyed by my appearance. He was disgusted in fact, said I wouldn't do at all, that I was from the gutter, and I could return there, and left. Mr Paston was very angry with me, and went on and on about ingratitude and disobedience and dumb insolence (for I said nothing, having nothing to say). I found that by looking fixedly in his eyes, he lost steam and eventually left the kitchen, which is where all this took place.

To my surprise, Mrs Christianson did not share his anger, rather seemed pleased and, in a way, proud of me. Mr Paston's friend, named Graves, was a lawyer who had made the Pastons my guardians according to Mrs Christianson. She did not seem to like him.

Mr Paston had wanted me and my clothes washed and there was a strange scene in which Mrs Paston and Christianson set out a tub of barely warm water in a small room, keeping the door blocked while I and my clothes were washed. I was kept in towels and a dress-like garment while the clothes dried.

* * *

As a result of urgings, mostly by Mrs Christianson, I began washing my hands and face more regularly. I also began bathing in the ocean, though this was always very cold, so I soaped myself and rinsed very quickly. For some reason, I didn't want anyone to see me doing this.

* * *

I had been given some clothes, as my original wear was worn out in many places, but the new clothes seemed worn themselves. I had begun sewing up holes and tears under Mrs Christianson's direction, so again began feeling as though I could help my own cause. Now I was told I would be going to school.

* * *

The school was a single room with a desk and a chair at the front, where a chalkboard was, and a number of benches. Many of the other students seemed huge to me, and some demanded money. On being told I had none, one boy demanded I get some from my parents. I told him my parents were dead. This gave him pause. Another boy asked for my lunch. I didn't have any, so everyone seemed unhappy with me.

We herded into the room when a bell was rung by the schoolmaster, a big unhappy-looking fellow. I looked at him with some interest, for my father was a schoolmaster taking up a post at a new school on that last disastrous journey. The schoolmaster, noting I was new, had me sit where the most ignorant pupil was. I had brought a slate and chalk and listened attentively.

The lessons in reading seemed easy after *Little Dorrit*, the book I was reading. Arithmetic was less familiar but at least I could see what was required and do the lesson. So by the end of the first day, I had moved upwards scholastically several seats. My reading was, it seemed, some years ahead of my age, though I did not know how to write anything. I resolved to work on the writing and counting. My cause was not helped by the fact that I favoured my left hand, the only one in the class who did so. The teacher took no notice, however.

* * *

By my calculations, I had turned seven. I couldn't remember my exact birthday or where we had come from or whether I had a middle name, but I was doing well in school; in the kitchen in the vicarage, I was working through Dickens and looking to start Scott. My handwriting was getting easier to read, thanks to working on it every day and arithmetic seemed simple, so I wondered at my fellow students who seemed to make such heavy going of it. I was careful not to say anything to them, or indeed much to anyone. I was a silent, sad little boy. Mrs Christianson was teaching me some simple cooking operations, chopping and cutting, so I was becoming helpful to her.

However, I heard Mr Paston's lawyer friend, the one who thought I really wouldn't do, was coming. I didn't want him to see me, so went quietly out the door – Mrs Christianson saw me, but said nothing – and went into the "tufty grassy" (as I called it) and hid. Mr Paston had sometimes come out in search of me, and I had learned how to keep out of sight: stay below the horizon, not leave obvious tracks and angle away from him. This time, the two of them seemed determined to find me, and I had to stay down, sometimes crawling, working myself into a very frightened state. A dozen times I thought they would see me but I made myself as small as possible behind bigger clumps of grass, keeping my hands and feet tucked in and being thankful my clothes were drab and, after a while, soiled. Eventually they went in, but I stayed out all night, eating carrots from the garden, rinsed off in a water barrel. Next morning, Mrs Christianson gave me some food and I went to school, still rather shaky. But no one said anything.

* * *

I had become ten by my calculations and on checking my own height, noticed that I was beginning to grow faster. I was already near Mr Paston's height and for a reason I could not precisely explain wanted to be taller and if possible stronger than him. I avoided being alone with him, and I had noticed that both Mrs Paston and Mrs Christianson were helpful in this. I had begun being more active in the kitchen, as I was now tall enough, though only just, to boil eggs and prepare the minces for Mrs Christianson's most noteworthy dish, the Cornish pasties. She herself was from that shire, and I was entrusted also with measuring the flour, lard and salt. I could also get the eggs unaided now, as I was no longer afraid of the roosters, but merely shooed them away. I cleaned the coop, turned the dung into fresh soil, and was the planter, weeder and harvester of vegetables from the garden. I still liked to eat raw carrots and potatoes while doing my reading, so I was not too thin or particularly hungry.

* * *

I was eleven now and growing rapidly. I was taller than Mr Paston and the lawyer but still avoided them. I began spending time with an old fisherman, George Japes, who had a rowboat that fascinated me, probably because I remembered the section in *Great Expectations* in which Pip, as an aspiring gentleman, learns to row. Since Mr Japes' boat generally was half-full of water, partly from rain, I started by bailing the boat. When the water was low enough, I would ask Mr Japes for the oars, which I would try to get into the oarlocks. They seemed very heavy and awkward indeed, but Japes was a very nice, patient man, and gradually I was able to actually pull one, then two oars. The boat was tied to a crumbling dock, and so I could eventually cause the boat to move using the oars, but it was all very slow work.

* * *

Becoming taller was a mixed experience: aside from greater dimensions, I had gotten too long for the top of the wardrobe; in fact I was a bit long for the cot where I was supposed to sleep. Eventually, I would every night move it to the door and set a box at its foot so I could stretch out. The door opened inward, so this meant the door was blocked while I slept. I liked this arrangement.

* * *

I was, and had been, the top reader in the school for some time, so was tasked with helping some of the new pupils. The older, larger boys seemed to be mostly waiting until they could leave, and the teacher let them be, as long as they weren't too disruptive or rude.

Actually, in my dealings with them, I gradually realized they had good qualities, moments of kindness and affability. Perhaps my orphan status was a sort of talisman, but I began to think all, or nearly all, human beings possessed some elements of a better nature, and so I provided help to the younger students as needed, unmolested. I was, I reflected, after all the son of a schoolmaster.

* * *

Our village consisted of the parish church, the vicarage where I stayed, a few small shops, the school and a fair number of houses, including farmhouses. People in our village mostly shopped in a much larger village, actually a small town, to our east. It was separated from us by tidal marshes and channels so that people from our village who bought things in the town had to walk several miles inland – there were no footbridges – carrying what they had bought.

With time and practice, I got a bit "handier" with the oars. Mr Japes told me that I should be pulling with my legs, not just my arms, and since my legs were quite strong, this was very

9

helpful. Soon the tidal flows could be overcome, and it occurred to me that folks might pay to be rowed back to the village.

I talked this over with Mr Japes, and he agreed with the idea. He even made and set in the boat a sort of low platform on which people could set their purchases without having them sloshing in the "bilge". We agreed sixpence was a reasonable fare, of which I would keep half.

Accordingly, on a Saturday I rowed over to the town and offered my services in a kind of water taxi. Several people accepted, and one or two even had me row them to the town. After splitting with my patron, I had two shillings sixpence, a half crown, for my efforts. I also was very tired, so that I welcomed Sunday.

* * *

My education, or rather lack of it, bothered me greatly. I particularly wanted to learn Latin, for my readings showed this to be the mark of a gentleman and, above all, I wanted to be a gentleman.

I forced myself to go to Mr Paston. He was writing something; when I knocked lightly on the door, he looked up and bade me enter. I told him I wanted to go to school, as I had learned everything taught in the village school. Very much to my surprise, he brightened up at the idea and told me he would write to the headmaster of Earl's Cross School, whose name seemed vaguely familiar, and get me admitted. I began to feel ashamed of having spent so much time avoiding him (though not of avoiding his friend) and thanked him sincerely. He beamed at me, and I retired, delighted but confused.

* * *

My water taxi business was a success from the first. In term, I could only row on Saturdays, as the teacher seemed more dependent on my help with the younger students than ever, not that there was any question of paying me. Once term was over, I was in business six days a week, some days making only a shilling and on others as much as four or five, though days like that left me exhausted. I kept a book in an oilskin bag to read when I wasn't rowing.

* * *

I collected a passenger, a young woman, to take to our village. I had not seen her before. She had no purchases, so was visiting someone in the village, I guessed. She sat down in the stern and as I got well under way, pulled her skirt back. Her legs were apart so I could see her legs – black stockings, a hint of white thigh above, and darkness between. She seemed to be looking elsewhere, and I was intrigued but embarrassed, so kept looking over my shoulder to stay on course while not looking too obviously. At some point, I met her eyes, briefly. She did not seem conscious of what she was showing and I wondered what she expected me to do, if anything. Once we arrived, I had to remind her of her debt, and while she gave me the sixpence, I could not fathom her expression: was she sneering, affronted that I should demand payment after showing so much of herself, did she enjoy doing what she did, what?

I had one or two more passengers, a fair day's collection, then took the boat to have Japes look at it, as I thought she was taking a bit more water. He and I hauled it out and turned it over – quite a change from two or three years ago, when I could hardly stir the thing – and helped him renew the caulking of a seam.

When I got to the house, I found Mrs Christianson requiring my assistance with the pasties. I had gotten to the point where I could nearly make them myself, but needed to wash my hands (and face) before I could help. The meal was a little late as a result, and she took about ten of them in, along with some other things. I never ate with the Pastons, probably for sanitary or aesthetic reasons, but was more comfortable eating at the kitchen table with Mrs Christianson anyway. When she came back from serving them, she had a letter in her hand. It was for me, from the headmaster of Earl's Cross School, a singular event for me, as I had never gotten a letter before.

The letter said I was admitted, with a scholarship. I could not imagine such good fortune. Mr Paston must have made an extraordinary case for me, an orphan and conscious of being very badly educated, at least in some respects. I told Mrs Christianson about my good fortune, about my happiness, and asked her to tell the Pastons and to thank Mr Paston especially.

I lay down in my cell of a room that night, my head awhirl with plans, projects and dreams. It would be hard, but I would do my utter best, and if I were not to be a gentleman after all, it wouldn't be for lack of application.

Eventually my mind turned to what I had seen in the boat this afternoon and recalled once seeing a couple lying on the beach. The woman, her skirts above her waist, her legs wide apart, was lying under a man with his trousers down to mid-thigh. He was rocking back and forth upon her, both were engrossed in what they were doing, and I retired quietly, deciding not to inquire what they were about. I was about ten at the time and now had a better picture, obtained from overhearing comments and talk from the older boys, about what I had seen. It was all very disturbing, but I wished I had looked more closely. Eventually I got up, dressed, and tired as I was, went outside to run on the beach, yet what I had seen remained, a nettle of memory.

In preparation for Earl's Cross, I obtained a copy of *Tom Brown's Schooldays* and read it. I gathered I would be bullied and harassed in various ways, but not much was said about what I would be learning. I also gathered that having money for buying things to eat was essential, so I paid more attention to my business. I never saw the girl again (though I hadn't paid much attention to her face) and had no idea who she was or why she was there.

For school, I would need better clothes, a "wardrobe". I picked up some things from a shop in the village that sold second (or third or possibly fourth) hand clothes, but eventually had to declare holiday, walk into town – I didn't want to leave the boat unattended – and buy better, including shoes and a valise to carry all in. I did some sewing, polished the shoes, walked about wearing them, donned my "gay apparel" on Sunday when the Pastons were in church, looked at myself in the mirror in the parlor. I could make no judgment of how I would look to others, but I guessed I could travel about without having dogs or constables set on me.

Between my business, working in the garden and keeping the chicken coop decent, helping Mrs Christianson in the kitchen, sewing etc. my days, even the long summer days, were very full, so when I had to go off to Earl's Cross with my valise, I felt relief as well as anxiety.

Earl's Cross was perhaps 15 miles inland, about four hours' walk for me. It sat in a village rather bigger than the one I came from was, and consisted of a largish two story brick building, a two story wooden one and one or two small outbuildings. I was sweating as it was warm, and went into the brick building and eventually found where I was to report. I had brought the scholarship letter, and was duly noted as having arrived. I was sent to the wooden building, where I was to sleep, eat, bathe (perhaps) and study.

My bed was upstairs in a sort of alcove, with a flimsy door, a small desk, a chair, and a cot not much bigger than the one I used in the vicarage. There were other boys about, but no one seemed to take much interest in me, not that I minded. Eventually, I wandered about enough to see where we were to eat etc. and became bold enough to introduce myself to some boys who were sitting at one of the dining tables, not talking, I noticed. These gave me their names, which of course flew right out of my head, and I learned I would probably be in the upper fourth or perhaps the lower, that there were about 500 boys in the school, some day students who lived in their homes near-hand, and that the school was named for a ceremonial cross erected by an Earl for his dead wife, some hundreds (opinions differed on this point) of years ago.

More boys showed up, none seeming too happy at being back in school, so it was a rather subdued gathering. Meals would not begin until breakfast tomorrow, and no one was much looking forward to that either. I went out and wandered about the village, and then the grounds of the school, neither of which took very long, then went back to my alcove and put my clothes in drawers in the desk, as there was no dresser or hooks or closet. The window rattled with the wind, so I knew it would be cold in winter. I lay down on the cot – I had slept many times on boards, so it was no hardship – and noted that the blanket smelled. Eventually the sky darkened and I slept.

* * *

After a week at Earl's Cross, I was overwhelmed by the work and beginning to feel chronically hungry. The food was poor: gristly meat, vegetables on the edge – or over it – of spoilage, and, worst of all, very limited in amount. I had begun trading the meat, or what might be called that, with other boys in return for their vegetables. I hated gristle, disliked fat and what we were served seemed mostly just those. There were shops in the village where pies, etc. could be bought, and I began to patronize these, but soon realized the thirty shillings I had brought, which seemed a very ample allowance, was not going to last the term. My situation was, it seemed, universal but unavailing.

While I wasn't badly off in one or two of the subjects, I was very far behind in nearly all, so much so that I asked the masters for copies of primers so I could try to catch up. I insisted I wanted to learn, and everyone provided me with the lower form texts. So I was in effect taking nearly double the courses, but there was no alternative. After a few days of floundering about, I began a systematic plan where I would try to do a chapter or part of a chapter of the lower form Latin text, say, in addition to trying, quite unsuccessfully, to do the lesson for the upper fourth.

As I was new to the school, I was ranked at the bottom of each class to start, and in some classes, it looked as though there I was going to stay. So rather than join the other boys in games and sports, I worked and worked. A few of the other boys asked whether I wanted to join them, and I always said I would be delighted to, but was very badly prepared and had to catch up.

I was not too sorry about this, as the other boys mostly played cricket, at which I immediately and obviously demonstrated my complete uselessness. I had never played the game, didn't know the rules, couldn't throw, catch or hit. When I became too restless I would go for a fast walk or a run through the country lanes. This would clear my head, settle me down, and I could go back to work revived.

I gradually was putting names to faces, and beginning to get a sense of the students. If there were any aristocrats' or squires' sons, they kept that to themselves; tradesmen's sons, farmers' (tenants, that is) sons and a few "working class" sons were all I met. I was something of an anomaly, though being a schoolmaster's son seemed to enable everyone to peg me and feel comfortable with me.

One or two of the bigger boys attempted to throw me to the ground, for no obvious reason, but soon discovered I was hard to throw, being now close to six feet tall and rather strong. So I was let alone, which once more suited me.

* * *

More than halfway through the term, I was getting low on the money I had brought. For next term, I was going to need more like fifty shillings or even three pounds. Even toast and butter (and not much of that) were inadequate, and talk of food supplanted even talk about sex, obsessive though that sometimes got.

Studies were going better, I was no longer at the bottom of any class, and cases, declensions and tenses in Latin and English began to seem at least more familiar if not understandable. Some subjects were easier: maths, history and German. Earl's Cross was a German school: its modern foreign language was German, as opposed to French. Since it started in the upper fourth, I was equal in ignorance to the other boys so could show what I was capable of in this class. I did want to keep the scholarship, as it was my only hope for an education of any kind.

* * *

The end of my first term was marked by exams and hunger. I was out of money and worn out from my study regimen. After the last exam, I filled my valise with filthy clothes needing repair and carried it in the rain back to the village. On entering the house, I was struck by how worn Mrs Christianson was. I had been in the house more than nine years and of course she was ageing, and now showing it. I was ashamed and began helping her, with the garden, the chicken house and the cooking, as much as I could. Of course, I had to carry people back and forth between the town and our village as well, so my resolves of studying over the holidays went unfulfilled. She made light of her health, noting that we all died and that she had a few years yet but I felt very guilty about leaving her alone to cope with all her duties. She said I had to return if I would be a scholar, and so I did.

* * *

I had brought more money, taking some of the money reserve I had kept back from first term and had a better idea of what to buy and where – loaves of bread and some butter, for example, were cheaper and more filling than pies and tarts. My studying had also, I thought, become more efficient. I had made top of the form in maths and German and was well above halfway in all the others.

One problem began to bother me, however. As I rose in forms, I was moved farther from the chalkboard, and I noticed I was having trouble making out what was written. On two occasions, I got math problems wrong because I had misread the numbers. The master suggested I needed spectacles. Just what I needed, I thought, another expense. But there was, again, no help for it; I had to get some after end of term.

I was on good terms with the other boys, at least most of them. I liked to tell jokes, make amusing remarks, and soon met every meal with a convivial group. This was the first time I was regularly conversing, on equal terms, with peers, extensively, and I was enjoying it. It was informative too: I learned much more about the other boys (and they about me) and when we occasionally digressed from the two main topics, sometimes learned something about art, music, politics and culture. I saw that not all learning occurred in a classroom.

* * *

My idea of getting a loaf of bread and some butter to ease my hunger was taken up by my circle and improved, as one boy suggested a tin of jam as well, and I thought a bottle of milk would be good. Soon the idea expanded to where we would buy these things in turn. We decided to call ourselves the Earl's Cross Gourmet Society. I suggested the Earl's Cross Gourmet and Incessant Discussions About Sex Society, and another colleague thought that Earl's Cross Gourmet Society (for short) would be a reasonable compromise.

My room became a sort of refectory for the group. We were in fact able to make our money go very much farther and the casual meetings over slices of bread, butter and whatever jam we had decided to try were very enjoyable though distracting at times. Two of our group had next to no money, so we made them *"vivandières"*, sent out with money from the rest of us to do the actual purchases. Of course, anything edible we purchased had to be eaten promptly or likely be stolen, but we simply had to plan our purchases around that possibility.

* * *

Exams at the end of the term felt easier, and I hoped my scholarship would be continued. On returning to the parish house, I found Mrs Christianson further declined. She was having trouble doing all the standing and moving needed, so I basically took over much of the cooking, at her direction. I noticed her feet and ankles were swollen, her shoes must have been very painful, so I foraged about for a box of suitable size so she could sit and prop her feet up while she instructed me.

I had to do the serving too, which surprised (and I thought displeased) the Pastons. So I added waiter to my duties, as well as washer-up. I worried about what would happen when I went back, and could only hope the rest I was giving her would enable her to recover.

* * *

One slow day, I ran to the town, to a shop that sold spectacles. The shopkeeper had me read letters on a chart, pronounced me to be nearsighted, and sold me a pair of gold-framed spectacles for four shillings (or sixteen passengers, as I always calculated). I could indeed see much sharper at a distance, so carefully carried them back in my breast pocket. Since I didn't need them for reading or rowing, I often left them with my other things to keep them safer.

* * *

I was becoming stronger from the rowing. Mr Japes gave me some hints about technique, such as rolling my wrists as I pulled, which also helped. So, with my services also being taken more as custom, I cleared over nine pounds over the twelve weeks between terms. This should suffice for next term – my scholarship having been renewed, my marks being tops in all but two subjects and close to tops in those two.

I was conscious of growing something of a beard, so I needed a razor, but here Mr Japes came to my rescue. He had a full beard so didn't shave but had once (had he been married? courting? with children? I wondered, but did not ask). He made me a present of his razor and strop with instructions to boot, and I made my first essay at shaving that evening. The results were very mixed: my face looked cleaner of whiskers, but with a number of scrapes and cuts. I told myself I had yet another thing to work on.

* * *

I left the parish house on a rainy morning, saying goodbye to Mrs Christianson, and I was afraid it might be for the last time. Her feet and ankles were still swollen and she really needed help with the garden, chicken coop, etc., but there was no sign Mr Paston would hire anyone.

* * *

One item I had taken – stolen, I suppose Mr Paston would consider it, though Mrs Christianson said it was not used or needed – was a bread knife, for the one we were using at school was clearly not worth the stealing. It was of course necessary to make the slices as uniform as possible. Our group was increased by a new boy, a German, Hans-Jeorg Fetter, from some village with a name none of us could follow, but he said it was near Hamburg, the port on the Baltic. We joked that he should have no trouble with the German, and he agreed, saying his father, a merchant staying in the capitol, Norwich, wanted him to perfect his English. I commented that I had found the Latin very helpful with English, and this prompted a general discussion.

* * *

Hans-Jeorg was a very affable fellow, and he and I began to take walks together and do some running as well. I seemed to have a bit more free time and he enjoyed a "ramble". (He used the English word, though I pointed out that it was somewhat archaic, going back to the eighteenth century, which he took in good part.) We agreed to speak only German on the way out and English back, so I think we both benefitted. He liked telling stories, funny stories, and I tried to tell those I knew. One of his stories, about a "night club" – I hadn't heard that term before – that had a loo with a golden seat, sent me nearly into convulsions, once the mental image the last of the story evoked came into my head.

Gradually, we grew more intimate, exchanging confidences. He thought, for example, that the behavior of Mr Paston and the lawyer friend of his was odd, and that I was wise to avoid them when I did. He had a sweetheart back in Germany with whom he corresponded, and I gathered that exchange of letters between a boy and girl was, in some families, tantamount to betrothal. They had grown up together, which I am sure helped. I envied him his sweetheart; since I was a year or so younger than he was, it would likely be a while until I had one, even if I could finish my education and get a job.

Hans-Jeorg was a new phenomenon in my life: a friend. I had made acquaintances, was on good terms with nearly all the boys, but he was my first actual friend.

* * *

The term went on. The "feast days" became more widely spaced, though perhaps even better appreciated. Hans-Jeorg was going back to Germany for the holidays, two or more days each way, but I guessed reunion with his sweetheart was ample compensation, and wished again that I had one.

Partly by accident, I was top of the form in all my subjects, which I was very happy about, but of course couldn't speak of. So I carried my valise, filled with my traditional dirty clothes, back to the parish house, wondering what I would find there.

It had begun to rain with perhaps a mile left, and I was getting soaked despite the oilskins given me by Mr Japes. When I arrived, Mrs Christianson wasn't there. Instead there was a small, waspish, middle aged woman who said she was Mrs Cord and that

I needed to put the chicken house to rights, it was filthy, too filthy to walk in, and the garden needed weeding and the Pastons wanted pasties and she didn't know how to cook these. All this in a breath, as it were, but I asked about Mrs Christianson. Dead, was the reply, dead two weeks or more ago, and the master and mistress wanted dinner, and I should get on with it.

I stood a moment, blinking, then said, "Mrs Christianson stood my friend when I had none, and was a comfort to me when I badly needed comforting, and I would go visit her grave, now, in the rain, it was little enough, but I would do it." My voice was breaking as I said this, and I felt tears (or it might have been rain) in my eyes as I went out the door.

There was a new grave in the churchyard, and the stone was freshly carved. It said "Nancy Tregellis Christianson, 1842-1909, wife of George and mother of Scott". She was 67, a fairly good run, but she had never said anything about a husband or a son, and I reproached myself for never asking, though of course she probably didn't want to talk about them if there were tragedies. I stood in the rain, regretting her loss, trying to bless her memory, not praying as I had never prayed, to my knowledge, but wishing her a happy journey to wherever she was bound, surely a happy place, if there was such a thing as Justice.

I squelched back to the parish house and began the meal. Mrs Cord had of course moved everything about, and this vexed and slowed me. The bell for service had rung three times before I got the pasties from the oven, set ten of them on the tray, keeping back seven for myself and Mrs Cord. She bridled at this, but I pointed, as emphatically as I could, at the tray, pointed to the dining room and stared her into submission. When she returned, I gave her two, took the remaining five for myself and sat and ate them silently.

The next day, the chicken house – Mrs Cord did the break-fast, not as well as Mrs Christianson (or I) did – and then, in the rain, put the garden to rights. The wind shifted toward the northeast, and turned cold, cold, cold. Aside from the noon meal, also not very good, I ate about a dozen carrots, eliciting a glare from Mrs Cord. Since I had planted them myself for myself, I ignored her.

I thought about Mrs Christianson. As a child, I was of course entirely filled with my own concerns, but I really should have done more to get to know her. She had been so helpful in so many ways, and I had just accepted her helpfulness. As I had gotten older, I had, I remembered, been more of a help to her, but I had never tried to get close to her, which I now regretted when it was too late.

Returning after the holidays, in the snow, I remained cast down. There wasn't much business, no one was very venturesome because of the weather, but I had been very busy trying to teach Mrs Christianson's replacement how to make the pasties, cleaning the chicken house and serving the Pastons as a sort of waiter. Mrs Cord thought my removal of fat and gristle from the meat wasteful, which I suppose it was, but if I was going to eat some of them myself, and I was, that is how they were going to be prepared.

I usually put the gristle and fat deep in the ground, so dogs wouldn't dig them up, but on one of my few rowing ventures, it occurred to me that boiling the scraps for soup stock might be thriftier. Of course, then I would have to strain out the rendered remainder, say through some muslin cloth. On another trip – I had been trying to figure out how this could be done – I thought of putting the scraps in a muslin cloth, tying the whole into a sort of bag and boiling that, with the string clamped under the lid of the pot to make it easy to remove the bag. I was able to try this, once I had myself paid for the cloth and string, and it seemed to work. I would make soup stock in the summer between terms; in the meantime, Mrs Cord was having none of my innovations, and our relationship remained somewhat strained. What the Pastons made of all this, I had no clue, nor cared.

* * *

Hans-Jeorg had returned and I told him about my feelings of guilt over Mrs Christianson's last days, as I simply wasn't there to ease her end. He took a more pragmatic view, noting her age, her symptoms, and the fact that I had never been paid for any of my services. Also, I had a duty to myself, to get my education, for the scholarship was meant for that purpose. Specious or not, these reasons, or perhaps just my being able to talk to a friend, my only friend, about these things, made me feel less unhappy. Still, I would miss Mrs Christianson, her quiet good nature and the feeling I had always had that she was in my corner, no matter what.

* * *

The fifth form, including me, was obliged to run in the Hare and Hounds, a race over several miles. After an apprehensive start, I settled down and wound up roughly in the middle of the pack, well out of breath, but glad it was over. I was persistent, it seemed, but not very fast. That was the only sort of formal athletic effort I had made in two years at Earl's Cross, and looked to be the last.

* * *

This time, my marks were tops, no accident, in all subjects. My walks with Hans-Jeorg had improved my spoken German so much that I could now actually carry on my share of the conversation. His English was, of course, much better than my *Deutsch*, but I was improving. He was now accepted fully into my circle, with his flair for storytelling, which was something, I felt, for an English public school, not the most welcoming place for anyone at all unusual.

* * *

I was not looking forward to between terms spent at elbows with Mrs Cord, but when I returned, she left for a month, she said to visit sick family. This left me as cook, waiter, gardener, and chicken house maître d'hôtel, as well as attempting to make enough for prevention of starvation fall term. It seemed I was doing a better job at meal preparation, since I did it as Mrs Christianson had taught me, so run-ins with the Pastons were limited to complaints about my clothes as I served them. One more thing to worry about, though I wondered if the cost of my lodging and such food as I ate was really so much that I was obliged to be so busy.

I got a letter renewing my scholarship for next year, my third at Earl's Cross, no surprise but I told Mr Paston about it. He seemed vaguely pleased – he was a vague sort of person most of the time – asked again what the tuition was and dismissed me, or rather ignored me out of the room.

A second letter arrived, from a lawyer in the nearby town, requesting my presence. This meant a walk there and loss of time for rowing clients between town and village, so I ran there early to see what I was needed for.

The lawyer kept me waiting, to my increasing irritation, but when I produced his letter, he told me that Mrs Christianson had left me some money in her will: fifty five pounds odd, after costs of the tombstone and fees were subtracted. This was a windfall. I had begun thinking of attending university, but couldn't see how I could possibly afford it. Now I had perhaps a year at university paid for. It was a wonderful thing to do, and I blessed her memory again.

There was a problem: where to keep the money. I really didn't trust Mr Paston, perhaps unjustly, and my opinion of Mrs Cord was, if anything, lower, though she had never actually given me any reason to question her honesty. In the end, the lawyer agreed to keep the money in an account, that I could withdraw when, and this was in the will, I required it, no matter my age. I had the document saying I was the owner of the money under the law, so that should suffice.

I asked the lawyer if he knew anything about a husband or a son but he said he had no information, so the matter remained a mystery. I returned to the village at a dead run, to find impatient clients at both ends, so took two each way until I had to prepare and serve lunch. So the day went, but my head was filled with dreams of a university education and unquestioned status as a gentleman.

* * *

Returning to Earl's Cross was a relief, though I knew I would soon be longing for my summer activities. Hans-Jeorg had bad news: he would leave after these two terms, back to Germany to work in the family firm, which he had said was importing and exporting anything anyone wanted anywhere. Our "rambles" weren't the same; I had hoped he would finish the sixth form, but we agreed to write, alternating English and German, of course.

I had begun to think more of university, and went to talk to the headmaster. He was vaguely encouraging but pointed out that I had three years left, and needed to think of a subject to read at university. For some reason, I asked him if my father had been coming here to teach, perhaps some memory of the name of the school was retained by me. He was after that time, but sent me to the clerk who looked after the files, who promptly went to one cabinet, looked at a few papers, then pulled one out.

It was a handwritten letter from my father to the headmaster at that time. My father, unlike me, wrote a good hand. He had graduated Rugby school (on scholarship), was married, had a son and his wife was expecting another child. He had taught six years at a Council school in Taunton and was applying for the position at Earl's Cross that was advertised. His name was Richard M. Dobbs, and I guessed the M. stood for Matthew. He listed two people as recommenders.

Since my father had a middle name, then I was likely to have one, but I had forgotten it if I ever knew what it was. It was likely to derive from some family connection or some personal friend of my parents but of course I didn't know that either, a double loss as it were.

Naturally, I wanted to keep the letter, as it was the only thing of my father I had ever found, but this, I was given to understand, was sacrilege if not blasphemy, for the letter was part of the Files and Files were Sacrosanct. I was permitted to copy everything I could but I would greatly have preferred the letter.

Returning to my alcove, I began to wonder what I should read. I was good at the academic subjects; my real strength was my ability to focus on my reading, to the point where I would lose track of everything else. But for the moment, that did not provide much in the way of insight.

* * *

My history master commented one day, that names of towns, districts or geographical features, given by a people to mean something about whatever it was, something meaningful in their language, would often be adopted by a displacing people, who might pronounce it faithfully or might try to convert it to some meaning in their own language, but the name could retain some information about the language of the original people. I was fascinated by this. Some names were obvious: Norfolk for North Folk. But Norwich was harder – what was a "wich"? Come to think of it, the suffix "wich" was found in a number of places, I thought all in England. I got a gazetteer and began checking on this. When I talked to the master, he was very encouraging, and we talked about my reading History at university. I began to think more extensively about migration of peoples and languages and whether place names such as Penzance had some meaning in a language now utterly, or nearly utterly, lost.

* * *

I returned from the parish house after the holidays thinking sexual/homicidal thoughts about Mrs Cord. She was a short, slight, waspish woman, and I had tried and tried to help her to perform her duties, but she seemed to have a constitutional objection to tutelage from me. I had no clue as to what the Pastons thought or how they would deal with the situation, but I had had enough of that woman. Having to deal with her over two more summers deeply depressed me. At least I would only have to concern myself with academic problems for a while.

* * *

More changes: aside from Hans-Jeorg, one of my other friends, for I now regarded them as that, didn't return. His father couldn't or wouldn't pay to keep him at Earl's Cross. This made me feel guilty about my scholarship and I kept quiet about it, not that I had ever mentioned it. I realized that my circle wouldn't last forever, that we would say goodbye someday and someday soon. I noticed that the ranks of the fifth form were a bit thin, and felt the injustice of giving support only through the fifth form or part of it. I realized again how lucky I was, able to get a complete education, and told myself not to slacken my efforts.

* * *

The end of the upper fifth: goodbye to Hans-Jeorg; when would we meet again? Another of my friends also wasn't coming back: the cost of education at even as remote and cheap a school as Earl's Cross was just too much for some families. My marks were tops again, but I couldn't feel as happy about that as I once had.

* * *

Meanwhile, back to my oars. I was very surprised to find Mrs Cord not only still there but seemingly humbled, asking, actually asking for my assistance. I dismissed my visions of violating her – I wasn't too clear on the details of how "violation" was to be done, but was willing to experiment – then tying her to some bricks and heaving her overboard, and tried to help. Since she was so short, it occurred to me that she might be having trouble reaching the pots, etc. on the stove. I tactfully asked about this, and then got some boxes for her to stand on, boxes that wouldn't wobble. This did help, though I couldn't shake the feeling her penitent mood had been forced on her. Still, better forced amity than the bickering we had before.

The garden had been left to lapse, and I planted vegetables as fast as I could, hoping for some sort of harvest for myself (I usually took as large a bunch of carrots back with me as I could stuff into my valise). At any rate, these would keep the Pastons in vegetables through fall, not that they ate that many.

Between rowing customers, I helped supervise Mrs Cord's preparations of meals. Again, I had the feeling she was coerced into being cooperative, but I tried to be as unassuming and straightforward as possible. She had finally gotten the pasties done as Mrs Christianson had (modified by me), so together we made them, and quite efficiently too, with me working hard (and I hope not obviously) to assist her. So this aspect of the summer was much more pleasant than I had hoped, setting aside my previous plans for her.

Curiously, no one ever seemed to try to pinch my rowing business during the long months I was away. Mr Japes thought the men my age were simply too lazy, and, to be sure, the effective wage scale wasn't high; still, it was a way to make some money. I could do as many as twenty trips a day, six days a week, which was as much as one pound ten a week, though with rain, etc., I was lucky to clear ten pounds this summer. My scholarship renewed once more, I headed back to Earl's Cross for my lower sixth form, one of the elite of the school.

* * *

A rapidly dwindling elite, my circle of friends now consisted of just four, two of them the boys with no money of their own. It looked to be a spare term. One of the *"vivandières"* had met some boys from Eton and Winchester on a trip to London and told us that the fare at those schools was as sparse and wretched as what we got, so there seemed to be some sort of perverse national tradition involved. I thought our method of supplementing the fare as actually ingenious, cheap and effective, and my three remaining friends agreed.

* * *

The history master challenged me one day: had Stonehenge been built by the Celts? We discussed the issue, that is, he asked leading questions until I saw the point: the Celts came from Central Europe, where there were no henges. So the henges must have been built by an earlier people. And, I realized later, "an earlier people" could be many earlier peoples. History, very ancient history, was becoming more intriguing as it began to appear that some rational conclusions could be drawn from the surviving evidence.

* * *

Toward the end of the second term, the headmaster asked me to see him. I was confident of my work, so when he told me my scholarship would not be renewed, in fact he would rather I not return even if I paid my own way, I was dumfounded. I could get no explanation from him, only that since I had spoken of going to university, it was time for me to leave Earl's Cross. He said he would write a strong letter of recommendation – which was only just – to wherever I was planning to go, though he thought London was most likely to take me. He added that there wasn't that much more I could or needed to take, and it was best I "moved on". I was bitterly disappointed, confused, and angry. I had done my part; why wouldn't they do theirs? Did they need the scholarship money that much?

* * *

I worked very hard, to make it obvious to them that a top student and scholar was being driven away. I was beginning to have headaches by the end of most days, which I attributed to all the reading I was doing. Mornings I felt fine, so gave the headaches little attention, just endured them. I also began to think what I needed to do. I would have to take the test for Matriculation if I were to attend London. I could always get a job teaching, though I was not confident of being able to deal with boys nearly my own age in a classroom. I also needed to get information about the University of London, since I would almost surely need to work to help support myself while at university, and jobs were far more likely to be obtainable in London than in Oxford or Cambridge or so I thought.

On writing to the authorities, I got a return letter, telling me the Matriculation Examination would be given at City College of London Saturday the second week of July. So, after the end of my last term at Earl's Cross, I began preparing: a suit of (marginally) better clothes, an extra fountain pen and a map of London, along with a train schedule.

I decided it was far better to take the train from Norwich, so I would walk there, take an obscenely early train to London, and try to get some sleep on the train.

The walk was tiring, but I found I couldn't sleep on the train, perhaps due to memories of my last train ride. So when the train pulled into the station in London, I had managed to shave but not sleep. I got off the train (I was carrying no valise), and began walking to the doors of the station.

I was passing another train just in and saw the backside of a woman, struggling with what appeared to be very heavy luggage. She seemed to have white hair. I looked about: no porters at hand, of course. So, to the rescue: I walked up to the woman and doffing my cap, asked, "May I be of assistance, Madam?"

The woman turned and we looked at each other. I saw she was actually young, perhaps my own age, with very light-coloured hair, not white or blond, just light coloured. Her eyes were a kind of dense blue I had never seen before, and she was the prettiest girl I had ever seen.

Her eyes were nearly on a level with mine, so she was tall for a woman, and I had the impression she had a slender, willowy figure. She was looking me over as well. I was actually respectively dressed, for me I mean, but I think the decisive factor in my appearance was the spectacles. She evidently made up her mind and said, "I'm afraid my trunk is stuck. It won't budge."

I walked round her, saw a wooden case, a small trunk, bound with metal strapping nailed in, and tried to raise it. I stepped into the compartment, pulled back on the handle of the trunk and freed it: a metal strap end had wedged in the bottom of the compartment door. I lifted the trunk with a great effort. It was extraordinarily heavy. I was preparing to step off the train with it when I realized that stepping down with such a load was probably not a good idea. I set it down on the edge of the compartment, stepped out and pulled it after me.

Still no porters. I said, "Which way, miss?" (Madam seemed inappropriate). She indicated the doors I had been heading to, so I heaved at that damned box and began accompanying her. She said,

31

noting my efforts, "I'm afraid there are rather a lot of books in there," I said, "The books I understand. It's the anvil that has me puzzled."

She looked surprised, and then laughed. She had a pretty laugh, which of course was appropriate. She said, "I'm going to stay with my aunt to study for the University of London Matriculation Examination next week."

I set the case down with a thump. "That is today." "Oh no", she said, as I began frantically rummaging through my pockets for the letter.

I pulled several pieces of paper out and hastily looked at them before realizing that the first piece of paper was the letter. I opened it and showed it to her: "That is today, isn't it?" She said, "Oh it is. I will have to go there directly." I said, "I don't know London. Do you know the way?" I was looking at the station clock, and the time was getting near. She said, "Yes", so I hauled the case to the porter's area, checked it, got a ticket which I gave to the girl, and we set off, out the doors. She pointed in the general direction we were to go, and we risked our lives crossing what seemed a very busy street, filled with very impatient drivers of all sorts of vehicles.

We were walking along a sidewalk, with me going at my usual gait, when I realized she was keeping up with me, stride for stride. With the shoes, hat and hair, she was as tall as I, a shade under six feet. I asked how far to the building the exam was to be given in, and she said, perhaps a mile. I pulled my watch out, which for a miracle was keeping time, and noted we had just over 20 minutes. I pointed this out to her and said we should be there with perhaps five minutes to spare. She said, "Are we walking that fast?" I said, "Easily four miles an hour."

At one point, she said, "Oh, no." I asked what the matter was, and she said her fountain pen was locked in her trunk. I said I had brought an extra one, loaded with ink, and gave it to her. As we walked, I snatched up a drifting piece of newspaper, and as we waited on a street corner, I uncapped my remaining pen and tested it. It worked, and she tested the one I had given her. Also good. I noticed she was left-handed like me. We proceeded, thinking, incorrectly, we had a gap in the traffic. The drivers swore at us as we dodged past, and I muttered, "Same to you, only sideways". She heard me, laughed before I could apologize, and we continued.

We took our lives in our hands twice more, and then were approaching the building she said was our destination. We got there with nearer ten minutes to go, with a great swarm of people, some milling about, many going into rooms marked "Gentlemen" or "Ladies". The girl turned to me and introduced herself: "I'm Alice Millwood." I said, "My name is Dobbs, Matthew Dobbs." I paused, and said, "According to my calculations, which are nearly infallible, your room is there", indicating a room where the Ladies were to go. "And you, I believe, should go there," she said, smiling, pointing to a room for the Gentlemen. "Good luck", she said to me, and I replied, "The Germans say, '*Gluckauf*'; so: '*Gluckauf*'". She waved and we separated.

In the room, we had to write our names and addresses on a form, and then pick up the test, which was sealed, and write our names and addresses once more on the test itself. I decided I would not comment on the irrationality of this procedure, being on my best behavior.

I had just finished, when we were told to open the exam and begin. The first question indeed appeared to be written using English words and after the initial turmoil, I was able to read the question, then to understand what information was being requested and finally to provide it. After that, I found I could answer all the questions, none seeming to be very difficult.

I turned a last page and found I had finished. I looked at the clock, and saw I had forty-five minutes, so went back to be sure I hadn't turned two pages thinking they were one, and rereading the questions and my answers. Nothing seemed amiss, and I finally got tired of waiting, so turned in my paper fifteen minutes early. I was the only one to do so; the proctor opened my test, looked through it and looked at me with surprise. I shrugged as if to say I had expected something more challenging, and went out.

There was more than an hour until the second half of the test, plenty of time to get something to eat. Of course, I hadn't eaten since yesterday noon. However, I waited, telling myself that Miss Millwood would probably have a better idea of where to eat than I did.

She came out a few minutes later, also a bit early, saw me and walked over. I asked if she knew of a nearby place to eat, but she didn't. We went out together and descried a scone and tea shop across the street. We made for that, got a table and sat down. The waitress handed me a menu, not her, and I realized I was to order for us both, possibly after consulting with her. I asked if she had had breakfast, and on being told she hadn't, replied no more had I, and perhaps milk instead of tea would be better (I hated tea, and I had never had coffee.) She agreed, and I told the waitress to bring two milks – large, I emphasized – and a plate of scones and jam.

While we were waiting, she told me about herself. She was, it appeared, the older daughter of a baronet, Sir Edward Millwood, MP (though he no longer sat for his district), and my heart sank. My spirits revived a little when she told me her family had a small estate, named, unsurprisingly, Millwood, but there was no money to send her to university, so she was going to get a job teaching at a nearby girls' public school. Her school wanted her to take (and preferably pass) the Matriculation Examination so they could say one of their teachers had matriculated at the University of London. She had an older brother, Richard, who was a captain in the Indian Army. She also had a younger sister, whom I somehow gathered she did not get on with.

I told her my story, including my water taxi job, for I didn't want to hide something like that from her. She didn't flinch, which caused me to think she was a very liberal girl (her father had been a Liberal MP) and very amiable; she asked me if the work was very hard. In reply, I showed her my hands, which this early in the rowing season were cracked as well as calloused. She said I had to do what was necessary for my education, and my feelings for her warmed decidedly.

Our orders arrived, and we ate. Afterwards, she asked me, rather hesitantly, what I thought about women's' suffrage. My feelings on that subject were about the same as most public school boys, but I began to recast them. I didn't want to lie, but then I remembered a comment one of my circle had made once, and said, "It's just the next extension of the franchise". I went on to remind her of the extensions in the last century, at about thirty-year intervals, and commented that the extension to women was inevitable, that the essence of democracy was that everyone participated, that is, could vote. I went on to say I thought the tactics of some of the extreme "Suffragettes" had actually hurt their cause but, I said, earlier efforts to extend the franchise had sometimes turned violent.

Alice asked why it couldn't be done sooner, and I had an answer ready: Britain was a very conservative country and people needed time to adjust to new ideas. I went on to elaborate on one of my previous remarks, that nearly every boy had been bullied at some point in their lives and so understood that giving in to bullying was simply an invitation to more bullying. That was why, I thought, the Liberal government had backed off on votes for women.

She agreed that violent tactics were unsupportable, but asked if the anger of some of the campaigners for the vote for women wasn't justified. I considered that, then commented that in America, several of the American states had enfranchised women, that a woman now sat in the American House of Representatives, and that this had been done with none of the violent tactics employed in Britain. I suggested that some of the more violent campaigners were simply very unhappy, disturbed people and would be just as unhappy, disturbed and prone to violent behavior even if this particular goal were achieved. She nodded. I was pleased with what I had said, because it actually made sense to us both.

She commented that Hardy's novels were angry, this time at the British class system. I said I had written a review of *Tess of the D'Urbervilles* and the master hadn't liked it and said so. He had marked me down, saying that I could like or dislike a book as I chose, but that I had to give a literary reason for doing so. I hadn't understood what he was talking about then or since.

She said *The Mayor of Casterbridge* wasn't a much happier story and I agreed. Then I said that Hardy was a very angry man, and she said that this showed in his plots. I said, "But that means in his characters, too". She picked this up: "So his characters were drawn to advance his plots". I hit the table with my hand, and said, "Of course, his characters were written to be victims, not human beings, like Austen's characters" "Have you read her novels?" "All six, over and over again." "Her characters are real." "Yes – they make mistakes, but they are not as passive as Hardy's characters are. I guess that is what irritated me, their passivity, as if they had only two, or rather one dimension." "So you think an author has to distance himself to some extent from his creations?" "Take an Olympian view, in other words, yes, at least to an extent. This is amazing: a few minutes' discussion with you, and I now realize what I should have been thinking and writing." She smiled. The waitress wanted to be paid. I had brought nearly a pound in silver, so had plenty of money for the bill, but Alice insisted on paying the tip. I acceded, since I wasn't sure how much this should be, so we each paid, got up and returned to the building for the second half of the exam, with again about ten minutes to spare.

I remembered the pens and pulled the bottle of ink out of my pocket – I pointed out that with a black coat, leaks wouldn't be as noticeable – and refilled both. We checked them on another scrap of paper, wished each other "Good Luck" and "*Gluckauf*" and went inside.

The second half was more mathematical, no problem for me, and this time I had finished a full hour before the scheduled end. I went back over the test, actually finding I had made a mistake on one of the problems and corrected it. Then I sat and thought about Alice. She too was left-handed, and we had commented about how we were ignored by the right-handers. It was a bond, and her height would have made her a bit shy and self-conscious like me. She was also a bookish person, so we shared that interest too. Still she was a "lady of high degree", or at least much higher than mine, which was at best ambiguous. I sighed. She was so attractive and so easy to talk to. Not that I had that much experience, of course.

About fifteen minutes before the scheduled end of the exam, I turned in my paper. Again, the procter looked surprised, leafed through my paper, looked more surprised. I smiled blandly and left. Then I stood, waiting for Alice. She appeared a few minutes after the scheduled end, looking tired. We walked together, away from the building towards the train station. Eventually, she commented that she had found the second half of the test harder: her school had very limited math classes, and she had had to take her brothers' old texts and go through them for subjects like algebra and trigonometry. She never got to calculus. I asked if she had problems with maths in general, and she said no, she had a good head for numbers, like her aunt. She was simply frustrated by what her school hadn't offered: she wanted, she said, rather stiffer fare than table settings and etiquette. I sympathized, commenting that for such an isolated, little-known school as Earl's Cross, we had at least access to a reasonable curriculum.

We walked on. I couldn't think of anything else to say. Then, finally, I commented that, at least for the purpose of getting a job, the girls' school she would teach in probably placed less emphasis on maths. She said it was the same school, but went on to say it was frustrating because she wanted to learn and was denied some opportunities because she was a woman. I said she had made a convert of me, for whatever that was worth, and she smiled.

When we got to the station, she gave her ticket in to the porter's lodge and the case was duly produced on payment. Without asking, I heaved it up and walked toward the track where her train was. At one point, she had me stop while she made two telephone calls, one to the aunt, and the other to her parents, apprising them of the situation. Then I hauled the case to an empty compartment on the train, set it in the compartment so the broken strap wouldn't catch and asked her if someone would meet her. She said yes, hesitated, and then apologized for the weight of her luggage. I smiled, noting that she was prepared, in case of encountering a horse that needed shoeing. She laughed at that and thanked me for my help. I in turn thanked her for guiding me so efficiently to the right building and helping me with my literary analysis. The train began to move and I bade her God's speed and fare well, breaking each into its constituent parts. She raised her hand in goodbye and I noticed how long and slender her hand was.

I went back to Norwich that evening and walked through the night back to the village, my head full of Alice. Back in the parish house, a full dose of reality quenched but couldn't extinguish my dreams of her.

About ten days later, I got a letter from the University of London, its Registrar admitting (provisionally) my matriculation. A list of fees for tuition, etc. was included. My legacy would cover this, but money for food, rent, perhaps clothes would also be needed and I wasn't sure I had enough, having no clear idea of London prices. I proceeded to bend to my oars, in addition to helping Mrs Cord, tending the garden, chicken house, and every time-consuming task the mind of her and Rev. Paston could conceive.

* * *

Two days after that, I got a letter addressed to Matthew Dobbs, Esquire, written in a somewhat eccentric hand. The return was A. Millwood, as nearly as I could make out. A letter from Alice! I opened it and was able to read:

Dear Matthew (if I may be informal)

I thank you again for your assistance, conversation and pen with ink. I made use of your comments on votes for women to write an article which has been published in our county newspaper. A cutting is enclosed. Perhaps it will restore some civility to the debate.

I still have your pen, though I used the ink. Should I return it? I have not heard yet about the Matriculation Examination. I hope your taxi business flourishes.

My best regards,
Alice Millwood

* * *

I eventually got time to write a reply:

Dear Alice (be as informal as you like)

You may keep the pen, and my rates for the ink are very modest indeed. I still cannot write with more than one hand at a time, so have a sufficiency.

38

Your article reads well, is cogent and factually correct. That was enterprising of you – are you a scribbler? Remember Johnson's dictum on writing, though I suspect scribblers must scribble; certainly it must be easier than rowing women weighing eighteen stone, with five stone or so of shopping aboard, against the tide. But I digress.

I haven't heard definitely about the Examination either. Presumably the markers are still awestruck by our erudition. That will pass, however.

Pray consider me, at need, your esquire

Matthew Dobbs

* * *

The Matriculation Examination people claimed I had gotten one answer wrong, which surprised me. Which? But I had been admitted, that was the important thing. As the time was nearing when I had to leave, I took the letter to the lawyer who handled Mrs Christianson's estate. She had been adamant that I could claim the money when I chose, even if I was under age, as long as it was for my education. Satisfied on these points, he prepared a draft for the money, which I secured from the local bank, though he accompanied me to avoid delays. I then went to the buried jar where I kept my rowing earnings and counted the lot: just under £20. That would have to do.

* * *

I was packing my things when Mrs Paston appeared. She hesitated, and then wished me well. I thanked her, not knowing for certain whether she had been a friend to me or not, then asked about Mrs Christianson's husband and child. She hesitated again, and then told me they were fishermen, lost at sea, and Mrs Christianson had answered her advertisement for a cook-housekeeper. I nodded, said she had never mentioned them in all the years we were acquainted. Another hesitation, then Mrs Paston said that Mrs Christianson regarded me as a sort of son. My eyes stung a bit at that, and I thanked her again, not knowing what else to say.

Mr Japes also wished me well. The new old age pension, five shillings a week, seemed to cheer him a great deal; with the fish he could catch, he would not starve, though he said the money I had brought him was very welcome. I thanked him again for his help, for being square with me (as I was with him), and wished him well.

Mr Paston appeared just as I was leaving. He wanted to know how much the tuition at the university was. For a moment, I thought he was going to give me some money, and I told him the amount, but he just nodded and walked away.

* * *

Another trek to Norwich, this time carrying my worldly goods, arriving sweating and exhausted at the train station, for the same train, as I felt I needed the entire day to find lodgings, orient myself etc. I hoped this time I would sleep, but no, and got into the same station where I had met Alice worn and badly shaven and dirty.

I eventually got to University College, paid my tuition, found a board where rooms to let were offered, and began a selection. It occurred to me that if I had a place with a functioning kitchen, I could perhaps save some money by preparing my own meals. There was one that sounded suitable; I got the approximate location from my London map and found the place. Since the houses were jammed together, distinguished as separate only by the steps in front, I missed the one I wanted, until I realized there were numbers for identifying each.

The apartment was the bottom level of a three story house, that is, the below street or basement level, and consisted entirely of a kitchen, pantries and a small bathroom. It appeared I would once again have to bathe in a sort of very large bucket, standing up, just as in the parish house, though I would at least be by myself. It wasn't in the least comfortable, indeed it seemed hot, but I couldn't recall being comfortable, so I was prepared to stay there. I would have to sleep on a bench against the wall. The rent seemed low, perhaps suspiciously so, so I paid for four months. The stove/oven was fed by a gas meter that took pennies, so some familiarization was going to be necessary. Still, I had a place now, an address.

II. LONDON

For the lectures, I was prepared to take notes and did so. Otherwise, the various masters each seemed to assume our time was entirely at their individual disposal, so required reading, papers etc. amounting overall to multiples of the hours in each day. I subsisted on sandwiches and tinned stuff for a week, then finally assembled what I needed for a pasty preparation, including two new, sharp knives. Everything was unfamiliar, everything was awkward, everything was slow, but I managed a set of 17 that was edible, didn't leak (much) and would keep, though the flat was very uncomfortable even on cool days. It occurred to me that perhaps it wasn't a good idea to keep the pasties several days at such temperatures, so could I sell them, and to whom?

By ostentatiously eating my pasties, I began to attract customers. I charged sixpence each, figuring a profit of four pence, so began to bake a new set at first every third day, then every second. One of my customers was a middle-sized bespectacled slender fellow, a medical student, named Eddie Partington, evidently (I was told) one of the Partingtons, the real ones, as opposed to the character in the Conan Doyle story. Eddie was more than a bit of a gourmet, and, while pronouncing my pasties "very tolerable", opined that a small amount of garlic would greatly improve them. So I bought some and some olive oil (another of Eddie's suggestions) and tried the experiment. A medium sized clove of garlic, minced and thoroughly mashed (for I feared the consequence of a customer biting into a piece of garlic; this was England, after all) did indeed improve the taste and savour almost miraculously, and my circle of customers widened to where I had to cook a set every day. I bought another valise, an old, cheap one so I had one for my books and papers and the other for the pasties, lining it with newspapers at first, then (still another of Eddie's suggestions) butcher's paper. My preparations required early rising, which I hated, but my efficiency improved with practice.

* * *

My fellow students were a very heterogeneous, cosmopolitan lot, all races, religions, classes mixed. I found it extremely interesting; I felt intellectually alive, meeting and talking to Sikhs, Muslims, blacks, Jews, Catholics, Dissenters, Chinese, all of us equal, each with new ideas, points of view and experiences. Earl's Cross was as nothing – here was the world! Groups of us would meet casually and talk about whatever was on our minds, no arguments or rancor, just exchanges, all stimulating of thought and reflection. Some of the lectures were fascinating and all the masters were on top of their subject.

* * *

About two months into term, I got another letter from Alice. She sent it care of the Registrar, who doubtless was not pleased at the extra duty, but I was delighted, since I had been fretting about the propriety of writing to her unbidden.

Dear Matthew

I am sending this in the care of the Registrar, who is a friend of Father; I do not know where you are staying.

I have been teaching two months now and still do not feel comfortable in front of the students. They are not much younger than I, and seem inclined to be, how I can put this, challenging. Not on the ground of knowledge, I am ahead there, but they seem to question my authority. I had not expected this, and am not sure what to do about it. Talk to the headmistress? Let me have your thoughts.

I still use your pen, it gives good service, and I thank you for it. My old one is inclined to leak and blot, and with my handwriting, that is not helpful.

Let me know how you are faring. It is not our tradition to go to university, but I am curious.

Your friend,
Alice

* * *

I thought about her letter a few days, while I dealt with cooking, attending lectures, reading and generally trying to complete what seemed to be twenty-eight hours of work piled into a twenty-four hour day, not counting sleeping, eating etc. At length there was a "smooth" as I think sailors call it, and wrote back:

Dear Alice

I think your problem was basically what sent me to university rather than trying to make some money teaching at a school, the knowledge that I really wasn't much older than the boys I would have to teach, and I was not confident they would accept my authority, without, as I think the French expression is, *force majeure* (no, I am not confident of the spelling). I am a bit surprised that girls behave in the same way, though that probably is naïve on my part.

On the one hand, developing the self-assurance and authority probably simply requires time and experience, which is no comfort. On the other, I suspect every new fledged teacher has the same problem, some overcoming it faster than others. I do not think you should go to the headmistress; I suspect she would be annoyed at you, not at the students. You are probably taller than any of them, and if my memory serves, physically robust. (Yes, I do think this a factor in the presence of a teacher). So be persistent and firm; stand your ground – you are meting out the marks, after all. Don't be impressed by what is essentially juvenile behaviour. If disrespect ripens into mutiny, write me and I will sally forth to sort them out, proper, as they say hereabouts.

The Registrar was sufficiently accommodating, but I fancy deludes himself into thinking he has more important tasks. Hubris everywhere. So my address is enclosed on a separate piece of paper as on the envelope.

My place of lodging was once the kitchen of a family dwelling, in the basement. I have a real appreciation now for the phrase "sweated labor", as I rise at a most unchristian hour to make a set of 17 pasties – the Cornish substitute for a sandwich – 15 of which I sell to fellow students at sixpence each. This actually keeps me afloat financially – just – and incidentally spares me from temptations of concerts, plays, conversations, sleep, etc. no doubt all tending to the building of my character into a towering edifice of, well, character.

Actually, and you should think about this, with all the work, I have felt as if I were freed, liberated, from my earlier life: the talks with fellow students, a very heterogeneous bunch, the lectures (some better than others) and the theoretical opportunities for the aforementioned concerts, etc. make me feel alive. I am learning so much. It may not be your family tradition, but traditions can change, and with your mind, you should think about coming here, and yes, women can and do obtain degrees from this university (not like Oxford).

Let me know how things go,

Matthew

* * *

Another six weeks had passed, and my pasty-making efficiency had developed to the point where I could sleep an additional half-hour, though I worried constantly about the alarm clock I had to use. I had written several papers, to fair applause by the masters, and was actually able to attend a concert, my first, and indeed almost my first exposure to what was called classical music: symphonies by Beethoven (his eighth) and Haydn (his 96th) with its bright, busy, joyful fourth movement. I was unsure of how these names were to be pronounced, so when I saw Eddie Partington with a girl I had seen him with before, I asked him privately. He told me, and when the girl, introduced to me as Christine Soames, reappeared, left with her. I had the impression he was more interested in her than she was in him.

* * *

The following Monday, I found another letter from Alice, waiting on the floor behind the door to my abode, as there was no mail slot. I put the burner under the soup stock pot on, poured myself a glass of milk, sat down at the kitchen table and opened the letter. It said:

Dear Matthew

Things seem to be going a little bit better in class. Your comments about using physical intimidation somewhat shocked me, but I found the tactic helpful with one or two of the ringleaders, and this seems to have cowed the others. Experience really does help. In another year, I will feel much more comfortable in front of a class. On the other hand, I try and try and do not seem to be conveying the knowledge. Is there a better way? Can I do it better? How?

The holidays are coming up and Mother and Father have arranged for me, booked me might be the better expression, to attend some dances and parties at their friends. I am not very happy about being "shopped" about, which is what it amounts to. I do not dance well, am very poor at small talk, and find what conversation occurs extremely limiting and uninteresting. The talks with you, and your letters, actually were the first really adult conversations I think I have ever had. However, my parents feel it is necessary for someone in my social position, whatever that is.

Please write again. I greatly enjoyed your letter, and hope you have finally gotten some free time.

Alice

* * *

My concert was the only spot of free time I was to have for the rest of the term. I was buried with demands for papers, with exams, my product, rudimentary hygiene etc. In one way, I was glad of all the demands, as Alice's letter had depressed me. Country house guests had to include eligible (for her) men, some of whom were likely to be students at Oxford or Cambridge and clever and amusing, even intellectual. I fancied she was warning me not to get too serious about her, and I realized the warning was too late. Her dismissal of the state of my hands when we first met may have simply been good manners, but had, I now realized, captured me.

* * *

After end of term, upon consideration, I decided to change my business approach. I could bake up to ten sets of pasties in what would be a murderously long day, but how to sell them? I had noted several shops that sold pastry dishes, meat pies and such, and felt that they might be willing to sell my pasties. I went to several, with samples of course, and found three that were willing to trust me to deliver a standard product that would not actually make their customers sick. More to the point, they would pay me for them on delivery rather than after they were sold. I was figuring on a profit of two pence each, but found the hours these shops were open meant my deliveries had to be by about two in the afternoon, so I had to get up even earlier to make my quota of six batches of 17, but, on the other hand, could rest after the last delivery.

My marks were quite good, and put me in line for a possible scholarship next year, though not next term. I was supposed to read some things, but for once had time for that.

* * *

A second letter from Alice arrived after I had begun adjusting to the holiday routine. She noted that I had not replied to her last letter and was afraid I had been offended by something she had said. She also was very unhappy that the headmistress had changed the marks Alice had given one or two of her students, who were basically academic drones at best, to less unfavourable ones. Alice rightly took this badly, as an affront to her judgment and a violation of academic integrity. Since I now had time in the afternoons, I replied.

I told her I had not replied because I had been absolutely swamped with work, that my work had been to good effect, and that my new business routine, which I described, as I didn't want to conceal anything from her, left my afternoons free. I expressed shock at the headmistress' behavior – had money changed hands? Surely these girls weren't going on to university, so no questions of scholarships or admissions were involved. I suggested she talk to her parents, as this was in a sense an attack on her professionalism. Otherwise, she had done her duty, and could continue with a clear conscience, though perhaps she might consider teaching someplace else (perhaps in London?)

As far as her efforts to instill learning, I referred to my experience assisting the day school teacher, and told her that learning required work and only each individual could provide that work, she couldn't pour the knowledge into their heads, so could only make it clear to each of them what they needed to learn. I confessed to a feeling of helplessness when confronted with a student who just wasn't interested, but holding a pistol to their heads was unfortunately not considered an acceptable tactic, though one could always hope for greater liberality in these matters someday, perhaps just involving use of hat pins, electric shocks etc. as a compromise. I said I was possibly joking about this.

* * *

Although I really needed to go to sleep early, there were a number of concerts I felt I had to attend, one or more nearly every evening, so struggled each day with effects of sleeplessness. Still, Alice's letter had left me feeling better, though I told myself sternly I was "imagining a vain thing" if I entertained any hopes of obtaining her affection. Friendship was all such as I could hope for. So I kept telling myself, over and over each day.

* * *

The new term, my second, started much like the first. During the holidays, I had made more than a pound a day profit, so could buy my books from my earnings, and the beginnings of a better wardrobe, suitable for concerts etc. Two weeks into the term, I got a reply from Alice, thanking me for the counsel – me, a counselor! – and noting that the two visits she went on were every bit as pointless as she had feared. My spirits rose at this, and were only slightly dampened as she said her parents were not inclined to be helpful, as they were not sure how they could help, and that she thought the headmistress was not being bribed directly, but one of the other teachers indicated that the headmistress just wanted all the students to graduate the school. Alice said she would just pass the marks she thought the students had earned on, that was all she could do. Alice said nothing about my suggestion she try another school, and I reflected that Alice was living at her parents' expense, so had her entire salary, whatever it was, to spend.

* * *

We exchanged short letters, then, nearing the end of the term, she informed me she would be visiting her aunt in London in July, and were there any concerts or other entertainments on the dates? I got in touch with Eddie, who kept track of such things, and was told there was a concert on the Sunday and an opera, one of the Italian composer Verdi's, the Saturday. I wrote back despite the massive and peremptory demands on my attention, giving her the dates and times and offering to (e)squire her to either or both.

End of term was endless. I wasn't sure I was keeping up with all my obligations, and began having nightmares about missing exams, forgetting papers due and so forth in addition to the standard (for me) ones about being buried alive. After the last exam, I sat on a bench, completely drained, staring blankly at the rest of the world until Eddie and David Cohen, bless their souls, rousted me and hauled me off to a pub. I declined the beer, which I really didn't like, but found something called "ginger beer" quite acceptable. We talked till dark, and then had some pub sandwiches, which Eddie judged marginally acceptable, and David, who as a rabbinical student seemed remarkably indifferent to what he ate, consumed without comment. Our talk continued on until closing time, when we reluctantly separated. I went home and found a letter from Alice, giving me her aunt's address and saying she wanted to attend both events. I wondered how much the tickets would cost and guessed I would pay whatever was required, and went to sleep on my bench in a very much better mood.

* * *

My fortunes were in flood. I was told by the University that I would be given a scholarship for the next year. This meant next year was easily affordable, "easily" meaning working myself into a middle aged, as opposed to an early grave. Then I realized midway through the fourth or so batch of pasties that morning that I would require decent clothes, clothes suitable for appearing at the events I planned to attend. After four more batches, a new record for me, I decided to consult the expert in such matters, Eddie.

So I went to his family's house, an impressive pile in Portland or Posh Place (as I dubbed it), was (reluctantly) admitted and asked to see him. I had to send in my name. I had no card, and for an instant I thought I would be thrown out, but Eddie appeared promptly. I explained what I wanted to get and asked for his advice. He sat down, asked what I could spend, and I told him I had a reserve of £15 or more, but that evening clothes were probably too limited an investment, so it would have to be respectable, not more.

Eddie wrote down what he thought I should get and, more important, where I should get it, mentioning his name of course. He also said not to wear the flat cap that was almost a badge, he said, of lower middle class-ness. So new shoes and a hat were added to a rather long and unquestionably expensive list.

There wasn't much time, so I was measured for the clothes, got the shoes and hat, and went back to my place. I had told Eddie of my plans, and was very surprised to find a note from him, inviting Alice and me to his family's box in Albert Hall. He was going with Christine, and there were seats for four. Evidently no one else in his family was going. He would furnish the tickets but asked me to buy two librettos when we got there. I wrote a note, saying I would, and thanked him. This meant less expense for tickets, as the librettos couldn't cost that much – could they?

* * *

My new clothes seemed stiff but looked fine, and when I showed myself in regalia, he was judiciously favourable. They cost nearly £10, but I told myself that eventually I had to appear less scruffy, and went back to my occupation.

* * *

Alice was due to arrive about four that Saturday, so I made eight batches of pasties, delivered them, went back and bathed in my bucket, though it was so hot in that place and I was sweating so much that the bath water seemed redundant. Eddie had also suggested I shave before the meeting and splash some cologne – just a little, he cautioned – on my face and a few other places. I got dressed in my opera togs, as I thought of them, and emerged into the afternoon, redolent and (for me) resplendent.

I was nervous as her train pulled in, as I hadn't seen her in a year. She looked magnificent, and I thought quite a few passersby were giving her overly much attention. Her luggage this time was smaller, lighter, and I took it from her with the statement that carrying it for her was part of the service. She smiled and seemed pleased with my appearance.

We took a taxi to her aunt's. Her name was Lydia Lark and while I thought her husband (dead) must have had a hard time in school, I merely nodded. We talked about her first year as a teacher, and I tried to think of some strategy or approach to crush the ringleaders, but she said she would be dealing with a new set of girls, so I merely noted that with a years' experience behind her, she would feel more at ease. She had turned in her marks, but didn't know what the headmistress had done with them. Since Alice had gone to the same school, I commented that certainly made her job harder. She agreed, and we arrived at the aunt's house.

Mrs Lark was above middle height, slender, taffy-haired – no sign of grey yet – with pale blue eyes. The only aspect of her appearance similar to Alice's was her hands, long, with slender fingers. Eye color and height apparently came from the other side of her family, whatever that was. She was hospitable but a bit distant; I felt she didn't know what to make of me. She questioned me about my plans, eyed my (restrained) consumption of the tea she served as though looking for breaches of manners, and seemed relieved when I didn't do anything unseemly. I didn't like tea, but sipped it as decorously as I was capable of. Both women were impressed when I acknowledged obtaining a scholarship for the next year. Since we were to dine after the opera, we sallied forth about six, as Alice said she wanted to walk.

We had walked a few steps when I turned to Alice and said, "I've been waiting for your appreciation of my unwonted resplendishousness. No doubt you are still somewhat awestruck, but even halting praise is acceptable."

Alice glanced at me, knitted her brow, and replied, "Resplendishousness is not a word, and I cannot be certain how wonted or not your appearance is, so I must absolutely decline comment."

I said, "Oh very well, then, if we must be confined to the covers of an unabridged, then my unaccustomed splendor surely merits comment. Here you will have to take my word for it, but I can get testimony for my normal scruffy condition from friends, or even enemies – well, especially enemies."

Alice, trying not to smile, looked me up and down and said, "I suppose it will have to do."

I made a theatrical gesture of appeal to the Gods, and remarked, "I must even bear this damnation with no praise at all. Let it go, I will bear it."

Alice said, "I hope in silence," and I laughed and so did she. She then said I looked fine, and why was the man cadging compliments, when I was supposed to be praising her appearance. I told her, "You look magnificent, transcendently beautiful, Goddess-like." I then added, "I meant the attractive ones, not the others." She said, "I'm glad you clarified that, but thank you. Are those new clothes?"

I said, "At last, yes. I went to Eddie, our host, for some counsel on dress."

She said, "I haven't heard of the family." I replied "The Partingtons are wealthy, I don't know from what source, but their house in Portland Place is impressive. I asked Eddie because he dresses well, he's not a dandy but has what I take to be good taste. He is something of a gourmet; in fact, his suggestions on my pasty recipe were very helpful."

We walked on a bit in silence. I continued, "I went to the house, knocked on the door, and the fellow who opened it looked at me like I was something undesirable on the sole of someone's shoe and asked what I wanted. I told him I wanted to talk to Mr Edward Partington, the university student. He asked me for my card, and here my mind was thrown into turmoil. I began thinking I wasn't aware I needed to be carrying a deck of cards around, and even if I had one, what card should I send in, the three of clubs or the ten of diamonds, and if I did send one in, would I get it back or would I have to carry an incomplete deck of cards around, and then I realized he meant a card with my name printed on it, which I didn't have as I can usually, though not always, remember my name, but I seem to be digressing again. Anyway, Eddie received me inside, sat me down and I asked his advice on what I needed to get and where I should get it. I think I was putting his tact to something of a test, but he said to get a tailored suit, ready-made just wouldn't do and gave me the name of a tailor, and here I am, contributing to your dazzlement."

Alice had been amused by my recital, objected again to "dazzlement", but I insisted it was indeed a word, at least *pro tem*. Still amused, she asked, "I hope you didn't pay too much. I know you have to work hard to support yourself." I said, "A little less than two week's profit, but I told myself, and Eddie agreed, that I really needed some good clothes, for concerts and such, or perhaps formal parties, though doubtless those wouldn't be as much fun as informal ones."

After a few more steps, I said, "After exams, I was absolutely flat. Eddie and David – Cohen (another friend), got me to my feet and took me to a pub near university where we talked to closing time, then a bit longer outside. I've mentioned this before to you, but these casual talks with friends, one's intellectual peers, are a very important part, unacknowledged to be sure, of an education." I thought some more, then said, "When I came here, for the first time I felt myself to be an adult, a man, a freeman. With all the problems, with all the work, I am at last on my own, following my destiny on my own terms." More silence, then I said, "I hope my comments are clear to you, about how I feel about this place. I really think I am where I should be." Alice and I looked at each other and we both smiled, and I thought, she really does understand.

An hour allowed us to cover about four miles, and I hailed another taxi for the ride to Albert Hall. I had told her about Eddie and his request for the librettos (libretti?) for the opera and we had talked about musical events we had attended, a fairly short conversation on her side. I had already gotten the tickets to the concert Sunday and gave her the bill of fare, musically speaking: more modern works, Mendelssohn, Brahms and Strauss. We agreed we were looking forward to it.

I bought two librettos, not too expensive, got four programs, and we looked through them, waiting for Eddie and Christine. About a quarter to eight, they appeared: Eddie perfectly dressed, I thought, Christine not quite up to his standard, though I am a very inexperienced judge, and she seemed a bit uninterested, nothing new there.

The box was very posh, and I was impressed. Eddie had a pair of opera glasses which he passed about for general use, though, as I remarked to Alice, with my eyesight, holding my hands up with the fingers curled would probably do as well for me.

The opera was wholly engrossing: the music, the singing, the costumes, the sets were a world transformed. We tried to follow the singing using the librettos, but sung Italian seems to transcend the written word. After the last ovations, we went out into the summer evening, and I told Alice I would always remember this evening and her being there to share it with me made it perfect. I thought I had been too forward, but she did not seem displeased.

We saw David and the girl he was with; he gave us her name but for some reason, perhaps the distraction Alice seemed perpetually to produce, I didn't catch it. It was a very cheerful group and we decided to go to a Jewish restaurant that David claimed was the best in London, a claim provoking mild skepticism from Eddie, mild because he felt that wasn't saying much. So we went, again by taxi and dined there.

The fare wasn't too familiar, so we let David order for us all. The prices seemed very high, but when the meals arrived, they turned out to be very good indeed. Everyone was pleased, and Eddie conceded David had a point. Eddie and Christine taxied home, as did Alice and I. When we got to her aunt's, we made plans to meet for tomorrow – actually, as I pointed out, today, clasped hands and said goodnight. I wanted to kiss her, but it would have been too awkward and probably entirely too forward. I walked all the way back, partly from happiness and partly because I wanted to keep my spending down at least a little.

Mrs Lark had invited me to her house for lunch, a command performance, I judged, but felt my table manners had been refined sufficiently by Earl's Cross refectory, hints from Mrs Christianson, and Eddie's example to avoid being sent to eat outdoors. So it proved; aside from commenting that I ate like

Alice, to which I agreed, she seemed to accept my presence more easily.

The concert was at two and we again took a taxi, if only because it threatened rain. I enjoyed all the pieces; Alice wasn't too keen on the Brahms but liked the others. Then we walked to the station, where we had left Alice's things on our way over. I was now more at ease with her, and talked about the pasty business. I said I supposed I could go into it in a much bigger and more systematic way, renting a bigger kitchen, hiring assistants, etc. In fact, I had made calculations about what I would need. But I said my experience of my first year at university had convinced me that I was by nature an academic, a don in embryo, and what I was I should do. It was, after all, the family business. She seemed sympathetic, and said she had been thinking herself about making a living with her pen, perhaps eventually writing novels. I commented that writing was very hard indeed to make a living at, that Jane Austen herself never made much money, though every novel she wrote was still in print after a century. Alice wondered if the poor financial return was because of her sex but I argued that what Jane Austen had written was new, fresh and original and that it took time for the public to adapt to and appreciate something new, fresh and original. I then put her things on the train, we clasped hands again (and I again resisted the impulse to kiss them) and she was gone. I was significantly poorer but rather happier and Alice's visit had gone well.

* * *

We exchanged letters nearly every two weeks after that. I was again cast down by Alice's attendance at several country house weekends, expecting every one to bring news of a more suitable admirer, but the summer passed into fall with a return to academic routines for both of us.

* * *

The holidays brought my pasty production back up to between terms levels, though the owners of the pie shops were annoyed by the "holidays" I was taking, as they put it, during term time. I explained, but they wanted the product, not explanations.

Since there was nothing I could do about my career choice, I shrugged and left in silence.

Alice was at yet another country house, up near Leeds, and I again became anxious and depressed. My suit, such as it was, seemed not merely hopeless but absurd. Her parents were putting her on exhibit in as many places as possible. Like me, she was eighteen, I supposed, ripe for at least an engagement. I swore, and told myself only five terms to go.

* * *

Spring term was as hectic as ever for me. The headaches were getting worse, lasting longer. I told myself if my education demanded I bear them, then bear them I would. Alice and I continued to correspond, and I wondered if her parents approved the connection or whether, in their family, letters counted for little. They must have gotten a report on me from Mrs Lark. Perhaps I was really considered to be nothing at all, at least in romantic terms, no threat to their dynastic plans, and this greatly distressed me. Apparently this years' crop of students was not as obstreperous for Alice, or, as I suggested, she was simply becoming more experienced. I kept thinking she ought to be at university, but didn't dwell on the point, as she had already heard my opinion.

* * *

Flat again after exams at the end of my second year, I mean emotionally and physically, Eddie, David and two other pals tracked me down – it wasn't hard, as I wasn't moving – and, following our tradition established last year, adjourned to the same pub, ate the same sorts of sandwiches, and talked about anything that came into our heads, this time till daybreak at the rooms of one of the pals, Charles Digby, a maths student and steady customer, a "Regular". I returned to my place feeling oddly happy and, not so oddly, very underslept, and decided to start production right away, though it was a late start for me.

* * *

On the one hand, my scholarship was renewed, so I would almost certainly be able to get a B.A. I wanted a M.A., which would qualify me to teach at university, but told myself, just two more years.

On the other, Alice had either become very popular at country house weekends, or her parents were shopping her more aggressively. Either way, I was surprisingly cast down by the fear that her next letter would describe this fellow she had met in such terms as would leave me with no hope of ever securing her. I found myself weighing each letter, uncertain whether a long one or a short one would be better.

* * *

Despite the roiling commotion over the assassination of the Austrian heir, Eddie's parents went on their usual tour. Eddie was now "on rounds" in the medical school so could not go, though I suspected he wanted to stay close to Christine, even with what I thought was an obvious lack of enthusiasm on her part. I had noticed her with a tall fellow, a student at university I didn't know, and saw her much more animated. This concerned me, as I naturally supported Eddie's suit.

Eddie sent a note round to me, saying performances of *The Marriage of Figaro* were to be presented two weeks ahead, and invited me to join him in his family's box, with a guest if I liked. I immediately wrote to Alice, offering her Friday night's performance or that Saturday night (Eddie hadn't been clear as to the exact days). Alice wrote back promptly, to my delight, saying Friday night would be best, as there would be a family gathering at Millwood Saturday-Sunday. I went by Eddie's domicile, and found him also opting for Friday, as it was Christine's preference also. I didn't mention Eddie's apparent rival, and felt a bit guilty as a consequence.

* * *

I made my deliveries Friday morning into afternoon, warning the shop owners of tomorrow's holiday. They were not pleased, and I listened with surprising patience to their lectures. To put it mildly, they felt I lacked commercial instincts, which was not quite true. The day was cooler than last year, not that that made much difference in the temperature at my place, but I bathed as before, donned my concert apparel after careful shaving and dashes of cologne. So fortified, I went to the station and waited for Alice. It was not a long wait, but would have been worth a longer: she had a different dress on, and if anything looked even more captivating than ever. She seemed happy to see me and received my compliments with a smile. I took her bag, not very heavy since she was staying only overnight, managed to secure a taxi, and was with her as we drove to her aunt's.

We exchanged news of our summer so far. The only noteworthy event in my life was a Sunday concert I had attended a few weeks ago. I described the program, and she said she was sorry to have missed it, as two of the composers, Strauss and Tchaikovsky, were her favourites. I was sorry too and quietly resolved to hear more of those composers' *oeuvres* – another French expression I had picked up from Eddie.

Her summer, she said, was spent reading, mostly popular works (I resolved further to check a few of the titles she mentioned out of the library) and – my heart sank – in country house weekends. She seemed to sense my feelings, for she added that they were, as she put it, "replete with *ennui*" as she didn't hunt, shoot, fish or play bridge. I felt slightly better as we reached her aunt's.

I felt fractionally more at ease with the mandatory tea, and even was able to smile blandly when the aunt asked me if selling pastries from a barrow wasn't very difficult in rain. I gently corrected her: "Pasties, not pastries, and no, selling anything from a barrow would be a most inefficient use of my time. I bake them in batches of seventeen, sell them to pie shop owners for them to retail, but I would have no shame about selling from a barrow, even if I had to wear a kilt and dance doing it, although I would do it badly – dance, I mean. I suppose I could wear a kilt as plausibly as anyone." Here I glanced at Alice who was looking amused, though the aunt looked blank.

Feeling oddly encouraged, I began to warm up, "My aim is to earn money for my education, and I will do anything, well, anything legal, to that end. I will say that frequently, arising at the ghastly hours I must to start preparations, I find myself swearing a blood oath that once the diploma is in my hand", raising my right hand to illustrate, "I will never prepare, eat, look at or think of a pasty if I can help it, though realistically, if I have children some day", refusing to glance at Alice, "I almost certainly won't be able to deny myself the opportunity of throwing my experiences, my efforts, my struggles into the faces of my children, at frequent intervals, to encourage them to greater efforts, for their own good, of course. And it is likely that they in retaliation will encourage, or rather require me to make them for the family to eat. So I shall be hoisted on a pasty petard, if such a thing exists."

Alice was trying to keep a straight face, and the aunt was beginning to show some signs of amusement. Perhaps she does have a sense of humor, I thought as I sipped my tea.

She commented, "It is unusual to find rooms for students which are supplied with a kitchen, I suppose." I replied, "My place – I am not really sure what to call it, as apartment or flat seems too grand, and it is more than a room – was once the basement, the "downstairs" as I think it is called, of a family house. There is a kitchen, a sort of bathroom, and some other rooms, probably pantries or such, which I have been really reluctant to explore. What impresses me is how hot the place is, except now and then, when it is hotter. I really wonder if I am on top of or next to a set of boilers, and I find myself, at times in the night, listening for the sounds of stokers. Perhaps I am being given a foretaste of Hell, so that I might mend my ways, not that I have had time or money for 'ways'". I sipped more tea, glancing at Alice: she glanced back, evidently still amused.

Her aunt, apparently feeling a need to keep up her end of the conversation, noted that such places sometimes had wine cellars beneath the kitchens. By now I had the bit in my teeth: "Well, that is where captives will be kept, chained to the wall with a few human skeletons, also chained here and there for effect. I haven't taken any captives myself, of course, lacking leisure, at least so far into my course of studies, but I would probably have to hire a headsman, by the day I suppose, wielding a rusty halberd, and with a tasteful collection of whips, scourges and so forth on one wall." I glanced at Alice, who began to laugh, and I started to laugh too, while saying, "the room for Satanic Black Masses occupies comparatively little space of course." Then we were all laughing together. When I had recovered to some extent, I said, "I fear I exaggerate." Silence, then, "Somewhat." More laughter. I drank more tea, as it had cooled enough.

Smiling, Alice's aunt asked how much longer I would be at university, I said, "I am halfway through. Next year I could get a B.A., which would let me teach at a public school at least, but I want to get a M.A. the following year, so I could teach at a university. Then," I raised my arms grandiloquently, "the riches of Peru."

Both ladies laughed aloud. I glanced at them both, and qualified myself: "Of course, some parts of Peru are richer than others." More laughter. I said in explanation, "The family business, so to speak; my father was a schoolmaster."

The aunt nodded. Evidently Alice had told her of my background. I glanced at the clock, and then pulled my watch out of its fob: six o'clock. I said this to Alice, and we rose to leave. I thanked her aunt for her hospitality, to me and particularly to Alice, as it enabled us to attend the opera together. The aunt was gracious, indeed seemed less distant than previously.

Alice and I set forth again. She liked walking, as did I, and I thought it would be a fine thing to go on walks with her, talking or silent as our moods took us. After a space, she said, "You do run on at times, Matthew. Whips, scourges and skeletons, indeed. Where do you come up with such things?" I replied, "Rubbishy literature allied to an overactive imagination. Perhaps I will check the place for a wine cellar. All the wine will have been taken, I am sure, but perhaps such a place would be cooler."

Alice commented, "You didn't mention a bedroom. Where do you sleep? "I said, "There is a sort of bench along a wall next the kitchen table, where I suppose maids and footmen sat, waiting. I sleep on that." She said, "That must be uncomfortable." I thought about the top of the wardrobe where I had hidden, the cots supported by ropes, in the parish house and at Earl's Cross, and said, "I may have slept in an actual bed before my parents were killed, but I have no memory of that or indeed of much of anything before the train wreck. I have slept on bare boards, and survived. Sleeping in a bed is something I suppose I may someday aspire too." I didn't look at Alice, lest I seem too forward, indeed suggestive. Then I said, "I suppose I'm not being very original, but Fate or Providence or God deals us our hands, and it is up to us to play them as best we can." Alice asked, "Do you believe in God?" I was a little confused, and finally answered, "I don't know. Despite, or perhaps because of, growing up in a parish house – I never went into the church, I don't know why – I am not agnostic or atheistic, just unsure. We had church parades at Earl's Cross, but these weren't very inspirational, at least not of religious feeling. Someone told me of a saying of the writer, Joseph Conrad: It is only the inexperienced man who doesn't believe in luck."

We walked on in silence. I began to fear I had offended her, but she said her silence was reflective, not resentful. I looked at my watch: nearly seven. I told Alice we needed to look for a taxi. We were eventually able to secure one – weren't these people looking for business? Once inside, I told Alice I was obliged to get two librettos, or were they libretti? – Alice said she suspected either would do. We also got four programs, as before. We looked through them, waiting for Eddie and Christine.

They arrived a little later. Eddie seemed glad to see us. Christine seemed reserved, more than I remembered from last time.

The opera was magnificent. Song after song, melody after melody. Staging, costumes, all perfect to my assuredly inexperienced eyes. The plot, as opera plots go, rather moving. No wonder the reputation it had, according to Eddie.

After a very large number of curtain calls, we eventually got outside. I thanked Eddie for the opportunity to see what was surely, I agreed, one of the finest operas ever staged. I was quite enthusiastic, which cooled a bit when Eddie said he had to take Christine home, so we would have to dine alone.

I asked Alice what her pleasure was, perhaps the Jewish restaurant? She said she had heard that Londoners dined mostly on fish and chips and wanted to try that. I didn't know if she was trying to ease the financial drain on me, but I had to agree, so we began walking in the late evening air, smelling, to be sure, of exhaust and coal fires, but still cool and invigorating. After several streets, I began to entertain the desperate (for me) resolve to actually ask some passerby for directions, when we saw a chips shop in the distance. When we got there, we saw it was open all night as well as in the day. It seemed crowded, which, as I pointed out to Alice, might be a good sign, Eddie's low opinion of the culinary expectations of Londoners in general notwithstanding.

We ordered "the usual", along with tea (Alice) and milk (me) and found a table next to the wall. We ate in companionable silence, and then Alice asked me what was the state of Eddie and Christine's relationship. I frowned, then said that Eddie had told me he had known Christine all his life, and had been in love with her as long as he could remember being able to be in love. Either Christine didn't wear her heart on her sleeve, or was not encouraging Eddie. I sat in silence a while, and then told Alice about seeing Christine with another man, a student whose name I didn't know, and she seemed much more forthcoming with him. I said I hadn't mentioned this to Eddie, but feared he had an effective rival. After another pause I said I had grown up friendless until I went to Earl's Cross and to university, so valued my friends, and while Eddie often seemed to be playing the dilettante, I knew him for a very serious man indeed when it concerned his profession and had always found him to be a good and loyal friend, so I was apprehensive he was headed for a severe disappointment.

Alice nodded and said she had gotten the same impression, that Christine thought of Eddie as a friend only, one whose aspiration shouldn't be encouraged. When she said this, I wondered whether she was placing me in the same category. We finished our meal, and I asked her if the meal matched her expectations. She smiled and said that it wasn't too bad and that now she could say she had had a typical Londoner meal. I grinned and said, "No expense spared." She laughed, and we got up.

I managed to hijack a taxi by the expedient of nearly getting hit by one, and took Alice back to her aunt's. I paid off the driver, and Alice asked how I was going to get back. I said I was walking back with an evening of Mozart in my head. I might hum a bit, but promised not to sing, out of consideration for anyone in earshot. She told me I was invited to breakfast tomorrow – actually I told her, today – and then I could escort her to the station, perhaps after a walk about the neighbourhood. So I said I would call at eight, and we said goodnight.

* * *

After minimal sleep – the music and scenes coursed through my head all night – but a thorough bath and shave, I took another taxi to the aunt's house, getting there at 8 AM exactly. The aunt seemed cordial, Alice delectable, and the meal edible. The aunt asked if I did all my own cooking, and I said, glancing at Alice, "Except for occasional Lucullan dining experiences with guests, yes. Breakfast for me is usually a pasty though I am capable of producing a reasonable Spanish omelette, eaten with toast – I am also capable of toast. Weekends I usually prepared a soup for evening meals for several days." "What kind of soup?" she asked. I said, "It usually is a very rich, thick beef-vegetable-barley soup, though I will sometimes venture a split pea with ham. I don't starve", I added smiling.

"Alice says you greatly enjoyed the opera." I replied, "It was, I hate to use the expression again, a transcendent experience. I thought the song the soprano playing a young boy sang the most beautiful song I had ever heard, and of course it was followed by one of the most famous. But the rest didn't fall much short, and I can see why my friend Eddie Partington calls it one of the two most popular operas ever staged." "Is his family the Partingtons, of Portland Place?" "They do live there, yes; at least, I don't know of any others." "Have you been inside the house then?" I said, "Yes, twice, though getting admitted by the servant guarding the door the first time I called was a rather near thing." I glanced at Alice, who smiled.

The aunt seemed impressed, and I ate my eggs – good, not outstanding, Eddie would have said – in silence until the aunt asked, "Is Mozart a favourite of yours?" I said, after wiping my mouth and swallowing, "I heard so little music growing up that I really haven't been able to develop a taste for any particular composer". After thinking a little, I said, "Several of us had a very long discussion, at a pub I am sorry to say, about music. Well, some of it was about music. Eddie said that when he was feeling down, he liked to listen to Haydn, and we eventually decided this was because Haydn's music, some of which I have heard, was so – joyful. We talked about why this was the case, whether it was because of the composer's personality or his background, or both. Mozart, Eddie said, and I can see what he is talking about, is purposeful – he always seemed to know where he was going and how he was going to get there – but with an underlying sense of sadness, loss, tragedy, yet the purposefulness ensures that – this was our conclusion – the dance, the dance of life if you will, requires the music to go on", I reviewed what I had said, and, smiling, "No, we hadn't had that much to drink, and I was quite sober and as much in my right mind as I ever am."

Both women smiled, and Alice rose, saying she wanted to see a park, not far away, she had been told of. The aunt agreed it was worth walking through. Alice's suitcase was at the door, ready for her departure, and we walked out together. Alice knew where we were going, and I walked beside her, at our usual rapid pace.

The park was very nice, though not very large. We encountered a wall we wanted to cross, about three feet high overall, of brick topped with a foot or so of metal spikes held upright by two horizontal rails. I stepped on the top of the brick part below the railing, set my other foot on the other side of the railing, lifted my first foot over and jumped to the ground. Alice, on the other side, was wearing a dress of course, so I reached across the wall, lifted her in my arms and swung her over the wall. I set her down. Our faces were less than a foot apart, and our eyes, nearly on a level, met. At that instant, I realized Alice understood I was in love with her – and that she accepted this. My right hand, almost of its own volition, rose and gently caressed her cheek. She didn't flinch or draw back, and I bent forward and kissed her on her lips. It was my first kiss, at least that I could remember. I drew back, still looking into her eyes with their remarkable blue colour, and said hoarsely, "If that was a liberty, I apologize; if not, then I rejoice." She said nothing, merely sustained my look.

We continued our walk, this time holding hands. We wandered along a street, then another street, saying nothing – what was there to say? – until we were in a section of shops, one of them a jewellery store. We were passing it when something caught my eye: a ring in the window with a blue stone. I stopped, and pointed it out to Alice, then looked again, and said, "The stone is the same colour as your eyes." She looked at me, and I opened the shop door for her and we went inside.

The proprietor seemed pleased to see us together. I pointed out the ring, and he presented it to us. It was, he said, a very fine sapphire of somewhat unusual colour, set in a platinum band, very tough metal that wears very well. The light was better, at least different, and the colours of eyes and stone still matched. I looked at Alice. She looked at me, not saying a word. I asked if the ring would fit her. He took out a gauge and measured the fourth finger of her left hand, those long slender fingers, and gauged the ring size and said, yes. I asked the price, and he told me. It was a lot, £3/10, but I had the money, and, after all, it had become something of a tradition to spend a good deal on her, as she was worth it, I thought, and bought the ring.

He gave it me, and I turned to Alice, again meeting her gaze, and raising her left hand, put the ring on the fourth finger. We looked at each other again, and then walked together out of the shop. We headed back to her aunt's house, still hand in hand, still silent.

When we got there, I picked up her suitcase and we went back in the direction of the station. Because of the time, I got a taxi and we rode the rest of the way in silence, though I was thinking about what I was going to say.

Her train was waiting and I placed her suitcase inside, then handed her into the carriage (though she was perfectly capable of entering it unaided) and we stood facing each other. I said, "Alice: the Jews, I am told, hold that an unmarried man is a being who is essentially incomplete, unfinished. He becomes a complete, whole man only when he takes a wife. I have thought a great deal about this, and, perhaps because of my upbringing, feel there is merit to that position. Certainly I am conscious of lacking someone to be a companion, a friend, a confidante, a lover, a partner, a wife. I will, I think, never be very great or very grand, a teacher of history at a public school or perhaps at a minor university. I expect to make a modest living, enough to support a family in a reasonable style, nothing more. Yet, if you will join with me, stand with me, whatever may befall, sustaining, comforting and loving me as I sustain, comfort and love you, I believe we shall be happy together. I pledge my first object shall be your happiness; if you pledge the same, and if children result, which is likely, then we will be able to bring them up in a household filled with music, laughter and love. I do not believe a better household can exist for children or for a husband and wife."

The train began to move, and Alice continued to gaze at me, her lips slightly parted. I raised my hand to her, and said, "God speed and fare well." She raised her hand in reply and then was gone.

I walked back to my den. *Iacta est alea*, I thought: the die was cast. I had told her what was in my mind, in my heart, for better or worse.

* * *

Three days later, a letter from Alice:

Dear Matthew

Mother and Father are not pleased at our engagement, and asked me to ask you not to say anything to anyone about it. They think it imprudent – you have no job yet – and premature – we haven't seen each other, in person, I mean, that much.

Sincerely,
Alice

I immediately wrote in reply:

Dear Alice

I have said nothing to anyone, and of course shall comply with your request.

Please understand that love, true love, is giving, is generous. I wish you to be happy because I love you, and the last thing I wish is for our relationship to cause you any unhappiness, embarrassment or contention. If you feel you would be the better

66

for ending our relationship, do so, though it would grieve me. Your happiness is my object.

I am no longer humble, since your favour, irrespective of how long it lasts, has made me enormously happy and proud. I remain, however, your most obedient esquire.

Matthew

A few days after this exchange, I was delivering to one of the retailers when I noticed the headlines in the papers: we were at war, evidently with Germany and Austria-Hungary. Normally I don't read the papers; as I explained at one point to David Cohen, it was an unnecessary expense, and if something important were immanent, the end of the world, say, someone would tell me.

I thought of Hans-Jeorg. We had been exchanging letters since he had left Earl's Cross, and I knew he had completed his military training and was a reservist. Would he be called up? I couldn't imagine anyone less interested in the military: he only wanted to work in his family's business and marry his sweetheart. His opinions of the Kaiser and his entourage, and the military in general were quite expressive, and I prayed German Military Intelligence hadn't intercepted and read them.

I went on with my deliveries. After the last, I was going back to read an assignment in the library – my place was hopeless in this weather – when I was stopped by a parade. A regiment of Highland soldiers, accompanied by a band, was swinging by. The rhythmic crash of the boots, the swaying of the kilts, the rattle and thump of the drums stirred me, I admit. The music was fine, a martial tune I didn't recognize, and the crowd roared their support. I thought again of my friend, my first friend, perhaps marching off to war in similar scenes, and grew sad.

* * *

Term started with the usual excess of assigned work, but with significantly fewer students, male students, and even one or two fewer masters. The ranks of my Regulars had fallen also. Eddie, who was the only man I knew with eyesight worse than mine, and David were still there, though David was considering joining up. A letter from Alice arrived, asking me if I had enlisted, which I thought strange, as she knew of my nearsightedness. Nonetheless, I replied as soon as I found a spare ten minutes, remarking that no, I hadn't enlisted as I couldn't imagine the depths of crisis that would lead to such a collapse of (optical) standards: if she did hear of my being accepted as a recruit, it would signal a very serious situation indeed. I added that the headaches that accompanied prolonged use of my spectacles worried me; I hoped I wasn't going blind or anything like that, but would see, in a manner of speaking. I noted the drop in numbers here at university, but guessed her place of business didn't have such problems. I ended by saying that perhaps the artillery would be a better choice for me, though I still thought with regret about my friend from Earl's Cross. I signed my letter "with conflicting emotions."

* * *

Alice's next letter seemed a bit peremptory. She gave the arguments for my enlisting as though there were no other considerations, and hinted that her continued favour, which I took to mean our engagement, depended on my donning a uniform forthwith.

I had no intention of doing any such thing: standing in queues for hours struck me as a major waste of my time, and, aside from what might be called sentimental considerations, I couldn't imagine any serious military unit accepting me. Still, I felt I had to compromise. I had promised obedience, so made an appointment to see an eye doctor, no easy task as all seemed to be very profitably employed in examining recruits. The fellow seemed in a hurry, too, and only had me look at a chart with capital letters of various sizes with and without my spectacles. He promptly told me what I suspected: my eyesight was far below military standards. I was going to ask about the headaches, but was instead ushered out and charged a guinea for the experience. I wrote to Alice, telling her what had happened and what the fellow's opinion was, and hoped that would be the end of the matter.

It wasn't: she didn't seem to believe me, and I began to resent her hectoring tone and especially resented her apparent feeling that I was lying. I promptly, or as promptly as my overnumerous duties allowed, replied, giving her the name and qualifications of the doctor, the date of the examination and the numbers describing my vision, which I had fortunately written down. I invited her to check with the fellow if she really thought I was making anything up, and concluded with what I hoped was a more conciliatory résumé of my activities, trying to keep the tone of the letter light and, I hoped, amusing.

* * *

The end of the term had arrived before I heard from her again, a prolonged lapse that made me think she was planning to throw me over, which was most distressing. The letter was short, a bit brusque, and was mostly about the dances and parties she was going to attend. She didn't refer to the eyesight dispute again, but I was once more cast down: if she did consider herself engaged, why go to all these events? Obviously, her parents disapproved, and hoped to weaken our connection. I went about my discreditable commercial activities in a most un-holiday spirit. I spent a great deal of time and thought, composing as eloquent and beautiful a reply as I could.

* * *

The new term, my sixth, showed a further drop in numbers of my fellow students, leaving a residue with real physical problems and some with what they called conscientious objections to war, or at least to this war. The women students fell a little in numbers, too, as some were evidently going into nursing, ambulance driving, etc. Alice's correspondence continued brief and infrequent. She said she was planning to become a nurse: there was a private home near her house for convalescent officers, and she would start there. I was certainly not happy about her exposure to no doubt decorously bandaged, handsome heroes, but could only praise her spirit and wish her well.

* * *

My sixth term went well, academically. My papers got good marks, some actual praise. Exams went well, but Alice's letters kept getting briefer and more widely spaced. I tried to reply using an even tone, reminding myself that I had essentially given her *carte blanche* to jilt me. Well, I had meant what I said, especially about my grief over losing her, but I had, after all, given her my word as well as my heart.

Eddie, David and a remaining Regular, Robert Jones, another Classics reader, continued our end of term tradition. David and Robert were going to enlist, as both had gotten M.A.'s – they had stayed on to finish because of promises to their families. We talked about the war, wars in general, music, painting (I could only listen), prices of things in general, and on and on. After closing, David and Robert went off and I accompanied Eddie back to his house, as I sensed he had something he wanted to talk about.

Talks with Eddie normally involved listening to his descriptions of symptoms, medical procedures, anatomical and physiological details, etc., in excess of what I really wanted to hear, but he was a friend and I was patient. And I supposed I was learning something, so I counted that a gain. Tonight though I realized a very different topic was on his mind. He began by telling me that Christine had effectively given him his "walking papers", as he put it: she told him she was engaged to marry another man. She suggested, vaguely, that she wanted to retain Eddie's "friendship", whatever that might mean, but Eddie merely wished her and her fiancé joy and bade her goodbye.

I had been expecting something of the sort, and I suppose so had he, but I could see he was very hurt. I asked if the fiancé was a fellow student, fairly tall. Eddie said yes, mentioning the fellow's name. I then told Eddie I had seen them together some time ago, but forbore to tell him. I apologized for this but Eddie merely shrugged, said it would have made no difference – I agreed with him there – and commented it would take a great deal of time and work to get over her. I told him I was sorry, that perhaps she had known Eddie too well, in the sense there was no mystery, no depths of character unplumbed, while this other fellow would serve as the basis of romantic fancies. Eddie shook his head, and said he wished he knew what women wanted in a man. I said if I knew, I would patent it, bottle it and make a fortune.

At my tone, he asked how things were with Alice. I was silent a bit, and then decided if I simply didn't mention the engagement, as I had given my word not to do, I could be open. I said our relationship was at best strained, there was strong family opposition, that I thought Alice herself was looking for an excuse to end our – I almost said engagement, and then corrected it to acquaintance. I added she was playing nurse to convalescent officers in some neighbour's house and expected to be thrown over at any time, perhaps the next post.

Eddie was silent as was I. He then commented that love was a mental and emotional habit, a habit of mind, very strong, so hard to break. I said, so, an endless stream of diversions would help. He said focusing on the short term, the day to day, would help, or perhaps a total change of scene. "The Army?" I asked. "I am not sure of that. Perhaps another girl, a new interest of that sort, but saying that and finding someone are very different things." I nodded, wondering where one could find a new "interest", especially between terms. I suspect he was thinking the same thing, for we were silent the rest of the way to Portland Place. There, he thanked me for my company, said he was sorry I was having the same sort of problem, and remarked that I had pasties to prepare and he had rounds. We bade each other goodnight, and I walked the considerable distance back to my place, arriving in time to once again begin my lower class tradesman's efforts.

* * *

I worked very hard between terms, averaging eight batches of pasties six days a week, reading every book and article I could get the masters to recommend. Alice wrote very little, and what she wrote was not informative. I tried to reply using as even and neutral a tone as possible, but seemed to be avoiding saying anything of substance myself, talking mostly of concerts. My headaches were not too bad, and I realized I hadn't needed to use the spectacles as much (for reading anyway). On the other hand, I began getting nasty looks and even muttered comments from women who wondered why such a fine specimen – I should have been flattered, I suppose – wasn't in uniform. So I resorted to wearing the things out of doors, as they in a measure shielded me from popular reproach.

* * *

The new term began, my penultimate, I told myself. Owing to increases in prices, my added pasty production hadn't been translated into more profit, but I told myself I had enough to continue, a real measure of my anxiety over Alice.

One of my Regulars, who had enlisted early, had returned, out of the Army as he now lacked his left hand. Eddie, I and one or two others took him to the pub despite, in my case, a tower of tasks. After he had a few pints, he began to tell us about his experiences: being sent against enemy defences almost unscathed by our shelling, entire battalions with 100% casualties for no gain at all, a relentless catalogue of stupidity and mistakes that left the rest of us open-mouthed. He went on to note he was well out of it, his only problem being he couldn't wipe his bum now, which stirred us all to comments I hoped no one else could overhear. He had a fiancée and now had a future, so Eddie and I at least envied him. We broke up at the usual time for the usual reason.

* * *

One of my Occasional customers, a rather emaciated fellow, was having trouble paying. I tried to ease the situation with humour, but succeeded only in humiliating him, it seemed. I tried to apologize, and explain, but he turned away and walked off. I didn't see him again. I told Eddie about the incident, and he thought it was too easy to misinterpret attempts at humour. I had to agree, only too late.

Fall had arrived, not that my place was any less unbearable, just not more unbearable. A note, it couldn't be more than that, arrived from Alice:

Matthew

Please visit me at Millwood this Sunday at 1 PM.

Alice

I had been dreading this or something like it for months, but the reality of the death of a dream left me numb. My idyll was ended. I had to reply. I wrote as brief a note, couched in exactly the same tone, saying I would be there at that time. Best to go out with dignity, I told myself.

* * *

That Sunday I dressed in my second best clothes, not my concert garb, but shaved carefully and looked as dignified as I could. I took the train out, got out with, I thought, a reasonable amount of time, asked directions to the place, and set off briskly. The condemned man... The way was longer than I was advised, so I had picked up my pace radically. I found the lane – there was a signpost – and walked down it, over a bridge across a small creek, then around a curve and saw the house. I was only two minutes late.

The house was no palace, two stories, made of stone, but I hadn't expected magnificence, so walked to the door and pulled at the bell. I heard it, then some steps. The door opened, and a rather hostile looking servant asked who I was and what I wanted. I said clearly, "Mr Dobbs for Miss Millwood." The fellow asked if I was expected. Becoming irritated, I said, "I am here at her invitation."

The door was shut in my face. For a minute I stood, stunned. This was rude. Angered, I turned and began to walk away. Then I heard the door open and Alice's voice said, "Matthew."

I turned and stared icily at her. Birth or no, I was her peer in intelligence, education and probably her superior in push. She was dressed plainly, and, after hesitating, advanced toward me. She had something in her hand, which she extended to me. It was the ring. I took it, put it in my pocket, looked her in the eye, and said, "I wish you happiness. Goodbye." Then I turned again and walked rapidly away.

I had rounded the curve in the path, thinking I would throw the ring into the creek. The Celts were always throwing valuable things into wells, rivers, etc., presumably as offerings to water gods. I wasn't sure what my motive was, just that I felt the need to do something dramatic.

I heard some dogs barking, then suddenly a pack of four or five were on me, and attacking me. I fended off one or two lunges at my throat but felt them tearing at my leg. I roared with anger, grabbed at them, caught one who was tearing something from my leg, and raising him, threw him at the others as hard as I could. I was a strong man and I was enraged. I caught another one and swung him at the others. I heard yelps of pain, hurled the dog I was holding at the others, and grabbed at them again. The dogs decided they had made their point, and retreated. I followed, beside myself. They ran off, leaving me bleeding and torn.

I looked down at my legs. One trouser leg had several pieces of cloth torn off, and I could see that leg, my right, was bloody. I looked more closely and thought I could see a chunk of flesh had been torn from my calf and several slashes, also bleeding freely. I remembered some of what Eddie had told me: there was no spurting so, apparently, no arterial blood, but plenty of the other kind. I thought briefly of going back to their house but for all I knew might be attacked again, perhaps even shot, given their general level of hospitality, and I wanted nothing more to do with the Millwoods. I could stand, so I could walk, and began limping back to the station.

I tore a branch from one of their trees to use as a support, and headed in the direction of the track. As I walked, I found I had lost the half-crown I had taken for the return journey, so could look forward to walking the entire way back.

Reaching the track, I discarded the branch. One shoe was filled with blood, but I was on my feet and on my way home. The mile marker said 33 miles to the London station, and on I walked. Trains roared by, and once I caught the scent – and perhaps more than that – of a W.C. being flushed, and I cursed and raged at the Millwood's, at their entire damned class, at England, at Alice and whoever was her new beau...

I walked on and on. My leg hurt badly but I could move and swing one leg past the other, sometimes feeling more blood running into my stocking and shoe. I was not going to be able to make my usual four miles an hour or anything near it: the track bed was hard going and I was tired and badly injured.

In the event, I reached home about four thirty Monday morning. I drank some milk, then some more, then sat heavily down and looked more carefully at my right leg. A chunk of flesh had indeed been torn out of the leg and several deep slashes made elsewhere. Bleeding had been abundant from all, and I remembered Eddie saying that free bleeding was good, as it washed the poisons out of the wound that might cause gangrene or death. I pulled off the shoe, wondering if it could be worn again. I decided it would have to be as I hadn't a replacement except for my concert shoes. This brought Alice to mind again, and I remembered the look on her face as she had handed me the ring and I thought it was a sneer, and I swore again that I would be successful in whatever I did, so successful that no one could again treat me like something to get rid of, something to sweep away.

I took off my coat. In doing so, I found the coin I had meant for my return trip; it had fallen through a hole in my pocket and lodged between the outer cloth and the lining. I extracted it, cursed, and then took the ring out of the other pocket. I was unsure where to put it, there being no well or stream at hand, so dropped it prosaically into the valise with my books and papers.

It was nearly time to start pasty production again. I hadn't slept, I doubted I could sleep for all the pain, and got to my feet and went to the counter to start the preparation.

* * *

I was sitting, waiting for lectures to start, when Eddie walked up. I handed him his usual two pasties in butcher paper and he gave me the shilling. He noticed my exhaustion, asked what the matter was, and I told him. He was shocked. He said I could sue the family, that setting dogs even on an uninvited tradesman was illegal, but I said I wanted nothing more to do with any of them. He sat down next to me and gently raised what was left of the trouser leg. He looked for some time, said the injuries needed stitching or would leave ugly scars but they seemed to have drained clean. I said I would leave things alone; stitching at this stage seemed a waste of time. He then pulled a newspaper, folded so one page was displayed, out of a side pocket and gave it me.

It announced the engagement to marry of Miss Alice Louise Millwood, elder daughter of Sir Edward Millwood, Bart, MP and Lady Edith Millwood, of Millwood, Berkshire, to Captain Charles Darrow-Frazier, MC, of the Twelfth Lancers, son of Mrs Laura Darrow-Frazier Ingleby, Pennville, Yorkshire, and the late Robert Darrow-Frazier. The wedding will take place Dec. 24 at the Candlefield Church, C. E., on the groom's return from service in France.

"How very posh," I thought numbly, and handed the paper back to Eddie. He got up, finished the pasty, gave me an appreciative nod and went off on his rounds. I got up very painfully and limped off to my first lecture. As I gained a little speed, two thoughts occurred: first, that the notice must have been sent in earlier, probably several days earlier, and second, Alice must have been accepting his attentions while still nominally engaged to me. That struck me as dishonourable, but given my other experiences with the family, probably nothing out of the ordinary for them. Going into the lecture hall, I put on my spectacles, preparing for the day's headache, and felt nothing but rage. I supposed I could hope for the bastard's early death, but given what I had been told about the value of the cavalry in this war, that seemed unlikely.

End of term was accompanied by no emotion whatever: I merely altered my schedule and activities to grub some more coins through my miserable pursuits. After deliveries, I did some reading – suggested, not assigned of course, while munching on a bunch of carrots I had bought. I had developed the habit, whenever I was tempted to lie longer on my bench, or nap, or just avoid doing whatever my duties required (most of the time, that is), of conjuring up the image of Alice handing back the ring while sneering at me. That got me moving.

* * *

Christmas day, 1915. No work, no deliveries. I did lie late this time, till nearly ten. It was a holiday after all, I told myself. When I got up, I noticed a newspaper pushed under the door. It was folded so I saw an announcement of a wedding, of Miss Alice Louise Millwood to Captain.... I read through it, then realized I hadn't remembered anything much of what I had read, and forced myself to pay attention. Not that it mattered: it was done. I set the newspaper on the table and sat staring at it. Suddenly it was all too much, all the grubby work at tasks others despised, all my efforts, all the frustrations, and my shoulders began to shake and I began to sob, uncontrollably, as I hadn't since my parents had died. Eventually the racking sobs subsided and I sat with my head on the table, despising myself.

* * *

My last term had begun like all the others; now, two months into it, I had the illusion, routine at that stage of term, of getting a handle on things. One of my papers had been highly praised by the master, even though he had some comments, and he summoned me to his office and suggested I rewrite it, expanding one or two parts a bit, and send it to a professional journal. I was flattered, said I would if I had the time, but talk of conscription was increasing, and I wondered if vision standards would be lowered to capture me. We discussed the situation: my headaches were about the same, but I didn't feel reassured.

* * *

March 24: my 21st birthday, or so I guessed. There was a letter for me, from a solicitor in Norwich I didn't know, informing me I could claim my inheritance. Since I had never heard of any such thing, I was curious enough to take holiday and travel there. I thought I would visit my parents' graves, since I had been told years ago they were buried there, at shire expense, after the inquest. I had never been, and felt guilty as a consequence.

I left early and got there by midmorning. I had a map, and made my way to the churchyard. I eventually found a single stone, cheaply carved, with the name Dobbs on it but not much else that was readable. I pulled weeds away from the plot to make it more presentable, and stood for a while before it. I tried to tell their spirits I was still alive and hoped to do them honour.

I turned to go to the solicitor's and passed a much newer grave with a much better carved stone. The name was that of Mr Paston's lawyer friend, the man who had come to the parish house, all dressed as a swell and perfumed, to take me somewhere, only to find me filthy and stinking. I had felt humiliated but did not want to go with him. The date of his death was recent, and there was no mention that he had a wife or children.

The solicitor's office contained only the solicitor and when I identified myself, he looked at me curiously and said, "You've been a rather expensive young man, Sir." I stared at him and finally said, "I have never before heard of any legacy and my upbringing can hardly have been more modest or cheaper, as I earned much of my support, and still do. Please explain what this is about, Sir."

He looked at me a minute, then produced a sheaf of papers with the heading, "Claims on the Dobbs Legacy". I read charges for clothing, meals, tuition, trips to France, expensive watches, and said, "This is unbelievable. Charges on what? And I never saw, still less wore, these clothes, ate these meals, bought such a watch" – here I hauled my old, still serviceable but clearly cheap watch out of its fob – "and as far as these charges for tuition, I was on scholarship to Earl's Cross for four years – I still have the scholarship letters, and for that matter, I am sure the headmaster there will confirm what I say – and the last three years I have been on scholarship at university, and I have those letters also." Here I paused for breath, then went on: "I am sure the Registrar will confirm what I say, and the first year I paid out of my own pocket." I was growing angry. "This is some sort of swindle, Sir. And by the way, I have never been out of England. I have no passport."

He was looking at me, then apparently made up his mind, perhaps a look at my clothes helped convince him, and said, "When your parents were killed, the attorney, Graves, who got himself appointed, with Reverend Paston, as your guardians, managed to extract a £2,000 settlement from the company that employed the lorry driver who caused the derailment. These charges were made by them, presumably in your name. Since the attorney controlled the settlement, he authorized payment of these sums."

My mouth had fallen open. £2,000? I looked again at the charges – I had been used in a swindle. I said so to the solicitor.

He nodded. "I believe you. After he died, I fell heir, as it were, to his affairs, including this." I said, "I saw his grave. What did he die of? He did not seem that old." The solicitor looked at me a bit oddly but answered, "Of his exertions in a brothel. A boy brothel, in London." I was stunned. "Jesus Christ," I said. Then I thought. I said, "On second thought, I am not too surprised." He looked at me, and I hastily added, "He never buggered me, if that is what you think. But I believe he was planning to. The housekeeper and, I think, Paston's wife protected me." It had been a damned near close-run thing, though.

He continued, "There is still a small amount left in the account, about 146 pounds odd. I will write you a cheque for that, close the account, and deny the current claims. In fact, I think I will write Paston a letter, suggesting a case of criminal fraud can be made against him." I said bitterly, "I don't suppose any of the rest of the money can ever be reclaimed." He said, "I doubt it: the attorney's estate was in arrears, and I suspect Paston spent his share."

So I walked out of the solicitor's office with a cheque for £146/10 shillings/2 pence in my pocket, over a year's earnings for me. I had been assured the London banks would honour the cheque, so decided to open a banker's account; after all, I would soon be a university graduate.

Going past the churchyard, I felt an urgent desire to desecrate the bastard's grave, but there were other people about, so decided I would use the loo on the train instead. I hoped his soul, if he had one, would take the wish for the deed.

Returning on the train, I kept my spectacles on, even so drawing hostile looks from some of the women in the compartment. In spite of my outrage, I actually felt better, for two reasons.

First, the money in my pocket. Even though it was only about 7% of the original settlement, it seemed a very handsome sum. I realized that if those greedy buggers had played fair, the settlement, invested, should have brought me 100 pounds a year, more than enough for my upkeep. I would have been a gentleman. I could have gone to Oxford. I wouldn't have had to work so hard at demeaning tasks... perhaps Alice and I would still be engaged to marry. But that seemed unrealistic now, given her family's expectations for her, and I thought of all the friends I had made, at Earl's Cross and particularly the university. Now I no longer needed to get up so poisonously early to bake pasties...

The other reason was that I now had a much better understanding of what had been going on: a number of incidents in my life, many that I had pushed out of my mind, now returned and made sense. There was a very tall wardrobe in the little room I was assigned, and one night I hadn't slipped out when I heard Mr Paston coming. I climbed onto the cot, stepped on the window sill and climbed onto the top of the wardrobe. It was very dirty and dusty and very close and I began to sweat, fearing I couldn't move my legs and arms again. I pulled my shirt over my mouth and nose so I wouldn't sneeze or cough and made myself as small as possible as the door opened and Mr Paston came in. He looked for me, said "boo" several times, I supposed to startle me into revealing myself, poked here and there, and even opened the wardrobe. Then I heard Mrs Paston calling for him and he reluctantly left. I remembered the bulge in the front of his nightshirt and now realized that he had an erection. After that night, I made sure to leave earlier.

Another incident: my second year at Earl's Cross, another student, a boy I only knew slightly, gave me a book to look at. No one else was about. I opened the book and found it full of photos of boys and men with enormous cocks, putting them into each other's mouths, hands or bums. I closed the book, handed it back with the comment, "I say, you had better not let the masters catch you with this, or you'll be sent down for sure." I then walked on, leaving him looking puzzled and disappointed. Perhaps my guardians' reputations had filtered over to him and he thought I shared their predilections. On that thought, I realized that the reason I hadn't been allowed to take a fifth year at Earl's Cross may have been because the headmaster had heard about the sexual activities of one or both and decided I was a bad influence.

Another memory: early in my stay at the Paston's, he had invited me into his study and asked me if I wanted a sweetmeat. I promptly replied, "No thank you, Sir." and left the room. Apparently someone, almost certainly my mother, had impressed on me never to accept sweetmeats from strange men, and Mr Paston certainly qualified for that category.

Bad and bleak as my upbringing in that house had been, I realized it could have been a great deal worse.

* * *

Back in London, I told Eddie and my other remaining Regulars of my (somewhat) good fortune, assuming I wouldn't have to make any more pasties. Here however I was gently but unequivocally informed that I was expected to continue my efforts, which had evidently become necessary for their happiness if not survival. Since the rise in costs of my ingredients had nearly wiped out any profits I was making, my efforts had become a labour of friendship if not love. I cursed each morning – nothing new about that – but rose betimes and did as I was bidden.

* * *

I had set my spectacles on the kitchen table prior to bathing, taken off my shirt and somehow thereby swept them onto the floor. I picked them up and saw one lens had broken: two pieces fell to the floor as I raised them. I cursed, picked up the broken fragments, cutting a finger in the process and erupted with the filthiest language I could conceive. There was nothing for it. I staunched the bleeding with some butcher's paper, appropriately enough, put my clothes back on and went out to get the lens replaced.

There was a chap who called himself an optometrist a street or two away, so I headed for him; the fellow who had examined my eyes a year ago hadn't inspired much confidence, perhaps unjustly. I felt constrained to wear the spectacles, even with one broken lens. The eye doctor had time, so I handed him the spectacles and said I needed a lens replaced.

He proceeded to examine my eyes, each in turn, rather thoroughly I thought, wrote down some numbers and told me my eyes had differing near-sightedness and having proper lenses ground would take a week, and in the meantime, he had a pair that I could use until then. I told him about the headaches and he took my old spectacles and held them up to the light, snorted, and with a gesture of complete contempt, tossed them over his shoulder so they hit the wall behind him and bounced into a dustbin. He looked at me and said, "Those won't do at all; just gave you those headaches, I'll be bound." He said flatly that the headaches were caused by inappropriate lenses making my eyes work against each other and the spectacles he was loaning me would not do that. I put these on, and everything did indeed look sharper. I paid a pound, with another due when the new spectacles were ready and left, feeling very foolish indeed.

* * *

The people who lived in the upper floors were recognizable but I didn't mix much with them, being always busy it seemed. One of them was a woman, middle height, middle sized, not very attractive, a shop girl or rather woman as I guessed her to be in her forties. One afternoon I saw her struggling with some parcels and offered to help. She accepted gratefully and I carried several up to her room, on the top floor. She told me her name was Elsie, Elsie Cross. I told her my name. She asked if I was a student and I admitted I was. She seemed impressed, asked me to sit down, produced a bottle, gin I think as it was clear, which I declined. She took a glass herself, said it helped her relax after a day's work, and then suggested there were other ways to relax, didn't I know? She pulled up the hem of her dress as she drank, and seeing I was intrigued, proceeded to show me more. She suggested I feel the texture of her silk stockings, and it would have seemed grossly impolite to refuse.

It was all very strange: one part of my mind was telling me I needed to start writing a paper due soon, but another part, a part that grew rapidly more dominant, was urging a very different activity. I was quite aroused yet oddly detached, almost a bystander, as I helped her undress, fondled her breasts, looking for signs as to what she preferred, then began fondling between her legs. She had to tell me sometimes exactly what to do, all very instructive; the smell was very strong but of course I didn't comment on that. Eventually she was breathing quite hard, and invited me to take off my trousers and lie on her – not her exact choice of words, but the gist – and again, I complied. While riding her, I saw her eyes grow glassy and her head jerked back and forth, and I felt more pleasure growing as the pressure inside me did. Then I felt the pressure ease, and knew I had discharged. Immediately I thought of the paper, of other papers I had to write, chapters to read and I felt ashamed of myself. After my cock fell out of her, I got off. She seemed pleased; in fact, I think she felt pride in seducing a university student. We exchanged compliments, but I wanted to get out of there as soon as possible. I went back to my quarters, bathed, and vowed to remain pure, while hoping I hadn't caught anything; she seemed too old to get pregnant. Still, my first sex left me remorseful, anxious and ashamed.

* * *

This mood lasted about three weeks. I encountered Elsie on the street again, and again she invited me to her room. This time I was much more knowledgeable, felt more pleasure, less remorse and, while I again felt guilty, realized that I would fall again as the opportunity offered. I thought of Alice and how she would despise me if she knew.

* * *

My last exams: all my papers were in, and I sat with a scattering of the remaining students, a much higher proportion now women of course, writing short essays about whatever was asked. I had to read the question, figure out what was required for an answer, and then organize the answer so it read well, and on and on. Eventually I realized I had written answers for all the questions and began rereading them. I made a few corrections but actually my answers read well and I handed my papers in with relief – I didn't dare feel confidence.

I celebrated with Elsie. She had never asked me for money, and I realized she was just lonely and was perhaps a bit of a tuft-hunter. However, I went to a jewellery store and, after looking at a great many items, selected one, a pin shaped like a flower, which looked stylish in a restrained way and was not too expensive. She was delighted, and insisted on my lingering until my lust had revived, and had a second essay into the rites of Venus, or, in plain terms, had fucked again. I took my leave after, as usual burdened with guilt and self-disgust, but less than before.

I looked up Eddie at the flat his family had bought for him. It was reasonably near his practice, he said, which consisted of dockers and their families, so was not on the road to riches, but then it had plenty of patients, so was exactly what he wanted: lots of work, the "anodyne" as he put it, for disappointments elsewhere. I told him of my doings with Elsie, and my fears of venereal disease. He asked about symptoms, describing these in his usual vivid detail, and on hearing I had none, told me what to look for and suggested using condoms. It was a bit late for that, but I thanked him for his counsel.

He showed me around: two floors plus an actual wine cellar in the basement: Eddie's family did not stint on anything, it seemed. He invited me to dinner, and I accepted partly from friendship, for I sensed he was as lonely as I, and partly because I had, at that moment, nothing else to do.

As I expected, the meal was quite good. He had two servants, a cook-housekeeper and a butler-valet. When the meal was served, he excused them, saying we would do for ourselves. Over the meal, he confided his sexual experiences with his mother's maid, a liaison that went on or off, depending on his relation with Christine. Right now it was on again, of course. I mentioned that I expected the constables any day, for I had never registered for the Derby scheme or at all. He suggested I talk to our colleague, my one-handed Regular, about enlisting if my eyesight permitted. I said I would and took my leave.

My colleague was with his fiancée, planning their honey-moon, but he listened to my story, had me take off my new spectacles, look out the window and tell him what I could see. I did so, and he thought I might pass, the visual standards, like some others, eroding. Also, I noted that, aside from cessation of the headaches, my eyesight actually seemed to have improved, even without the spectacles. Perhaps not reading so much was a factor. He nodded and asked if I had been in OTC at Earl's Cross. They had no OTC program, I said. I hadn't been in the OTC at university either, as I hadn't the time. He said there were rules for commissioning officers, but these tended to be ignored when demand for second lieutenants was high, as now, so he suggested I enlist in the Artists' Rifles. Since I would probably be taken in anyway, I might as well try for an officer's commission. This made sense, so I went to enlist, first passing by the board on which the last exam results were posted.

Everything was there: I looked and eventually found "Dobbs, M. (Norfolk)" near the top of the list. I had taken a first, First Class Honours, M.A. in History, though by only two marks. Still, it would serve to carve on my tombstone, I thought mordantly, and went looking for the recruiting station for the Artists' Rifles.

However, my maimed former customer had said if I wanted to "see some action" – I was not sure how serious he was – I should enlist in an Officer Cadet Battalion: the training period was shorter. I asked several people for directions to either place, got confusing replies, and wound up in a building, rather run-down, that seemed associated with the military. I went in. An officer at a desk looked up and asked, "Officer Cadet?" That seemed what I wanted to be, so I said, "Yes," then realized from a look the officer gave me that I needed to add something, so said, belatedly, "Sir." He looked at me a long moment, then pointed to a side door.

Once through that, I found myself in a room with an Army doctor. He examined me, especially including my eyes, and said I was fit for service, provided I wore my spectacles. He said I should get another pair in case the first got broken. Then I was sent across town to a barracks, where I was interviewed by two rather busy officers. At this point, I realized I didn't really know which organization I had wound up in, but guessed I would find out soon enough. "Your vision now passed muster?" one of them asked. "Yes, sir, with the spectacles." "You went to school?" asked the other. "Yes, sir, then university." "Which university?" "Here, sir, London." "Did you graduate?" "Yes, Sir." That was all they seemed to want to know about, and I was dismissed. I was issued boots, uniforms and kit and went with a few other new men to where we doffed our civilian clothes and put on King George's own – some of us, perhaps all, for the last time, I thought, still feeling rather mordant.

The new uniform felt stiff and uncomfortable, like new clothes generally did, but the uniform seemed to be meant to be stiff and uncomfortable. Then we were mustered outside, to be given preliminary instruction in drill. A corporal gave the orders and put everyone through our paces, at least the others through the paces. It seemed they all either had been officers or sergeants. Shortly, they were sent in to join the others: I was having trouble distinguishing between my right and left foot, getting the steps wrong, like some sort of dance, and the corporal, who was very patient, kept working on me, but it was very frustrating: I would at last get, say, about turn right, then try something else, then discover I had forgotten about turn. At length we stopped for lunch, not a gourmet experience, as Eddie would say, and my appetite was not helped by the clear expectation among my colleagues that I would be rejected, as apparently I was supposed to have been in OTC or a sergeant at least six months before being considered for a commission.

The afternoon went much the same; I gritted my teeth, conjured up that last image of Alice for motivation, and resolved to take what extra time and pains were necessary.

* * *

Day followed day. I sought out the corporals, sergeants or experienced colleagues to give me extra drill in all my spare time.

Gradually, I became less clumsy, though my performance still tended to be erratic.

Marksmanship wasn't much better. Again, I tried to get as much extra time on the range as possible. I could see well, at least with the spectacles, and gradually improved to the extent that I passed with minimum marks.

Map reading was another matter. I had always been fascinated by maps, especially topographical maps, and had no trouble locating where I was and telling where I wanted to go. In fact, in map reading I was top of the entire class. I was conscripted to help other cadets, which of course I did willingly, considering how much extra help I had gotten in other areas.

Military subjects could be considered an academic discipline, albeit a sometimes bizarre one, and again I had few problems there. My colleagues however continued to regard my presence among them as a mistake and in fact were taking wagers as to how long I would last before being sent back to the ranks, where I deserved to be. My plight seemed actually to inspire joy among the other cadets, and I thought, with very mixed emotions, about all the happiness I was bringing them. I worked extremely hard trying to master whatever I could, and I thought with some success. Eventually, however, I was summoned to a board or panel of officers to be questioned about my qualifications. They seemed to think I must have lied to be admitted, but I insisted I had been absolutely truthful: "Sir, I was not asked about OTC anywhere, or previous military service, only about my education. I thought I was joining the Artists' Rifles, Sir." There was silence at this, they looked at each other, then one of them said I could go, and I did. I went back, assuming I would be rejected as a candidate for a commission.

* * *

After that, nothing happened. The list of successful candidates was posted and included Dobbs, M. (Norfolk). I was to be a second lieutenant, a "temporary gentleman" after all.

I had the feeling this caused consternation among the bettors. They muttered among themselves, looking sideways at me, but I could only shrug: "the mills of Mars grind exceeding coarse" I think someone said – fatalism seems the prevailing philosophy in military matters. However, one of my colleagues, who had or claimed to have connections with the War Office, said that the reason I had been retained was that casualties, especially among second lieutenants, had been so heavy in our attacks along the Somme that it had been decided that every effort should be made to turn out more. This made sense, but was not encouraging.

Accordingly, at our final parade, I marched – badly – among all the others, my insignia of rank gleaming, Sam Browne belt, boots, etc., polished to perfection, uniform spotless, the picture of Mars. The song we marched to seemed familiar, and the other cadets began singing. I heard "Tipperary" – that was it, a jolly tune for our farewell to England, at least for the time.

I had a bit of leave before reporting to my division, the number of which meant nothing to me, and I had no clue as to where I would be stationed. Eddie invited me to stay at his flat, and I was happy to accept: good food, good company. Elsie was very impressed with my uniform, calling me her "young officer". I bought her another trinket, so was received as well as it was possible to be. Still, leaving was melancholy: unfamiliar comrades, unfamiliar duties and dangerous ones at that, left me pensive.

III. IN FLANDERS' FIELDS

I travelled by train, then boat, then train again. I at length located the division I was to belong to, and after many hours actually got there. I was sent into a sort of office, very roughly constructed, containing a desk, a chair and an officer I recognized as a colonel sitting therein. I came to attention, gave my best salute and told him who I was and the division to which I had been assigned. I spoke loudly, because many guns were firing, and some shells were exploding to the east. He told me I was to go to D Company, Second Battalion, First Brigade and report there. He also said Second Battalion was to attack tomorrow, and I was expected to lead. I nodded. He moved in his chair and I suddenly realized he had an artificial left leg. He looked older, too, perhaps in his fifties. He glared at me as though it was all my fault and dismissed me.

I went out to get directions, did so and was told I was to take five new privates to the line. I met them, told them to follow me, and took out my new electric torch to help light the way, only to be told by the orderly not to turn it on, as German snipers or gun layers might see it. Gun flashes, Very lights, and light from exploding shells would be enough, he said. So off we went.

The approach trench zigged and zagged to keep the effects of a shell burst in the trench confined to one zig (or zag). It was also muddy, and I could smell things, faeces or carrion or both. At intervals, I stopped, checked to be sure my party was intact, and then continued. We saw no one else.

We were perhaps halfway there when German shells began landing nearby. A flash, the ground heaved, a roar, pieces of something flying by, and my insides heaved. Another flash, this time in the approach trench itself only a couple of zigs away and I decided we needed to seek cover. But where? Off to the right was a large hole, and I ordered my party into it, though thinking about it, one spot was exactly as hazardous as another, but I hoped my men – so I was thinking of them by then, as they were my responsibility – weren't thinking that deeply about our situation.

We sat down in the hole, a large shell crater, so our heads were well below the ground. It was dry, too, so was probably a new one. We looked at each other. I could see they were frightened (as was I), and for some reason I decided to introduce myself. Then I asked each man to do the same, asked each what he did for a living, where he was from, etc. I think this helped, though nearby shells landing tended to make for interrupted discourse. Eventually I decided to tell them the joke Hans-Jeorg (where was he, I wondered?) told me so many years ago, the story of the cabaret or pub or nightspot with the golden loo seat.

I told the story. I tend to get a bit animated when I tell stories, and for an instant actually forgot where I was. At the end of the story, there was a moment of silence, and then everyone roared. This broke the ice: one man after another told a story, usually filthy and vile, which we all enjoyed very much.

At length the shelling by the Germans eased. Our own guns were turning the western sky into an aurora throughout the night. We went back to the communication trench and continued on up the line. At the front line trench, I found a sergeant, was directed to the battalion commander, reported myself and my five men, and was sent off to D Company. To my regret, none of the five would go with me.

The section of trench D Company held was, for some unfathomable reason, deeper than the other sectors, walls well over six feet high, made partly of sandbags toward the Germans, but still high to the west. I found the commanding officer, a Captain Frye, who seemed to have some stomach problem. I gave my name and rank and was told I was the only other officer in D Company, the two other second lieutenants being on leave or recuperating from wounds. I was to lead the left wing of D Company when we went "over the top" at 6:00 A.M. I automatically checked my two wristwatches, and established they were both correct. I then looked more closely at Captain Frye.

He seemed pale, sweating and in some distress. I asked him about his symptoms, was brushed aside, persisted in my questions and eventually was told he had had diarrhoea, rather persistent and when I asked, persistent pain in his lower right abdomen. I felt my forehead, felt his, and noted he had a fever, and told him I thought he had appendicitis, an inflamed appendix, and on being told he had had this problem before and had his current symptoms several days, told him he needed to have his appendix removed, before it burst and killed him of peritonitis.

He bent over suddenly, I could see he was in a great deal of pain, and then he straightened himself and asked, or rather gasped, if I was a doctor. I said I had a good friend who was, and the symptoms were unmistakable. At this point, he bent over again, moaned and tried to say something. I called for the sergeant, told him to get a stretcher, two bearers and a blanket and take Captain Frye to the Advanced Dressing Station. I wrote out what I thought was the matter, as I didn't think the stretcher-bearers were likely to remember "appendicitis" or "peritonitis" and ordered them on their way.

Which left me the only officer, completely new to everyone, in a company I had to lead into an attack in – I checked my watch – three and a half hours. I asked the sergeant to come with me and show me the sector, introduce me to the other sergeants and corporals, and see what preparations had been made.

First, however, the sergeant, White was his name, showed me where I was to sleep. The fact that our section of trench was so deep meant it was muddy; in fact I could see a trickle of water down it and could hear a pump going. The dugout where I was to stow my effects was even deeper, actually had two or three inches of water in it, air saturated with water and with a smell consistent with the circumstances. The bunk I was allocated had damp bedding and the closeness of the place made me start to sweat and my old nightmares of being buried alive threatened to revive. I tossed my effects on the bunk, first pulling the bedding away so my things wouldn't soak up (too) much water.

I met my company, names given but of course exiting my head immediately. I saw two ladders where observers or snipers perched, but there appeared to be no other way across the parapet. I asked Sergeant White about this, and was told ladders were supposed to be delivered, but he didn't know when. I checked my watch again, a bit over two hours to go.

I organized our attack as best I could, being sure sergeants and corporals were in their places with their men. I climbed one of the ladders with my field glasses and looked towards German lines. The light of gun flashes and shell bursts showed the glasses were made by Karl Zeiss of Germany

I could actually see fairly well, noted a great quantity of barbed wire still in place in spite of our bombardment, which seemed to be hitting the enemy trench frequently. God help them, I thought, still thinking of my friend, and God help us.

The field glasses weren't likely to be of much use during the attack, so I went back to my quarters, more like eights or sixteenths, I thought irrelevantly, and left them there. My service revolver was one of those with a very long barrel, very accurate I was told, though this advantage was wasted on me, and I remembered the fellow with connections with Olympus (War Office) remarking that a) the long barrel made quick drawing difficult, and b) in the trenches, fights were usually at two or three foot distances so accuracy was unnecessary. I drew it, checked the loading, rotated the drum and put it back – on my right side, as Sam Browne belts for left-handed officers did not exist or at least hadn't been issued me yet. I checked my watch – one hour – and went out.

Still no ladders and Sergeant White commented that to get through barbed wire, cutters were needed, and these also hadn't been issued yet, only one or two for repairing our own wire. I was beginning to become concerned myself, and asked him to send a corporal toward battalion HQ, to our left, to ask. He did so, promptly, as he was getting worried. The two ladders we had were too short to allow fast movement out of our trench. I wondered if they could be set on the lower (west) side of our trench and across to the top of the parapet (east) side, but then how to get everyone, loaded as they were with 50-60 pounds of ammunition, bombs, boots, kit, etc., up onto the top of the west side? Well, there was the other ladder...

I checked my watch: a little more than half an hour to go, and <u>where</u> were those bloody ladders? I decided to assemble each section and go over the orders, if only to pass the time: at five minutes to six, over the parapet, line up, bayonets fixed, then advance when the whistles blew – I realized then that I hadn't a whistle, presumably Captain Frye had one, but that didn't help me – 50 paces a minute, towards the German lines, keeping in line. Our bombardment, which certainly seemed very fierce indeed, was supposed to reduce opposition to a minimum.

One of the privates asked what we would do if the ladders didn't arrive in time, and I replied that we would take shovels and tunnel to the German lines. This prompted a laugh, which eased matters, but meantime, we were waiting...

Almost time to go over and I saw a stir coming from our left – ladders at last! I only just recognized the corporal I had sent. He saluted and gestured toward the ladders, each borne by two men. They were accompanied by another corporal with a bag, presumably holding the cutters. The corporal, my corporal started to say something, but I was busy, moving the ladders, four of them, into a useful distribution while opening the bag of cutters, taking one and telling my corporal to give one to each sergeant, and corporal, too, until they ran out. He took the bag and went, and one of the sergeants swore, turned to me and said, "The bloody ladders are too bloody short, Sir."

It was true: our trench was too deep, and while I or anyone unburdened with a pack could lever themselves over, the packs would have to be put over separately, and the damned things were, I noted, too damned heavy to do that easily or quickly.

It was almost six. The other companies were already over. I ordered three of the ladders set so the men could climb onto the west side of our trench and the remaining three (including our two original ones) across the trench, like stair flights. This took time, each had to be secured so it wouldn't turn under the weight of a fully laden soldier, and I was panic-stricken at being so late. I pulled my revolver out of its holster, transferred it to my left hand, and climbed the first ladder, then across the second, saying, "Follow me."

I fell down the face of our parapet, by God's Providence remembering to roll out of the way as another man, then another, fell down after me. I scrambled to my feet, noted my revolver had stayed out of the dirt and started towards the German lines, dodging posts, stepping on barbed wire, running when I could over incredibly broken ground, feeling rather than seeing the men behind me. Orders for the advance were forgotten as I was late and had to catch up. I moved rightward along a sort of path or clearer land, tried to cut a strand of wire with the cutters, found them completely inadequate: the German wire was very thick. I cursed, kicked hard at a post holding the wire, it went over and several of us crossed, moving as quickly as we could. Now a huge roll of wire stretched across our way, we could not cut through that, then a private breathlessly said, "Clear over that way, Sir." And there was a path, oblique to the German lines – they must have some way out themselves, going on patrols – well, we would come in the same way.

Not a shot so far from the Germans. Had they all been killed by our bombardment? I glanced to my left and saw lines of our men, lying before the German lines, and had the impression from the way they were lying that they had been cut down by machine-gun fire. A few were moving. Now we were at the German parapet, and I ran onto it, roaring, "At them, by God!" And we were over, the trenches full of German soldiers, who were utterly astonished at seeing us, more and more of us.

I stopped two men who were trying to bayonet Germans who had put up their hands, ordered the men to disarm the Germans, asked a corporal to assemble a strong party to take prisoners back, saw some German machine-gunners, grinning, still unaware of our presence, firing onto the lines of our fallen soldiers, became enraged and fired my revolver at them, without effect, though a private emptied his rifle into their backs and they fell over.

I organized parties of men to move down the German lines in both directions, shooting any resistors, taking others prisoner, tossing bombs around any corner where the trench changed direction. Another party I posted where a communication trench joined the front line trench, to ensure no surprises from that direction, made sure the German prisoners were being moved to our lines, then got another corporal and his squad to check the German dugouts for sick or wounded or skulkers. Then I got some more men to swing the German Maxims around to fire into their own lines. I could see a reserve line forming up outside our own line, and wanted to help them as much as possible.

The corporal who was checking the German dugouts, there were three in the sector we had captured, found about thirty sick and wounded, no skulkers. He also brought several boxes of German bombs, which I had placed near the communication trench and along the trench. More German prisoners were conscripted to carry their own sick and wounded into our lines. Another strong party of guards was sent and I began to feel the need for more men. Our parties had taken a total of over a quarter of a mile of German trench and the fire from the captured German Maxims had silenced many of their machine-gun posts, though a few rifle bullets were starting to come our way.

I asked a sergeant to prime a German bomb, toss it back and see if it exploded, and if it did, train several men to do the same. We had a great many German bombs and it seemed as well to put them to use. I asked him to find men with good arms, cricketers, as I was sure the Germans would counterattack, and goddamn it, this was now my trench. I had the German Maxims, those not firing on the Germans, brought across the trench and set to fire to the east, in the direction of any counterattack. I asked if anyone knew how to reload a Maxim: one man said he did and I set him to instructing the newly made Maxim gunners.

An officer stood in the trench, asking me who was in charge. I looked at the relatively immaculate uniform and the staff insignia, and what I thought was a captain's badges, and said, rather rudely, "I haven't had any volunteers to replace me, so I suppose I am." He looked at me and said, "Orders are to retire immediately." I swore, and told him we had the damned trench, all those others had to do was saunter, rifles slung, across no man's land and escort the prisoners back. He seemed about to say something, when the cry, "Lieutenant" came, and the Germans were advancing in line towards our trench and I ordered bombs thrown with abandon – but prime the bloody things first, I had to order two or three men – and the Maxims to open fire, with some more men to pile sandbags from the German west parapet about the Maxims to protect the gunners, and the sandbags tended to be rotten and burst when we tried to shift them, and more Germans were coming up the communication trench, so more bombs had to be thrown, many of them, and some were being thrown at us and the air was filled with explosions and bits of metal and I saw a bomb land nearby and grabbed a sandbag which mercifully didn't burst and threw it on the bomb, which exploded under the bag but did us no harm...

Now our reserves were reaching our sector, having mastered our ladder system, and I deployed riflemen along the east side of the German trench to fire on the advancing German line which seemed to have melted away but here came another...

I became aware of a captain at my elbow, realized I had been ordering his men about, but also realized the situation was obvious, and merely nodded at him.

The fighting continued past dark, more and more Germans trying to retake the trench, and failing, as we used our and their bombs with abandon, more boxes being found in their dugouts, compensating for our own rifle ammunition running low by using the German rifles – they had plenty of ammunition, and my men were able to master the reloading, clearing, etc., quite well. We were taking casualties, but not many, and their own Maxims were cutting them down. I wondered when the German snipers would show up: our men were relatively unprotected, but the German command didn't seem to think about that.

* * *

We were relieved after dark as things had quieted down, though I felt the Germans were not going to give up completely. Still, I was exhausted, we all were, my water bottle was long empty and I had spots in front of my eyes, the result, I noted with relief, of bits of dirt on my spectacles, which I had forgotten to remove.

At any event, we swaggered out. Because of the very heavy losses taken by the rest of the battalion, we went into reserve. By now, I was aware of how incredibly lucky we had been: our late start because of the business with the ladders had led the Germans to think no attack was coming from our sector, and our crossing the quarter mile or so of distance between the lines as quickly as we could improved our chances. Still, the Germans should have kept someone watching but neglected to do so and paid the price. I remembered Conrad's saying I had quoted to Alice, another life ago, and settled down to some leisure, very relatively speaking. We had had eleven wounded, but no dead, so I didn't even have to write any letters. This was as well, as I discovered next morning when we were given tea to drink that my hands were still shaky. I kept them in my pockets as much as possible as a result. I didn't think anyone was fooled by this, but nothing was said.

I was summoned to the colonel's office, made myself as presentable as possible, and reported. In the office were a major I didn't know and the staff captain I had, I realized, been insubordinate to. The colonel was not happy – with me, he explained: I had disobeyed an order to retire to let our artillery resume firing on the German trench. The captain had had to run back to the observation post to call off the bombardment. Luckily (more luck!), he had been successful. However, said the colonel, orders had to be obeyed even when the need for them was not apparent to officers in the field, did I understand?

I thought of several things I could say, none of them likely to help my case, so I said, "Yes, Sir." There was a silence, and then I said, "Sheer fighting madness, Sir." Another silence, although the colonel's face moved. I didn't understand what that meant. Finally, the colonel said, "Return to your company, Lieutenant, while we decide what to do with you." I saluted, made an about-turn, stumbled but recovered and left, returning in a chastened and apprehensive mood. I didn't think I would be shot, but I might be broken to sergeant or even private. I wandered through a French village, where things were of course for sale. It occurred to me that carrots grew in France so I hunted about, not knowing the French, but found some and a few raw potatoes, and returned to my company, for I now thought of it as mine.

I wrote a letter to Eddie and another to David, who was stationed to our south, I thought, and yet another to my one-handed Regular to tell him about the wire cutter situation. I washed the carrots and potatoes and crunched away at them while I wrote.

The next day, there was a parade of the battalion, a miserable spectacle, some companies reduced to a handful, mine alone presenting a truly martial appearance, owing to our victory. I stood in front of D Company, the only officer still, and was surprised to be ordered before a brigadier general. "Now I'm for it," I thought as I marched as smartly to him as I could. Very much to my surprise, I found I had been awarded the Military Cross and promoted first lieutenant. I stood stunned, then, after the decoration was pinned to my tunic, I recovered, saluted, said. "Thank you, Sir." He nodded, and I marched back to my company.

More initials for my tombstone, I thought, yet once I had recovered, felt elated. Now I was the military equal, in terms of decorations, to Alice's husband. She read the papers, and would see my name; would she regret her behaviour? I eventually sighed: it really didn't matter.

* * *

We were in reserve some time, a trickle of recovered casualties and new recruits slowly bringing the other companies back to some semblance of strength. The two second lieutenants who had been absent for our attack returned, and were not pleased to be under the command of a "wart". They tended to be a bit insolent, but I found that since I was bigger than either of them, things went no farther. Also, I found I simply had developed enough self-confidence to be able to insist on having my orders obeyed.

Captain Frye, I learned one evening at the officers' mess, had died, of what my informant said was "pery something." I said, "Peritonitis." He said yes, that was it, from a burst appendix. I was sad, sorry I hadn't come even a day sooner, but then, if he hadn't felt so wretched at the end, he would have ignored my warning.

I also learned that the reason I was not court-martialed was that news of our successful attack had been published, including my name, and it would not do, my informant said, to court-martial the man who commanded a successful attack and defence of the captured position the next day, as it were. This dimmed my lustre somewhat, but I still remembered the feeling of a conqueror marching out.

* * *

We were back in line, in exactly the same place I had reported to. The Germans, led by a German Matthew perhaps, had mounted a surprise counterattack and turned the men holding the captured German trench out, killing some, capturing some and forcing the rest to flee to our original trench line. My company had plenty to say to the defeated battalion, and I had to intervene several times to break up fights.

I really couldn't stand sleeping in the "wading pool", the dugout that seemed to permanently have two or three inches of water. I began sleeping by day, on or wrapped in, depending on whether it was raining, a ground sheet in one of the recesses carved in the side of the trench for observing or sniping. It was cramped, yet not as oppressive as the dugout. Nights I roamed my sector: sentries sleeping on duty were a real problem, and German patrols had kidnapped or killed some sentries. I kept an eye on my own men but also on the German lines.

One night I spotted movement: a German patrol was coming across. I could detect three shapes, and decided enough was enough. I would go myself, alone since the more men the more noise and difficulty in coordinating them. I quickly notified the two sentries nearby that I was going into no-man's land to deal with a German patrol.

I rolled over the parapet and was able to land on my feet quietly, then headed towards them. I had my revolver out and could actually see well enough, in fact, I wondered why the Germans seemed oblivious of me. I moved carefully among posts, barbed wire, pieces of what had once been living men, helmets, bits of clothing and kit, keeping as low as possible and trying not to move where they were looking.

They drew nearer. I saw one had a large knife in his belt and wondered if this was for an assassination. At length, I let them get between me and my trench, so I was behind them. They didn't seem to suspect I was near. When they were close enough to my trench, I quietly told them, "*Hande hoch*." Then I quickly yanked the knife out of the belt of one, the rifle off the shoulder of a second, pushing him down in the process, and the Mauser pistol out of the hand of the third. I moved very quickly, pushing them, constantly changing my position, forcing them to face into our parapet. Then I quietly called to the nearer of the sentries, who seemed to take a long time responding.

After accusing him of being asleep, I ordered him to get a sergeant and four men to take three German prisoners back. I kept moving around, pushing the prisoners, keeping them off balance and intimidated, letting them know I understood German and would shoot them all and be back over the parapet before their own side could react.

It seemed to take a long time, but the sergeant arrived with three men and I tossed the rifle, the Mauser and the knife over, then grabbed the smallest German and boosted him over. The other two were permitted to climb over.

I questioned the man with the knife, who insisted it was only for intimidation, and quieter than a pistol, so I sent them off, wishing them "*Gluckauf*", and telling them they had perhaps two or three years to invent truly outrageous lies about their exploits to tell their families and friends. Two of them smiled, the one with the knife didn't and I figured him for a bad one. I told the sergeant this, and he nodded and led them off, strongly guarded. One of the Germans, not the bad one, had wire cutters, good ones, evidently, which I kept.

* * *

I figured the Germans were likely to respond to the loss of their patrol by sending out a bigger one, and, sure enough, three nights later, I again saw movement. It was a very dark night, but I could detect five shapes. I briefly thought of using the captured knife myself but decided if I could surprise them, I could probably capture them. I again alerted the sentries, and this time I felt they would stay awake.

I went over the parapet again – the occasional gun flashes from our side would be blocked by our parapet. I didn't wear my spectacles as they would reflect light and my uniform was dirty enough, as were my face and hands, to allow me to remain hidden from them.

The same stalking routine began. I realized they were being very cautious, not knowing what they were dealing with. I moved with more confidence, quickly getting first behind their lagging member, then between them and their trench. They took their time getting close to our parapet, but once close enough, I struck again, moving very quickly to disarm them and knock them down. Two or three seemed of a mind to resist but I conveyed to them that I had a loaded pistol and could see them very well, and when one or two tried to creep away, pistol-whipped them into obedience. The long barrel of my revolver came into its own now.

This time the sergeant came more quickly, and one by one, the prisoners went over the parapet to be secured. They had several knives, pistols and what I was told were brass knuckles concealed about them, so I sent them back under a stronger guard. I shook hands with the German sergeant, wished him and all his men luck, and bade them goodbye.

* * *

After this, there was no more muttering by the two second lieutenants. I had more than proved myself; in fact I was told that the men talked of me with some awe and definite respect. Indeed I was told I had been "mentioned in dispatches", an honour I supposed. (My initial reaction to this news was to ask, "Favourably?")

* * *

Look as I might, after the loss of their second patrol in three days, the Germans stopped sending men out, at least in our sector. I was somewhat disappointed, as I had enjoyed being out of the trenches, playing cat and mouse with the Germans, especially as I seemed to be able to see them better than they could see me, so had the advantage.

Subsequently, I was told, the Germans had become rather nervous: any noise out in no-man's land, even from the rats eating pieces of dead men, prompted a barrage of Very lights. I thought this was good, as the Germans wouldn't do this if they had men out there, so we knew when to start looking for their patrols.

* * *

In line, routines dominated everything: daily inspection of the men's feet – actually quite important – supervision of the rum ration (when available) – once it was realized that I was a teetotaller, I became the supervising officer for the battalion – posting sentries – and roaming the line at night to make sure they stayed alert – censoring mail, etc. These were, I fancied, designed to take the place of thought. So I was busy but bored and feeling increasingly hemmed in.

We were back in reserve when I was again summoned to see the colonel. Since I couldn't think of anything I had done wrong, at least anything he would know about, I went with no emotion but curiosity. The colonel told me I was wanted at Corps Headquarters, as they had a project I might be able to perform. There was a staff motor to take me, what seemed a considerable distance, to the Corps HQ.

There a staff captain told me what was wanted: someone to take a time-bomb across enemy lines to a munitions dump and set it off. This would cut down on German shelling while they replenished the dump, perhaps saving lives, but at least disconcerting the enemy.

He showed me a device consisting of three sticks of dynamite, some cells, a clock, a switch and some wires. He explained how the device was supposed to work, and then reached over to throw the switch that was supposed to enable the clock to detonate the dynamite after a set time.

One of the many virtues of Earl's Cross School, I was coming to realize, was the thoroughness of the curriculum: it had some physics, including electrical circuit theory. I had been tracing the wires and came to the conclusion that this man didn't know what he was talking about, so I stopped him and said that if he was determined to throw the switch, to allow me to get several hundred yards away first, because the dynamite would go off the instant he did.

This prompted an argument, which ended only when I disconnected the wires from the dynamite, held their ends near and told him to throw the switch. The resulting spark surprised, then quieted him. Still the idea intrigued me, even more the idea of roaming freely behind German lines, so I began reworking the device.

The clock first: it was an alarm clock and noisy withal, so I opened it and wrapped string to quiet it, and removed the alarm.

Instead, I secured one wire to the minute hand and the other to the hour hand, so the free end of one wire would connect with the wire on the hour hand, completing the circuit. I set it so removing a pin would start the mechanism, allowing me an hour to get clear. I got rid of the switch and rewired the device. Now it would work as intended. All I needed to do was get it there.

I studied the map: nearly 40 miles to the place, near Tournai. I would need two days to get there and two days back. I talked to an officer on the staff: he told me where to set the device – anywhere, especially if the shells were fused. I needed a compass; eventually one was found.

The moon had nearly waned completely; with clouds as well, it should be dark enough. I went to the front line with two water bottles and four tins of bully beef, each wrapped so they wouldn't clink, told the battalion commander what I was about, and waited in my usual recess. I fell asleep, waking about 11 and decided I had better start. I had darkened my hands, face and brass; I put my spectacles in a pocket and rolled over our parapet with the device.

I made my way across no-man's land bent low but moved fairly quickly as I knew the way, and even with fairly complete cloud cover could see well enough. I assumed German sentry discipline was better than ours, so listened carefully at their parapet: arrival of replacement troops, for example, had to be waited out.

At length I decided I could move, peered very cautiously over their parapet, now repaired, saw nothing and rolled over the top, dropping as gently as possible. Still nothing. I moved to the east side, rolled up onto that side and began moving east, crouched and glancing back to our lines for gun flashes. It was a fairly quiet night and after orienting myself relative to their communication trench, began walking more upright at my usual pace, though much more quietly. The German wire cutters worked quite well.

I crossed two more trenches in the same way. No one seemed awake. I was very surprised but began moving even faster, past some artillery batteries, also quiet. Didn't they post sentries anywhere?

As soon as I could detect some light to the east, I found the largest grove of trees around, moved into the middle, drew out my ground sheet, wrapped myself up in it, and went to sleep. The only concession I made to my location was to keep my revolver at hand, though I doubted this would do any good if a party of Germans approached.

I was able to sleep to mid-day, emerged cautiously, emptied my bladder, ate a tin of bully beef – I figured that gave the best nutritional value for the weight – and checked the device, then went over my map. I had gone over ten miles, but would have to pick up the pace if I was to get to the munitions dump by tomorrow. I then realized I would need three days to get there if I was to plant the device at night, so my rations were going to run short. I shook my head at my shoddy planning, and went back under cover to doze the rest of the day.

Fortunately the clouds were thicker, with some rain, so I started probably sooner than I should, but was not challenged. I passed more batteries, some encampments and many billets, trying to stay downwind of anywhere there were dogs. Otherwise I moved quickly.

Dawn again and I sheltered in another copse. There were still leaves enough on the trees to shelter me reasonably well. I had to be close to the dump, but was very tired – the nervous strain was affecting me. I slept on and off the next day, ate another tin of bully beef, decided the dump couldn't be more than five miles away, say two hours including getting by the sentries, because some sentries had to be about a munitions dump. Dark again, full dark this time. I could hear locomotives operating, which would help cover any noise I would make.

There were sentries, so I had to crawl, sometimes on my belly, which was awkward because of the device. However the sentries had their routine, and after seeing what it was, I was able to move behind one and into the dump itself. It was perhaps midnight.

I found a place between stacks of medium-sized shells, which appeared to be fused. Carrying those had to be a nervous task, I thought. I used my torch to inspect the device, set it concealed under and between some shells, and removed the pin. The clock started and I was startled by how much noise it made. There was nothing for it but to leave however. I checked the time and headed back west.

I again crossed behind a sentry and moved as fast as I prudently could. The sound of the munitions trains should cover the clock, I thought, and anyway the sentries didn't patrol everywhere.

I was crossing a meadow when I saw lights flickering behind me. I suddenly realized that the Germans would be looking east, towards me, and I was silhouetted by the lights, and I dropped to the ground. Then I heard rumbles and explosions like a Guy Fawkes fireworks. Looking back I could see an auroral flickering, growing in intensity and spreading as I watched. Now all I had to do was get back in the face of any onlooking Germans.

I crawled on my belly across the meadow, hiding behind bushes, moving in ruts and depressions in the ground. I heard no voices, no conversations, but stayed down anyway. Once I was in trees, I could move faster, but tried to stay in shadows.

When I stopped, I figured I was about twelve miles from the dump. I saw several groups of Germans and some civilians, all watching the show, which grew and grew most gratifyingly. I hoped some of the munitions trains had gotten caught in the explosions but they were probably able to move away. I slept, ate what was my last tin of bully beef, though I couldn't remember consuming three tins previously, only two. It was going to be a hungry twenty eight miles back.

A thirsty one, too. I had taken two water bottles with me, and both were empty. All the wells had German soldiers about, and I didn't dare drink from streams, not with an army camped across the countryside. So I started as early as I could: fortunately it was wooded country, so I could make good progress for a while, but then began to encounter German rear area facilities – corps and division command centres, counterbattery guns, etc. As dawn became visible, I stopped again and tried to sleep, hoping for a good rain.

* * *

About ten miles to go: I had moved off my original course, so was in *terrae incognita*. This slowed me, too, though I was able to move fairly rapidly parallel to the German communication trenches. Crossing their lines still presented no problem.

I had crossed the parapet of their front line trench when I realized getting across all the barbed wire to my own lines would be very hard, and dawn was approaching. I had the cutters but there was a great deal of wire to cut. I looked for a path the Germans would use for their patrols and eventually saw a trodden area. I moved down it crouched over, saw a way to my lines and crept to the British parapet. After listening and hearing nothing, I climbed to the top and rolled over, landing upright in a British trench, enormously relieved and enormously thirsty and hungry.

Eventually I found a sentry, asleep of course, and roused him with some difficulty. I explained my presence, which greatly relieved him, since I wasn't going to order him punished for sleeping on duty. I got a sergeant to show me where the battalion commander worked. He was out on some errand. I asked for something to drink and eat and eventually got some tea – unsweetened – and a tin of bully beef. Then I put my head down on my arms on the battalion commander's desk and fell asleep.

Fortunately the battalion commander accepted my story, especially once I had told him about the original version of the device the staff officer had rigged. Belief in the thorough incompetence of any member of any staff in our army was profound.

He provided me with an escort, as I assured him I hadn't the faintest idea where my battalion or division or corps was, so I was able to report back, my mission accomplished (as everyone for miles had been able to see), adding to my military laurels.

* * *

I sat in my recess in the trench, thinking how lucky I had been – again – despite my miscalculations. The staff captain had wanted to send me around to blow up all the German munitions dumps on the Western Front, until I pointed out the impossibility of such a project, even if the Germans remained oblivious throughout. The basic problem was water, but after that, food became limiting. I figured 20 miles was about the limit. I was perfectly willing to attack anything within that distance, remembering how free I had felt, once across enemy lines, but that seemed to rule out any target of real significance.

It had started to snow again, and I pulled the ground sheet closer around me as the wind was cutting. A messman with tea came along and offered me a cup. I drank some, and discovered there was no sugar in it. To me, tea was bearable only when heavily sugared – milk was a distant memory – and I said, "Bugger." The messman nodded, taking no offense, and went on. As I stared at the liquid, something splashed in it. I looked closer, hoping it wasn't some insect or clod of filth called dirt around here: then another splash and I realized it was starting to rain. "Bugger" I said more loudly and pulled a corner of the ground sheet over me.

We were back in reserve, eating – dining was an inappropriate description – and I was listening to the lieutenant colonel commanding our battalion. He had been wounded in the attack but was back. He told the three of us listening to him that our attack, that cost us so heavily, was a diversion, to keep the Germans from responding as strongly to our Somme offensive. He didn't know if it was successful. He added that the colonel was a "dugout", meaning dug out of retirement when the army urgently needed officers as it expanded early in the war. He had lost his leg in the Boer War, I was told. He had been kept on because he seemed very capable, despite his missing leg.

I asked about the wire cutters, a sore point with me, and was told the new ones worked well, that we had been given surplus old ones. This enraged me: our attack should have been as decently and strongly supported as any; giving us ones that were known not to work was worse than careless, it was criminal. I used the word deliberately, and the battalion commander sarcastically suggested I write to the War Office about the matter.

After thinking about it, I did just that:

To whom this may concern:

My company, sent into action against well-armed and supported German trenches would, but for a lucky accident, have been wiped out, partly because we were issued wire cutters that were known to be inadequate to cut German barbed wire. To do this knowingly, whatever the reasons, strongly suggests either our lives are of no concern to the War Office /General Staff, or that some no doubt elusive official or officials are guilty of criminal negligence. While I doubt any will be actually brought to trial, focusing public attention upon official misconduct will allow us to more effectively prosecute the war.

Sincerely,
Matthew Dobbs, MC, First Lieutenant

I gave the letter to the colonel, who I assumed would see it went no further, but I misjudged him: he sent it on. I wondered what the response would be, probably my transfer to the Sinai or even farther afield, but nothing happened.

* * *

We were moving up the line, from support to the front line, at night of course. There was German shelling, not too heavy, so we were moving steadily, changing directions with the communication trenches. A German shell burst ahead and to my left at some distance, seemingly a safe one, when I felt I had run against a post or something with my right shoulder. I couldn't see any post, and continued. My shoulder began to hurt, and then throb – I must have hit whatever it was hard. Another flash from a shell, and I could see a jagged piece of something sticking in my shoulder. I said, "I say, I've been hit in the shoulder by a piece of shrapnel." No one responded. I continued, figuring I would report my injury, then turn around and go to an Advanced Dressing Station. I began to feel blood running down my arm, and said, "I think I'll have to go back." Still no response. Now my knees were becoming heavy, I was beginning to breathe heavily and perspire, and I tried to turn around. I felt myself beginning to fall, tried to stop myself with my left arm, and hit the ground, running the shrapnel further into my shoulder and causing me to cry out; then there was nothing.

I was lying on a hospital bed, evidently in England. My shoulder hurt like hell. I had vague memories of riding on a train and a ship, lying on a cot, too drugged to even worry about my arms being bound and immobile. Now I watched nurses and soldiers and civilians, relatives of the soldiers I assumed, moving about, some on their feet and some in wheeled chairs, feeling quite detached except for the pain. I imagined all sorts of fantasies involving Alice, Alice having lost or divorced her husband, Alice trying to make amends, coming to an understanding with her, except my imagination kept running into a wall of reality: I could not trust her. Gradually my fantasies wore out, leaving me a creature of hospital routine. My shoulder had been repaired, severed ligaments sewn back together, muscles stitched, skin sewn over all. All I had to do was heal, but it still hurt badly. I remembered telling a nurse and doctor who had asked if my wound was very painful, "only when I laugh," then telling them the joke with that ending. They seemed more surprised than amused and I put them down as having little sense of humour.

As I watched, I saw a nurse suddenly sink down and begin to weep hysterically. Two other nurses came to her side and helped her away, and I reflected that the nurses had to bear a great deal, day after day, awful wounds, sorrow and death, and what they were seeing were relatively cleaned up, presentable patients – the ones just off the battlefields were mercifully past imagining.

* * *

Eddie showed up in the afternoon. He said he had just seen my name in the papers and came over as soon as his patients permitted. He looked at my dressings, looked under them, sniffed at my wound, said there was no sign of gangrene or infection, so I should heal. I had a "blighty wound", allowing me a stay in "old blighty" (Britain). It still hurt like hell.

Eddie went off to talk to the resident doctor, and came back to tell me I could move to his place tomorrow to recover; he had permission to keep me there. I was quite happy to leave. Despite the bustle, the place depressed me, as I had no one else to visit or talk to. I sensed Eddie wanted someone to come home to, some friend to listen to his day's doings, talk about music or anything else. He had been kind enough to let me leave my things at his place when I had gone a-soldiering, but then he was always kind.

* * *

The next day I was resurrected, as it were, put into my uniform with the help of an orderly and a nurse, which embarrassed me, but I could stand, so I could walk, and I did, though supported on my left, down to a taxi brought by Eddie. Sitting down was better, but I was able to walk up the steps into Eddie's flat. He had his man draw a bath and I was able to bathe all of me save the shoulder in actual hot water with real soap, even one-handed, for the first time in – years, I realized, probably since before my parents had been killed. Then clean pyjamas and sleep in a real bed, and I hadn't been in that many of those over most of my life either.

* * *

When I awoke, I felt nothing: I was completely relaxed, warm, and safe; I couldn't even feel my shoulder. I thought this must be what Nirvana was like: bliss. I could not recall ever feeling so good and for an instant wondered if I was even alive. I glanced to my left and saw the sun setting, some birds flying and smoke rising from chimneys, and decided I was indeed alive and at that moment my shoulder began to hurt again.

Eddie sent his man to help me into a dressing gown, one of Eddie's as it was a bit small for me, and I went down to dine. He had even stocked some ginger beer, which brought tears to my eyes, though he pretended not to notice. The meal was excellent, and the music – some Strauss waltzes, songs by Caruso and Melba – from his gramophone superb. I asked him about his practice, not just to be polite but because I was genuinely interested.

His practice was growing, not surprising as he charged his patients, dockers and their families and anyone else who wandered in, pennies. He told me of the diseases he was treating, sometimes in more detail than I really cared to hear, and I could again see he was a man who loved his work. I told him about the captain with appendicitis, and we talked about the war. I told him about our attack and our luck.

He was curious, asking what it was like to serve in the trenches. I sat and thought and groped for words, and finally said, "Squalid. Squalid and beastly and boring. Farm animals wouldn't be kept the way we live. It is a combined latrine and charnel house. I am amazed there aren't epidemics, of sickness or madness. Human beings are incredibly tough and adaptable. But, in the midst of life, you are surrounded by death and all its consequences. I have really begun thinking, how little life, how brief, we have, and how important we are all to each other." I stopped, a bit embarrassed. I added, "The cuisine could stand a deal of improvement, too." Eddie laughed.

He told me he had been thinking of joining the Medical Service, in fact he had begun filling out the paperwork. I reminded him how important he was to his patients, many of them dockers, and how vital their work was to the country. In France, I said, in quiet times the doctors were probably bored, while during and after offensives, no number of doctors would be enough. It wasn't as though he was one of many doctors with a suburban practice; he was really making a contribution, and was irreplaceable where he was. He listened, and said he would think about what I said.

He went off to bed early because his patients sometimes came early, while I stayed up, listening to recordings, and rereading Austin's *Mansfield Park*. Eddie had all her books.

I sat on the patient's cot, bare to the waist while a nurse removed the stitches from my shoulder. Then the doctor looked at the scar. He said I should be ready to return in a week, after having me move my arm about. I got dressed, went to the bank for some money, went to a jewellery store to get a trinket for Elsie, then, after walking until I was sure she was back from work, paid a visit for my usual purpose and with the usual result. She was very impressed with my MC and was very generous indeed with her favours, leaving me exhausted and disgusted with myself. I was careful not to give any indication of the latter. I had been visiting her nearly every day, and I prayed she wouldn't see anything in my motives except lust, though I felt ashamed of that, too. I talked to her about her work, which was utterly boring to her (and to me), but was careful not to ask about anything personal. She sometimes asked me about being a soldier, and I answered honestly, or as honestly as I thought she could stand, but our relationship had but one real dimension.

There were opportunities for diversion of a young, unmarried officer, but I didn't care for most. The concert fare was mostly now confined to French, Italian, Russian and British composers, some of which I liked but were not my favourites. I still tended to be shy and awkward, so had difficulty "mixing" with the women in canteens serving tea (which I didn't like), etc. I didn't dance or drink either, which further limited my activities. Since I had an outlet of sorts with Elsie and an intellectual/gastronomic refuge with Eddie, I otherwise spent a fair amount of leave time reading or walking. What I wanted, of course, was a romance.

* * *

I had been "passed fit" and was to leave in two days when I got some letters. One was from the second lieutenant in acting command of the company. Apparently a sniper had been exacting a toll on our battalion: my company had four deaths alone – I recognized two of the names. I thought about the situation, and then continued reading. There was the usual farrago of requests for things I was to get from Fortnum's. I hoped I could carry everything I was asked to provide, but decided to go there tomorrow morning to reduce last-minute confusion.

Another was from the Corps staff, asking me to report there on my way to my battalion. I guessed my letter had finally provoked a response. I was not going to move an inch towards accommodation; if they really didn't care for my attitude, they could send me home, I thought.

The third letter was from David, and had followed a very circuitous path getting to me at Eddie's. David had lost his lower right leg at the Somme, so was out. I was sorry about the leg, but glad he was safe. His parents had insisted he forget about the rabbinate and manage the family pawn shop and jewellery store, which he was doing without much enthusiasm, though he had decided against becoming a rabbi. I could understand his disillusionment. His sweetheart had married another man, a man who owned a furniture store and had bad eyesight so probably wouldn't wind up being entertained by the Imperial German Army in France. Again understandable but very depressing: I could easily imagine his feelings.

When Eddie returned, a little earlier than usual, I showed him David's letter and suggested we descend on him, perhaps going to the Jewish restaurant we all liked. I offered to host the meal. Eddie told me I was on, gave his servants the evening off, and we went outside for a taxi.

David's family's shop was ready to close when we went in. He was just ushering the last customer out when we arrived. He looked at us a moment before realizing who we were, not just late customers, and gave a grin like I had never seen on him before. We hugged, slapped each other's shoulders, and could hardly be more affectionate than reunited lovers. Eddie mentioned the restaurant project and David ushered us out, locked the door and we all went on foot to the restaurant, David limping somewhat but manfully keeping up.

The place wasn't too crowded but as lively as I recalled: exuberant talk, some in Hebrew or other languages, everyone evidently on good terms. Eddie and I weren't regulars, but David was known and our presence apparently caused no constraint. We sat and ordered, ate, drank and enjoyed, as we were bidden by the waitress, who was apparently something of a "character" well known to the regulars.

We decided to move on to Eddie's and got another taxi. Our conversation had moved beyond boisterous, and I had to reassure the driver we weren't drunk, just meeting again after months of separation. He didn't seem reassured and was evidently glad when we got out. Once inside, I made up the fire while Eddie got a bottle of wine, ginger beer for me. David sat in the place of honour on the couch. I showed them a recording of a Strauss waltz, which was approved as we could talk while enjoying the music. I put it on, telling them I wasn't going to waltz with either of them, as they had a reputation for taking liberties with their hands. I was hit by cushions from a chair and the couch in reply, tossed them back and sat down to my ginger beer.

Eddie showed David the wine. David examined the label, was impressed, and accepted a glass. We all drank, and I suddenly realized that all three of us had been jilted. As if this thought had somehow been transmitted between us, David turned to Eddie and asked about Christine. "Still engaged to that tall chap," said Eddie. "Haven't heard from or about her since she sent me away."

David turned to me and asked about the light-haired girl he had seen me with at the opera. "Threw me over," I said. "Parental opposition. Married a cavalry officer." David made a comment about cavalrymen in general that I recognized. It was not complimentary. "But very posh," I argued. This prompted more terms, also uncomplimentary. I wasn't about to disagree. I asked David about his girl: "Much the same story," he said. "Got a letter a month or so after being sent to France: married this other chap. Married. No warning at all – must have been seeing him on the sly while I was training." Eddie and I both cursed. I asked, "Didn't he know she was engaged to marry you?" David replied, "We weren't actually formally engaged, no ring or announcement." He paused. "But there really wasn't any doubt. No, she threw me over for fair." He took another drink of the wine, savoured it, and nodded appreciatively to Eddie. Eddie and I both cursed again; not very original, but heartfelt.

David was philosophical. "It isn't confined to women, of course. You hear about fellows doing the same thing. I think anyone who does that sort of thing is simply selfish, and, really, unworthy of the love of any decent human being. But," he paused again, "Still, it hurts like hell." Eddie and I nodded in silent agreement.

I got up and put on another recording. This was the Emperor Waltz, the *Kaiserwaltz*. We listened in silence, until I had to turn the recording. When the second side of the recording ended – it was almost a small symphony – I went over to shut the gramophone off. Eddie said he had heard that piece playing in Vienna, when he had visited with his parents. "When was that?" I asked. "In '12, before the war." Eddie said. He went on, "I tried to get Christine to come with us, but she refused. A sign of things to come, evidently." I asked, "What was Vienna like?" Eddie thought, and then said, "A very musical city. And wonderful food. Consider: it sits between the Hungarians, Italians, Germans and Czechs, so you have their cuisines and their folk tunes all mixing. The people don't get on that well, but I think the mixing or perhaps modifying of each by the other somehow improves them all. Except that Christine wasn't there, it was a marvellous visit. I should like to go again, once things settle down and I can get away." I thought I should like to visit myself, especially if I ever had someone I loved to do it with.

We sat in silence a moment, and then began to talk about friends, an often painful exercise: ranks thinned so much by death, so soon. At length Eddie made what was becoming a standard toast: "To absent friends." We all drank, and then David said, "When we Jews gather, we have a toast. The Hebrew is '*Lachaim*'; in English, 'To Life'; so I give you" – holding his glass out so Eddie and I did likewise – "*Lachaim!*" "*Lachaim!*" Eddie and I repeated and drank.

We put on more music, talked about music. I thought of how important music had become to me, and how deeply I had been moved by some of it. It had made a great many things in my life more bearable. By now Eddie and David were down to the last of the second bottle of wine, and showing the effects a little. Both realized they had to be at work tomorrow and Eddie noted I was returning to France that next evening, so our gathering broke up. I accompanied David back to his parents' place, telling him I didn't want the responsibility for leaving him on the streets of London unescorted, being blamed for the trail of rapine, vandalism and common nuisances he would undoubtedly perpetrate. He feigned indignation at the vandalism part, but I got him home and we bade farewell, possibly forever, though we were careful not to say this. I walked back to Eddie's, several miles as I disliked the Underground: it seemed too confining.

* * *

The next morning, not early, I headed towards Fortnum's. I was passing a clothing store, and assistants were putting out manikins and clothing them. I saw one set the head on a manikin, noted how lifelike it looked, and got an idea.

I went inside, got the manager and asked about obtaining one or two manikin heads. He wanted to sell me one at what I was sure was an outrageous price, and I became stubborn. I argued, said even damaged ones, ones useless for display, would do, invoked King, country, his country's soldiers, and finally was allowed to take two damaged ones away for nothing. The damage wouldn't affect the use I had in mind for them, and I was pleased with myself. I was, I thought, becoming rather pushy, and I liked being so.

On to Fortnum's: I produced my list, bought the items (and a few more), got them and the two manikin heads packed in a box they provided, for a fee to be sure, and persuaded them to rope the box so I could carry it easily. I carried it back to Eddie's, and was rewarded with lunch. I packed my things, cleaned and resewn by me, and sat on the couch in front of the fire, drinking ginger beer, listening to some opera overtures by Mozart, although not the *Marriage of Figaro*, as I didn't want to evoke memories, and rereading *Bleak House*. It all seemed very civilized.

Back to my last: I paid the solicited visit to Corps HQ, and was even asked to sit, so I assumed it wasn't a disciplinary matter. Indeed it wasn't: first, I was told I was promoted captain. This actually made sense: I was effective commander of what was still the largest company in my battalion, and, I told myself, had not done badly. The staff colonel even gave me the additional diamonds for the captain's insignia, which was helpful. Then he got down to what I guessed was the purpose of the meeting: my letter had in fact stirred things up. He assured me that the business of the cutters had been a "simple oversight": the original cutters purchased by government had proved inadequate, so were replaced by better. However, the inadequate ones had been stored, and when Corps had requested some, the old ones had been sent by mistake.

I was unmoved. I pointed out that inattention to such seemingly trivial details could prove lethal, the difference between success and failure, and that the men were not convinced of the competence or even the good will of staff when such incidents multiplied, and I reminded him about the ladders. I went on, saying that staff had to check and if necessary recheck every detail, it was their duty to not just the cause but to their fellow citizens. I was out of breath, and the colonel, still trying to be conciliatory, remarked that the staff was run ragged with details, but he would pass my remarks on. I thought briefly of the immaculate uniforms, including the one the colonel wore, and then was caught by what the colonel said next.

Apparently the Germans had decided that I must have been assisted by Belgian civilians on my sabotage mission, and had executed about a hundred. I cursed. I told the colonel that no one, no other human being, had either assisted or even seen me over the entire mission. I was prepared to take an oath on this, I said, not that it would help any of those executed – murdered, really. The colonel said this incident was pretty much according to form for the Germans. I cursed again; I had heard the stories, some obviously ridiculous, like the "Belgian corpse factory" but now I realized the German occupation was harsh, even brutal indeed. The interview over, I arose, saluted and returned to my company, now mine officially. We were in reserve. I distributed the items I had brought and showed the battalion commander the manikin heads and explained my idea.

He looked at me, smiled and said he had thought I would come up with something. He sent for the other captains – we had no major – and we had a conference. The senior captain, Castlefield by name, served as assistant to the lieutenant colonel. He was considered very capable, and after I had explained what I thought would work, amended my idea, and I realized actually improved the chances for success. We would need the shortest soldier we had, a wide cardboard tube for holding the manikin head on his, and at least two snipers of our own. Our short soldier would walk at a reasonable pace, with the top of what the German sniper would assume was his head moving just above our parapet – not my company's section as our trench was of course too deep. The German sniper would try to lead the target as it reappeared just above the parapet, shooting when he could get a good bead on the target. Our snipers would try to locate him, and shoot him if they could. I thought three or even four snipers would improve our chances if they could be concealed. I also pointed out that our snipers should be warned that if the German sniper was left-handed, he would be firing from the left hand side of an embrasure. Everyone seemed pleased – at least we were doing something other than serving as targets (though in a sense, that was about all the infantry were doing anyway). So the meeting broke up. I took the manikin heads back to my quarters, the battalion commander sending to other units for snipers.

In my billet, I wrote to Eddie and David, extolling the culinary delights of pommes frits and raw carrots. Also, for a while, real chocolate, although no milk, still less cream. Then, after brooding on what the staff colonel had told me, I wrote another letter:

To the Foreign Office/High Command,

Government of the German Empire:

I was informed that about one hundred Belgian civilians were murdered – I use the term deliberately – in reprisal for their supposed involvement in my mission to destroy a German munitions dump near Tournai on November 16, 1916. I give my word, as officer, gentleman and, I hope, decent human being, I had no assistance of any sort whatsoever from anyone else, nor did any Belgian have any knowledge at any time of my presence behind German lines or of my intentions.

Accordingly, those who perpetrated this disgusting massacre, and those who ordered it, are murderers and deserve the punishment meted out in all countries that consider themselves civilized, which is to be hanged.

I add, that the guard mounted by the German sentries was wretched, which was no small help to:

Matthew Dobbs, MC, Captain

I sent the letter to the British Foreign Office for transmission to the German government. At least it made me feel better.

* * *

Back in line, we put the plan into operation. Although the sniper might be back in reserve, we paraded our decoy duck as realistically as possible along the lower parapets. We had three snipers, all borrowed, with orders to concentrate on the German sniper. We prepared loopholes for our snipers, we hoped inconspicuous ones. Then we waited.

The third day back, one of our snipers fired, then, after a bit, said, "Got 'im." I was called over, looked and saw a rifle with a telescope lying muzzle down in front of a machine gun position. Our sniper said the German was indeed left handed, and he saw the man's hands come up as the rifle fell forward. Our short decoy had done his job; both our manikin heads were still intact, in case they were needed again.

We doubted the Germans would retaliate with increased shelling: snipers weren't that popular in either army. So all we had to worry about was the normal hazard of a shell hitting too closely, and so there was a distinct increase in cheerfulness in the battalion. The commander wondered if I could sneak over at night and retrieve the rifle, which he thought looked expensive. I said I would try, but by dark it was gone.

* * *

In line again: the Germans were sending up balloons for artillery spotting, nothing new about that for either side, but there were now more of them in our sector, and their guns were hitting us more accurately. I got a request from Corps, and went immediately even though it was day as I didn't think a single, rapidly moving soldier would draw any fire.

When I eventually got there, I was told my letter to the German government had been published in the *Times* – no mention if the Germans had been given it. (I doubted they would accept it.) Also, the staff wanted me to go across German lines with another explosive device to blow up one of the German balloon stations. I looked at the map: the distance wasn't very great. The balloon station was surrounded by antiaircraft guns, but everyone would likely be asleep at night as there would be no aeroplanes flying. And the station would probably be quiet as well, although I had no idea what their routine was. So, as I commented, I could probably do one station, but my experience of my supposed triumph with the munitions dump was that the Germans simply produced more shells and re-established the dump (and murdered some Belgians "*pour encourager les autres*").

So I said I thought our artillery was the agent for the task. Thinking about the situation, I asked for a gunner to consult. There was a staff officer who dealt with artillery matters, but he, I was not surprised to hear, was not actually a gunner. At length a gunner captain was obtained, and I talked the situation over with him.

The initial problem was spotting: we would need a balloon of our own to call our shots. Communications were then essential to the guns. At length I decided I would do it. It was five days past the full moon, giving me time to rig the device.

This I did, using five sticks of dynamite. Also I wanted to be able to set the time to detonation, rather than have a fixed time. This took thought. Eventually I removed the minute hand entirely and would have to set the device using the hour hand alone. The other arrangements were as before, and I carried the device back, again by day, and disconcerted the two second lieutenants in my company by leaving it wrapped tightly in oilcloth on the table in the "wading pool" where they slept.

* * *

It was two days until the new moon, but very cloudy. In fact, it began to rain just after dark, uncomfortable but otherwise perfect: the sound of the rain would cover sounds I would make and help keep the Germans under cover. I decided to leave about 10 to give myself plenty of time: I figured on about a 20 mile round trip. I carried the German wire cutters – good ones – and only one water bottle and no food.

There wasn't much gunfire to possibly reveal me to sentries so I moved fairly quickly. There was more barbed wire laid between the lines which I cut through as quickly as possible. When I got to the balloon site, I was somewhat surprised to find no watch being kept at all: everyone was asleep in dugouts. I found the hydrogen generating apparatus with the collapsed balloon nearby, checked the time, risking using my torch, and carefully set the device for about 6 AM when my observations indicated the balloon would be ready for the observer. The idea was not just to destroy the balloon, the Germans would merely supply another, but to kill, if possible, the observer, as, I was told by the gunner captain, trained experienced observers were precious. I realized I was growing callous, even homicidal, but told myself I was perhaps saving the lives of my men, or even myself, a rationalization to be sure, but an effective one.

I pulled the pin, starting the device. I hid it under some sacking so the ticking, muffled but clear to me, would hopefully escape German notice. Probably there would be a lot of conversation, banter and other noise. It was now past two and I started back. I used the path I had taken as I had cleared it through the wire. It was raining harder and pitch-black; even I had trouble seeing where I was going but wasn't going to complain about the weather. I got back to our lines near five, slowed a little by the darkness.

I wandered our sector, managed to get some tea, with sugar this time, and drank it while waiting. As I paced, the east began to lighten. Then I heard an explosion in the German lines. I checked my watch: six or nearly. I paced some more. By seven, the rain had stopped. I began thinking of retiring to my niche, but used my field glasses to look across: no balloon.

I was sitting on the couch at Eddie's reading *Persuasion* once more. Elsie had rather coyly informed me she would be "indisposed" for the next two or three days, which gave me pause: I thought she was past that, and wondered if I should employ condoms, as Eddie had suggested. Eddie himself was very late – I was thinking he might need to take an assistant, although I had no idea about the finances of the practice or how much would have to be paid. At length the front door opened and Eddie came in. He looked more tired than I had ever seen him, and seemed utterly cast down.

He began to change as I put a marker in the book, set it on the table where the glass of ginger beer was sitting on its coaster, and got up, rolling down my sleeves, buttoning the cuffs and picking up my tunic as I moved towards the butler's pantry. The butler was reading the newspaper when I pushed the swinging door open. He looked up; I nodded once, and then pushed through the second swinging door into the kitchen as I put on the tunic. The housekeeper-cook was also reading something, recipes perhaps, and looked up as I nodded once to her.

I buttoned the tunic as I passed the butler-valet who had filled a glass, actually a goblet, half full of wine. I raised a finger, indicating more wine seemed necessary and he filled it two-thirds full. I took the glass of whatever it was out as I finished buttoning the tunic, and set it at Eddie's right hand as he sat back in his armchair. Then I went to the fire and rebuilt it. I went to the gramophone and selected a recording, turning to show it to Eddie.

He glanced at what I was holding, nodded and raised the glass; I blinked: most of the wine was gone already. I had never seen Eddie put it away that fast: this was a very bad day.

His glass was empty, and I took it back to the butler for a refill. The butler was in the kitchen, helping the cook, and seemed shocked when I showed him the empty glass. Nonetheless, he filled it two-thirds full again and I went back in.

Eddie had gotten up and moved to the dining table. He accepted the glass, set it down and sat down himself. I set my ginger beer glass with its coaster at my place, at Eddie's left. The door opened and a cart on wheels was pushed in with the evening meal. I helped place dishes, silver, napkins, everything in its proper place. Eddie liked to eat – dine was his term – "*en grand tenue*," everything in its place, everything appropriate, hence my uniform.

Our plates were filled and passed to us. Eddie suggested leaving the wine bottle, which was done, and then he told his two retainers we would do for ourselves. They both thanked him and left us to ourselves. It was late, after all.

The meal, only one dish, was essentially Shepherd's Pie, although delicious. We ate and drank; I noticed Eddie's consumption rate had dropped, although he refilled his glass again. I went into the kitchen for another ginger beer.

We had each taken another helping, I serving Eddie and myself, when Eddie began to talk. Three of his patients had died that day. The first, an elderly man, had coronary problems; Eddie described the symptoms. His death was expected and probably unavoidable. The second was harder: a young woman, pregnant, began complaining of headaches as her pregnancy progressed. She was near her term when her husband brought her in, nearly comatose. She died as Eddie was examining her, and he had performed an emergency Caesarean with his pocket knife. The baby, a boy, was alive, and Eddie thought would be all right, but the husband was distraught. Eddie felt there was probably an arterial weakness, an aneurism, blood leaking into the brain causing the headaches, before the artery burst because of the onset of delivery. Eddie had told the husband there was nothing anyone could have done about the situation, that their son was her legacy to him, and he must live and work for him and for her memory.

The third was a docker, seemingly in good health, who collapsed and died just at day's end. Eddie said he had no clue as to what had happened, "heart attack" was all he could suggest, and no idea how to prevent it. He said he had never felt so helpless, so much a failure. I pointed out that he had saved the child, and that two of the three at least had untreatable conditions. He agreed but said he couldn't help feeling the way he did. He liked his patients (and I am sure they liked him), and, while knowing intellectually no one lived forever, hated being reminded of that reality.

The recording had finished, and I went through Eddie's collection, eventually selecting something that I hoped would lighten his mood. After both sides had been played, he noted the cook would be off two days hence, and, while he didn't want to appear to be asking me to "sing for my supper", he wondered if I could be persuaded to make pasties. My cooking gear and the rest of my possessions were in Eddie's box room, and I had been thinking of making some. I suggested we invite David again, that would give us five each, and I would also bake a walnut cake, given walnuts. I asked him where he got his meat, that being currently in short supply in Britain. I figured he would have some sort of special arrangement with a butcher and indeed he had. For that matter, I was supposed to get an extra meat ration myself, but Eddie waved that aside. So I said I would get the ingredients, but he had better tell the cook an interloper was going to be disrupting her kitchen.

* * *

That night, I lay thinking of the dance-like routines the three of us had performed for and around Eddie. He undoubtedly was exacting in some things but never ill-natured, and we all did what we could to please him because, in our different ways, we liked him.

* * *

The *soirée*, as Eddie called it, was a great success. I felt it was so, and the other three – a stray Regular was on leave – also said it was so. In the end I made two batches of pasties, since I didn't know the oven, and a walnut cake, and although I think I strained Eddie's arrangement with his butcher, the result seemed worth it. We had a surplus of pasties so all of us could have a couple for breakfast and lunch the next day. We listened to music and had a lively conversation involving seemingly endless digressions and I went to bed very late after escorting the other two back to their lairs, as I put it, and felt happier than I had in a very long time.

We were in billet near Ypres, where the army was pushing the Germans very slowly east. Our brigade had been sent north, but with the sort of Corps staff efficiency I had come to expect, my company had arrived late, and was being sent separately into the line to replace, temporarily we were assured, a unit that had "lost effectiveness", meaning they had had very heavy losses. This was bad enough, but I had no idea where I was supposed to go or how to get there. Finally, the brigadier, formerly the "dugout" colonel, had given me my marching orders. On the map everything seemed straightforward: I noted our destination, got a map and marked everything down.

That was in the afternoon. We were to move up after dark, fairly early in the evening this time of year (November), and hold on until relieved. This itself seemed odd as I had thought we were supposed to be attacking. At any event, I was sitting in a chair in a reasonably intact house, listening to music, this time some songs by the soprano Melba. The recording was showing signs of wear, but I was lost in the music.

A corporal came in: time to go. I got up, lifted the arm of the gramophone, a wrenching experience, shut the thing off, and turned to a table full of my things. I picked up and checked the time on both wristwatches – both correct, set at HQ yesterday, both wound. I put one on each wrist. I picked up the electric torch, turned it on, turned it off, opened it and removed the cells. I replaced them with a substitute set, turned the torch on to be sure the substitutes were also charged, and set the torch and cells in a pocket of my trench coat. I put that on, and then strapped the holster on. I took the revolver out, rotated the cylinder, opened it, removed the bullets, checked them, replaced them with new from a box of bullets, closed the pistol and put it in the holster. I picked up the compass I had brought and checked it briefly. It probably was unnecessary, and with all the iron in the ground and air, probably was off, but I might need it. I put it in another pocket.

I had a copy of the sector map, up to date I was assured, although I had long lost faith in assurances by staff, and studied it again. Out of habit, I took a compass bearing to our destination once we were clear of Ypres. Presumably we just followed the proper communication trench. We were supposed to join the line at a point just to the southeast of a village called Passchendaele, a name on the map, nothing more. I hung my field glasses around my neck then put on my helmet. I strapped on a water bottle after checking to be sure it was full, put a tin of beef stew – an unwonted luxury in the line – in a pocket, and I was girt for battle.

The corporal and I walked out after extinguishing the lantern and walked side by side to the road, where a dark mass spotted with lights from cigarettes waited. Out of habit, we had fallen into step. I was greeted by the senior sergeant; the lieutenants were towards the rear, by design. "Let's go, Sergeant," I said, and the sergeant relayed that order, some men getting to their feet, most simply starting the march. I was in the lead as we advanced into a night broken by flashes from our guns and from German shells exploding. It looked very busy.

I set the pace, occasionally glancing to left or right. Once I saw a huge flash, the light showing a great gun, probably 14-inch, mounted on railway trucks. It rocked backwards, the flatcar it was mounted on moving with the recoil. The angle of the gun suggested medium range, not so good for us.

The flashes lit up railway lines, narrow gauge, and many of our guns, 6-inch rifles for counterbattery work with gunners moving about. They were firing often, the guns at a variety of angles, suggesting many German guns as targets. Again, not good. Ahead, flashes from our 9.2-inch howitzers. "It's like a great machine," someone remarked. "Yes, and we're aye caught in the gears," was the reply. I waited for a sergeant to rebuke whoever said that, but suddenly there was a great roar, the sound of the 14-inch gun finally reaching us.

I checked my watch. After 50 minutes, I called a halt for 10 minutes. Many of the men used the break to empty their bladders, with accompanying commentary. On we went. A short column of men coming back reached us: the officer at its head and I exchanged salutes: he seemed dazed. His men walked unevenly, clearly exhausted, some without boots, all appeared stunned. This was looking nasty.

A second ten minute break, this time in Ypres, what had once been a living town, now badly smashed into fragments of walls and heaps of bricks. We set out again, leaving the town. I soon saw there were no communication trenches and also saw why: the landscape was interlocking craters, all filled with water. There were trails of duckboards, some fairly intact, some interrupted by craters or duckboards upended by a near miss. I took out my compass, tried to get a bearing – I didn't dare use my torch as this would surely draw unwanted attention – and eventually picked a trail that was more or less in the right direction. I decided to change the marching orders, and went from group of men to group, repeating my instructions: no halts for any reason until we reached the line; if someone fell, leave him, trying to help would just result in another casualty. Someone, I assured each group, would give aid, and I hoped that was true. We would need every man in line. I had concentrated the two lieutenants, many of the sergeants and corporals towards the tail end, to cut down on straggling: everyone must keep up. Our greatest safety was in speed.

My company followed as I moved along the line of duck-boards. Flashes from guns or shell bursts showed corpses bobbing in many of the craters, an awful skeleton which after a moment I recognized as that of a horse blown into a tree, hands, washed white with rain, clutching at the rims of some of the craters, a man lying as though running, arms and legs outstretched – I couldn't see if he still had a head – a corpse under a shattered limber, booted legs sticking up out of another crater, all in addition to booted legs lying about, horses, up to their shoulders in mud, apparently (and hopefully) dead, helmets, rags and filth of all sorts, everything wet and covered with dirt, everything stinking.

Our duckboard trail vanished at a large crater, the ground very slippery, and anyone who fell into a crater probably would not be able to get out unassisted and assistance would be very difficult. I stood as solidly as I could on the edge and helped my men who of course had the usual 50-60 pounds of gear pass to where the duckboards resumed. At times I was afraid I and the man I was helping would both go in, but as soon as what I took to be the last man passed, I pushed on to regain the lead, as I was, I realized, probably the only one who knew the direction we were supposed to go, and had the only compass.

The air occasionally hummed with bits of metal, some shell bursts closer, some farther away. I took another compass reading, selected a trail and moved on. I had no idea what time it was, no point in checking: thank God it was nearly winter, but we had to be in whatever shelter was available before light. Surely there was some sort of trench, although of course it would also be full of water or mud, and it was very slow going through either.

I could see bombs going off up ahead, a sign of the front line, and could hear machine guns, although mercifully nothing coming our way. The duckboards ended where a trench was, water in it as I feared, sandbags forming a low parapet. Perhaps we had arrived. I splashed into the trench, saw a man facing the east behind a Lewis gun, put my hand on his shoulder to ask him where we were but saw he was dead. Then I saw an officer, moved to him, saw blood on his tunic, tried to ask him the same question, but all he could say was, "Don't let them put me in there," gesturing with his hand towards the parapet. I nodded, lifted him onto the rear of the trench as he was in the way, then gestured to my men to file left and right to man the trench, which seemed nearly empty of the living.

I splashed along the trench, crouched of course as the trench was shallow and the parapet low. I asked everyone to fill the sandbags they had and build up the parapet. Two live inhabitants of the trench were found, but I couldn't tell whether this was the place we were supposed to be or not. However, it was obvious someone had to be manning this section of line, so while I sent men further to my left and right to make contact with the flanking units, I decided to stand here. Passing the place where I had moved the dying officer, I saw he was gone. I had the feeling I knew where but didn't ask.

It became light. The German shelling increased. We needed protection from our rear (west) but were nearly out of sandbags. Two underwater obstacles turned out to be dead soldiers, so these were laid on the west edge. Wounded men also – there was no place else to put them – and the packs every man carried, all helped the living and functional in this way. I found the sergeant who was carrying the periscope, got it, cleaned the dirt off the upper window, saw the upper window was broken, cursed, tried to see what was going on, then heard Lewis guns open fire and heard men cry, "Germans." I had the men who weren't manning the Lewis guns throw bombs, many of them, indiscriminately, and the German attack subsided.

We needed more bombs, and dug about, finding a box or two and distributing them: I didn't want to expose riflemen to the German fire. Even so, casualties piled up: Lewis gunners fell back, slumped and died. I couldn't tell if this was from sniper fire, so I had the survivors stay out of direct fire, but look towards our flanks. One of them caught a group of Germans attacking the unit on our left in flank and cut them all down. I sent men to see if the units to either side had any bombs to spare.

My water bottle was empty, although I couldn't recall drinking from it. I took a bottle from one of our dead – others were doing the same – and I was afraid we might run out of water. I repositioned our Lewis gunners to fire to our flanks; we had barely enough to cover our entire front with flanking fire. I had to detail riflemen to assist our remaining Lewis gunners. Some I put to digging out submerged boxes of Lewis gun ammunition: they found some, but not much.

German artillery fire re-intensified; evidently another attack was coming. I had done all I could with the Lewis guns and posted our remaining riflemen to assist with the flanking fire. They had our bombs also. More men were hit by shrapnel: the company sergeant who seconded me in our attack on the German lines when I had first arrived fell forward onto his face, a piece of shrapnel in his neck. I think it severed his spinal cord, so his death was quick. Others took longer: I tried to stop haemorrhages with field dressings and bootlaces, with indifferent success. I felt totally frustrated at being unable to staunch heavy blood loss; surely there was some way?

We were short of stretchers and could send wounded back during quiet times, trusting that German snipers wouldn't target the bearers, only there weren't many quiet times. At night, bearers might lose their way or fall into a crater, and we were desperately shorthanded and getting more so, but if our wounded lasted long enough, the risk, I finally decided, had to be taken. I had to guess who had the best chance of surviving the journey, and then ask for volunteers: I couldn't order anyone to undertake such a task.

At some point, the German attack eased, and we took out tins of food and ate. Water was already short, and that could prove critical. We could scavenge only so much from our dead. Then it began to rain, and I ordered ground sheets set out to collect rainwater.

Attack followed attack: we kept losing men, one or two at a time, all irreplaceable. Still, the Germans could make no headway, but how long would that last? At one point, German bombs began to land nearby, exploding sometimes in the water in our trench. Here our limited numbers helped us by limiting our casualties. I had one or two men who claimed to be cricketers throw our bombs, and managed to quell this attack, too.

* * *

Darkness: I was very worried about a surprise German attack, and kept looking out of our embrasures but saw nothing. The ground sheets helped greatly: I was careful to let the earliest rain rinse off the sheets, then was able to refill our water bottles.

* * *

Another day, more German attacks, more casualties. Lewis gun ammunition was short, bombs were short. We had to rely more on riflemen firing from the embrasures. I had no idea how the units to our flanks were doing, but there didn't appear to be any German breakthroughs.

At one point, I got my field glasses and trained them towards Ypres, hoping to see reinforcements, stretcher bearers, rations, help of some kind. What I saw was absolute devastation: blackened tree trunks, sticking harrow-like out of ruined land, ruins of men and horses and their gear everywhere, all water-filled craters and mud and random heaps of dirt, black and brown. The only things that were functional were our 60-pounders, mostly under camouflage nettings, and as I watched the gunners move their shells, I realized that they had to <u>clean</u> the things, remove the mud before they could fire them. That certainly didn't help the rate of fire, I thought disconsolately. Then I heard, "Captain!"

We were receiving German bombs and small arms fire. I hit a flying German bomb with the palm of my hand as it flew towards me and knocked it back over the parapet where it exploded. I picked up one of our bombs, primed it, and tried to throw it. It didn't go very far, and I cursed. Then it exploded. I heard, "*Liebe Gott.*" The Germans were very close to our parapet – how? I tossed two more bombs, heard two more explosions, a cry and the attack ended. How had they gotten so close?

* * *

I sat on some sort of box. We were all in a tunnel below Ypres, fairly safe. I had counted 49 of us, a few wounded, of 151 who had advanced to the line. I was tired past sleep, and chaotic memories of our stay in the line (2 days? 3? 4?) kept running uncontrollably through my mind. The air in the tunnel was misty; the walls glistened with damp as did the uniforms of my men, lying against one another like the human sandbags we used to stop the Germans. Someone had given me a mug of hot tea, and I kept both hands on it because my hands were shaking so badly that even two were hardly enough.

* * *

I reported to the brigadier, or tried to. All I could say was we had returned with 41 men and 8 wounded. The brigadier asked how many were missing and dead. I opened and closed my mouth several times before saying I didn't know. At length he told me to go get some rest. I swayed, hesitated, then saluted, about turned, stumbled and nearly fell, righted myself, and went to my billet.

* * *

Over time, a few stragglers returned: several men had gotten lost, or so they said, wound up in other units, and some, about 11, had survived the experience. Another five had been wounded on the march up the line, and had either been able to make it to an

Advanced Dressing Station on their own or had been picked up by "Conshies", conscientious objectors, who, without pay, uniforms or protection roamed the battlefield in quiet times to pick up any man who needed aid. I thought them the bravest of the brave, the best of men, but was aware my opinion was likely to add to my reputation for unorthodoxy. A few wounded who had been evacuated might survive and return.

There were two other men, who had been caught in a rear area and were considered deserters, which was punishable by firing squad. They insisted they had simply gotten lost, which was barely possible, and eventually the Army sent them to me for punishment. I had each man empty some dustbins then stand to attention before me. I said, "We needed you in the line and you weren't there. You let all of us down, badly. I want you to give me your word of honour you won't let us down again." I waited. First one, then the other, gave me their word of honour they wouldn't let the rest of the company down again. I then noted in the company records they had been disciplined, and told them to return to their duties. They said, "Yes, Sir," then, "Thank you, Sir." I replied, "Thank me by doing your duty to all of us." They again said, "Yes, Sir", saluted and left.

* * *

We were sent to another sector south of Ypres, to rebuild our numbers. There was talk of reducing the number of battalions in an infantry division from 12 to 9. Something of the sort was needed, owing not only to the expansion in gunners and tank men, but to the very heavy losses taken by infantry. I thought the new men would be hard to assimilate for some time, but again kept my opinion to myself. Meantime, I still had many letters to write. The shakiness took several days to subside, keeping me from writing decipherable letters to the families of the lost. Even after, these were very difficult letters. For most of our losses, I had no idea when or how they occurred.

I was sitting in Eddie's flat, on leave. I was glad I had missed the holidays, which were cruel to men like me with no wife, fiancée or sweetheart. I would repair to Elsie tonight for a spell of rogering. I had already bought my customary piece of jewellery. Despite the shortages, I was sure of good food and, although Eddie likely had even less time to spare, good company. Good music, too.

* * *

After leaving Elsie, who was as always delighted by my gift, and impressed by my uniform, I entered Eddie's flat about 9:30 and found him just sitting down to eat. Perfect timing, I thought, as he insisted I take a plate and dine with him.

After, we sat down before the fire with drinks. Eddie commented that there was a lot of criticism, muted but growing, about the casualties at Third Ypres. He asked if I had been there. I said, "Yes." Silence while I tried to fight off memories of that place. They seemed to gather, to loom. I felt everything darken. Eddie sensed my reserve, and said gently that I didn't have to talk about it if it was painful. After more silence I blurted, "I-It was Armageddon. It was C-Calvary, a Calvary of soldiers, a C-Calvary of nations. We were so m-many shovelfuls of d-dirt thrown into a hole in a d-dike." I became emotional and Eddie jumped to his feet and disappeared. After a few seconds, I composed myself. Eddie reappeared with a bottle of ginger beer, though I still had a glassful.

I then told Eddie about having to decide what men were most likely to survive evacuation. The others, lying wrapped in ground sheets on the west edge of our trench, were left to die. "Men I knew and I-liked. I c-couldn't help them. We c-couldn't evacuate m-more than a few, we didn't have m-men or st-stretchers. It was d-dangerous but there were always volunteers. There j-just weren't enough of us." I was getting emotional again, and Eddie stirred as if going for another ginger beer. I forced myself to calm down and told him about my failures to staunch blood flow. We talked about this for some time. He gave me some helpful advice, and we talked about giving every soldier training in some aspects of initial medical assistance. Eddie thought it were better to train a few soldiers in every company in these procedures, to make them specialists like mortar men or machine-gunners.

I was going to put on some music, but Eddie gestured for me to sit down. He said, "I've just learned that Christine's fiancé was killed in this Passchendaele battle, about ten weeks ago. I thought I should write, but of course it's a delicate situation. What do you think?" I sipped my drink and asked, "When she sent you away, how did she do it? Was she scornful, contemptuous, dismissive, anything like that?" "No. She was quite definite but, as I mentioned, said she hoped we would remain friends. I took my leave politely, wishing her and the fellow well."

"A friend – surely a friend would at least send a letter of condolence? I wouldn't recommend calling, but I don't know the entire situation. What were her parents' attitudes towards the match, the one with you, I mean?" Eddie in turn sipped his wine, and said, "Favourable. Actually, favourable on both sides." "Very well then: you have advocates in her family. I would send a note, make it brief and dignified and basically remind her and her mother of your continued existence. And sympathy too, of course."

Eddie sat for a while, and then commented, "The thing I worry about is Christine basically going into mourning for the rest of her life. She has very deep feelings, feelings I fear I never aroused, I suppose because of my shortcomings." I protested, "I think the problem might be more that you were too well known, the match had no mystery, hence no romance, and perhaps she wanted to show her independence of her family. Her decision to go to university might suggest that." I stopped, and then went on: "I once suggested that love, true love, was generous and giving. The spirit of a dead lover would not want the survivor, the beloved survivor, to be miserable, to pine the rest of his or her life, but would want the survivor to be happy."

Eddie smiled. "Somewhat speculative, surely. But that is a point one could argue." "Perhaps telling your mother might be useful: she could transmit it to Christine's mother. Have your parents called?" Eddie said his mother had, but again, it was a delicate situation. I nodded, sipped my drink, and put on some Mozart songs at Eddie's suggestion.

The next day, Eddie showed me the draft of a note. It seemed too long to me. We discussed the matter. Finally Eddie sent a very brief note to Christine:

Dear Christine

I have only just heard of your loss. Please accept my sympathy and condolences.

Sincerely
Eddie

We were in line to the south of the Ypres salient created at such cost. We were getting more and more detailed information about a planned major German offensive. New German tactics were supposed to be employed: sending small groups of heavily armed men through our lines to attack flanks and rear. The tactics had worked on the Eastern front, and although Corps staff seemed to think there was nothing to learn from Russian experience of anything, I remembered how easily I had been able to cross enemy lines. I knew if I could take a small number of heavily armed men, very fit and active and well trained, I could cause a great deal of disruption to the enemy, so I took these tactics seriously. Figuring how to counter them was another matter.

I talked to Castlefield several times. We agreed we needed to organize our lines differently, but morale was low and our men were still exhausted from Passchendaele, the weather was incredibly cold and the ground deeply frozen. There was no possibility of preparing new fortifications, even if morale had been good.

Talking to Corps staff, I became aware of a great gap between their ideas about effectiveness of different weapons in combat and my experience. They seemed to think rifles were the decisive arm. I had lost all faith in the value of riflemen: the men in my army would have machine guns, bombs and, if such could be obtained, small cannon. Volume of fire seemed decisive to me. But I was in contradiction to Doctrine.

Castlefield agreed, commenting that the (people) (he used a different term), on staff had had their ideas fixed by novels written fifteen or twenty years ago, when the rifle's mystique was established. I remembered thinking of joining the Artists' Rifles, obviously organized on the basis of the same idea.

I wanted more Lewis guns. Established strength was 32 per battalion. We had 15, but because we were so understrength, I could not get more. For close encounters, the best thing was bombs.

So I tried to get more bombs. I wanted at least 8-10 per man, instead of two or three. Predictably, my request was dismissed, my arguments blandly considered the result of hysteria. I was seriously considering a raid on our depot, when I encountered the brigadier. I made my case to him, expecting little, but he surprised me by agreeing with me. He then went to staff and managed to get enough bombs – they seemed, weirdly enough, to be in short supply – for 5-6 per man, helpful but perhaps insufficient.

Then I began redeploying the men. I had roamed the area before and behind the support line, and tried to guess where the Germans would likely come through. There were two or three places in my sector, ravines and slightly sunken roads, and I began ordering stand-to's at midnight, then two. I set the men in groups of ten or fifteen, each with a Lewis gun, although I emphasized the bombs, because it wasn't likely they would be seeing the Germans initially at any great distance.

Aside from the cold and exposure – it wasn't possible to dig anything – the main problem, almost prompting a mutiny, was my ban on smoking. I pointed out that lighted cigarettes, even pipes, could be seen for hundreds of yards, and our survival depended on surprise. I threatened to confiscate the fags, and gave my version of the St. Crispin's Day speech from *Henry V*, that we all depended on each other and that meant every man must, must do his duty. Not exactly the Bard, but, on my skulking around my positions at night, apparently effective.

* * *

We were to go back to reserve in two days. It had been a very busy five days in support. Late in the evening, a runner came from the brigadier, saying the German offensive would start tomorrow morning, March 21. I checked with the two flanking captains. They had the report, believed it, but were planning to stay in the entrenchments. I could not order them to do otherwise, and the battalion commander and Castlefield were both at the front line for some purpose.

At two, I got my company up and out. It had turned very misty, bad for us, good for the Germans. I told them the German offensive would start in a few hours. There would be a tremendous bombardment, but it would concentrate on our known positions. It would not be scattered about the countryside, so they would be as safe where they were posted as in the trenches, probably safer. However, the mist made it even more important they first be sure who was approaching, friend or foe, and second use bombs, plenty of bombs, on the German raiding parties. I repeated the message at each of the groups of men then sat down with a centrally located group to wait.

It was cold. I got up, circulated and made the men get up, move about to warm themselves, then shelter as best they could: ground sheets were little protection. The mist seemed to get thicker and thicker. Then, as there seemed to be a hint of light in the air, the German bombardment started.

I had not thought there were that many guns in the world. Shells overhead seemed to form a canopy of sound. Many were landing to our front, on our front line, and on our support trenches, but most were going to our rear, to stop reinforcements. This argued confidence, I thought, trying to make myself as small as possible, as shards of metal and clods of earth raked the air. East the mist lightened by the minute, a light that flickered and danced.

The bombardment of our front lines lifted, keeping our support lines under fire, and I knew the German infantry patrols were on their way. I had told my men to expect the Germans then, and waited. I had also told them to make no sound at all. One of the men in the group I was in, a man I could barely see in the mist, moved forward nearer the ravine, bomb in hand. He waited, looking into the mist. Then, just as I thought I saw something move, he primed the bomb and tossed it into the ravine, then grabbed another, primed it just as a shout came from the ravine, tossed it as an explosion flashed in the mist. Cries, in German, I was thankful to hear, then more bombs were tossed. More explosions, then silence.

I then heard the same thing off to my left, where another patrol had been ambushed. I ordered five men with bayonetted rifles forward, to explore the ravine. They found two intact

144

Germans and six wounded ones, and made them prisoner. The German patrol consisted of eleven, at least when they had reached us. I went over to my left. I had to use my compass, as the air was still very thick. I found two of my groups in possession of eight more prisoners, three wounded. I crossed my sector end to end and there was no more activity. I could occasionally hear a shot or two but otherwise everything was quiet, a quiet I found ominous.

We waited. Waited for the mist to burn off so we could see. At length, we could see, to our left, a large group of our men, prisoners, escorted by twenty or so Germans. We lay down, waited for these to pass us going east, then fell in behind. I had two of my groups, and we smoothly took the German escorts prisoner, and released what was our entire left flank company. We gave them the Germans' weapons, and escorted the prisoners towards my centre; I wanted the unwounded Germans to carry their wounded comrades. The captain sent some of his men – armed – back to our trenches to get their weapons.

When I got back, I found my lieutenant, the one who survived Passchendaele, had done the same thing on our right, so we now had over fifty German prisoners and three intact companies. I praised him for his initiative, reorganized our group, and sent patrols to see if any more of our men could be rescued if taken prisoner. The patrol sent by my left hand, fellow captain returned with rifles and a dozen more German prisoners, caught as they were looting our quarters. I sent more men to our right as they were certain to encounter the same thing.

They did; this time there was some resistance. We had a man killed and three wounded but we took another 10 German prisoners.

By now it was full day, the mist was rapidly burning off, and I felt it was time to go. I could see in the distance more of our men, prisoners, but couldn't get to them. I realized the German patrols were behind us, to our west, and we needed to move as cautiously as our numbers, now over three hundred counting prisoners, permitted. I had the unwounded Germans carry their wounded comrades, mounted a very stiff guard on these men, as I could see they were big, fit men, and we moved off west.

I sent strong patrols ahead and had flank and rear guards as well: I was not about to be surprised myself. We tried to stay in what vegetation there was, but German aeroplanes were overhead and must have realized what was happening, but fortunately did not attempt to strafe us. On two occasions, our advance patrols were able to get behind groups of Germans escorting British prisoners and reverse the situation. I learned these men were from our reserve line. We had been badly defeated.

* * *

I finally found the brigadier. We had taken more Germans prisoner, coming up behind them, so I could report 106 prisoners taken, but my battalion now consisted of three understrength companies. The brigadier said our battalion commander and Captain Castlefield were both missing, presumably captured, so I was made acting battalion commander. This made sense as I was the senior captain, after Castlefield.

We had been assigned a sector easily half a mile long, to be held by my battalion. Now, with returns from hospital and leave and some scattered refugees, we had just over 300 men, not even a half what I thought were needed. A "road", actually more of an overgrown track, ran through our position. I was told this had to be held, or the Germans could advance up it and flank the divisions to either side. I decided to set my men out in groups of 15-20, each with a Lewis gun, no trenches. We hadn't time, men or energy to dig them, even if the soil was deep enough; I suspected the ground underneath was mostly rock anyway. They would have to support each other, but if the Germans tried "infiltration" tactics again, they would be taken in flank; if the Germans tried a frontal assault, we would inflict heavy casualties, but could not hope to hold. I had talked to every group, and also to commanders of the units to our left and right, but the day was advancing, already past noon, and no sign of an attack – I had men in trees scouting. I was surprised: the Germans needed to push on as rapidly as they could, not stop to organize or for anything else. However, if they were going to give us more time, well, I would do my best to receive them.

The brigadier arrived. He had been surveying our "line" as it might loosely be termed, and I told him what I had done and why. Rather to my surprise, he nodded and asked what I needed, aside from a great many men, which were not available. I said, "Guns. I want guns – eighteen pounders, a battery at least, and mortars, all with plenty of ammunition, and we are still short of bombs." He pointed out that batteries were being set up to our rear, but I told him I wanted a dozen or so guns in line, to fire at the enemy over open sights. I wanted everyone concealed as much as possible, to ambush the Germans. It was our only chance of stopping a frontal attack. My groups of men would protect the gunners and the gunners would put weight into our response to an attack. The brigadier said. "I'll see what I can do." He stumped to his staff motor and was driven back up the road we were to hold.

Meanwhile: water. Our map showed a few dwellings, and these must have wells if inhabited by anything, so I sent parties of men to find these, put the wells under guard, and begin filling every empty container we possessed.

I spent the next hour checking my flanks, repeating my instructions, and wondering where the Germans were. Their aeroplanes occasionally flew over, and I had instructed everyone to stay as out of sight as possible, hiding in brush as the trees were still bare.

We were facing what could generously be called a "ridge", actually not much bigger than a ploughman's furrow, but to someone who grew up in Norfolk, the term seemed apt enough. It lay about a quarter mile distant, perhaps less.

I heard noises to my rear, turned and saw a line of 18 pounders drawn by horses, limbers as well. I went to greet the commander, a captain. He had 8 guns, he said. I explained my dispositions, asked him to set his guns along our position about 100 yards apart. He apparently had plenty of ammunition. I was delighted. I was even more delighted when lorries containing boxes of bombs, shells, and about 10 mortars with another captain in charge, arrived. The boxes were dumped unceremoniously on the ground, some cracking as a result, but I got men from my groups to take the boxes and move them, some to the mortar crews, whom I dispersed to support us. They wanted to fire to establish the range, but I told them no, I wanted our surprise to be as complete as possible. So they set up as best they could visually. The horses were sent to the rear. Camouflage netting was set up over the guns.

Time continued to pass. Still the Germans didn't come. I shrugged and went up and down my sector checking deployment of guns and mortars, supervising movement of ammunition to where it would be needed. To pass the time, I had some digging done, anything that would provide protection, especially if the German artillery started its work on us.

It was getting late in the afternoon. I realized that if the Germans attacked now, they would have the setting sun in their eyes. I looked up at one of my sentries or scouts in a tree, then down, when the man said, "Sir, the Germans are coming." There had been no artillery, but when I climbed up into the tree with my field glasses and looked, I could see the tops of helmets, German helmets, many of them, moving and moving towards us.

"They are coming." I announced to my men nearby and sent runners to my left and right, to warn everyone. I looked again, from the ground, and now could see tops of helmets again, seemingly in line. Still no artillery. The helmets filled with heads, tunics appeared, and on they came, several lines in a formation that, allowing for changes in uniform and weapons, might have been seen a hundred or more years ago.

The men reached the ridge and crossed it, weapons in their arms, evidently not expecting any opposition. That explained why no artillery: the gunners didn't know we were here – no fortifications – so had no targets.

I had sunk down, and then lay down, watching them with my field glasses. The second line had crossed, and I decided to strike. "Welcome to Hell, gentlemen," I said, then turned to my right and roared, "Fire!" then to my left, and again, "Fire!", but the 18 pounders were firing and so were the mortars. Looking again, I saw the ridge and ground nearby erupt in fountains of dirt and bits of things. The third line reached the ridge just as it exploded, the 18 pounders and mortars firing as fast as they could.

Yet another line appeared, but seemed to be faltering. The captain commanding the mortars, who had also been keeping an eye on things, very intelligently got his men to lengthen range. Now fountains of earth from the mortars appeared behind the ridge. And by God, they were running! We had beaten their attack with guns alone, and from what I could see, inflicted terrible casualties. I felt nothing but joy, seeing arms and legs and bodies in *feldgrau* strewn everywhere.

The sun was setting. I knew the German survivors would be relating their experiences and the staffs would realize there was a British force opposing their advance along the road. They would even know approximately where. They might start shelling, but I figured that wouldn't be until morning, when their spotters could see. Our position was somewhat ahead of our flanks, so when the other officers gathered, I told them I wanted to move about a third of a mile back. Hopefully we could avoid the bulk of the German shelling tomorrow morning. We couldn't move forward, as we would no longer be in contact with our flanks, which, so far as I could tell, had not been attacked at all today. So move we did; everyone helping even with the 18 pounder and mortar shells, through the evening into the night.

I informed the flanking units that we were now "refused". I had the men dig holes to lie in for some protection, trying to keep these as hard to see from the air as possible. The horses for the 18 pounders were sent farther back. I thanked the gunner captain and the mortar captain, said I thought we and the Germans would arrange that they wouldn't have to carry much surplus ammunition back. They and I expected tomorrow to be noisy and busy.

* * *

At 6 AM the Germans opened fire on our previous position, sending some shells long, towards us, but mostly hitting where we had been with admirable precision. They used gas, but the usual westerly wind kept much of that from us. We put our masks on just for practice, enabling me to spot a few men who were confused as to how to do it and a few masks that were defective. So, as an exercise, it was helpful.

The barrage lifted, moved towards us, and now the air filled with shards, and we began to suffer casualties. Then we saw the Germans advancing, in formation as before, and our guns and mortars opened up. Some of the Germans seemed to be moving very light guns; these became prime targets. We fired as rapidly as we could, and soon the German attack, pressed with great determination I had to admit, faltered and dissolved in eruptions of dirt. The German barrage lifted further, hitting our rear, including the horses I feared, and the road we were defending.

Another German aeroplane flew over. I checked my watch. How much time did we have? We couldn't move further back without forcing a general retreat. I decided to advance, back to our original position, if I could.

150

I met with the captains again, and we worked out a plan to advance back. The mortars would keep firing on the enemy positions, forcing them to keep down, as they had no trenches either; the 18 pounder gunners were to shoot at anything involving a live German they could see; and our riflemen would advance, but not in line: I wanted them running forward, no packs, falling to the ground if fired upon, then firing themselves at German muzzle flashes while everyone else moved forward. I sent the flank groups forward first, then when I hoped the Germans' attention was focused elsewhere, led my centre groups out. We ran in open order, got some German fire when we were halfway across, fell and began firing at them, jumping up and running forward a few yards, falling down, firing while more of us ran forward....

We took the position. The Germans, and there were a great many of them, seemed bewildered. We had them carry their own wounded back under guard. We took over 300 prisoners, but had nearly 50 casualties, over 10% of our infantry force, and of course more than we could afford. We had the unwounded Germans carry our wounded as well, which they seemed perfectly willing to do, a rebuke, I told myself, to my joy at seeing their losses earlier. I waved our mortar crews and 18 pounders forward, halting movement across an open field when German aeroplanes flew over. If the pilots were paying attention at all, they could well figure out what had happened, but there was no point in making things obvious, was there?

A number of the horses for the 18 pounders had been killed, so I had some of my men haul the things across. This they did with a will. After their performance in the attack on the German position and their Herculean labours with the guns, shifting the shells back, I was immensely proud of them. I sent runners to our flanks, telling them where we were, and wrote a report to the brigadier, telling him of our new (or old, depending on how it was defined) position and requesting more ammunition for the 18 pounders and mortars. I also said our numbers were dwindling: we had taken 66 casualties, including the gunners, so we were down to below nine-tenths of original strength.

While I was reorganizing the position – fewer and smaller groups, to be sure – two German staff officers walked into our position and were taken prisoner. I thought that a very good sign, although their disappearance might alert the Germans to the actual situation. I sent them to our rear, under guard of course, depleting our little force still more.

* * *

The day passed. I expected the German Staff responsible for this sector was thoroughly confused. Given the mistakes they had made already – attacking on too narrow a front after first failing to do the most elementary job of reconnaissance, and using small groups, not entire battalions – I was hopeful that they would bite again by shelling our rear while sending more formations into our guns.

It seemed unlikely our position was the primary objective. We could hear their guns to the south, so perhaps they were trying to get reinforcements, which were always in short supply. As I walked our sector and thanked officers and men for their efforts, a trickle of reinforcements and returnees began to appear, but no ammunition. I figured we could stop another attack, but after that we would have to retreat.

* * *

Night fell. I had napped and so had most of our force; I had had little sleep for days and days, it seemed. I had very strong patrols out: I did not want to be surprised. Some went almost a mile back down the road, reporting that the Germans were apparently asleep. I thought that good news and a good idea and did the same myself, asking that I be awakened at 4.

* * *

A cold morning and a starry sky. I walked cautiously back down the road to see if there was any early morning German advance. I saw no sign. The air was calm; a peaceful night.

On the way back, I passed the German dead from their first attack. Because of the cold, they hadn't yet started to smell much. From a distance, they looked like fallen leaves.

We ate cold rations – no fires. Anyone wanting to smoke had to retire behind some half-built German parapets. I told the gunner captain that his surviving horses should be kept close – the Germans, I hoped, would be shelling our rear. We shook hands and I continued my rounds. I told my flanks the Germans would probably begin another attack shortly, possibly on a wider front. I couldn't believe they would keep making the same mistakes.

* * *

6:30 AM. The German guns began firing, an avalanche of sound, of metal and gas. We all put on masks, but the shells were clearly aimed at our rear position. Evidently they thought they still occupied the position we were sitting in. There was no wind, and the gas cloud simply grew and spread. If the usual westerly winds began, the Germans would be attacking into their own gas.

At 6:45 the German infantry appeared, marching up the road in order, evidently expecting to deploy when they reached where we were. We let them get within two hundred yards of our position when I gave the order to fire. The effect was staggering: the German column, some ten abreast, simply flew apart as every rifle, Lewis gun, mortar and 18 pounder hit whatever part of the column they could. Within minutes, I had directed the mortar gunners to begin firing down the road, out of our sight, but sure to be filled with more troops marching towards us. I sent some men out to bring in some wounded for intelligence purposes. There was certain to be a very large number. I could hear firing to our right, sent to find out what was happening and was told another German column had deployed and began advancing on our right hand neighbours. These had managed to throw the Germans back also. Nothing to our left.

The German guns methodically rained shells on our former position, and then extended their range farther and farther. Sooner or later someone would inform their staff that their attack had been aborted. Sooner, actually: we saw another German aeroplane fly over, surveying the situation. I checked my watch, decided we had perhaps two hours before the German guns shifted to where we actually were, and decided to order a retreat. I had received a message from the brigadier, saying I could, as the Army had established a line four miles back.

I contacted my flanks, told them we were moving back; they were already withdrawing. The German shelling had moved far up the road, and then stopped. We brought back every gun, mortar, Lewis gun and all our wounded, although not much ammunition: we had fired most of it.

* * *

We were put into support, to recover. I wrote more letters, this time with much better ideas how each man had died, and filled with praise for their courage and devotion, all of it meant.

Castlefield appeared. He had been taken prisoner, marched with many other prisoners towards Germany, but had escaped. A noteworthy feat, but badly rewarded, for he found me in what should have been his place. I sympathized with him, told him to talk to the brigadier, that I would cheerfully step down in his favour if that was ordered.

I didn't hear what was said in that conference, but Castlefield remained a captain and my second in command, and I got a letter from the War Office, addressed to Major M. Dobbs (Norfolk), Acting Battalion Commander. Castlefield, who had been friendly, now became very formal, saluting and Sir-ing me on all occasions. I felt badly: he was a Sandhurst graduate and but for bad luck should long since have had his own battalion as lieutenant colonel. The mills of Mars again.

* * *

My battalion was on parade, everyone "*en grand tenue*", including myself. We marched past our Corps commander, the first I had ever seen of him, and came to attention before him and some of his staff, one or two of whom I recognized. I was called forward to receive a decoration, I didn't know what decoration, and on advancing and saluting as smartly as I could, had a medal pinned on me. It was a DSO, distinguished service order, the general said. I saluted again, about turned and marched back to my battalion. There were other decorations: a couple of my men got M.M.'s, and then it was over: the general and his staff left.

I was suddenly tremendously moved. I turned to my battalion and said, "This was given me in my honour. But I tell you it honours all of us who were there with me. We all have a share, an equal share, for we equally risked our lives for our King, our country and its cause and for each other. So, to each and all of you, especially not excepting those of us who are gone, I salute you and thank you." I stood back and saluted them.

I then said, hoarsely, "Battalion: dismissed", and walked back to my quarters. I could hardly see for tears, a weakness to be sure. But, I had meant it. Otherwise, it was that many more initials for my tombstone, if I ever had one.

* * *

One of the officers had gotten hold of a newspaper in which my alleged exploits were recounted. It embarrassed me, making me out to be, at the least, Roland at Roncesvalles and, at best, Richard I at Acre. Anyone reading it must have wondered why the Germans had not sued for peace.

We were back in line. We had enough replacements to constitute a company for Castlefield. In fact, we were perhaps 500 souls in total. I got Castlefield to be in charge during the day, while I roamed about our sector at night, invigilating sentries, especially preventing smoking. Lecture as I might, the fact that a lighted cigarette gave their position away seemed of lesser importance unless I was physically present to make it greater. As it was, the men seemed quite tolerant of my demands, I didn't know why.

Corps informed me they wanted German prisoners to question, not an irrational request considering the well-known fact the Germans were planning new offensives. I could certainly get into the German trenches, cosh a sentry, but then I would have to haul him back. I didn't want to take anyone else across with me, as I felt I could move more quietly and surely than anyone else in my battalion. Since the Germans were patrolling no-man's land, perhaps a bit aggressively, it seemed better to let them come to us, as it were. A prisoner was, after all, a prisoner, no matter what he was doing when he got caught. Also, I was getting restless again, wanting to roam, and I thought the Germans needed taking down a peg.

So for the next night or two I watched no-man's land with my field glasses, looking for movement and patterns of movement. The second night, I saw two Germans moving. I looked as carefully as I could but I couldn't see any more. So I told the sentry nearby, "Two Germans on patrol. I am going to get them. Stay alert." The sentry nodded.

I darkened my face and hands with dirt, looked at the sky — thick clouds, not much moon, reasonable. I had long stopped wearing the spectacles as my eyesight had gotten better, probably from not reading so much. I rolled over the top of our parapet, and began stalking the two Germans. They usually sent three or more, but two was easier for me. I looked very carefully to be sure these two weren't decoys, but saw no one else.

I threaded through the barbed wire, quietly cutting a few strands of the German wire. I got behind them, then, when the way to our trenches was reasonably clear and close, knocked them down and disarmed them, my pistol in their faces to help them understand their survival depended on keeping quiet. I pushed them back to our lines, moving constantly, keeping them off balance and moving in the right direction. When I got to our parapet, I found not only that the sentries were alert but that the sergeant and two other men had been called, so there was no delay in searching them – recovering the customary knife in the boot – and escorting them back. Evidently everyone was confident I would succeed, which gave me pause.

* * *

We were back in support when I heard that the lieutenant, who had done so well rescuing a company of captives, had been promoted to captain. I was pleased although we would lose the services of a capable man if he were sent to another battalion.

The girl in my arms was beautiful, even though I couldn't see her face; she was dressed in a full ball gown. I was in evening dress and we were waltzing, moving, feet perfectly synchronized, around the dance floor, other couples moving as well. The music propelled us, turning, turning, holding each other, moving together, dancing, dancing.... I awoke with reluctance. It was a beautiful dream, a vastly superior one to that two or three days before: I was in a shell hole, trying to crawl out, and my fingers kept slipping, I could gain no purchase, the water, ice cold, stank, and there was a corpse in the water with me. The corpse kept tangling in my legs, as though it was trying to keep me in the crater, keep me with him, drawing me into whatever world he inhabited, a world I didn't want to enter...

I reflected that the dancing dream probably resulted from recordings of waltzes the adjutant had been playing. We were in reserve, a nervous reserve, as information about another German offensive became more circumstantial and detailed. We would be going back up the line soon, and Corps would insist on prisoners. Well, the moon was waning, so if the Germans sent out any more patrols, I would try to catch a few.

* * *

There were three of them. Watching, I somehow got the opinion they were a little too obvious, and I couldn't see what they were looking for, what purpose they had wandering along in no-man's land. So I looked behind them, searching for movement, men following them.

There appeared to be only one, look as I might. He was certainly big, probably aggressive, but I had learned there were ways of dealing with such. So I turned to the sentry, told him what the situation was, and that I was going to get the trapper, leaving the three decoys. So over I went, moving parallel to our parapet, crouched, until I was behind the trapper, as I called him, and then closed up behind him.

He didn't give me as much trouble as I thought he should. He had an elaborate looking pistol, as well as a knife, both of which I grabbed, and hauled him to our lines. I put him over the parapet. The sergeant was waiting with two escorts, as before. I examined the pistol and realized it was actually a small machine gun. I had heard about these and decided to show it to Castlefield before sending it up to Corps.

I went back to watching the three decoys, evidently unaware their reserve was gone. After a while, I became irritated, and decided to bag the lot. "In for a penny," I said to myself before telling the sentry what I was up to.

None of the three showed any fight; perhaps they were waiting for the other fellow. I basically threw one of them, the lightest one, over our parapet while disarming the other two. I sent them over at pistol point. Another sergeant, this time with four escorts, took possession of the three. They had ordinary pistols and only one knife between them. I told them in German their colleague was already on his way to our cages and asked why there was only one. One man said there were supposed to be two, but one had been sick; they called him "the hunter" ("*der Jäger*"), which meant they were stalking-horses, but I didn't say that, just wished them luck. They asked for food, and we gave them some. They ate like they had been fasting for a week, and I privately told Sergeant Number 2 to tell the intelligence people to ask them about their rations. I had heard stories that the previous German offensive had faltered when their soldiers had reached our supply dumps.

* * *

Corps Staff asked me to visit, which meant a project. If it meant throwing a spanner into the gears of the next German offensive, I would do it, if feasible; Corps Staff's ideas were quite variable in practicality.

When I got there, I was greeted cordially, which made me wary. I was offered scotch (declined), cognac (also declined), some sort of wine (ditto), and finally, chocolate, which I gladly accepted; I couldn't remember when I last had chocolate. What is more, they had, not milk, but cream, real cream, to add to it, and I poured some in with reverence, stirred it and began to sip. I thought I would go into an ecstatic culinary trance, but a staff major brought me to earth by beckoning me over to a map.

A German Corps headquarters had been identified rather close to our lines, closer than usual. The major wondered if I would carry an explosive device with a timer and set it somewhere in the building so it would go off when everyone was up and working. An assassination, in other words. The major seemed embarrassed at the suggestion, but I had by now no qualms. I looked at the building, a farmhouse, and decided it was rather extensive. That was the problem: I could make a device with, say, six sticks of dynamite, but I doubted it would do enough damage to wipe out or even inflict serious casualties on the staff. The distances and other circumstances, military installations nearby, would present no insolvable problems, but, again, mass of fire was needed.

I accepted, or rather took, another cup of chocolate (with cream) and looked at the map more carefully, calculating distances. I explained the problem: I couldn't carry enough explosive to demolish the place. What was needed, I said, was artillery: three, four, five heavy guns, firing two or three salvos. I asked what was the range of our longest-range, most accurate guns, counterbattery pieces.

The major looked blank, then sent for the staff officer in charge of coordinating artillery. He didn't know either, not that I was too surprised. I suggested they call in the gunner captain I had dealt with before. They agreed, although he was now a major, and I accepted, rather aggressively, I admit, more chocolate (with cream) and sat down to wait in an armchair, an actual armchair! I smiled blandly at the mess steward, and suggested more chocolate be made.

We waited while I enjoyed their increasingly reluctant hospitality. The major arrived, saw me, noted my rank, smiled and we shook hands. I presented him with a cup of chocolate (with cream) and we sipped appreciatively. I didn't know if he would have preferred any of Corps Staff's other offerings, but he certainly liked the chocolate (with cream). Then we went over to the map and I explained my idea: bring two or three counterbattery guns up what appeared to be a minor, yet apparently well-metaled road running roughly parallel to our lines, set them up in the dark, wait until the German staff were up, then fire two or three salvos into the farmhouse. Then hitch up the guns using lorries, not horses, and return. I doubted the Germans would even be able to figure out what had happened for several hours, let alone retaliate.

The major looked hard at the map, measured distances, looked at the roads, considered, then said he would have to go over the route, and if it was firm enough, and he thought it was, let everyone along the route know what was going to happen. Otherwise, he was sure it would work: he had three new guns, knew their ranges to a yard, and said three was in fact optimal in terms of weight of fire and ease of getting there and back. He would start today, he said. We toasted the effort with more chocolate (with cream), shook hands and left an unfortunately rather sullen mess steward.

* * *

Two nights later, I was wrapped in my ground sheet in a recess in our front-line trench, trying to sleep. It was nearing daylight. I was startled by a crack of heavy guns firing near our trenches. I had seen the flash, but didn't know what it meant. A couple of minutes later, a more ragged flash, with the crack following enough later to suggest a distance of four miles. I smiled and waited; sure enough, another flash and, after about 20 seconds, a sharp crack, a perfect salvo. Then silence and I dozed.

I walked into Eddie's flat. It was Sunday evening and I hoped I was in time for the evening meal. As it happened, I was. We dined in Eddie's usual style. I thought he seemed considerably more cheerful, and I doubted success with his patients was the reason. After the meal, I put on a recording and we sat, I on the couch and he in his armchair, sipping our drinks.

When the recording ended, I got up and, glancing at Eddie, selected something pleasant but not compelling complete attention. I asked Eddie how Christine was coping with her loss. He said, "Still sad, but resigned. I called about a month after I sent the note. She had replied, thanking me and hoping my practice was going well. Her mother sent me a note, suggesting I call, and I did. We talked, Christine and I, for the first time since she had sent me away. She seemed to realize I had suffered, too. Since then, I have called once and taken her to two concerts. I think she is coming around. I have been as delicate in my attentions as I could, and I think she realizes this and appreciates it. So I am, obviously, in a better mood. I am to take her to a performance of *The Mikado* next month."

I nodded. I would have liked to see *The Mikado* myself, but wouldn't be here. Eddie and I discussed the war. My battalion had been in reserve during the latest German offensive, and, once again, our sector didn't face the brunt of their drive. Still, it had been ugly for a while. Evidence of hunger among the German prisoners was now routine. I commented that, since Germany was now a military dictatorship, I could hardly imagine how German civilians were faring. I felt we would now almost certainly win. Eddie agreed with my assessment and we talked about a peace. We agreed also that a generous peace would be in everyone's best interest.

I stared into my glass of ginger beer, and then said to Eddie, "Christine has known you since childhood, so you have been part of her entire life. I think you are, or can be, a comforting figure, someone who represents stability, normal living if you like, so I suspect she will come to be increasingly emotionally dependent on you. I don't think this will require acting ability on your part, just behave as you always have, though as you have guessed, restraint and tact will help." Eddie nodded, and we went off to our beds.

* * *

Matters seemed to have altered for David also. I tried to set up a *soirée* with the three of us, but either Eddie's practice or visits to Christine or David's elusiveness in terms of when he would be available defeated me. Visiting David one day in his shop, I found a young woman, whom David introduced as Esther Goldman, a refugee from Latvia, helping behind the counter. I began to see the source of David's preoccupation, and although sorry not to be able to get together, I was pleased to see the two of them clearly taking an interest in each other. Well, I thought, two out of three, perhaps.

We were advancing now. The Germans, driven back in one sector, had to withdraw in adjoining sectors to conserve their forces. When I returned from my leave, sexually relaxed but self-disgusted, I found we were to attack the Germans within two days. This was a diversionary attack: we were to seize the German front line trenches and hold off any counterattacks, but not to try to advance further. In my absence, Castlefield had drawn up the plan. He was still somewhat overformal, but went over his plan with me.

I could find nothing to change, and said so. We were to have the support of four tanks, probably older models, which even so should help greatly. We went among the battalion, telling everyone what was going to happen, when and what each of them was to do. At night, I walked our sector. This was partly to keep everyone on sentry duty alert but also to foil any German attempts to raid our trench to get a prisoner. We did not want our offensive signalled prematurely.

The day before, we had some shelling, but no casualties. Wire cutters appeared, wire cutters that would work on the German wire, and even heavy gloves so the men cutting the wire could pull it away without slashing their hands. I remembered my first attack, when one private grabbed a coil of German wire our shellfire had cut and pulled it away: I thought his act very brave indeed: his hands required extensive stitching. I felt perhaps our army was acquiring efficiency.

That night, I kept a close watch on the German trenches. Nothing. At 4, we roused the men, got them into position, and went over what they were to do. At 5, the sky to the west suddenly began flickering. A few seconds later, we heard the sounds of shells overhead. Some more seconds passed, hundreds of explosions to our front, and then the roar of our guns enveloped us. I knew the tanks were starting their engines: they were noisy, and we wanted the sound of the guns to mask their approach. Our reserves were by now moving up towards our line.

At 6, we could hear the machines approaching, and put up the signal flags to show them where they were to cross our lines. Our trench had been reinforced at those points. Then the monsters appeared, rhombohedral with tracks along the sides, each with six pounders projecting from their sides as well as machine guns. They crossed our trench. We put up our ladders, each the right length this time. Up went the second lieutenants, revolvers in hand, then the men, labouring under their packs, then the sergeants, captains and I.

Our barrage was still hitting the German lines and would continue until we were halfway across no-man's land. Then it would lift to hit their rear areas. We were supposed to move in dispersed order at 50 paces a minute, a very moderate walking pace, no faster. The sergeants were supposed to regulate our advance so we didn't walk into our own barrage. The top speed of the tanks, Mark IV's by the look of them, wasn't much faster. At least none of them had broken down yet.

I was near the centre, Castlefield on the far right, advancing into what seemed a very accurate and heavy bombardment by our guns. Then our barrage began to move back. We were more than halfway across. Suddenly I saw a German Maxim begin firing and felt bullets overhead. I cringed, then a six-pounder gun on the nearest tank fired and I saw an explosion where the Maxim was. No more bullets. I stood up straighter, very relieved. If that Maxim gunner had been up to standards of a year or so ago, I and many more of our men would be on the ground: he had fired too high.

Our men with the wire cutters were clearing paths through the German wire, though I saw men edging behind the tanks, which were crushing paths of their own, with sparks occasionally jumping when metal met metal. The tanks lurched and jumped, but pushed on. We were getting close to the German trenches. Occasionally, the machine guns in the tanks would fire, but we were now getting no return fire at all.

The tanks reached the German parapets then stopped. They weren't supposed to go any further, not that they really could: they weren't carrying fascines to drop into the German trenches to cross over on those. We all reached the parapet shortly after, and found the Germans, with their hands up. The tanks had convinced them to surrender, otherwise they could have hurt us badly.

I jumped down into their trench, holstering my revolver. I asked an officer if there were many wounded or sick in their dugouts. He said there were, and everyone was hungry, not having received rations for two days. I got the Germans to bring up their wounded, which were numerous. Some of our shells had penetrated far enough to do much damage, and I saw appalling wounds; some men had to be actually dug out. I shuddered at the thought of such a fate. We began to send parties of prisoners with their wounded back. I handed out all my tins of rations and many of my men did the same. I asked the Germans if they had tin openers, and they all did, it was the tins themselves they were lacking.

Gradually we cleared our sector of prisoners, and I began having my men move the Maxims across their trench, to support our Lewis guns. I wanted any German counterattack met by an enormous volume of fire. My men began moving the German sandbags to build revetments about the machine guns.

Three of the tanks withdrew. The fourth threw a tread and would have to be fixed or towed. I went to that machine, to ask the commander to support us with his six-pounders while his machine was there. As I approached, a hatch opened and a bottle flew out, landing without breaking on some dirt. I picked it up: some sort of Scotch. I rapped on the side with my knuckles, and another hatch opened. A man's head appeared, and I made my request. He nodded, said they would be there a while, but the top gunner would stay alert – the top gunner was a teetotaller, he said. I held up the nearly empty Scotch bottle. The man said the Scotch, a full case of it originally, was the tank commander's. He was handing it out to the other crew members. I pleaded they show some restraint, as we might need their support. He said he would see what he could do.

Bemused, I walked along our captured sector. The work mounting and shifting the machine guns and moving the sandbags – still fairly intact, being new – was proceeding. I checked with the captains, asking about our casualties. I had seen none, and each captain reported none. Finally I got to the end of our sector, where Castlefield was.

"None here either," he said. I exhaled with relief. "That means we had no casualties at all," I replied, and he nodded. He looked at the bottle in my hand, and I handed it to him. He stared at the label, said, "Damn: this retails at a guinea a bottle." "Damn," I said in turn, "the commander of the disabled tank had a case of it, so I was told." I tried to think how many bottles were in a case: eight, twelve, perhaps sixteen? Castlefield was eyeing some brown liquid that had collected in a corner of the bottle. He raised the bottle and poured the residue into his mouth, swallowed and said, "Very good stuff indeed." I left him with the bottle – he was holding it carefully to collect a bit more – and went back, lest the tank commander decide to start a more general issue.

The fact that Castlefield was no longer saluting or Sir-ing me I took to be a good sign for our relationship. And the plan, his plan, had worked flawlessly: we had no casualties ourselves and had captured over 250 Germans. The other battalions weren't so lucky – in their sectors the Germans had anti-tank guns – but all had taken their assigned sectors.

* * *

The brigadier asked me to see him shortly after our attack. He congratulated me on our success. I said, "It was Castlefield's plan, sir; I couldn't think of any changes to it, and it worked perfectly." I added, "Castlefield is a very good man, Sir." The brigadier nodded. He said he was trying to get him command of a battalion as soon as one opened up. He went on to tell me that Corps Staff wanted some reconnaissance. The Germans were retreating, but were presumably going to make a stand somewhere. They wanted someone to see where the Germans were fortifying, so we didn't run headlong into their entrenchments unawares. This was to provide a check on aerial reconnaissance. I said, "The moon is full now, Sir. I can go in, say, 10 days. My range is about 20 miles, unless I can find a spring or unattended well." He nodded, and I saluted, made an about turn, stumbled slightly but managed to get out the door without falling. I fancied I could hear or sense the brigadier wincing.

It was eight days later: still a significant moon, but heavy clouds with some rain. This was uncomfortable for me, but the sound of the rain plus the discomfort of being out on sentry duty would help me. I was very restless. I made my preparations, and then waited. About 11:30, there was enough rain to mask my movements, and the German movements had quieted, so I decided to start then. I went over our parapet, moved crouching, occasionally on all fours, cutting my way across no-man's land. I waited at the German parapet until I was sure where they were – trying to smoke cigarettes, which allowed me to cross their lines easily.

Once across, I struck through the wire belts until I spotted their second trench: again, sentries smoking. The discipline in their forces seemed to have slackened sharply in the last few months. I crossed again, again easily.

The third line seemed very poorly prepared – not much wire laid – but I suddenly became very cautious, as that meant not everything was where or as it usually was. Still, I could again see the sentries and crossed quietly and unchallenged. Now I was loose in the German rear.

I moved quickly and upright. I could see the German gun positions – same behaviour. I wondered: the German prisoners universally complained of hunger. Was the smoking an attempt to curb the feelings of hunger, so strong that their officers felt compelled to allow the practice? Well, it certainly helped me. I could see a lighted cigarette easily a quarter of a mile away, and I felt the Germans who were smoking weren't as alert to the rest of the world.

* * *

I was sitting in a copse. I speared a piece of meat in the tin of beef stew with the point of my trench knife, but cautiously, lest I simply cut the piece, and transferred it to my mouth. I chewed, swallowed, and reflected that a tin of cold beef stew was a very small luxury, but one I was glad to have. It was hard enough to lay hands on the stew. I had been shameless in appropriating six tins for my journey, but couldn't muster any feelings of regret at all.

I was watching the Germans build what appeared to be the first line of what I took to be a series of trenches to fall back upon. I had marked the position of the trench on my map and intended to survey a five or ten mile section prior to returning. It was the first day after the crossing. I would sleep or at least nap until night, then be on my way.

* * *

I noticed the denseness of the vegetation in the hillside even in the dark. On looking into the brush, I discovered a spring. Nothing was nearby. The water seemed to be disappearing into vegetation, but the flow was adequate to fill my water bottle that was nearly empty and allow me to drink my fill as well. It certainly tasted all right, actually it seemed almost sweet, the way good cold spring water should taste. I tried to note its position on my map – the wisp of moon was barely bright enough. Then I decided to stay an extra two days, move east farther into Belgium. I could see a road on my map that should have military traffic; I could at least count what there was. I hoped perhaps I could actually somehow stop a staff motor and steal documents. These would give a much better idea of German preparations. It was a thoroughly insane idea, but I had mapped a good segment of the new German front line trench – I could see little evidence of a second line as yet – so I decided to try. I was still too restless to want to return yet.

* * *

I found the road easily enough. At night, there was significant traffic, some on foot, some horse-drawn, a few lorries. When it was light enough, I moved along, looking for a tree I could push over into the road. Eventually I found a small tree whose roots were partially exposed. I cut some with my trench knife and pushed at the tree: it moved but not enough. I cut more, pushed again. This time the tree fell over into the road, blocking it. I concealed myself and waited.

Two lorries with soldiers in them pulled up. The soldiers got out, pushed the tree aside, got back in and the lorries drove on. I got out, pushed the tree back, and waited again. A single lorry this time, only the driver and another man, but the same performance. After they left, I returned the tree to across the road and sat concealed.

The next vehicle was indeed a staff motor, which duly pulled to a stop at the tree. In it was a driver with two men in the rear seat. One of these got out, a large, fleshy man, no uniform but with the mandatory Kaiser Wilhelm moustache. He said in good colloquial German he needed to empty his bladder. The driver and the other man got out to do the same thing, presumably inspired by their chief's example. The other man was shorter, slighter, what I took to be a toady/dog-robber. However, he left the side door open and I could see on the seat a fat black valise looking for all the world to be stuffed with important documents.

The three men were standing with their backs to me. I prayed their bladders were very large and very full and emerged, revolver in hand, from the brush and quietly but quickly went to the motor, grabbed the valise and pulled it up and out. It was surprisingly heavy, yet I thought I had made no sound at all as I moved back into the woods. I heard a shout behind me, fired several shots in their general direction and ran. I may have hit something, but I probably merely caused the three men to duck. As I dodged behind some trees, someone fired at me and I ran faster downslope, perpendicular to the road.

As soon as I was sure I was out of sight, I turned and ran roughly west, parallel to the road. The valise was very heavy and I was already sweating and my right shoulder was becoming painful. I switched the valise to my left after holstering my revolver – an awkward business cross handed. I moved closer to the road, and as soon as their motor was hidden behind a curve, crossed to the other, southern side and began climbing the hill, trying to get behind trees.

The staff motor roared past me down the hillside. I could barely see it and was sure they couldn't see me, but I pushed myself to the limit, because they were probably going for help. I began to wonder what was so heavy. It couldn't contain books, shoes or papers and weigh so much. Bricks? Gold bricks? But if the official considered it that important, not just dirty laundry, then important it was and my duty to carry it off. I considered hiding it so I could move faster, but I was curious about its contents.

I kept moving, panting now. Both arms were tired, one shoulder very painful, shift the valise as I would. I kept to the high side of the road, which was fairly straight for a couple of miles, dodging trees, brush, rocks, holes and trying on top of everything else not to leave too obvious a trail. Then ahead I saw a glimpse of German soldiers deploying, forming what I guessed, slowing to look more carefully, to be a line perpendicular to the lower side of the road.

Good luck with that, I thought, then saw more men on the upper side. There seemed to be quite a few of them, and I didn't think climbing higher would help – they were already higher than I was. I could turn around, but I was nearly exhausted. Ahead was a very large oak, one side torn off, perhaps by lightning. I crouched, moved to the tree and found I could easily climb it.

This I did, trying not to leave obvious footprints. I pulled out my ground sheet and stepped on it, pulling it up after me as I got higher. It was very awkward with the heavy valise, but I managed to move to a spot where I could rest it and myself, about 15 feet above the ground, a place where several big branches extended from the damaged trunk.

I could hear and occasionally see German soldiers approaching. I tried to keep my feet back, the valise as hidden as possible and my breathing quiet by opening my mouth. They came closer and closer. It was like my childhood, hiding from Paston and his homosexual lawyer friend, only now I might be shot as a spy even though I was in uniform. The foliage in the oak was dense, thankfully, but if anyone stood at the base of the tree and looked up, I could hardly be missed.

The Germans were spread about 10 feet apart, kept in line by *feldwebels* – sergeants. They reached the tree. They passed the tree. They kept moving. I waited, then heard more Germans approaching, a second cordon about a half mile behind the first. The valise must be very important indeed, I thought: capture of a lone British officer behind enemy lines would hardly call for such a deployment. The official must himself be very high ranking, but I saw no uniform; perhaps a military governor or some such, even an ambassador?

The second cordon came on. A small group of officers with them chose to stand under my tree and talk. I could follow what they were saying fairly easily, allowing for the accent – Saxon? Bavarian? They were in plain view, and in no hurry, which distressed me doubly: if any of them looked up, they would see me and I had a full bladder myself. If it were to rain, I thought, I could deal with that problem, and I wondered if my sense of humour was edging into madness.

They seemed irritated at having to spend their time thus, and were not unduly respectful of the official, whose name I caught. It meant nothing to me, but he was a "*von*", so presumably noble. One of the officers leaned against the tree and I froze, so as not to dislodge any bark, etc., which would give me away. They continued to talk: leave, the war, sweethearts, food – the same things my officers (and men) talked about. I was paralyzed by fear. Didn't anyone ever look up into a tree they were standing under and leaning against?

Their conversation flagged. Then a more senior officer appeared and beckoned them forward. As the leaner walked away, I caught a slight movement of his head as though he was finally going to look up, but an irregularity in the ground took his attention and off he went. I felt relief, but wondered if there was a third cordon. Also my bladder felt close to bursting.

I stood in the tree another hour without seeing a third cordon, and decided I had to move. I got down and began moving west again, very cautiously, after dealing with my most urgent problem. I re-crossed the road, then saw more German troops, more dispersed, yet moving towards me, both sides of the road. There were no trees to climb that promised sanctuary, so I crouched in a ravine, very awkward with the valise, moving to try to skirt the German line. At times I had to move on all fours, even more awkward, and finally crawled under a bush, lying flat as groups of Germans moved along both sides of the ravine. I thought of simply going to sleep there, but it was marshy, and I thought I needed to keep moving. So I kept moving.

More German troops, all apparently on the same errand: my capture or death. I was by now past exhaustion, and if I had seen any place I could have hidden that damned valise, I would have gotten rid of it. I crossed the road once more as the cover on the other side was thicker and I could move more upright.

It was close to sunset when I emerged from a rather sparse forest and spotted a ruined building close to a road. I looked as cautiously as I was capable of by then and crossed to the building, climbing into it through an opening for a window. Inside there was some cover. Also a great many loose bricks knocked from the walls. I couldn't figure what the building could have been: not a home or a church; perhaps a school. Crouching next to the brick pile, I examined the valise.

It looked of good quality, black leather, shiny though scratched by its passage. It was locked and of course I had no key. I took out my trench knife and levered it under the lock holding the leather flap closing the case. I abruptly pried, and the lock broke. I opened the flap and looked inside.

It was not full. On top was a sort of book that on opening seemed to be accounts: a name, a set of letters and numbers, and a sum, although in a few cases there were some abbreviations I had no clue about. Under this was another book. Opening this, I found it was in French. It was also lavishly illustrated, with photographs, all of men and women performing every conceivable sexual act – it was a book of pornography. I wondered if this was the reason the "*von*" was so determined to retrieve his valise. Then, under the second book, I saw the actual reason, and the reason the valise was so heavy: a large number of coins, all gold, Belgian, French and even an English guinea or two. There were also quite a number of pieces of jewellery: brooches, pins, rings, earrings, a bracelet and some loose stones. A small fortune, and the account book, I suddenly realized, was highly incriminating: the fellow had been taking bribes, probably to let some hapless Belgian civilians off for some offense or other. The Roman numerals and numbers probably referred to the section of German military law they had run afoul of. The abbreviations, I imagined, may have been sexual bribes. I thought I could guess what they referred to. The bastard! I wondered what sort of shame he had imposed on wives, mothers, daughters, sweethearts. I was very, very glad I had taken his gains and decided the Foreign Office should see the account book. I was far too tired to carry that damned valise another step.

After some thought, I tore the first three pages from the account book, folded them small and stuck them down one stocking, lacing the boot so they wouldn't work out while I moved. If I was caught, it was unlikely I would be searched that thoroughly. I folded the flap of the valise down, dug a hole in the loose bricks, and then buried the valise. After making sure it couldn't be seen from any angle, I cautiously came out, moved crouched to the road where I saw a Belgian milepost. I copied the markings inconspicuously on my map, and then forced myself across the road into the brush and trees on the other, western side. As I moved out of sight, a German staff motor suddenly appeared and drove quickly past. I shuddered, because I was nearly caught; I had been so tired I had to force myself to move across that road.

I moved on as darkness grew. I was nearly out of water, entirely out of food, and needed to re-cross enemy lines this night if I could. The blessed darkness clothed me in invisibility as I moved past the rearmost German gun positions, now firing on our lines, desultory fire, harassing only, but still very, very bad if you were where a shell hit.

I had gotten to the same copse I had hidden in on my way east. I could recognize it even in the dark, my navigation had been that good, and I decided I couldn't go any further. The physical stress, the nervous strain, each and together were too much. So I crept into its centre, pulled out the ground sheet, wrapped it around me and tried to sleep.

* * *

I was running from a German patrol, and they had dogs, and the dogs were loosed and gaining rapidly no matter how hard I ran, then they were on me, tearing at me, particularly at my right shoulder, and the pain... woke me up. I was sweating, it was bright day, after eleven by my watch and I threw off my ground sheet... and realized I was behind enemy lines and became very still. I looked cautiously in every direction, could see and hear no Germans nearby. Their guns were firing, but still just harassing fire. I began to get up. My shoulder hurt indeed but so did the rest of me: arms, back and legs, very stiff and sore. I tried to move about, stretched and tried to loosen my muscles, but I was still very sore. Also thirsty. I had only about a half pint left in one bottle, the other was empty, and I knew I would have to get back to our lines by tomorrow morning. Fortunately the nights now were longer, but I would have to endure the rest of the day dry. Going back to the spring, assuming I could locate it again, would cost another day. I went back to my ground sheet, lay down and tried to doze.

* * *

A new moon and clouds into the bargain. As good as I could expect, perhaps with some rain to follow. I emerged from my copse in full darkness and began walking, mostly upright, occasionally crouched, past the German guns. They were still firing only now and then, so hopefully the flashes wouldn't illuminate me too conspicuously.

The third line trench featured the same smoking German sentries, all focused to the west. I went across without detection, pulled out my wire cutters and crept, sometimes on all fours, cutting a new path through to the second line trench.

The second line trench had the same situation. The wire was heavier and I had to lie down sometimes, cutting away and pushing the wire away with my feet – I had no gloves – before proceeding. As I got to the rear of the first line trench, I checked my watch: not yet three. I reminded myself to take extra care – this was the home stretch.

Getting across was again no problem. The wire was heavier yet, and my progress slower. There were sure to be paths through where German patrols would go, but it had started to rain. This was good, but the darkness was absolute with only occasional Very flares and gun flashes to let me see what I was dealing with. I went across mostly on my belly, even cutting our own wire as I couldn't see our paths. Once I got to the British parapet, I called across cautiously. At once, a voice replied, "That you, Major?" I said, "Yes, who is there?" "Corporal Driscoll, Sir." "Fine. I am coming over." And I did. I landed in the trench, not two feet from Driscoll. I was home.

Sergeant Scott came up and greeted me, "Expected you back two days ago, Sir. We was getting fair worried." "I did a bit of extra work, as I found a good spring," I replied. "Speaking of which, I need something to drink." Cold tea was produced, which I downed, reluctantly. Again no sugar, but I needed the water. I asked about events, and was told nothing much had happened, that the battalion was due to go into reserve tomorrow night. I checked my watch: 4:30. A bit close.

* * *

I spent my first day in the relatively sybaritic delights of reserve, managing to write my report after I had reported to the brigadier. I stressed that the Foreign Office needed to see the report, and he agreed. I had attached the three leaves from that scoundrel's account book and I had the fellow's name and appearance. I said I had buried the coins and jewellery. I didn't say where, actually I couldn't be certain where I had done so. I had also drawn in where the German fall back entrenchments were being built, at least the first line. The second just had a few flags to indicate where it would go. I finally gave my assessment of German efficiency: still good, but slipping; and morale: ditto. Since I had overheard private conversations of several German officers, I felt my report would have that much more weight.

I recovered slowly from the muscle soreness; I knew the nightmares would be more persistent.

We had gotten some reinforcements, not many. I had the feeling we were not considered top priority for these. Our strength had otherwise increased a little with returns from hospitals, etc. The few new privates I saw seemed of wretched quality: boys, technically eighteen but looking fourteen, older men, not tremendously robust. The scrapings of conscription. I thought of the legions of fit men who had volunteered, now mostly rotted bits across dozens of battlefields, squandered while generals and their staffs learned their business.

We also got a new lieutenant, Pope, whom I interviewed prior to assignment, probably to Castlefield's company. He simply seemed green, but I was once green, too. He otherwise was mad for cricket, asked me what position I had played, was stunned to learn I had never played the game, and then asked about getting some men together for a few games. I had no objection – it would keep them busy – and off he went to report to Castlefield.

* * *

We were in support, to go back into reserve in a few days. I heard nothing about my report, but got some maps of Belgium and identified the place where I hid the coins and jewellery. As I suspected, it was listed as "*école*", a school, so I looked forward to getting my hands on a bit of loot, quite a bit, I hoped.

Occasionally the Germans would fire on us, mainly for the benefit of our character, keeping us praying for example, but usually without effect. Not so this time: a round landed squarely in our support trench, killing one man, Morris, outright and wounding Moggs and Hayman. I went over with some other men. Moggs had a piece of shrapnel in his left thigh. Provided it didn't become infected, it was a "blighty" wound. I sent him off on a stretcher, as he couldn't walk. Hayman was the battalion comedian (aside from me, that is): he loved telling jokes, funny stories, anecdotes, and was very well liked. He had a piece of shrapnel in his head, but was conscious and alert. Typically, he made a joke of the whole business, saying the Germans had picked his least vulnerable part, that he thought he had rather damaged the German shell than the other way about, etc. I looked at the wound. It didn't seem too bad, but I recalled Eddie once commenting that head injuries could be tricky. I looked at his eyes, noted the right eye seemed dilated, shaded it with my hand, and then tried the same with the other eye. The left eye responded normally, the iris widening in shadow. The right didn't seem to respond. I was concerned, despite his saying he could just sleep it off, preferably with one of the girls in a good French whorehouse. I wrote a note to whoever would examine him: "Right eye unresponsive to light. Suspect" – I then crossed out "suspect" and wrote: "Head injury indicated." I underlined the last sentence, put the paper in his tunic pocket and sent him off on a stretcher.

* * *

The next day, I got a note from the brigadier to report to him in my best uniform. I turned the battalion over to Castlefield. I went back to where the regimental baggage was stored, managed to bathe, put on my best togs, medals and all, and went on to Brigade HQ.

I entered and saluted. The brigadier looked me over, asked who my servant was. I said I never had one, I did for myself, always had. In response, he summoned several officers' servants, had me remove my boots and uniform and sit in a chair in my stockings and drawers while the servants buffed, polished and picked verdigris out of my brass. This while a continuous stream of visitors came and went, each with some comment or other he deemed witty.

As this was going on, the brigadier took time to tell me my report caused something of a stir, that an official at the Foreign Office wanted to see me, and that he (the brigadier) had promised I would pay a call on the official at 10 AM tomorrow at the Foreign Office. I was straitly enjoined to go to a barber shop, get a shave and haircut beforehand. Evidently I was expected to dazzle the official – "*en grand tenue*" again. Then I was to return. Since I would be gone only a day, I needed no luggage.

Otherwise, I was given the usual list of things to get at Fortnum's and the personal effects of Moggs and Hayman – Castlefield had somehow gotten wind of my mission and sent these. So I donned my martial apparel, was inspected by the brigadier, who eventually conceded I would have to go as I was, and given a ride on a staff motor to the port.

I got into London about 8:30 and left the two sets of personal effects with the porter's at the train station. The barbershops were open and I was shaved professionally for the first time and given a haircut. I then took a taxi to the Foreign Office. I got there at 9:40, went in and eventually was ushered into the presence of the official, exactly on time. We shook hands, and he asked me to look at some photographs of German officials, to see if I could confirm the identity of the man I had seen briefly getting out of his staff motor.

As it happened, I identified the man readily enough, although he had gained some weight while in office. Then the Foreign Office man asked me if I could retrieve the rest of the accounts. I said I thought I could. I didn't ask why Government wanted them and he didn't volunteer to tell me. I asked him how soon he wanted the book, as I would have to cross German lines again to get it, and this was best done during a new moon. He hesitated, and then said this might not be so much of a problem in a few days; otherwise as soon as I could. Instanter, I thought, and then realized he was hinting something was afoot. I decided to change the subject a little: I asked about the coins and jewellery – what was their legal status?

He smiled, and noted that they might constitute loot – and looting, he thought, was a court-martial offense. I nodded, and he said that if – he was speaking hypothetically, he cautioned – someone were to come accidentally into possession of property which was originally stolen but which the victims were unlikely to claim, then that person could convert the property into pounds and claim it as an inheritance. Provided Inland Revenue were to get its lawful (as an inheritance) share, no questions were likely to be asked. He smiled, I smiled, arose and we shook hands. I took my leave.

The bank where I had my account was near, and I decided to get cash for a lunch at the Jewish restaurant, for Fortnum's and for a trinket for Elsie, for I rather urgently desired her services. This I did. It was 8 November, Friday.

I then returned to get the personal effects for Moggs and Hayman. We would be happy to see each other. I looked forward to exchanging quips with both, especially Hayman. The two bundles were awkward enough that I decided to take a taxi to the hospital they were at.. After paying the driver, I took the bundles inside. The hospital was a busy place, unfortunately. I gave my hat and coat to a porter at the main entrance, then asked for the locations of my two comrades.

A rather starchy looking woman heard me, and called a nurse to be my guide, a very necessary service as the place was a warren to me. The nurse looked up their locations, and bade me follow her.

My guide was a tall, willowy woman with reddish hair, not red or auburn, but reddish, stray locks of which emerged Medusa – like from under her nurse's cap. I remembered one of my friends at Earl's Cross opining that red hair was "common", an opinion the rest of us naturally agreed with, although I couldn't remember the reasoning, if any, behind this judgment.

Common or not, I noticed my guide had very trim ankles and quick feet as she helped me past groups of people, patients, visitors or hospital workers, standing, moving about, on crutches or in wheeled chairs, propelled by their occupants or pushed by others. We went along corridors, up stairs, through wards. At one point, our way was clear and my guide asked me what my name was.

"Dobbs. Matthew Dobbs." I said. She asked if I was from London. I replied no but I had been to university here. "What did you read?" she asked. "History." I replied. She then asked where I was from. I said, "I am not sure. Somewhere in the west. I was orphaned when I was four and grew up on the north coast of Norfolk." More patients, nurses, visitors. I edged my bundles past them, sweating now, then we were in a long ward, and my guide pointed to the third or fourth cot.

It was Moggs. I grinned, and said, "Skylarking again." He grinned in response, said "Hello, Sir." "Which of these is yours?" I asked. He pointed to the one nearer him and I set it next to him. "Thanks, Sir." I asked how he was faring, and he said the shrapnel had been removed and the wound sewn up. I asked to see it, and raised the blanket on his wounded leg, which was propped up. The nurse moved away, which surprised me: surely she had seen all parts of sick and wounded men. I remembered Eddie saying that infections, if they were to occur, would do so over about 36 hours, so enough time had passed. I looked at the leg, saw no red streaks towards the torso, sniffed, and aside from unwashed Moggs, smelled nothing: no gangrene. I said, "If gas gangrene were to develop, it would have developed by now – I could have smelled it. And I see no signs of infection spreading, so it appears we have our archetypical 'blighty wound'. Five shillings, please." Moggs grinned. I had something of a reputation as a doctor, derived from listening to Eddie expound hour after hour.

"Well, Moggs, I trust you will behave with appropriate decorum and dignity; the honour of the battalion is in your hands." Moggs replied, "I'll do me best, Sir." I said, "That's what we are all afraid of." Then I asked if he had seen Hayman. "Come across on the boat with me, he did. He was all right, but he was sick on the boat, threw up. Came out like a shot, it did. After, he said he was all right, though, Sir." I noticed a shade of concern cross the face of the nurse, but the symptom meant nothing to me. I would have to ask Eddie when next I saw him.

I bade Moggs goodbye, picked up Hayman's things and followed the nurse along the ward. As we got to near the end of the aisle, I heard her say, "Oh, dear." She was approaching the last cot. Two nurses were making it up. It was empty. One of the nurses saw my guide and shook her head. There was no mistaking the message. I stood a moment, stricken. I dropped Hayman's things on the floor, turned on my heel, and walked away as fast as I could.

Along the corridor, down steps, through wards, around people moving randomly across my path, I blundered past them all, heartsick. Another meaningless death! Everyone liked Hayman, it would greatly depress morale once his death was known, and I would have to report it.

Somehow I arrived at the entrance, still crowded, new faces but the same awful business. I hesitated, looking for the porter to get my hat and trench coat. I wanted out of this damned place. I heard steps behind me and turned. It was the reddish-haired nurse. She was a bit out of breath, having followed me. As I stared at her, she raised a hand to push a lock of hair that had escaped back under her cap, an automatic gesture, done many times a day, but the movement of her hand drew my eyes towards it. The hand was Alice's hand and her eyes were Alice's eyes, and – of course: an inch or two shorter (and not nearly so pretty), this must be Alice's younger sister – I couldn't remember her name.

She obviously knew who I was from her questions, and we smiled at each other from mutual recognition. Then the memory of that empty cot returned and everything turned bleak. "Was he a friend of yours?" she asked, having moved closer. "No, not particularly," I said, "He was a thoroughly good chap – they most of them are, you know." She nodded. "He liked to tell funny stories and jokes," I continued, "and everyone liked him." I stopped, and then said, "The phrase 'brotherhood of arms' isn't just words. Men who have shared the experiences of war become closer than brothers." I thought some more. "And I daresay it is the same for you nurses." She nodded again.

The porter came by, handed me my hat and coat. Was I supposed to tip him? But he moved on, taking coats to another group. I turned back to my guide and said formally, "Thank you for your assistance," and turning to leave, heard her say, "You are welcome."

I put on my hat and was struggling into the coat as I left, moving as quickly as the people in front of me allowed. "So that is Alice's sister," I thought as I moved along the street. I picked up my pace, trying to shake off the depression constantly moving to fill my mind. My train left at midnight, and I decided a lunch at the Jewish restaurant would be just the thing, and I would call on David and try to get him to join me. Aside from the pleasure of seeing him once more, I wanted to ask him about disposing of the coins and jewellery, assuming I could retrieve them.

It was nearly noon when I got to the pawn shop. David was there, talking to a customer. I saw the woman, Esther Goldman, dealing with another customer. Both noticed me as I came in. I nodded to her, grinned at David, and waited. As soon as another clerk entered and the two customers left, David came from behind the counter and we shook hands. I jerked my head in the approximate direction of the restaurant. He understood, but gave me to understand that Miss Goldman was an inseparable part of our group. I nodded, and we three went out together.

As we walked, I told them I was hoping to be considered their host (acceptable), and that I was here only for the day. We got to the restaurant, which was naturally crowded as it was around noon, and had to wait for a table. I asked David to get us a place with some privacy, and he interceded with the characterful waitress. She got us a corner booth. I took off my coat and hat and sat down with them.

Miss Goldman, and David himself, were impressed by my uniform. I spread my arms, inviting their admiration, informing them the glitter and polish would be short-lived, that I was made resplendent because I had to talk to a man at the Foreign Office. I looked significantly at David, and moved my head fractionally towards his companion. He interpreted me correctly, and said Miss Goldman (he used her given name) was part and parcel of the firm and trustworthy. So I told them my story. Their faces both darkened when I told of the German official's bribe taking, and became grim when I hinted at his acceptance of other means of payment. They were delighted I had stolen his private treasury. I said, "So you know the provenance of this horde. I asked the man at the Foreign Office about it, and he suggested I convert it to pounds and call it an inheritance. He said, provided Inland Revenue got its share, no questions would likely be asked. So, are you willing to convert the coins and flog the jewellery?"

David and his companion looked at each other, then David said, "The coins you could probably convert yourself as they are current currencies of Allied powers. We can certainly sell the jewellery, but that will take more time." I said, "I would rather you handled it all, since if I began appearing in banks with Belgian and French coins, large numbers of them, claiming I had inherited them, questions might be asked." David said, "You understand our fee for all transactions is 20 percent." I said, "That's what I thought it was. That is perfectly acceptable to me." We shook hands on the deal, our orders appeared, and we ate. And enjoyed. David asked what the Foreign Office wanted if I could talk about it. I told them to keep quiet about the business, but the man wanted me to confirm the German official's identity and he told me they wanted the rest of the account book. I didn't ask why, I said. They nodded.

I asked how Eddie was, as I couldn't drop by his place and expect to find him during the day. David grinned and said, "He's married. To Christine Soames. I got a card from him yesterday, telling me. By registry office. Said they were 'at home' Sunday, so we" – glancing at Miss Goldman – "will call on them." I said, "By God, that is good news, good news at last. I suppose if I check there for any mail, Christine might be there – or are she and Eddie off somewhere?" David said he didn't know. I paid and we all went outside. We all shook hands, said goodbye for now and separated.

Christine was in. She greeted me pleasantly, said I had no mail, but would I stay for some ginger beer? I replied that I was on a mission, a quest even, to deplete ginger beer stocks in the homes of all my friends. We went in; I took off my coat and hat and once again elicited awe and admiration. I spread my arms, and said, "Gaze and be overwhelmed by my unwonted splendour. In another few weeks I will be verdigrised back to my normal, battle-hardened, heroic scruffiness and unsanitariness. You have been warned." She was amused, but asked whether I had a servant. I said I never had, always did, or rather didn't, for myself, with results my brigadier found less than satisfactory. I told her about my spell, sitting in stockings and drawers, listening to what I considered very feeble attempts at humour by a very large number of visitors. I asked if Eddie had taken an assistant now he had her to greet him when he returned. She hesitated, said she didn't know, that Eddie worked very hard, he had so many patients.

I said, "He worked so hard, partially because of his sense of duty and of compassion, but I think mainly because the practice, his work, was all he had." I said she should encourage him to get some help, so they might have a life together. I went on, saying that Eddie is not a saint, although if you told that to his patients, you would probably get an argument, but he was as good, loyal and generous a friend and man as any I had ever met. He was also, I said, a very lonely man, and needed someone, her, to fill that void.

She sat silently for a while. I thought I might have offended her, but she said she had spent so many years, trying, not to discourage his attentions, but not to encourage them. I nodded. I then said, "Eddie wants your love, not just your presence in bed and at his board. I think he is actually quite loveable, if you give him a chance." She was silent again. I finished my ginger beer, arose to take my leave, and Eddie himself appeared.

"Aha," he said. "Aha, indeed," I replied, grinning: "Behold and be dazzled. Don't hesitate to grovel; it is the usual effect I have on everyone." He laughed, said he had just come back for some medicine, had gotten it at the local apothecary, and stopped by for a glass of wine. So wine and more ginger beer were produced and I told them, for the second time that day, of my adventures at the Foreign Office. They were fascinated by the story, although not surprised at the German official's behaviour. Then Christine asked, "How much longer is it going to continue? Have you heard anything?" "No," I said. "However, when I told the fellow at the Foreign Office that I would have to wait for a new moon, or nearly, to go back across German lines, he hinted this might not be a problem. I took that at first as an indication that talks were going on, but the longer I think about what he said and the way he said it, I am beginning to think actual decisions have been made." They stared. I said, "I agree that raises more questions than I can possibly answer, but that is my impression. There may be an announcement in a few days. I hope so." They nodded.

Eddie and I got up. Eddie asked when I was going back. I said this evening, not wanting to be more specific. I wondered if Eddie had told Christine about Elsie, decided he almost certainly hadn't, but pulled my Fortnum's list out. "This is," looking at my watch, "my next stop. Fortnum's. The lists get longer and longer. I hope they can get all this in one box. Then I go back," I lied. Not quite directly, anyway. I wished them congratulations and best wishes, the former for Eddie and the latter for his bride, and left.

———

I was standing at the altar of a church, a heavily veiled bride-to-be carrying a large bouquet of flowers at my side. The priest asked if there were any reason these two persons should not be joined in matrimony, let them speak now or forever hold their peace. There was a stir, and we turned to see Elsie, clearly heavily pregnant, pointing at her belly, shouting something, then pointing at me. My intended bride tore off her veil, revealing the face of Alice's sister, her face contorted with rage, who swung her bouquet at my face...

I awoke to find my hat had fallen from its perch above my seat and hit me. My box from Fortnum's was beside me on the seat and I was on the train to Folkestone on the way back to France. "What a strange dream," I thought. My meeting of Alice's sister recurred to me; considering my relations with her family, I would have expected coolness at best, otherwise disdain, yet she had seemed ... nice. I couldn't put it better than that. Odd. My reunion with Elsie had gone as hoped: she had been delighted with my present, very impressed by my uniform and very generous with her person. I had managed three satisfactions of both of us, the last less from lust than the melancholy realization that this might be the last time, the last meeting.

My dream was surprising on another count: I had a hard time sleeping on anything moving, a very old characteristic, so I must have been very tired, perhaps from the sex. I sat back, my hat in my lap, looking at the faces of the three other men in the compartment, all of them sleeping soundly.

Getting back to my battalion was slowed and exasperated by the box, but also because we were suddenly and mysteriously in reserve. We were not scheduled for this for several days, and into the bargain seemed to have shifted position. I finally got to my new quarters, which otherwise looked depressingly like my old ones, long after midnight Saturday, technically Sunday morning. Entering, I woke the orderly who had been sleeping on his arms folded on a table. He told me the brigadier wanted to see me tomorrow – actually this – morning, early. I nodded, set the accursed box down to be opened and sorted by the orderly. I then located my cot, took off my boots, coat and tunic and lay down on it.

* * *

I was awakened at 6 AM, cursed vigorously if unoriginally, emptied my bladder, washed my face and hands, cleaned my teeth and shaved. Then I put my usual uniform on and, given directions, went to find the brigadier.

He was of course already up and well into his day. I saluted. He said, "Good morning, Major. Were you able to give satisfaction to the Foreign Office?" I said, "I think so, Sir. The man I talked to showed me some pictures. I was able to identify the fellow easily enough. The Foreign Office wants me to find and send the rest of the fellow's accounts book. I think I know exactly where to look, too." "Keep the gold and jewels, eh?" "Yes, Sir. The Foreign Office official suggested I have it converted into pounds, declare it as an inheritance, pay Inland Revenue their share and put the rest in my pocket." The brigadier nodded, and then asked me to close the door to his office. I did so.

The brigadier said quietly, "This is for your ears only, to be told to no one else unless authorized to. Do you understand?" "I believe so, Sir." He leaned forward, "There is an armistice being negotiated between the new German government and the Allies. We are proposing that it is to take effect at eleven AM, 1100

188

hours, tomorrow." I stared. I could hear guns firing, distant ones, but all at targets, human targets. I flushed: "Why in Hell don't they call it off at once?" I had spoken loudly, too loudly. The brigadier shook his head. "Not my decision, Dobbs, or yours either."

He leaned back. "This division is to be broken up. The men and junior officers will be sent to other divisions. I am recommending you be put on Indefinite Furlough. I want to promote Castlefield in your place." I said, "That's good, Sir. He's earned promotion." The brigadier nodded. "This will be done over the next month or so. You should be able to find your treasure trove, and then go home. I know you don't like the Army." I smiled, thinking of several responses, but kept my mouth shut. "That's all, Major," the brigadier said, and I arose, saluted, made an about turn, stumbled as usual, grabbed at the door frame, opened the door and went out.

As I walked across the field, I tried to cope with what I had heard. I was going home! I had survived one of the most awful wars in history, in terms of casualties. I thought of everything I wanted to do, everything I had tried not to think of, it being considered bad luck to dream of peace and peacetime pursuits. Now I was free, free to dream....

In the meantime, I had a letter or two to write, particularly to the parents of Hayman. I sighed, and on entering the battalion office, told the orderly to make a large pot of chocolate. To Hell with trying to make it last! I sat down and pulled a sheet of paper towards me and took out my pen, my old faithful fountain pen, and began to write.

* * *

The battalion was assembled. I had been told I could inform the men of the Armistice at 10 AM. It was now 10:13. The men were excited; rumours had been thickening for a day or more. They were called to attention and fell silent. I said, "I am ordered to inform you that as of 11 this morning, an Armistice" (noise growing), "between the Allies and Germany" (it was getting hard to make myself heard), "is to take effect." The men yelled, threw helmets and caps into the air, and began embracing and shaking hands, all grinning, all ecstatic. Who could blame them? I was torn between irritation at being unable to finish and the sheer joy of what I was communicating. Eventually things quieted, and I said, "We pray the Armistice will hold" (everyone more sober now), "but I know that, whether it does or not, you will continue to do your duty. No one can require more of you than you have given. Thank you again. Battalion, dismiss."

I went back into what passed for an office, grinning, although feeling very emotional. I ordered another pot of chocolate, staring down what I took to be reservations on the part of the messman. I sat down, put my feet on the table and leaned back in the chair, resisting the temptation to keep looking at my watch. I concentrated instead on the distant sound of the guns, hammering, hammering and all so useless.

The pot of chocolate was ready and I took a mugful. There was a sound of cheering outside, indeed it seemed to be everywhere. I raised my mug, toasted the legions of the lost: "*ave atque vale*", and sipped at the brew. Castlefield came in. I nodded towards the pot and he filled a cup, sat down and drank. "No cream, unfortunately," I said. He grinned, said I was *persona non* at Corps since my last visit. I laughed. "Serves them right, inviting a line officer to sample the extravagant comforts of staff work. They were lucky I eventually left, in an excess of politeness. I suppose that's why their clever ideas are now presented by the brigadier." He nodded, took a larger mouthful, sighed, and said, "Pope's got a cricket match going." I said, "I shocked the poor fellow deeply by admitting I had never played. I suppose you did." Castlefield said, "Some." He was silent a while, and then said, "I suppose you know I am to get a battalion and a lieutenant colonelcy when everyone gets reassigned." I said, "I didn't know about the rank, but I assure you I will be delighted to salute and be-Sir you. It is past time. Just don't expect me to click my heels: with my drill skills, I would probably manage to miss. But congratulations – you are on your way at last."

He was silent several minutes while we both sipped and listened to the happiness outside. The reassignment part had not been communicated to the men. Then he said, "When I graduated Sandhurst, I was determined to make the Army my life. Now, after this war, I am not sure I want to stay in. Last leave, I talked to my wife. Her family owns a number of wine and spirit shops in the Midlands, and they have offered me a job." I said, "What does she want you to do?" He said, "She was willing to be an Army officer's wife, but she would rather stay in one place, near her family. And I am leaning that way, now." I asked, "Is the job one you will like doing? Making the wife happy has to be a plus." He said, "Actually, I am sure I will like it; the question is whether I will regret leaving the Army and pitching my dreams of being a general into the dustbin." I commented, "Promotion will be slower in peacetime."

We had some more chocolate and sipped in silence. Then he asked if I was married or had someone. I said, "No, not anymore. Once I was actually engaged to marry, but was jilted." I reflected I had broken my word not to mention the engagement, but decided it didn't matter now anyway. Castlefield asked, "Did she marry someone else?" I said, "Yes, a cavalryman." Castlefield cursed. "But very posh," I objected. More cursing: Castlefield fully shared the line infantry's opinion of the cavalry. Come to think of it, so did I: their main achievement on the Western Front was to convert mountains of forage and smaller mountains of rations into still smaller mountains of dung. I laughed, and then told this to Castlefield, who also laughed, agreeing, and the conversation became, I was somewhat sorry to say, rather scatological.

* * *

Our division was dispersed. Instead of sending men in their accustomed units, as units, everyone was sent to units where they were strangers. The war was over, so efficiency didn't matter so much, but it was hard to break up comrades. Every man in my battalion, and some in other battalions, came by to shake hands. I would miss those men, and they would, although not saying so explicitly, miss me. Castlefield got his battalion, and said goodbye. We had become friends, and that made parting harder, although I was glad for him.

We had never been a "name" division like the Guards or 51st Highland, just there to stop a hole in the line two to three miles long, but that meant we hadn't usually been thrown into the forefront of attacks or desperate defences. This had been, no doubt, the saving of many of us. And the Germans, perhaps accidentally, had never made us a principal target, since we were never tasked with holding sections of line deemed important. Luck again.

* * *

I was attached, through the good offices of the brigadier, to another division's staff, becoming one of the military tapeworms I had loved to despise, and in the process discovered that staff officers were very, very busy people indeed. The brigadier, who was going home, had let the general commanding the division know I was supposed to retrieve something the Foreign Office wanted, but until the Germans had moved far enough back, I had to see to ration deliveries, routing and scheduling, movements of amazing quantities of supplies, all intricately coordinated, and all just for one division.

The Germans retreated slowly. This was not, as I discovered through going over to talk to them, because of recalcitrance but exhaustion. For that matter, we too were sluggish, but no one at the lower levels seemed impatient.

For my trips, I had a staff motor and driver, a real luxury. I loaded my pockets with tins of bully beef as presents, extremely acceptable to sentries and officers alike. Providing the Germans with food was, as the Germans would say, "*strenger verboten*". However, practicality and compassion were far more compelling, not that orders had ever elicited automatic obedience from me, which was probably why I was to be sent home after retrieving the accounts book. Which I found perfectly acceptable.

With the help of the illicit bully beef, I established a rapport with the German officers and the men that I met. It was a great help to speak the language, of course. I told Hans-Jeorg's joke about the establishment whose loo had a golden seat to a growing crowd, and, after the usual pause, got a roar of laughter. I followed this up with the story whose last line is, "Only when I laugh," and found I had a very appreciative audience. More jokes followed, although I noticed my driver didn't speak German, so I would have to give the English versions on the way back. We all stood about and talked about families, sweethearts and what we were going to do when we got home, men who had been doing their best to kill each other a few days ago.

* * *

The German army had moved far enough back so I could go to the *école* and see if the valise was still there. My driver stopped beside the place, and I told him to stay put. It was a raw day, and he was glad to do so. I got out and went through what was probably once a doorway, over to the pile of loose masonry, and began pulling bricks up. The pile looked undisturbed and after a few minutes the black valise appeared. I pulled it up, its weight now a source of gratification, opened the flap and looked inside. Everything appeared to be there. I wondered how it would feel to have several thousand pounds in my pocket, and decided I very much wanted to find out. I had brought two pieces of rope to tie the flap down, since I had broken the lock.

Once back at Division HQ, I told the general I had found what the Foreign Office wanted, so would take it back myself. The general knew of my Indefinite Furlough (although not of the coins and jewellery), shook hands and was kind enough to say he was sorry to lose a good staff officer. This surprised me, but I thanked him and went to get my own suitcase containing my things.

I could just fit the German official's valise inside mine, once I had emptied it. I stuffed my things inside the German official's valise and around it. I decided I wouldn't take the pornographic book back, as it added to the crowding and I really didn't think I needed that with me. I left it on the wardroom table, where it attracted the intense interest of the orderly and the officer of the day, whose last words I heard were, "By Jove, I didn't think it could be done that way."

I managed to get a ride back to the railhead in a Red Cross lorry driven by a woman. She was smiling at something, but managed to miss major holes, ruts and obstacles, manoeuvring rather skilfully, while I sat with several thousand pounds between my legs literally rather than metaphorically.

IV. LONDON

I had visited one of the Gent's at the Foreign Office, there ferreted the accounts book out and given it to the official I had met before. He took it happily, gave a significant look at my suitcase, which was obviously heavy, smiled and bade me goodbye. I went to a scone shop, got chocolate – sorry, no cream – and some scones and looked for a room in the papers. I didn't want to intrude on Eddie and Christine; they needed to adjust to each other. I wanted a room near the university, although not near Elsie, so I could see what jobs were available.

The second one I looked at was acceptable. The landlord would let me keep food and ginger beer in the room, so I got the key and set my things down. I pulled the German official's valise out, roped it shut again after removing my things and carried it over to David's family's shop.

David was talking to a customer. He saw me; I grinned, nodded towards the valise, and waited. The customer left, and David and I shook hands, each of us "out of it" through our different fates, but now both of us had a future, the great uncertainty gone. He let me in behind the counter, then into his office, a poky place, where I took the rope off and tilted the valise so the coins, etc. poured onto the desk.

It made an impressive pile, David catching one or two coins that attempted an escape to the floor. He began inspecting the coins, confirming my hasty observation that these were modern, not rare or old. He began sorting them into French and Belgian, a few guineas in a third pile. I set to helping him. The door opened and Esther came in – without knocking, which told me a good deal about her status with David. She sat down in the third chair and began helping with the coin sorting, occasionally looking at the jewellery in an appraising way.

Once the coins were sorted, they were counted, David writing the totals of each down on a sheet of paper. That left the jewellery. David let Esther look at each piece, writing down a brief description, making an inventory/receipt. All this took nearly two hours. No one else came in, confirming my feelings about how things were between them. It was past one when the business was completed. David put the loot in the safe, gave me a copy of the inventory signed by him. I proposed lunch. This was acceptable, and we adjourned to our favourite restaurant.

David said the coins alone would come to over £3,000 and as to the jewellery – he looked at Esther, who felt they would bring at least £2,000 more. David's shop would net at least £1,000, Inland Revenue probably about another £1,000 leaving me with £3,000 or more. Having a definite figure deflated me a little, but I told myself that £3,000 would keep me for a decade or more. After all, it was quite unearned, if you forgot how hard it was to carry it off in the teeth of what seemed a large part of the German Army.

David thought the coins would be sold within a few weeks: gold coins were at a premium. The jewellery would be sent abroad, probably to New York City in America, by special courier. Perhaps six months. I nodded, told David to keep the money from the coins in an account until everything was sold. I got a sheet of paper from him and wrote a brief will, making him and Eddie my heirs in case a tram did what the Imperial German Army couldn't. Esther signed as witness. I paid the bill and we got up and shook hands outside. I smiled at them, wondering how long before they were married, and walked back to my room.

I unpacked, set my things out, and then went over to the University to look at job listings. These seemed sparse, nothing for Assistant Lecturers in history. Not much in public schools, either. I bought a dozen bottles of ginger beer in a box, got some scones from the shop I had been in earlier and went back to my room. I was feeling tired, perhaps inevitable after the excitements of the last few days.

The German official's valise was a very handsome one even with the scratches, and I thought it would be better for carrying papers to be marked than my old suitcase, whose stitching was failing in several places. I decided to have the lock fixed, with two keys made. I went out to look for a locksmith. The first one shook his head – didn't do that sort of thing – and referred me to a second. He referred me to a third, some distance away, and I began to feel this was getting tiresome.

The third locksmith looked at the lock, and then gave me a most reproachful look, so I felt compelled to explain it had to be opened in a hurry and the key wasn't available, which in a way was true. He didn't seem to think my explanation valid, but eventually, once cornered, conceded he could fix the lock and provide two keys. I paid some money down and left, feeling more tired than ever. I decided I would get my old suitcase re-stitched tomorrow, although I was having trouble figuring out what sort of tradesman would do such a thing.

By the time I got back to where my room was, I was feeling very bad indeed: my joints and muscles were aching, my head was swimming, and all I wanted was to lie down. I took off my trench coat and tunic and boots and pulled the bedspread over me. The room seemed cold, and after a minute or two I laid the trench coat on top of the bedspread. This didn't seem to have much effect. I got out, crawled under the sheet as well, then laid my tunic over the trench coat and placed the second pillow on top of my head. I seemed to feel colder than ever, I was shaking, I curled into as compact a posture as possible, I couldn't get warm.

Time itself seemed frozen. I couldn't sleep, I was shaking and shivering so much. There were no blankets in the room, not that these would have helped, even piling all my clothes on top of me didn't warm me at all. I realized I had "chills" and wondered how long these would last.

At some point, I had no idea of time by now, I stopped shivering, and began a troubled sleep. Eddie lay on a bed before me, dying of the flu, caught from me, the life's light fading from his eyes, Christine at the bedside, her face a mask of grief, grief and remorse overwhelming me, was I bringing death to all my friends and grief to their wives and sweethearts? I woke, feeling very hot now and began to pull clothes off myself, then thought I shouldn't go too far as I might get chilled again...more dreams, confused dreams I couldn't remember upon waking, except they were awful.

Now I had a cough, a dry, hard cough, and my nose was congested and runny. My handkerchief supply rapidly shrank. I was thirsty, and looking in the ewer on the table near the window found it had liquid in it. I poured some into a glass next to the ewer. It didn't look like piss – by now I couldn't smell anything – so I drank it. I couldn't remember filling it in the first place, but drank more. My bladder was full, so I padded, in stocking feet with uniform shirt and trousers on, to the bathroom at the other end of the floor to refill the ewer after emptying myself. By the light and my watch, it was midday, but of which day? Back in the room, I ate a couple of the scones, which by now were quite stale, and tried some ginger beer. The ginger beer seemed very harsh on my throat (as were the stale scones) so I drank more water and returned to bed.

Time passed. I got up occasionally, still feeling shaky and weak, drank water, ate a scone or two, went to the bathroom. By now it was in the middle of the night, so I saw no one. I began washing my handkerchiefs, for there was, I was surprised to find, hot water even at that hour. Then I dozed, coughed, blew my nose over and over and drank more water.

After a reasonable sleep, waking about midday, I felt better, and decided to call Eddie and David, informing them of my sickness, although, to be sure, if they had caught it, my news would be useless. I found a public telephone and called Eddie's house. Christine answered. She was surprised I was in town at all, even more surprised that I had had the flu but told me what day it was, so I realized I had been sick nearly a week. She said there were some letters for me. I asked her to set them outside their door; I didn't want them to contract what I had. I said I would call David, and then call Eddie in the evening to get his recommendations.

David answered. He said he was sorry I had been sick, but he and Esther were well. I went to Eddie and Christine's, found the letters, took them back to my room and read them. The one from the War Office confirmed my Indefinite Furlough status; the other two were from soldiers from my old battalion, telling me how they were faring. I would postpone replying until I was sure I was well.

Eddie told me, that evening, over the telephone, to stay indoors as much as possible at least a week longer. After that, I should be in (and pose to others) no danger. He said my symptoms were standard. They were also very nasty.

Over the next week I gradually recovered and re-entered the rest of the world. My civilian clothes were at Eddie's and I was loathe to expose him or Christine to what I had recovered from, so I eventually bought new clothes from a store. They seemed uncomfortable, but were clean and presentable.

I still wanted my old suitcase re-stitched, so emptied it, in the process finding the ring I had given Alice Millwood. I stuck it in my pocket for lack of a better place. I got a cobbler to re-stitch the suitcase, and got the repaired German official's valise from the locksmith. He accepted my praise (and money) as each being merely his due.

The holidays were near, normally a bleak time for me, but I was alive, and feeling so much better I decided on a visit to Elsie. After buying a suitable trinket, I went to her room. No one answered my knock, although she should have been there. I knocked on the door of her neighbour, who did answer. She recognized me as Elsie's "young officer", and told me Elsie was dead – of the flu. She had died a week ago. The woman went back into her room and brought back a cigar box and gave it to me. Inside were the pieces of jewellery I had bought her over the last 2 1/2 years. She said Elsie wanted me to have them. I was touched, stunned, depressed: Elsie was gone. I had used her. Perhaps she knew this, I didn't know. There was so much about her I didn't know, hadn't been interested in finding out. As usual, I left that house deeply ashamed. When I got back to my room, I put Alice's ring into the box with Elsie's trinkets.

I kept looking for a job. The only thing I could find was as a substitute for a sick master at a day school in a posh section of London. I went to the school and talked to the headmaster, who was impressed by my qualifications, as well he might be. The salary worked out to about £12 a month, which I could survive on. A temporary job while I looked for permanent employment was what I wanted. I gave him my references, and he promised me a quick and, he hinted, a favourable reply. I went on to Eddie and Christine's, as they had invited me to dinner that night. Apparently Eddie would definitely be home at a predictable hour.

Predictable, but not early. I sat talking to Christine nearly an hour, sipping my ginger beer while she drank a glass of wine. She asked what I thought of men who never served in the war, as soldiers, she meant. I answered it depended: I knew of Conscientious Objectors whom I greatly admired and others I considered self-righteous and arrogant. Some men couldn't physically measure up to combat, some were merely lucky, some were cowards and beneath contempt. I began to guess the purpose of her question, and commented that I hadn't volunteered early in the war although pressed to do so (I didn't say who had done the pressing, but she probably knew), partly because of my friendship with a German and partly because of my eyesight. I eventually volunteered as an officer candidate because otherwise I would have been conscripted as a private soldier – not very noble, I noted. I went on to say that Eddie told me he was filling out the papers to join the Medical Service (Christine looked surprised), but that I had dissuaded him because of his practice. The nation depended very much on the work of the dockers, who controlled flows of foods and raw materials into the country and finished goods out, and Eddie was their doctor, perhaps their only doctor. I added that if he had joined the Medical Service, he would have spent most of his time being bored and busy times not being of as much help, as he was not a surgeon. Christine said, "He never mentioned this." I said she was engaged to another man while this was going on, so not in communication with Eddie. I pointed out that Eddie was not a boaster. She nodded. I could see I had impressed her.

Eddie came in, said, "Aha" again, and we shook hands. He looked me over, and then bade me sit at the table, as usual on his left. Christine sat on his right. We had roast beef and Yorkshire pudding, most excellent as expected. At one point, Christine got up to talk to the housekeeper-cook and her hand rested a moment on Eddie's sleeve, a trifling gesture but bespeaking affection. Eddie looked up, and smiled at her, she smiled back and I focused my attention on my plate, very pleased.

After the meal, I told them about the prospective job. Eddie said he had heard of the school, a good one, but the students he thought were mostly from wealthy families and tended to have a reputation for snobbish behaviour. I smiled and said I was forewarned and would be in full character-building mode for them. If hired, I added. We talked some more, then I took my leave.

* * *

The letter offering me the job arrived three days after the interview and asked me to come by to be given details of the work: classes, textbooks, etc. I took notes. The first class consisted of upper sixth formers, and I guessed these would attempt to cause the most trouble. I asked the headmaster when the school opened, that is, what was the earliest time I could get into the classroom, so I could prepare my lecture. He was impressed by what he took to be my zeal. I let him harbour his illusions. I asked to talk to the man I was replacing, to ensure continuity of coverage of the subject. The headmaster gave me the man's address. Then he asked where I intended to live. I replied, as closely as possible to the school. A woman, a widow he knew was willing to rent a room to a suitable tenant. He spoke her and her husband's names with what seemed almost reverence to me, and I gathered I was supposed to be impressed, although the husband's name, and her maiden name, meant nothing to me. I thought I would ask Eddie and Christine about them. The room was quite close, to be sure.

The headmaster hesitated, and then said the widow was quite adamant on one qualification: he asked me if I was homosexual. I stared at him, quite confused. However, my answer was

200

straightforward: "No, I am not." He explained she had an absolute distaste for homosexuals. Since the only such people I had any contact with were Paston and that vile lawyer friend (lover? almost certainly), I merely nodded.

I went first to the man I was substituting for. He had had a stroke, but was recovering, he said. I noted the tell-tale symptoms I had heard once or twice from Eddie, but expressed my sympathy and hopes for his full recovery. Then we got down to business. His speech was still handicapped, but I could follow him. More notes. The curriculum was familiar to me, and he was kind enough to let me have his copies of the texts. These would indeed help.

The widow's house was detached, in an enclave of such houses very near the school. I knocked on the door, was admitted by a maid, who ushered me into the prospective landlady's presence. She was of middle height, trim figure and very pretty, or would have been except for the stoniness, almost disdain, of her expression. I gave her my name, said the headmaster of the day school had given me her name, and that I wanted a place to stay while teaching at the school. She stared at me, asked me if I had served in the Army. I said yes, I was on furlough. She asked me what my rank had been and I told her. She then asked me what regiment I had served in, and I told her that. She was clearly not impressed. There was more silence, and then she said she would show me the room.

It was a room with a window and curtains, a closet, a dresser, chair and bed, not much different from the room I currently occupied, save for the closet and curtains. The rent was 10 shillings a week. I could have one (1) bath a week, Friday evenings. However, the main restriction was I had to be out of the house by 6:30 AM and could only return after dark. She emphasized she did not want the neighbours knowing she had a tenant. This, I understood, was absolute. Since I would be over early to the school and could busy myself elsewhere marking papers and preparing for next day's classes, I accepted these somewhat unusual terms and we went into the kitchen.

I would move my things in six days hence, except for those left with Eddie and Christine. I paid over the 10 shillings. She indicated I was to put them on the kitchen table, and she wrote out a receipt for the money, setting this on the table for me to pick up. This was a bit irritating, but I told myself the location was sufficient to put up with odd manners. The restrictions on my coming and going meant that if I wanted to go to a concert or other formally dressed event, I had to dress for it at Eddie and Christine's house. Still, the location outweighed everything else. As I was leaving, she told me her husband was in a Guards unit at Second Ypres. She asked if I had served there. I said I had, and left.

The school was opened at 7 AM, and I was there waiting, shiny black valise in hand, introductory remarks prepared for all my classes. I had passed the six day interval working in my old room. I had told the landlord I had had the flu in that room, meaning he had better clean it or air it or something before renting to a new tenant, but all he had said was there was a lot of it about. I had been given a key to my new quarters and had entered the house after dark, as instructed. No one was about. I had unpacked, dressed in new pyjamas and gone to bed. My alarm clock had done its job, awakening me – and perhaps everyone else in the house – at 5:30 for shaving, cleaning my teeth and dressing. As I was going out, I found my landlady, her maid and her son, who appeared to be about four, all in the kitchen. I said, "Good morning, Madam." She replied, "Good morning, Major", rather distantly. I nodded to the maid, who ignored me, smiled at the boy, who was asleep, and walked out.

The classroom where I was to teach was quite empty, I was glad to see. I sat down and began reviewing what I was to say. Half an hour or so before class was to start, the classroom door opened and four young men, apparently students, came in. They had the air, to me, of planning something and were quite taken aback to see me already there. I stared them into their seats, and then resumed my work. Silence. One of the students coughed, and then asked, what they were to call me? Another said, "You do have a name, don't you?" This was insolent, and I stared at the second speaker until his gaze shifted, and then said, "Yes, I do." More silence. The first speaker asked me what my name was. I gave him my best don't-trifle-with-me look, and said, "You may call me 'Sir'." I gave a brief smile, as insincere as I could manage. I said their commendable promptitude suggested an interest in the subject which, I imagined, would inspire them to extra work on it. I went on to say they would not find me slow in assigning such. They were not pleased at this, but the door opened to admit several more students.

Studying them, I guessed two were expecting to see the results of some prank while the rest were merely surprised at seeing me there. The pockets of the first four suggested they were carrying something for such a purpose. I did not trouble to ask any names, as I figured some would give other students' names to put me off. I pulled out a blank sheet of paper, turned it sideways and set my pen beside it. More students came in. I had been told there were twenty-two in all. The list was in alphabetical order.

The door opened again and the headmaster walked in. We all rose and I inconspicuously picked up my pen. The headmaster introduced me to them, then, one by one, introduced them to me. I rapidly noted names or sometimes just letters next to where they were to sit. I tried to fix faces with the names but knew that would take longer. When the headmaster left, I told them to sit and began my talk.

"The basis of history is of course human memory. Events, circumstances, people, all can be remembered, even though the remembrance is almost always flawed. Our observations and especially our knowledge are always incomplete. Memories fade or are displaced by other memories, so we all sometimes get things wrong. And of course our transmission of events, circumstances, and so forth is also always incomplete. We cannot convey everything, all the circumstances, ever. Yet this information is conveyed from generation to generation and eventually becomes written down in books." I picked up the text, "This interests us because we are a curious species. Moreover, by considering how our ancestors behaved, how they met the challenges of their days, we hope to decide how we may best meet the challenges of ours, for there always are and will be challenges to meet."

"So, we first must learn what others, the writer or writers of texts, consider to have happened. As to the significance, the moral conclusions, these we may judge for ourselves. But, then we must examine the written record sceptically to see if what is written is correct. Usually of course it will be. Some document called the *Magna Carta* certainly existed – we have some copies of it to this day – but some of the details associated with it may be mistaken. Some historians point out that the original writers, the original sources, had biases, Caesar for example, so their accounts need to be read with that in mind. But, and this is important, it is likely, not certain, that at least the facts noted are correct. Legends, for example, once divested of what we consider the miraculous or supernatural, may, indeed probably do, contain a kernel, a seed, a nexus of fact."

I then began questioning each student about Stonehenge, what they knew, what had been written and what was likely to be true, remembering the discussion I had on the subject so long ago with the history master at Earl's Cross. I managed to get them to the same conclusion, pointed out some implications: there were people and civilizations in the Isles before the Celts, and we knew almost nothing about them. The time being nearly over, I gave them their assignments, chapters to be read. One of the troublemakers objected that they had covered this before, to which I responded that the man I was replacing had said otherwise, but, even if the student's statement were true, rereading the chapters in question would hardly be an unbearable burden. I beamed at them, again as insincerely as I was capable of.

The remaining classes were younger and less disposed to question my authority. However, by the end of the day I was soaked with sweat and very tired. And it was only Monday. I sat at my place, reviewing what I was going to do tomorrow, and writing down outlines. The building was to be locked up and I had to leave. I wandered about until I found a place where I could eat, and did so, continuing my outlines.

It was past eight and full dark when I emerged from the restaurant. While not a gourmet experience, as Eddie would put it, I would survive another day, nutritionally speaking. I went to the house, found everything dark and let myself in. Evidently my landlady was an early riser. Once in my pyjamas, I lay down after setting the alarm.

I was drifting off when the door to my room opened and a figure dressed in a nightgown, a woman, entered. She pulled off the nightgown – definitely a woman – and pulled back the covers on me, lay down and pulled me onto her. I was in my normal night-time masculine condition, opened my pyjama front and mounted her. I tried not to hurry but she seemed very eager, rising quickly to what I recognized as satisfaction, although its characteristics were different from Elsie's. I released very shortly thereafter, her excitement communicating itself to me, and we lay together, breathing hard. Then she pushed me off her with surprising strength, got up, picked up the nightgown and walked out. I opened the door as she went into the bathroom after turning on the light, and got a most entertaining view of her bare bottom disappearing into the bathroom. It was my landlady, I was almost certain, although not a word had been spoken.

The next morning, after cleaning myself, etc., and dressing, I emerged with my valise to find her in the kitchen with the maid and the boy. I was confused by her pushing me off her so soon after we finished and wondered if she was dissatisfied by my performance. I stood in the kitchen door, unsure of what to say. Eventually she looked at me as though it was a duty and not a welcome one and I felt compelled to say, "Good morning, Madam," to which she replied, "Good morning, Major," as formally as one human being could address another. Thoroughly confused, I nodded to the maid, who ignored me, smiled at the boy, who was asleep, and went over to the school.

My second day I assigned written work, particularly to the sixth formers. I told them they were expected to be able to write and practice was the only way this could be learned. My message was not well received, but I was insistent. Provided they did the work assigned, I told them, I would most conscientiously examine, comment on and correct what they had done. If they intended to succeed in anything, they had to be able to muster the push to do what was needful. Again, a message not well received but I intended to keep sending it.

This day I had some papers to mark and sat doing so, then preparing for next day, until I had to leave. I found a new place to eat, and dawdled over the meal, working until I felt the management wanted me to go, and did. This night I was not visited, which piqued my vanity, but, being tired again, slept until the alarm went off. Up betimes, as Pepys put it, and back to business. I was beginning to suspect that teaching, if done conscientiously, was very time consuming if not physically draining.

———

Friday afternoon I declared holiday after the students left and went over to Eddie and Christine's to see if I had any letters. There was one, from Pope, the manic cricketer. He was in hospital: a blister on a foot had become, in his words, "troublesome" and he asked me to visit. I wondered at this, we had hardly been intimates, but decided to go Saturday evening. This evening I simply felt too tired, and I had papers to mark.

Friday evening my landlady – I could almost swear it was she – visited me again. Evidently my performance Monday was acceptable after all. Once she had left the bathroom, I went in to take my weekly bath ration. I noticed apparatus that Eddie once told me was for contraceptive douching. This might suggest I had a predecessor, or then again it might not.

* * *

The hospital was much less busy, thank the Gods. I found Pope in a separate room, a small one to be sure, but private. He looked odd to me, as though he had been out in the sun, and he gave the impression he felt he was dying. We talked. I was surprised to learn he was an orphan like me. An aunt had brought him up, most unwillingly I gathered. I realized that his only happy moments had been on the cricket field. He had written to me because he had learned from someone that I too was an orphan, although my childhood at the Pastons was nearly as bad as could be, and my happier moments mostly came from books. I left after an hour, deciding to ask Eddie about his symptoms.

As I was leaving, I encountered Alice's sister – what was her name? She recognized me but I saw she was a little shaky. In fact she began to collapse, and I caught her by her elbows and turned towards an older nurse and asked or rather demanded that a wheeled chair be brought. The woman, I belatedly realized, was Matron. She looked a bit put out, but did call to another nurse to bring the chair. I asked Miss Millwood if she had just had the flu. She said she was better, which I, as the expert *in loco* as I put it, disputed. I told her she needed to return immediately to bed and stay there a week. A week, I repeated, and told her to have water at hand to drink as desired. The chair came, I helped set her in it, and she was wheeled away. She whispered – I think she was starting the coughing phase – "Thank you" as she disappeared.

* * *

Sunday I spent working, preparing what I was to say and assign Monday and perhaps Tuesday. Eddie and Christine had invited me to dinner, and of course, as I told them, being the soul of politeness would not refuse. After the meal, which helped erase the gastronomic experiences of Monday through Saturday, I described Pope's symptoms to Eddie. He looked concerned, thought the blister had become infected, and that Pope seemed to be having trouble with his kidneys. Kidney failure, said Eddie, was fatal. I returned to my lodging apprehensive for Pope.

* * *

The second Friday of my teaching had me feeling much like I had during university: the target of escalating tasks and expectations. I was working later and later and getting less sleep, a process not helped by my landlady's, or whoever my visitor was, appetites. Every third or fourth day was the routine. I enjoyed the sex but with Elsie there was a human element: we talked, however superficially. With my visitor, it was as though I was considered an appliance, a venereal machine, nothing more. Certainly the daytime routine never varied. This annoyed, yet somehow intimidated me; I couldn't seem to speak to my landlady about any of this, or indeed about anything. I paid down my ten shillings, got my receipt and went my way. The only rebellion I attempted was to bathe after sex, Friday or no. However, since the boiler seemed to be off when it wasn't Friday, this experience was quite unpleasant and very quickly conducted.

* * *

Friday evening I found another note from Pope. The hand and the message were consistent: he was failing. I decided to visit Saturday, as before, since it was late when I went round to Eddie and Christine's.

* * *

Saturday afternoon I went again to the hospital, probably for the last time, I thought. Indeed, he seemed well on his way. He knew he was dying, but thanked me for coming. There wasn't much I could say. After a few minutes, I went out and saw an elderly woman sitting in a chair. She was crying. I asked if she was Pope's aunt. She said she was. As urgently as I could, I begged, exhorted, ordered her to go in and tell Pope that she loved him, cared for him and would mourn his passing. "Do it now, for God's sake," I said. She got to her feet and went in through the door I held for her. I went along the corridor, and had just gotten to the end when I heard a loud wail. I went on; the nurses would comfort her as best they could. They had much experience of that. I was saddened beyond expression. Perhaps the aunt had trouble expressing love, but it was hard, hard on both of them to be separated forever without that last tender exchange.

The lobby was nearly empty, except for the porter, a nurse I didn't know and Miss Millwood, the latter two talking. When Miss Millwood saw me, she excused herself to the other nurse and came over to me. I watched her critically, but she seemed steady on her feet and was not coughing. I asked her how she felt, and she said she had recovered and thanked me again for my help. I said it was nothing and we sat together in two chairs near a wall.

I commented that at first, I had been afraid I would die, but as it grew worse, I was afraid I wouldn't. She smiled and said she had felt the same way. Then she asked about the man I was visiting. At this point, the conversational sun became hidden by clouds. I said, "He was one of my officers. He was mad for cricket, which I never played. I didn't know he was an orphan like me. He grew up with an aunt, who he felt didn't really want him about. He said the only place he felt free, felt at home was on a cricket pitch. I found the aunt outside his room, weeping. Evidently she had more affection for him than he realized. I urged, begged her to go in to him and tell him she cared for him. I don't know if he heard her before he died. I hope so."

She nodded, and then hesitated. Finally, she said, "When you visited Millwood, I heard some commotion involving our dogs. When I went outside later I saw scraps of black cloth and blood stains on the ground. One of the dogs was injured and had to be killed. Were you attacked? Father and Mother and my sister didn't want to believe it."

I felt anger again, after so many years. "Yes, I was attacked. I grabbed one of the dogs who was tearing a chunk out of my leg and threw him on the others. That discouraged them. If you like, I will raise my trouser leg to show you the scars." I had half risen as had she. When I looked at her, she seemed stricken, and I felt instantly contrite. "Miss Millwood," I said, "Please forgive me, for making so much of a trifle." I sat down again, as did she. The silence lengthened. Finally I said, in a reflective tone, "I have been better received." This provoked a laugh, and she asked, "And where was that, pray?" "In France," I replied, "By the Imperial German Army." We smiled at each other: evidently we were on good terms again.

She then said, "It was outrageous to treat anyone that way, still less someone who had been invited there. As a member of the household, I assure you it was unintended and apologize to you on behalf of my family." I was a bit impressed: her statement took some courage. So I said, "Your apology is accepted, so I think we may consider the matter closed."

After a short silence, I said, "When I was wounded, two years ago..." She broke in, "Where were you wounded?" I said, "Right shoulder, blighty wound. Anyway, I saw something of what you nurses had to go through, and realized how hard your duties were. To see what you had to see, do what you had to do, hour after hour, day after day, must have taxed you emotionally and physically, and I honour you and your sisterhood, and thank you for that service." She flushed with pleasure, and I suddenly realized she was rather a pretty girl. She was about to reply, but Matron came in and called her to some duty in some ward. I thought she looked a bit vexed, but she went, of course. I sat some time, thinking, when the doors opened and Pope's aunt, still crying, carrying his personal effects, including a cricket bat, came out escorted by a nurse and orderly. I got up and opened the door for them all, the last service I could perform for her. Then I put on my coat and hat and went out into the winter darkness. I had papers to mark, tests to prepare and lectures to prepare also.

* * *

Eddie and Christine had invited me over that Sunday, along with David and Esther. They had brought a bottle of wine for Eddie and Christine. I was nonplussed: Eddie and Christine had been hospitable to me in so many ways, my things were still stored in their box room, that I felt I had been inconsiderate in not thinking of something to bring. After the meal and a very enjoyable conversation, I left with David and Esther. Once outside, I asked them what I could bring, some token of friendship and esteem. David and Esther looked at each other, and then David suggested I might get a bottle of champagne or brandy. I asked for names, as I knew nothing of wine or spirits. David gave me two or three names which I wrote down, or I would never be able to remember them, and we separated.

My life had settled into a routine: struggling to stay ahead of six groups of students in various forms, periodic sex with a woman who was either my landlady or an extremely randy twin sister. By day, there was no hint of what the situation was. Sundays I was a guest, generally with David and Esther, at Eddie and Christine's. This was a diversion from my academic duties, but one I embraced. The food and company were, I was certain, unsurpassed. I had taken David's advice and brought his recommendations, which were gratefully received, I was happy to see. Another Sunday, I had brought some expensive Swiss chocolates, also well received, so I felt a little better about dining there so often.

* * *

I generally went by Eddie and Christine's Friday evenings to see if I had any mail. I had explained to them about my landlady's strong desire that, aside from sleeping there, no hint whatever of my presence or existence should be given. They were good natured about that as about everything else. This evening, there was no mail, but Eddie, whose hours had become more regular and rational since his marriage, met me and told me he had tickets in his family's box for a performance of Bizet's *Carmen* tomorrow evening. Christine, he explained, was feeling a trifle indisposed and he was going to keep company with her rather than attend.

I was concerned about Christine, but Eddie said there was no problem: he said Christine was in the early stages of pregnancy, and wanted to stay at home tomorrow. I was delighted, congratulated them both, said this was the very best news, that I needed to get married, have a child so we could talk about a match, sexes permitting. Eddie laughed, he was delighted also. He gave me the set of four tickets, said David and Esther had been invited to use two of them. I decided to ask Miss Millwood, although it was very short notice. I went to the hospital, asked for her, then realized I didn't know her first name and asked the woman on duty at the desk what it was. I explained that I knew the family, which was in a sense true, but had never learned the first name of the younger daughter. A reasonable request, I thought, but the woman at the desk seemed to think my request was in aid of some vile machination, or possibly a compromise of some War Office secret, and refused. I attempted to reason with the woman, aware that she would call the porter (and the constables, perhaps) if I pressed too hard. Fortunately, Matron appeared, and despite my brusqueness to her earlier, told the woman to show me Miss Millwood's full name. It was Frances, Frances Margaret.

* * *

The bearer of the name herself appeared shortly after, and I explained the purpose of my visit. I apologized for the short notice, saying I had just gotten the tickets. I emphasized the opera, one of the two most popular staged (*The Marriage of Figaro* was the other, but I thought it better not to mention that), and the fact we would have box seats. She looked at me, considering, then said, "Wait here," and disappeared. I waited for what seemed a long time, but Frances reappeared, said she had exchanged duties with another nurse, and could attend. I showed her the tickets, told her what the arrangements were, and we settled on a time. The performance started at 8, so I would call on her at 7.

I went back to Eddie and Christine's to get my valise, and then headed for a place to eat that allowed me to linger and work. I had thought of Frances essentially because she seemed reasonably friendly and because she was the only eligible woman I knew. I didn't consider my landlady; she might be eligible but was certainly not willing to be seen socially with such as I. At least I could bathe beforehand.

Saturday afternoon, late, I went to Eddie and Christine's, changed into my Opera Suitables, got my field glasses, and took a taxi to the hospital. Frances was waiting, I was surprised to see; I thought I would have to send for her. She looked very nice, the first time I had seen her out of her nurse's uniform. We got into the same taxi, which hadn't left, and travelled to the Hall. I asked her what operas she had seen, and she said none, but had attended several concerts. She seemed fond of music, said she had an old wind-up gramophone and some nearly worn out recordings at home. I asked what recordings. She replied, "Some Mozart arias and Beethoven's 5th Symphony." I said I had heard some of the pieces and liked them. Then we arrived. She seemed excited, and I was eager to see the performance also. Inside, I bought two librettos – one for David and Esther, I explained – and we leafed through them while we waited.

I waved to them when they arrived. When they reached us, I introduced Frances: "Miss Frances Millwood." I saw David glance at me: the name was of course known to him. "Miss Esther Goldman. Mr David Cohen." I paused, was grandiloquent, "I, of course, am well known to all." David said, "Too well, perhaps. The tickets, of course, are far more important. Did you remember to bring them?" We stared at each other, trying not to smile. Finally, I produced the tickets, handed two to David, who handed one to Esther. I gave one of my two to Frances: "In case we are separated." I gave David a libretto and we ushered the two women to the box. David and I had been there before.

Inside we settled in. I put the glasses between the four of us. Each couple had a libretto open between them. Ten minutes to go. I pointed out the manufacturer to my companions, and told them that Government had apparently bought several thousand through Swiss firms after the war had started. This provoked some discussion, terminated when the overture began.

The ladies went to the loo at intermission, which seemed an invariable custom, leaving David and me to talk. He said he was surprised at the name of my companion. I explained she was the younger sister, that she seemed nice and that anyway she was the only eligible woman I knew. David asked about Christine and I passed on Eddie's news. David was also delighted; we agreed we each needed to marry, produce a child, and begin talking about a match.

When the ladies sat down, Frances commented she had seen details with the glasses she had never seen before. I turned sharply towards her and said I wasn't sure I wanted to hear an explanation of that remark. Everyone laughed, and Frances said she meant details of the sets, the shoes and costumes the singers wore, things like that. Esther said sometimes it was better to see with the imagination, at a distance as it were, but when I asked, the others liked having the glasses.

The opera over, the curtain calls taken, we went outside and agreed to eat at the Jewish place, which, David assured us, would be open. A taxi was secured; David said my glare at the drivers seemed to have almost magical results. I explained it was the result of my teaching technique, and had a similar effect on students. I did not explain.

The restaurant was indeed open and as lively as ever. I thought people were going to start dancing, the place was so cheery. Frances seemed to enjoy the atmosphere. We sat and ordered. David passed on my news about Christine to Esther, while I explained what we were talking about to Frances. Esther seemed delighted by the news. She looked significantly at David, who took the hint, and, after some hemming and hawing, told us that he and Esther were to be married in a month.

I threw my arms in the air, said, "By God, well played, David, very well played. I'll offer you both what I offered Eddie and Christine, congratulations and best wishes. You," to Esther, "get the best wishes." After some laughter, I said, "Two pieces of very welcome news in two days. I think we need a toast to the prospective bride and groom." I got the characterful waitress and ordered an appropriate wine, saying I, myself, would even take a sip in their honour. David wasn't through, however. After another look from Esther, he told me I was conscripted as Best Man.

"What about Eddie?" I asked. David said, "When we decided, we couldn't be certain Eddie would be available." That was true: his assistant was a help, but emergencies still sometimes kept him at work. So I said, "As long as it doesn't involve any swordplay." I pronounced the "w" in "sword". "I mean repelling unsuccessful suitors, raiders, importunate insurance salesmen and the like." Esther was a bit puzzled: she asked, "Is that how it is pronounced?" I adjusted my coat, looked mildly affronted, and said, "That is how it is spelled," as if that settled the matter. Seeing the amusement on the faces of Frances and David, Esther, who, I had noted, was quite sharp, caught on and smiled.

David gave me the time and place and told me my duties, basically handing him the ring at the appropriate moment, and then placing a glass tumbler down so he could crush it with his foot. He told me of the symbolism. I nodded, said, "I am delighted and honoured and will, of course, do my best, even to the extent of showing up sober and reasonably dressed." I added grandly, "No man can do more."

The wine arrived. I had ordered a bottle, as I knew David liked wine. It was opened and four glasses poured. I took mine, glanced at Frances, and proposed a toast, "To the happy couple." We drank. The wine tasted unpleasant, as my few sips in the past had. But I drank the glass, hoping David and Esther appreciated my gesture. Frances drank her wine, and accepted a refill. Our meals arrived, and we ate. Frances seemed impressed by the food, which was quite up to standard.

I paid. With the wine, it was quite a sum, but I insisted: their news merited no less, although, as I warned them, this was the last time – to celebrate their engagement, that is. We separated outside the restaurant, David with the rest of the bottle of wine and his fiancée and I with Frances.

I asked Frances, "Taxi or walk?" "Walk" she said, and after we were underway, "It has been weeks since I had a good walk." I commented, "Good is one way of putting it." It would be several miles, although if she got tired, I could get a taxi. We were some streets along before I realized I was walking at my normal clip, but Frances was easily matching my pace, recalling my first meeting with her sister.

We were silent. A number of topics were out of bounds: my family, because I had none; her family, for obvious reasons. Then I remembered she had an older brother – after a bit, I even remembered his name, Richard, and that he was an officer in the Indian Army. I said, "I am reluctant to ask about your brother." Frances smiled, "Richard is well, thank God. He served in Maude's campaign. He is lieutenant-colonel now, and is marrying a woman, Selena Patterson. She is a daughter of missionaries. I've never met her, but we exchanged letters. I don't know when we will see them. I suppose Richard will someday be able to get leave." She added, "The player I told you about: he sent me the money for it – it was second-hand, of course; I think the recordings were about fifth or sixth-hand – but it was most generous of him; he certainly didn't have much money then."

After a few more steps, she said, "He calls me his Magpie. My middle name," she explained, "is Margaret." I nodded. She looked at me and said, "You knew that, didn't you?" I said, "I was never told what your first name was, and rather than have to introduce you as Miss Anonymous or Incognito Millwood, I asked the woman at the front what it was. It seemed an innocuous request, I even showed her the tickets, but she apparently suspected me of some deeply discreditable motive – which," I turned towards Frances, "shows her to be an excellent judge of character, or rather lack of it." Frances smiled. "I really thought she was going to call the constables, but Matron intervened, and made her show me the nurses' register. I thanked her, but really should apologize to her for my brusqueness towards her a few weeks ago."

Frances asked me how I enjoyed the opera. I said I could understand why it was so popular. The combination of melodies and rhythms drew one into the music. The plot, I said, was at least as plausible as opera plots usually were. Frances wondered why Spanish music had rhythmic patterns so different from Northern European music, was that the influence of the Moors? This triggered a disquisition: I thought it was the composer's modification of the intrinsic music of the people there. I commented that Moorish, that is, Northern African or Moroccan music was, I believed, entirely different. I went on to note that some parts of Europe, Sicily for example, had been under Moorish control for some time but didn't show similar musical patterns.

I was caught up by now in one of my favourite arguments: invasions, which of course had occurred, had much less effect on indigenous populations than historians tended to suppose. Before the invention of the steamship and railways, movements of peoples were much more limited. My standard example was, I said, the Viking incursions. A raid by, say, 100 long-ships would have been a very significant effort by them, but how many men would have been involved? Assuming, I said, 50 men per ship, and, I thought, that would probably have involved some crowding, so we were talking about 5,000 men at most. This would be a large number certainly, but not enough to overrun a shire, still less exterminate the population. So invaders would have basically killed the indigenous leaders and imposed themselves on the rest of the population, as the Normans had done.

At this point, I caught myself and apologized to Frances, noting that I was, or had some aspirations to be, a professional historian, and it was all her own fault, asking me anything that had any trace of relevance to something historical. She said she found my analysis interesting, but did I think, then, that most peoples were descendants of the original population? I said I thought it likely. The languages spoken, I said, seemed to change fairly easily and readily, although some traces of the original languages spoken might linger in place names, again one of my favourite theses. I said that one of my masters had liked a paper I had written to this effect so much he had suggested I do more research, rewrite it and submit it to a professional journal to try to get it published. I went on to say that once I had time, I would try to do so, since its publication would make it easier to get a job at a university. I said that I was interested in doing the paper because – I hesitated, and then continued – it was my nature, that I was basically a scholar; I found ideas and research both frustrating but fascinating.

Frances asked if I was enjoying the teaching I was doing. I said I found myself in the same state I spent much of my time in university in: one or two weeks behind.

After a few more steps, I said, "I get the feeling, it is not even an impression, that the students seem less respectful of authority, I mean more openly disrespectful of it. I suppose that is inevitable, given the conduct of the war by authority, but perhaps it has implications, profound implications, in terms of politics." Frances asked, "Do you think we shouldn't have entered it?" I answered, "I now think we had to; I was originally hesitant because I had a German friend, my first real friend – I hope and pray he survived – and the thought of meeting him on some battlefield seemed grotesque."

I thought further, then said, "Teaching is inherently frustrating because you basically have to force, coerce, inspire, trick, whatever tactic works, to get the students to make the effort needed to learn. They must do the hard work. I really can't make it easy, just perhaps a bit easier."

Frances asked, "Was your father a schoolmaster?" I said, "Yes. When he and my mother were killed, we were all on our way for him to take a position at the school I eventually attended, Earl's Cross school. I was allowed to see the letter he wrote, applying for the position. I wanted to keep it, it was the only thing of my father's I had ever seen, but of course couldn't, as it was part of the Files, and the fellow from the school who showed it me reacted to my request as if I had suggested, well, never mind." Frances was amused, "And your grandfather? Was he a teacher, too?" "I don't think so: my father attended Rugby school on scholarship, so I imagine there wasn't much money in his family. That condition seems hereditary, at least so far."

I asked, "And your own ambitions? Nursing?" Frances said, "For the moment. I've been asked to stay on by the administration. But nursing was originally my way of contributing to our cause. I have enjoyed being self-sufficient, not dependent on my family, but I have mixed feelings about staying on." I nodded. Looking ahead, I could see we were approaching the hospital. When we arrived, I thanked her for her company and forbearance at listening to my sermonizing. She smiled – she had a sweet smile, I thought – and said the opera was magnificent, and the evening extremely interesting and entertaining. We hesitated, and then I said, checking my watch, "Good morning, Frances." She let me hold the door for her. I removed my hat and she said "Good morning, Matthew" in reply and was gone. I walked back to my lodging and to bed. The visitation by my landlady (or her randy twin sister) was not scheduled, somewhat to my relief, for I was tired.

I went to Eddie and Christine's both to change back into my School Presentable clothes as well as to dine with them and David and Esther. I didn't bring anything this time but knew what I would next time: a bottle of the "kosher" pickles we ate at our favourite restaurant. Eddie and Christine told the three of us that they would be dining at their families' to announce Christine's pregnancy, but would like to host not only the three of us but also my opera guest if she would be willing to come, in two weeks. I undertook to ask her, but had, I realized, no idea of whether she had a suitor or not. I decided to ask her this evening, at least so she could clear her schedule.

* * *

I asked for her at the desk, and was told she was on the wards. The woman at the desk, not the one I had trouble with earlier, was reluctant to send for her but finally agreed to send a note from me, asking for a moment of her time. Frances appeared, smiled when she saw me (I smiled back) and I asked if she would grace us with her presence at dinner at my friends Dr Edward and Mrs Christine Partington in two weeks' time. I explained the two weeks part. I said there would be good food and plenty of it and good company and plenty of that, to which she would add. She said she would be happy to come. I gave her the time – three Sunday afternoon – and we agreed to meet then. That night, another session with whomever it was I was having sex with, and Monday at 5:30 it was as though I had gotten no sleep at all for days. The combined mills of academe and Venus were getting too much for me.

* * *

The following Saturday afternoon, late, I had checked at Eddie and Christine's for mail – none – and was walking to find a place I could very slowly eat while working. I was hoping I could at last begin, not to catch up, but at least not to fall further behind. A man walking ahead turned for some reason, saw me and called

220

me by name. I recognized him from university, not as a Regular but as an Occasional. No matter: these days, seeing an old acquaintance was sufficient basis for joy, and we shook hands as though we had been friends since childhood. He invited me into a nearby pub for a pint, and it is a measure of my happiness at seeing him among the living that I accepted, and even, once inside, very slowly drank the stuff. Greater love hath no man, I said to myself.

We rather gingerly asked after people we had known, a process punctuated by sombre silences, then about each other. He had obtained a medical degree and was working at a hospital for the insane. As practitioners will, he talked about some of his patients, encouraged no doubt by my patience, developed from years of listening to Eddie. These illnesses were however much less easily treated if at all. He began telling me about a Guards captain who basically lay staring at nothing visible, except when he was crying. He had been brought there from Second Ypres and been in hospital since. His wife and small son visited him every Saturday, but he simply ignored them. After two hours or so, they would go away.

I was sufficiently shaken by his account to take a large sip, which I regretted, but asked if the child was about three or four. Yes was the answer. Was the wife very pretty? Yes, again. I mentioned my landlady's name. My host looked around, leaned over and said that was confidential. I nodded and said I was slightly acquainted with the family (which was true enough), and asked if any treatment might be efficacious (I had picked up medical jargon). He said people were thinking of electrical shocks, but no one knew how this should be done, still less if it would work. I suggested getting his wife to talk to him while she was there, just about household things or things they had done together in the past, just be persistent. Or have men from his company, if any survived, come by and talk. He considered and said it was worth a try. Perhaps that might break through whatever memories had him in their grip. I had some idea of what those memories were like, but simply nodded. We finished our drinks, arose and told each other how glad we were to see each other, which was absolutely true. Then we went our separate ways, I very thoughtful.

Unlike some men who gloried in sleeping with other men's wives or sweethearts, I was desperately sorry for my landlady's husband, and hoped he might be restored to her arms and his home and his child, his family. I was beginning to get some insight into my landlady's behaviour, if indeed it was she I was having sex with, and the more I thought about it, the more uneasy I became. Still, it would be very awkward moving now. I told myself I really didn't have the time to spare. And I knew I would continue having sex with her whenever she made an appearance. Only instead of what had been fornication, which was bad enough, I was now a participant in adultery, which was a great deal worse.

That night, a day ahead of schedule, she visited me again. I had been considering kissing her after we had finished, anything to contact the woman, but now I realized at some level in my mind that I had better leave things as they were. So I did.

* * *

The following Saturday, late afternoon, I went to the store where the pickles we all liked so much were sold, and bought a bottle for Eddie and Christine. I was sure they would be well received even if David and Esther also brought one. Then I carried it, with my valise, to a reasonably tolerant restaurant to dine and work.

* * *

I called on Frances at the appointed time, with my bottle concealed in a bag. I showed her the bottle, and she also thought the present would be well received.

So it was. Eddie and Christine were delighted, and proposed sharing the contents about, which made the delight unanimous. I introduced Frances, and although Eddie and Christine were curious, having met the older sister, they were aware, through Esther, probably, of her existence. Christine showed Frances Eddie's gramophone and collection of recordings, which Frances found fascinating. Eddie and Christine had a few new ones which attracted my attention. The housekeeper-cook pushed in the cart with the meal – roast beef and Yorkshire pudding again, although no one complained. I helped her with the serving, as I had during my leaves, which she appreciated but scolded me for, although I told her I was justifying my share of the tips. We had some music on, of the not-compelling-silence-for variety, and ate and talked.

Frances, after two or perhaps three glasses of wine, told us of her problems with the hospital administration. Although it was amusing, the way she told it, I was also annoyed that she should be treated in such a way. But I said nothing. David and Esther's wedding were discussed. As I expected, Christine would certainly attend but Eddie could not guarantee when or even if he would be there, Saturdays being rather busy for him. He said he would do his best, as he wanted to dance with Christine: it had been years, he said. Christine said she would keep a few spaces open on her card. Eddie asked David about honeymoon plans, and David said they would visit the Lake District. I asked if they had looked into a place to stay, and Esther said they would stay at a place which was highly recommended, although pricy. David noted that the price included breakfast and dinner, so was not so bad. I couldn't really imagine David doing much hiking with his artificial lower leg, but he seemed fairly mobile whenever I had seen him recently. It did sound nice and I wondered if I would ever be able to squire a bride about there or anywhere.

After the meal and some more music, Frances and I went on our way. She took my arm, which I quite liked; it seemed in a way an intimate gesture. After we had gotten into our stride, I commented, "Whatever are those people thinking about, treating you in such a fashion? How many years have you been serving as a nurse? Two years? Three?" Frances said, "Just fewer than three." The way she said it hinted there was more to the situation than I thought, something she didn't want to explain, so I shifted the direction of the conversation. "I thought that intelligent administration consisted of getting people who knew their jobs, getting them what they thought they needed to do their jobs, then making sure they were allowed to do their jobs." Frances said, "That is the ideal, Matthew."

We walked on a bit in silence, and then I said, "Too often these people try to play the bully." Frances looked over at me and asked, "How did you deal with people like that, in the Army I mean?" I said, "You salute, kiss their ring, salaam three times, then withdraw, stopping every three paces to bow again, and never letting them see you backside." A few steps. "Then," I went on, "I would go do whatever I thought was best to do in the first place." Frances was amused. "That is with relatively junior people. With generals, the procedure is nearly the same, except you kiss something else."

Frances stopped, doubled over with laughter. I was laughing, too. Eventually we were able to resume walking. "My dear Miss Millwood, you surely were not imagining I was implying anything capable of an indelicate interpretation, were you?" Frances, still laughing, said, "Of course not, Matthew." I said, "Then you would be profoundly and routinely mistaken." We both laughed.

A little farther on, I said, "You do understand you are also invited to David and Esther's wedding? I hope you can come with me. I shall need encouragement to perform my duties." Frances said she would attend with me, then. She said she knew a few Jewish nurses but had never attended a Jewish wedding. I said I had never been inside a synagogue or, except for church parades at Earl's Cross, a church. Frances asked if I was an atheist. I frowned, thinking, and then finally said, "I am confused. I do feel I should believe, and I think I want to believe, yet was never brought up to it, despite, or considering the character of the vicar in the house, because of growing up in a parish house." "Was he such a bad man?" Frances asked. I said, "I found out when I turned 21 that he and a lawyer friend of his got a £2,000 settlement from the railroad company or someone supposedly for my support, but they embezzled nearly all the money for themselves. Also, I eventually realized they were sodomites, and but for the protection of the vicar's wife and the cook, would have used me for their enjoyment. My first few years there were spent hiding from the two of them." Frances said, "My God, Matthew." Silence for a few paces, and then I said, "Well, I was able to claim £146 odd and as for the other, I did escape their attentions. It could have been a great deal worse."

I was thinking about the wedding. I asked Frances, "I am unsure if some sort of present to the bride and groom is required or at least acceptable, and if so, what sort of present." Frances said, "It isn't necessarily the custom. But perhaps something, silverware or table crystal, I am sure would be acceptable." I suggested, "Perhaps Christine should be consulted. Come to think of it, I never thought to give them anything. Of course I was in France when it happened." Frances said she would talk to Christine about all this, if I wished. I said I would be obliged if she would. She might send me a note, using Eddie and Christine's address, letting me know what was expected of me.

Frances asked if all my mail was supposed to go to their house. I said, "Yes. At the place where I lodge, I am not really supposed to exist. I really don't know what would happen if a letter addressed to me were to arrive there, and don't want to find out." Frances looked at me inquiringly. "The location is ideal. I can easily get to the school as soon as the doors are unlocked, go into the room I teach in, sit down and absolutely focus on what I am to do and how I am to do it. My effectiveness, such as it is, would be a great deal less if I lived much further away."

We proceeded in silence a street or two, and then Frances asked, "How long had Eddie and Christine known each other?" I said, "All their lives. They grew up together. Eddie mentioned their dancing together. They were in dancing classes together and were partners. Both families wanted the match. Eddie himself told me once that he had been in love with Christine as soon as he could be in love with anyone. He was badly hurt when she became engaged to another man."

Frances asked what had happened to the other man. I said, "Killed at Passchendaele." Silence. Then I commented, "I think Christine has been in a sort of rebellion against her family. Her coolness towards Eddie was one manifestation, her decision to go to university instead of marrying Eddie when she left preparatory school, another. As to the fellow she fell in love with, I saw him about once or twice, he was also at university, but never met him. When he was killed, I think Christine bowed to the inevitable, although I understand the wedding was at a registry rather than a big church affair, which might be her way again of asserting her independence."

More silence. "Despite her reluctance to accommodate her family, I truly believe, without saying anything or knowing anything about her fiancé, that she really made the best choice.

Eddie is my friend, but I have always found him to be a very good, capable, compassionate and generous man." Frances said, "I think Christine is genuinely fond of him and perhaps more than that." I replied, "It will take time, but I think she will grow to love him. And he does need her love. She is and has been at the centre of his thoughts for a long time."

We walked on. I had been about to relate David's romantic history, when it occurred to me that describing his jilting might be a bit near the mark, so kept silent. This was broken by Frances. She wondered if it were possible to completely recover from loss of a lover. I felt the conversation was heading rapidly into shoal waters, so tried to keep the tone as neutral as possible. I mentioned Jane Austen's opinions, expressed through her heroine Anne Elliot, about relative constancies of men and women. I added that this difference, from differences in level of activity, or busyness, was probably less as more women were working outside their homes, but said I felt that it varied so much between individuals, that generalizations were pointless.

Frances persisted, asking if finding a new love after loss of a previous one (and by loss, I began to understand she meant loss by death), was not somehow disloyal. I told her what I had told Eddie about true love desiring the happiness of the survivor, not his or her misery. But I acknowledged this was a mere point of view, although that was really, so far as we could know, all that mattered, perhaps. We arrived at the hospital, where I thanked her for her company. She asked if she wasn't keeping me from attention to my teaching duties. I said she was a major distraction and, I gallantly added, a most welcome one. She seemed pleased by my comment. After some hesitation, we said goodnight and I returned to my room.

Friday afternoon I visited at Eddie and Christine's. She had two suggestions of possible wedding presents. I wrote these down and told her I had never gotten anything for her and Eddie. She said nonsense, I had brought several things, although she added that if I was absolutely tormented by guilt – I interrupted, saying that was always true – that another bottle of the pickles would be welcome. I said a wish was a command, bowed and left.

* * *

David and Esther drank wine and one suggestion was a silver wine cooler, rather expensive, but I got it and the bottle of pickles Saturday afternoon. I took these over to Eddie and Christine's. She was glad to get the pickles – I vaguely recalled some legend about pregnant women and pickles – and undertook to wrap the wine cooler.

Eddie came in, said, "Aha", and I replied, "Aha, indeed", as had become our custom. He approved of the cooler and the pickles. He said he and Christine had bought a silver serving dish. He added, apologetically, that he and Christine were bidden to another conference of the two families in which names of the grandchild would hopefully be decided, so Sunday dinner was out. I nodded, said I could use the time preparing lectures and marking papers, which was true. Eddie went on that he thought frontier negotiations between adjoining sovereign states would take less time than the naming. Christine commented that she expected that, as a compromise, the child would wind up bearing six or seven names, and probably would employ, perhaps as a result, some nickname that was totally unrelated. Eddie looked at her and suggested that the obvious course then was to produce more children. Christine gave him a mock indignant look, but said the matter might be revisited, if he were good. Eddie protested he was always good. I added, "Except when he is better." This was received by smiles and I went about my business, leaving the cooler with them.

* * *

I had sent Frances a note outlining Saturday's schedule: I would call for her, travel with her to Eddie and Christine's, change into my Opera Presentables and accompany her, Christine, and the presents to the synagogue, in time, I prayed.

* * *

In the event, we were in fair, not good, time, to the obvious relief of the bride and groom. Eddie was with us, as it happened, so our party was complete. We were quickly instructed on custom: men wore hats, presents were quite acceptable, and I was given the ring and glass tumbler and told where I was to stand and when I was to place the tumbler where David could crush it with his good foot. David was nervous. I was very nervous. I asked him if he was sure no swords were necessary as I hadn't brought one. David affected chagrin, said he knew there was something he had forgotten to tell me but just then the ceremony began.

I had never been to a wedding before, so had no basis for comparison, but the bride was lovely and, since the service was in English, with some Hebrew thrown in, all went well. David shattered the tumbler as if he had been practicing for weeks, which may have been the case.

Food was served afterwards, quite good really, and there was music and dancing. Eddie and Christine waltzed very well I thought, as I watched. Frances, when I looked apologetically at her, said she had never had any dancing lessons. Then there was some sort of dance in a ring, and seeing David and Esther join, I took Frances's hand and we joined, too. The steps were simple enough even for me, so I danced my first dance at David and Esther's wedding.

Photos were taken: the bride; the groom; the bride and groom together; with the bride's family; with the groom's; with both; eventually with the wedding party (here I beckoned Frances to join); with a significant fraction of the population of London, it seemed. Finally, we threw rice at the newly married pair, which somehow did not seem a Jewish tradition. Then, as it was raining, the four of us went to Eddie and Christine's. There I returned to

School Presentable clothing and we all sat about listening to music and occasionally saying something. Since negotiations over names had reached a crisis point, no Sunday dinner invitation tomorrow, either. I shrugged. I still felt I needed all the time I could find, and Frances had a shift tomorrow. So, reluctantly, we said our goodbyes and thanks and I telephoned for a taxi as it was raining hard now.

Tuesday I was given a note from Christine while I was lecturing. Between classes, I read that a letter from a lawyer in Norwich had eventually migrated to their address. It had originally been sent to my address while at university and then was forwarded to the University, then to the War Office, finally to Eddie and Christine's. After class that afternoon, I went over to find Mrs Paston had died and left her estate to me. Evidently Mr Paston had died previously, at least I assumed so.

I thought. Saturday afternoon – Sunday were all that were available to me, and getting to Norwich early enough Saturday to be received was going to be touch-and-go. I checked the train schedule to be certain, and then wrote a note to the lawyer, not the one I had dealt with earlier, proposing to wait on him Saturday evening. I would probably have to visit the parish house, for the first time in how many years? Seven or nearly, I reckoned.

I gave the lawyer's letter to Christine, who was reading it when Eddie came in. "Aha" and "Aha, indeed" were our greetings. Eddie changed, asked Christine if she wanted wine, poured her a glass when she said yes, and poured himself one also. I was sipping a ginger beer, the first I had had since – the previous Saturday, actually. Eddie read the letter. I told them this provided me with camouflage: the money from the coins, already in bank, and the jewellery could be simply included in whatever had been left me by Mrs Paston, even if that were only six shillings sixpence. They nodded. Eddie asked if Mrs Paston seemed wealthy. I said no, so I didn't expect a great deal. I did think I would get the books, the books I had taught myself to read with, and asked them if I could have them shipped to their house and stored. Eddie said they could go in the box room, which, after all, was for boxes. I thanked them once more for their hospitality and kindness and thoughtfulness before leaving.

* * *

The lawyer was obliging enough to receive me late Saturday afternoon. He told me the books, her clothes and jewellery were mine. There was some money also; he didn't know how much yet. Perhaps £1,000. Mr Paston had indeed died last fall, of influenza. The lawyer didn't know Mrs Paston's cause of death. Mr Paston's estate was meagre and had gone to Mrs Paston.

There was now a motor bus to the village, or near enough, but Sundays there was only one trip, in the morning. I was tired, I seemed to be always tired, my landlady's demands were now every third day, which shouldn't have been that much a burden but for the class work which steadily pared the time I had for sleep, so I checked in at a hotel for the night. I had done some work on the journey up, but simply couldn't do any more after I had eaten.

The parish house looked much the same. Mrs Cord was still the housekeeper-cook. To my surprise, she greeted me as "Major". She seemed impressed by what she deemed my eminence. She explained that Mrs Paston had kept track of my doings in London and the Army, which touched me. I told her I would need to have the books boxed up, and she said she would get some lads to do this. I gave her some money for that, said I would be around probably next weekend. I also gave the address to which they should be sent.

She showed me Mrs Paston's jewellery box. I opened it. A couple of brooches, necklaces, some bracelets, sets of earrings and one or two rings. I pointed to one of the rings, and Mrs Cord said that was her wedding ring. She didn't want to be buried with that. I asked where she had been buried, and Mrs Cord said with her family, not beside her husband. I looked about and saw several picture frames, all empty. Understandable but very sad. Mrs Cord asked me for some of Mrs Paston's clothes. I looked at Mrs Cord: short and slight of frame, much like Mrs Paston. I opened the closet: there were a fair number of her dresses, coats, etc. and told Mrs Cord to take everything if she wished. She seemed very pleased. I asked where Mr Paston's clothes and personal effects were, and was told they had all been given away. Sad.

There was nothing more I could do today, and if Mrs Cord was diligent, and I thought I had at least obtained her gratitude, she would see to the books. So I took the jewellery box, and went out to wait for the return of the motor bus.

* * *

I returned the following weekend and found the books had been boxed and were awaiting shipment. I paid for the work done and the shipment to London. Mrs Cord, it seemed, had been asked to stay on by the incoming vicar, so at least was assured of a job. I had no idea where she would wear all those clothes; perhaps she would sell some – they were hers.

The following Friday I paid my usual visit to Eddie and Christine's to see if I had any letters and found the boxes of books had been delivered. Eddie was home, unusual at that hour of that day, and invited me for dinner. I accepted, of course. After the meal, we talked about Paston and his wife. I had decided the key to the fellow's character was he was a fraud. He pretended he was a man of God but was actually a thief, defrauding me of the bulk of the settlement, and a charlatan, defrauding his wife of her due and dreams as a woman and potential mother. There was no disagreement.

Christine told me that Frances had called, asking about me. I was a bit surprised. It occurred to me that perhaps I should take her to a concert. Busy as I was, and the nearly constant disruption of my routines aggravated the problem, I did want some good music. I asked them if they had the papers, so I could see what was on offer. There was one next weekend that looked promising, symphonic music that I thought I would like and some lieder of Schumann's that I was willing to hear, if only to extend my musical hearing experience.

* * *

The following day, I asked for Frances at the desk, endured the obvious disapproval of the woman behind it, and waited. Frances appeared, smiled and asked how matters were with the estate. I told her, and then asked if she would accompany me to a concert in one week. I showed her the program. She looked at the offerings, said she could attend the evening performance, so I said I would try to get tickets – no box seats this time, I warned. I would send her a note, I promised, telling her whether I got them and when I would call for her if I did.

* * *

We arrived at the concert hall in good time, got programs and found our seats. We talked. I was, I told her, going to have to spend even more time with my teaching preparations as end of term was approaching. I said, even with all the work piled up, I did need music, so, I rationalized, this concert. She smiled at my rationalization.

The symphonic part of the concert was very enjoyable. The soprano singing the lieder could have been a spear-carrier in one of Wagner's operas but certainly had a good voice. I didn't enjoy the songs as much because, I told myself, I wasn't as used to that form of music.

She was well received, and announced she would sing an encore, an English folk song. The name she gave meant nothing to me, but caused a sound of approval in the audience. She began to sing it, and suddenly I began to sweat, to breathe heavily. I had heard that song somewhere before, somewhere in my early life. I remembered where I had heard it, and the memory shook me to my soul. Frances noticed my reaction and I tried to steady myself, to endure the emotions the song called forth.

It ended to great applause. I had tears in my eyes, I was dabbing at them with my handkerchief, and my hands were shaking like they had after an action during the war. As I had done then, I tried stuffing them in my pockets. Also as was the case then, I couldn't conceal my shakiness, not from Frances. When the applause ended, we sat, letting people leave from both sides of us. At length, I was able to stand and move towards an exit, Frances close behind. I didn't want her to help support me; I thought I would be unmanned.

We got outside. Frances was trying, I noticed, to shield me from stares of passers-by. Eventually I was able to talk, to explain, "That song the soprano sang, I heard it before. I remembered my mother singing it as she packed our things for what would be her final journey. She had a beautiful voice, and I could see my father standing in the doorway, smiling at her. I could see he was proud of my mother, of her voice."

We were walking. I began to calm a bit, and suggested we eat somewhere, anywhere she wanted. Frances chose a fish and chips shop. We got the food, and tea – they only sold tea – and sat down. I had eaten about half of my meal, without tasting much;

perhaps there wasn't much taste to begin with. I looked at Frances, and said, "From time to time, I have thought of going to Somerset House to look up my birth records. They must be there. Do I have a middle name? My father did, so I must, but what is it? Do I really want to be known as Dobbs, M. (Norfolk) for the rest of my life? Where and exactly when was I born? What about my mother's family? I am almost certain to have relations. But I am very busy with my teaching, truly I am, so I put it off. And now I begin to think the reason I haven't is because I fear what memories of my early life, memories I thought lost, would have on me, and tonight's exhibition is not encouraging. Still," I looked down at my plate, and then up at her, "since it is something I should do, I will even have to do it." I looked at her, concerned. Did she despise my weakness? But she reached across the table and took my hand. "It isn't urgent, Matthew. Do it when you have the time. I think it is necessary, so I know you will do it." I felt warmed, comforted. I pressed her hand in turn and, after drinking some of the tea and grimacing, returned to the meal.

Frances took my arm again, and we walked back, all the way to the hospital, mostly in silence, but it was a companionable silence. At the hospital, we stood facing each other. I suddenly had an urge to kiss her, but didn't want to be forward. Finally, awkwardly, I thanked her again for her company, and said I would have to press my efforts with the students. Frances asked me how I dealt with the students. I said, "It depends on their attitude. If they are actually interested in the subject, or become interested, they are potential colleagues, essentially my equals, and I am just their guide. There aren't many of them. A larger number really doesn't care, and with them I feel rather helpless. I basically just try to keep them alert. A few seem antagonistic; I don't know why and frankly don't care. Those I try to keep off balance, on the defensive. This makes them sullen, but I consider that a compliment of sorts. Actually, now that I think about it, some of the antagonistic ones have come around, so perhaps there is hope for my efforts. I am speaking mostly of the upper sixth formers." Frances nodded. She seemed pleased, and I thought she was happy to get my mind on something else. I said I needed to rest up for the daily clash of wills, and said Goodnight. I couldn't interpret her expression, her face was partly and sporadically lit by lights from passing motor cars, but she replied, "Goodnight, Matthew." I held the door for her, suddenly reluctant to part, but she went in and away.

I walked back to my room. Tonight I wasn't scheduled to perform for my landlady, and I had very mixed emotions about that. I was thinking of Frances. Something was missing, something amiss with our relationship, and I realized that we had a relationship; she wasn't just a companion to escort to social events. This confused me.

I had indeed focused on my teaching, working even longer hours. I fancied I was actually catching up. One morning, one of the remaining Sullens, as I called them, asked me how much I charged to row people across the Thames. This was insolent, and I wondered how he came to know about my water taxi service. However, I walked calmly to the window, looked out – it threatened rain – and, walking back, observed that I had never pulled a boat on the Thames, that, despite my injured shoulder, I might like to do so if only for historical reasons, but it threatens rain and I doubted headmaster would give me leave to do so. The fellow again asked, "How much…Sir?" I could see he was now alone, isolated, and I smiled as grimly as I could and said, "You couldn't afford it." The room was silent, and I began talking about the Thames watermen, how important they were to communication along and across the river and began asking selected students about geographical factors in commerce and communication. I even managed to get the lone Sullen to contribute a thought to the discussion. Afterwards, I was angry at the fellow but felt I had dealt with the matter professionally and effectively. I wondered when he or others would get wind of my pasty business and what they would make of that.

* * *

The man I was replacing paid an unexpected visit to the upper sixth form class. He used a cane and I could see traces of the effects of the stroke still, but he was greeted cordially, even enthusiastically by the boys. I yielded my place at the front to him and sat in one of the student's chairs and watched as he questioned them about what they had learned. The students answered readily and clearly, and I felt some pride in them. The man seemed pleased and impressed and said to me after I had accompanied him outside, "You have done a good job, Dobbs. I think I will be able to return in a few weeks, perhaps by end of term, but I will be happy to recommend you for whatever teaching job you choose to apply for." I thanked him and said I would cheerfully resign my place to him whenever he could return. We shook hands and he

237

left. I was very pleased by the praise from a veteran teacher but told myself I had papers to mark, lectures to prepare....

* * *

I rooted around in my papers from university until I found the one that the master had suggested I write up for publication. I put it in my shiny black valise. I was leaving, there was no mail for me, when Christine appeared. She invited me to dinner – it was Saturday evening – and of course I accepted. Eddie was sipping some wine, music was playing, and I began to relax. I told them of my purpose, saying my replacement teaching looked to be coming to an end. They nodded, then looked at each other, then at me, and said they were going to attend a concert in their box this coming Saturday and would I join them? I said I would be delighted to, and asked about the musical bill of fare. This seemed interesting, I nodded, and then Christine said she thought Frances would like the selections. I said I would ask her, tonight if possible, so she could arrange her schedule. Then we went to table and ate.

On the way over to the hospital, it occurred to me that Christine and Eddie seemed almost to be bringing Frances and me together, but told myself that more likely they just liked Frances. As it happened, I managed to find Frances on duty; she seemed pleased at the invitation and accepted.

I called on Frances exactly on time. I had always tried to be punctual; being late was bad manners, rude to the lady. I thought Frances looked very attractive and wondered why I had not realized this during our early meetings. She took my arm again as I escorted her to the taxi. On the way to the Hall, I told her that signs were increasing that the teaching job would end soon, and that I was going to try to rewrite the paper I had mentioned and get it published. If I could, I added, it would certainly help getting a university job. Frances seemed interested, and asked where I would like to teach. Anyplace that would hire me, I said, but I would ideally like a place with some topography, some vistas, some places for rambles, unlike Norfolk, but if that was my only offer, I would have to take it. Frances nodded, smiled and said she thought a place like I described would be ideal indeed.

We went in, got a program apiece and found Eddie and Christine already seated. I hadn't brought my field glasses, but the others didn't think they were necessary.

As I had hoped, the concert was very enjoyable. There was an encore, from one of Gilbert and Sullivan's operettas that I also enjoyed. After, when we came out, it began to rain and looked to be in earnest soon. Eddie pointed to a nearby restaurant and we took refuge there. No one had thought to bring an umbrella.

We were seated at a side table next to the window. Once seated, I asked Eddy if this place was any good – I had never heard it mentioned. Eddie said, "No," but gestured towards the window, against which the rain pelted. A waiter appeared, unctuous even for a Dickens novel, and presented Eddie and myself only with menus: evidently we were supposed, through some mental wireless process, to know what the ladies wanted. The waiter did not seem amenable to our hints that the ladies would also appreciate menus, merely smiled, grovelled and sought our orders for drinks. We were, I decided, fairly trapped. Eddie ordered wine for himself and Christine and, after a glance at Frances, for her, too. I figured if I tried to order a ginger beer I would be summarily ejected, so insisted on a glass of milk. "Large," I said, glaring at the fellow. Surely they had milk somewhere. When the waiter, clearly shaken by my order, had slunk back to his hole, I glanced at Frances. Her eyes met mine and I realized she was enjoying the scene and so was I.

Eddie and I each shared the menus, I with Christine, Eddie with Frances. Everything looked grossly overpriced, with pretentious descriptions and eventually we decided to order Welsh rarebits all around. Eddie urged this, because, he said, there wasn't much damage the cooks could do to those.

The waiter returned with the wine, served with some cere-mony. My milk was placed before me with no ceremony, but I stared at the fellow, daring him to exhibit any emotion at all. Eddie sipped his wine, shrugged; the ladies sipped theirs. I looked at the milk, lifted it, sniffed it and drank some. Eddie looked at me inquiringly. "Watered," I said, "with the authentic City of London *eau ordinaire*. I can smell the chlorine, which in a way is reassuring." Eddie was amused as was Christine. I glanced at Frances, our eyes met, and it seemed we were both amused as well.

We sat in silence for a moment. Then Christine turned to me and said, "Matthew, were you at Passchendaele?" I looked at her, and then at Eddie, who was looking at Christine, then at Frances, who in turn was looking intently at me. "Yes, I was," I said. "For how long?" she asked. I shook my head, trying to drive away darkness, and replied, "I am not sure. We had been sent as temporary replacements to fill a gap in the line. It may have been two days, it may have been longer." Christine was confused, "How could you be uncertain?" The darkness was moving in, gathering and deepening. I tried to explain, "While we were there, it seemed as though we were outside of time. Things kept happening, but there was no progression, no direction to events." I closed, and then opened my mouth, but could find no more words.

Christine, warned by a look from Eddie, apologized for resurrecting bad memories. I said not to apologize, they were natural questions and I would try to answer any others she had. "Though," I said, "remember my view was almost literally from a worm's eye, and my experiences may be atypical." Christine said,

"My fiancé, whom you may have met," I shook my head, "was killed there and I was told he had no known grave. It is probably a foolish question, but I couldn't see how that could happen."

"It was a fairly common fate," I said, "A near explosion from a large shell, and literally millions of those were fired there, would leave little to bury, let alone identify. Or, if a man fell in a shell crater," hopefully he was dead when that happened, I thought, trying to fend off things I had seen there, "another nearby explosion might bury him. When my company went up the line, there were 151 of us. When we came out, there were 49. Eventually a few others trickled back, having gotten lost and winding up in other sectors, but our losses were heavy. I had to write letters to relatives of the missing, and try as I might, talking to all the survivors, there were twenty to thirty I could never account for. Those are listed as having 'no known grave'."

Christine was silent. Frances was still looking intently at me and I thought she must have known someone in that battle, someone who didn't survive.

Our orders arrived. I was not impressed. I informed the table after the waiter had left that I could do a much better job of a Welsh rarebit myself, and had in the past. Each had a large sprig of parsley. Glaring at Eddie, who smiled in reply, I picked up my sprig and began eating it. Eddie beamed, and with his fork, passed his sprig to my plate. I began eating this, and Christine and Frances also passed their sprigs to me.

I finished the lot, glowering at my companions, who were not at all nonplussed, and then began on the rarebit. I was chewing the second piece when Eddie asked me how it was. I swallowed and said it tasted rather of parsley, actually, and we all laughed.

The waiter arrived and asked if we wanted anything else. Eddie, who was the responsible party, as he put it, called for the bill. The rain outside had subsided, so we were imprisoned in this place no longer. The waiter presented the bill to Eddie, who took a fiver from his notecase and handed it, with the bill, to the waiter. I was somewhat appalled: £5 for what was, well, probably not worth five shillings. The waiter asked if everything had been satisfactory, and I said, "Quite up to standard," as if it were a compliment. The fellow chose to take it so and oozed away supremely gratified. When he was out of earshot, I said, "May God have mercy on my soul," and Eddie, Christine and Frances burst into laughter. We got up and went out into the night. The rain had stopped. Eddie and Christine went off by taxi. I hailed another and Frances and I were driven in silence to the hospital.

At the door, Frances faced me and said, "Matthew, I corresponded with a man, a young officer, who was killed at Passchendaele. Would you be willing to tell me how it was?" I swallowed, shook my head. It was no use: the darkness was on me, in me. I said, "One detail I spared Christine: all those craters were full of water, cold, muddy, stinking water. I was told that the area around Ypres has what geologists call a 'high water table', meaning if you dig a hole of any depth, two or three feet is enough, it will fill with water. Even if it doesn't rain, and it did rain." I broke off. "Frances, your duties bring you enough nightmares. I don't want to add to those." She said, "Please tell me, Matthew. The men I treated from that battle didn't want to talk about it, so it must have been very bad. But I want you to tell me what you can."

I was silent. Rage was building in me, but I tried to speak calmly. "Very well. You see, millions of shells were fired into an area perhaps the size of central London. It was unbroken craters for miles, all filled with water. So we were fighting, hundreds of thousands of men, in a man-made swamp, mire, bog, morass. Wounded men who fell into one of those, well, some of them were never able to get out." I swallowed, I couldn't stop. "There was a story that went around sometime after the battle ended. I don't know if the story is true, it doesn't matter. A high ranking officer came to view the battlefield for the first time. He burst into tears, and said, 'Good God, did we actually send men to fight in that?' And that epitomizes the entire experience of this war for me. We used inappropriate tactics on unsuitable ground, for objectives of du-dubious value, and the b-battle w-went on for months. It nearly broke our army. The men used to sing when they marched up the line. N-not after Passchendaele."

I fell silent, and then had to continue. "Higher staffs, Corps, Army and above, ensconced themselves in chateaux, thirty, forty or more miles from any unpleasantness. I'm not implying cowardice, just detachment from the realities of the consequences of their orders, the higher ranking generals surrounded by immaculately uniformed staff officers who spent their time sticking pins in maps. The pattern was set by Haig. Haig was a bonehead. Like all boneheads, he surrounded himself with other boneheads, who were there to tell him what he wanted to hear, not what was actually going on."

I swallowed, and then went on. "I'm n-not saying our generals were unique in any way. Generals in all the armies were caught sh-short and had to learn their trade as they w-went on, and the c-cost of that tuition was in … b-blood, a very great deal of b-blood."

I looked at Frances. She stared at me, transfixed. I said, "Frances, I am very sorry. This was a wonderful evening, and I've ruined it. I apologize." Frances said, "Please don't apologize, Matthew. I did ask you to tell me, and you did. Thank you. I understand better now what everyone went through." I looked at her. "Yes," I said, "I believe you do. You yourself have stories to tell, nightmares to relate, don't you?" "Yes," she said, "but I think enough nightmares have been exchanged for tonight." I continued to look at her. "A familiar spirit." I took her hand, kissed it. She looked at me. "I apologize for the familiarity. Think of it as tribute." She smiled, said, "No apologies are necessary. What are you going to do now?" I said, "Walk. I think that helps. Just walk and walk." She replied, "Yes, that does help." I didn't ask how she knew. I said, "Goodnight, Frances," and she replied, "Goodnight, Matthew," and I held the door for her as she went in. We raised our hands in farewell, then I went out onto the streets, walking and walking as images returned, images of faces as the life left their eyes…. I wondered yet again if the decisions I had made as to whom to evacuate were correct. I would never know, not in this lifetime.

My teaching ended the following Thursday. The man I was substituting for returned, no cane, looking quite recovered. I congratulated him on his recovery, and essentially watched him resume his duties, class by class. He had a loveable personality, I decided, watching him. That was his secret: his students would work for him, not wanting to disappoint him, because they loved him. I had no chance of emulating him there, yet he told me again he thought the students in all the forms I taught had learned a great deal. Even the last Sullen seemed to be willing to forgive me for having taught him despite his best efforts.

Friday I celebrated by taking my paper to the British Museum Library and began reworking it. I saw almost immediately that minor revisions weren't going to be enough. While the master was most complimentary, he had written many comments, questions and notes, and each had to be dealt with. I went out, bought some paper and began research.

Saturday I visited at Eddie and Christine's: no mail, but Christine told me she and Eddie were planning a party two weeks ahead, for David and Esther, and that I was of course invited and, looking me in the eye, could bring a companion. I said I would see if Frances could get free that Saturday. I added that if she weren't available, I would have to bring a cat. Christine thought that Frances would be available, although she didn't say why she thought so. As it happened, Christine was right; in fact, Frances seemed to know about the party. As Frances was on duty then, we couldn't talk much beyond setting up the time when I would call for her.

* * *

The research for the paper proceeded, but it was an erratic business. I had done this sort of thing before: each new source, each new reference pointed out further sources, a process that steadily expanded the reading required. Eventually, I had learned, the sources petered out, referring increasingly to each other. But at

244

the moment, what I had to read was increasing rapidly, not being whittled down. However, by Wednesday night, I had covered everything mentioned and rewritten the entire paper. Everything was now much more solid and better documented. On Thursday the manuscript was typed, corrected and personally handed to the editor of the journal, who was on staff at the university. He said he and another expert would look at it right away and reply as soon as they had read it. I returned to my room at the prescribed late hour and was visited by my landlady according to her current schedule.

———

I was now at leisure, so began again looking for a job. At university level, there seemed no current call for historians. Public schools were looking for people but the pay was comparatively meagre and the locations were not attractive. With my qualifications, I should be able to get a job paying about £200/year, possibly more, plenty for me, but perhaps a bit tight if I had a wife. For some reason, I thought about Frances at this point, but I really didn't know how she felt about me or I about her. I guessed on my part that "wary" would sum it up. She must have other suitors, I guessed; at least one who had been killed. We always seemed to get on well, but perhaps that was just her way. Given the attitude the rest – well, perhaps excepting the brother – of the family had towards me, I found it very difficult to believe she really cared for me, yet she seemed somewhat distant from the rest of her family…. And then there was my landlady (or her twin sister)…. I couldn't figure it out.

There was one thing I knew I should do: look up my birth records at Somerset House. I had now no excuse for delay, and remembering Frances's confidence that I would look into my birth when I could – her confidence in me was greater than my own in myself – I girded my emotional loins and went into the den of possible nightmares.

It was very easy and quick. My name and approximate birth location were sufficient. I did indeed have a middle name – it was Edward. I was Matthew Edward Dobbs. I was also six days younger than I had believed, although my guess as to my birthday had been close. My mother was originally Elizabeth Katherine Lewes, like the battlefield in the Wars of the Roses. Her family seemed to be in Taunton, where I had been born, so the next step was to go there.

* * *

I had to ask about, but it seemed a Mr Lewes lived, and I got his location and went to the house. It was a small cottage, well kept. I took a deep breath and knocked. The door was opened by a woman in, I guessed, early middle years. I asked for Mr Lewes. She wanted to know my business – I seemed to elicit suspicion – and I told her I believed he was my mother's father. At this, I was admitted.

Mr Lewes appeared to be in his seventies, yet was hale enough. He was very surprised at my name, telling me he had been told all of us had died in the train wreck. "Not quite all, Sir," I said. I told him the people who had brought me up had no knowledge of my family (not that they ever tried to obtain any), and I had lost my memories of my life before the crash. The woman went out of the room. I asked him, first, had he any other children; that is, had I uncles and aunts?

He had, as it happened: one son, a lawyer, and two other daughters, both married to lawyers. He gave me their names and addresses, commenting that he could see I resembled his dead daughter but also my father. I asked if he had any photographs of my parents. Only of the daughter, it seemed; everything else was lost. He showed me the picture: my mother as a young woman was very pretty. I was sweating, but not too badly, yet I could now recall images of my mother engaged in domestic chores. I began to shake and turned away. When I could speak, I asked him about Mother's singing. Was she hoping for a career in music?

246

He told me he was originally a carpenter then turned builder, and with four children to provide for, hadn't been able to pay for much in the way of voice lessons. Yet Mother did practice and did sing publicly. My father, he said, had first set eyes on Mother at one of these concerts. "Elizabeth had several suitors, of course, but your father beat them all out. He was a clever chap, with a future" (not a prolonged one, I thought) "in teaching, and they were happy together. He had a better offer from a school in Norfolk," "Earl's Cross School," I interjected. "Yes, that may be the name. Anyway, off they went." He sat silent for a while. "My wife, she's gone now these ten years, it shadowed her life. Elizabeth was her favourite. If we had known you had survived...." He didn't finish. I wondered how different my life would have been, growing up among family, among people who loved me and cared for me.

The woman came in with a tray of tea and biscuits. She set it down, sat down herself and distributed teas to herself and us. I guessed she wasn't a servant, but of course didn't ask about her status. She seemed quite at home at any event. I took several biscuits and washed them down with as much tea as I could stand to be polite.

I thought of something: I told my grandfather my middle name was Edward. He nodded, said that was his name. Another gap closed. I then asked if he knew anything of my father's family. He said my father's father, who was dead, was a guard on the Great Western Railway. This did not seem a surprise, so I may have heard something about that. My father went to Rugby School on scholarship.... I knew that, I interrupted, "I saw the letter my father wrote, applying for the position. Did he have any brothers or sisters?" Mr Lewes said Father had one brother who kept a store, but he couldn't remember where. I noted this also, and then asked where Mother and Father had lived after they married. He said he built the house himself, and gave it to his daughter as a wedding present. (Evidently there was no parental opposition to the match: a house, even a small one, was a magnificent present.) He gave me the address, and I arose and thanked him for his kindness and his help. By now, I could hardly talk, and he seemed embarrassed, but said he was very happy indeed I had survived. It in a sense brought his daughter back to life. I left quickly and used my handkerchief freely, catching the notice of passers-by.

I approached the house in which, I assumed, I had been born and had grown up, well, four years' worth. It was small, and I stood outside wondering if I could withstand the emotions of going inside. I decided, cowardly, that I didn't want to disturb the occupants. From the outside, there was little to evoke memories, which was just as well: I had reached my limits.

Riding back, it occurred to me that if the cottage had been given to my mother when she married, that would have been part of her estate, and the proceeds from its sale, surely several hundred pounds, should have gone to me. My parents might indeed have been carrying the proceeds with them. Of course if that vile Graves had somehow gotten his hands on it, it was lost. There was now nothing I could do about the situation, everyone concerned being dead, and damned in the cases of two individuals. Otherwise, if the money had gone to her family, I would let things be as I valued having relations far more.

During my return to London, staring out the train window, I became almost calm. Aside from not visiting the house of my early childhood, I had, I thought, managed well. I had kept my promise, for so I regarded it, to Frances, and I now had names and addresses of several relations. I had a family, however distant, at last.

I spent the following day writing and rewriting letters: to my surviving grandfather, thanking him again and giving him Eddie and Christine's address, to my uncle and aunts. The latter were difficult letters: I did not want them to think I was after money, just letting them know they had a nephew, and gave something of my plans and prospects. I thought of seeing Frances and giving her my news, but I kept thinking I might find she had a suitor or lover, and, irrationally, I was afraid of such a discovery. I did visit Eddie and Christine, was very kindly invited to dinner, and related my adventures. I was still, I told them, a bit shaken, I didn't know why, but at least the gap in my first four years was beginning to close.

They were sympathetic, always good friends, and I began to relax. We discussed the party approaching, and I received a hint that one, or better, two bottles of pickles would be appreciated. I replied that in some matters, I could be relied upon, at least more than in others. Christine went upstairs, leaving Eddie and I to talk. Eddie said her pregnancy was progressing normally – he had engaged a specialist – but that at times she needed to rest. Our conversation concentrated on Eddie's practice and wandered thence into some of his cases; his descriptions of symptoms and cases recalled so many years of listening to him talking about medicine. I was, as always, somewhat repelled, yet I listened attentively, partly because I had some interest in the topic but also because we were friends.

Returning to my room, I had the scheduled (as I imagined it), tryst with my landlady, and this time didn't even bother getting up to glimpse her bare bottom entering the bathroom, so jaded I had become. Saving her monthly courses, which seemed as precisely timed as the rest of her life, her lusts were entirely predictable. I wondered why sex should have been, in my experience, always such a source of shame, and decided it was because it was divorced from love, from responsibility, from caring. In isolation, it was pleasurable but meaningless, or rather exploitative and selfish. That, in the extreme, made it monstrous. My landlady, I would assume it was she, despised me, yet used me. Even if her husband were dead, that would almost certainly not change. Of course, I was using her as well, yet that made the act no different.

I called for Frances exactly on time. I had not seen her for weeks, and, I had to acknowledge, I had missed her. She emerged promptly, descending the stairs wearing a bluish dress I had not seen her in before. No jewellery, as usual. She turned towards me, and seeing me, smiled. My heart gave a great bound, she looked entrancing; I was awestruck, yet felt a wave of pride, I had so pretty a girl on my arm. I gaped at her, felt myself grinning idiotically. She took my arm and we walked towards the door. Two nurses, friends apparently, called to her, "Have a good time, Fanny." As I opened the door for her, I turned towards her and said, "Fanny?" She looked over at me and replied, "Of course, Matthew. You are the only person who calls me 'Frances'." I was taken aback. "Do you object?" She glanced at me as we went down the steps to the taxi and said softly, "No."

A bit confused, I helped her into the taxi, got in myself and gave the driver our destination. As we were driven, I told her about my paper and its submission. She asked if it would help me get a job, and I said, "Definitely, although how long it would take to have that effect, I have no idea. And it has to prove acceptable to the readers. If they want changes, I will try to provide them; if they really think it without merit, then that is over. But, I think it does have merit. We shall see. As I mentioned, I did it because, I suppose, it is my nature to do things like that. I am an academic; that is what academics do."

I went on to tell her of my trip to Somerset House and its results. For some reason, I had the feeling she knew about it, but that couldn't be. I described my trip to the West Country and meeting my grandfather, the only surviving one, and seeing my mother's picture. "She was a lovely woman," I said, "And although with little formal training, sang beautifully. That, I was told, is how my father met her. He had to fight off other suitors, but emerged victorious. My grandfather thought they were very happy together and news of her death and, he thought, of the entire family, was a heavy blow."

There was silence as we rode, and then I said, "On a brighter note, I have an uncle, my father's brother, although I don't yet know where he lives, and an uncle and two aunts on my mother's side of the family. I have written to them." I paused. "I went to the house where I was born and spent my first four years, but lacked the courage to see if the occupant would let me in. Perhaps on another visit."

Frances was sympathetic, and praised my efforts, although why I deserved praise for such obvious things eluded me. Still, I was pleased. I wanted to tell her I had missed her when we arrived at Eddie and Christine's, but was afraid of being forward. I paid the driver and we entered. I told her I was almost certainly acceptable this evening because I had earlier brought two bottles of pickles over. "So," I said, "they may even let me dine with the grown-ups."

We were received with cheer and music. David and Esther were the guests of honour. I suspected there was a reason, and seeing the two of them, David pleased yet embarrassed, Esther glowing, I guessed she was, as they say, "with child". There were two other couples, the men I was delighted to meet, also as they say, "aboveground", one a Regular, the other an Occasional, both either married or engaged. Looking around, I noticed that Frances was easily the prettiest woman there. For some reason, I had never thought of her in that way before, but the other men were, although in a restrained way, since their wives or fiancées were present.

Wine was served (ginger beer for me), and I got a chance to talk to David and Esther. David told me I would be getting a final account early next week, sales of the jewellery bringing the total to over £6,000, very gratifying even with David and Esther's 20% and Inland Revenue's 25% or so. I told David about the bequest from Mrs Paston and he agreed it would serve as cover very nicely, even if it was small. He and Esther had, he said, decided to buy a cottage outside London with their commission. They had in fact selected one. They seemed quite enthusiastic about it. I had thought of David as a Londoner born and bred, but he told me he always wanted a place of his own, with actual grass and trees. We talked about a garden, a hot house, and I volunteered, for a suitable share of the proceedings, to prepare walnut cakes, as they had, they said, three walnut trees on the property. My offer was accepted, pending negotiations over the exact details.

I noticed Frances closeted with Christine, talking very seriously about something. Eddie was being the good host with the other two couples, so I inspected the recordings. I saw two or three that looked interesting, new to me, and hoped they might be played this evening.

We were called to dinner. The butler-factotum and cook-of-all-work brought in the cart. I moved to assist as usual, but both the butler and Eddie waved me to my usual seat, on his left, Frances on his right, Esther and David facing each other in the places of honour either side of Christine at the foot of the table. We all sat and were served, the others with wine, I with ginger beer. Before eating, the now customary toast, "To absent friends" was drunk in silence.

As expected, the meal was excellent. Several courses were served, unusual for Eddie and Christine. After dessert, Eddie proposed another toast to David, Esther and to their child, drunk with acclaim, Esther and especially David blushing, the rest of us delighted. Their removal to the suburbs was also disclosed, and a general invitation to the rest of us issued. David gave their direction, which I carefully noted.

The Occasional began chaffing me for my choice of tipple, and I waited for silence to reply. I said, "This is all I'm allowed," gesturing to Eddie, "at least when ladies are present" (some amusement). "Eddie claims that when given the real stuff, I get rowdy and climb onto the table to dance..." (more amusement, which I let subside before continuing), "...without any clothes on." A roar of laughter followed; I was enjoying myself. I continued, "I have no recollection at all of any such event" (amusement again), "but Eddie assures me he has photographic evidence, although he refuses to let me see this." More laughter, then Eddie said with mock gravity, "No one wants to see those photographs, Matthew." We all laughed, and I clinked glasses with Eddie, in honour of his *riposte*.

Frances and I were outside Eddie and Christine's, walking back to the hospital. I noticed she didn't take my arm this time, which troubled me. I wondered what I had done to offend her and how I could put it right. We walked in silence a minute or so, and then Frances asked, "How long have you known David?" I said, "About seven years. We were at university, all of us." Francis asked what David had read. I replied, "Classics, I believe. Theoretically, David was studying to become a rabbi, but I began to realize he really wasn't interested in that." "What was he interested in?" "I think David's real dream was to become Reader in Hebrew at Oxford or Cambridge. He took a first, as did Eddie, but after he came back without his lower leg, his parents insisted he work in their shop, a pawn and jewellery shop. He has a married older sister, but her husband teaches school and has no interest in the business, nor had she. I don't think his heart was in it, but his father is getting on. When Esther arrived, I think things improved for him, and for her. I am very happy for them both."

More silence. Frances asked, "Why did you think he wasn't interested in being a rabbi?" I considered, and then said, "A number of things. Jews are supposed to keep dietary laws, one of which is they don't eat pork. When Eddie and I and David and one or two other friends got together at this pub, we would order a plate of sandwiches. These were a mixture, either ham or roast beef or cheese. I noticed that David would simply pick the sandwich that was nearest him, never mind what it was. The only thing that mattered was whether the sandwich was any good – to taste, I mean. And I never heard him comment on any religious topic. We would often talk for hours about words, about languages, including historical relations between languages. I have read a great deal about that, speak German, Eddie French and I think some German, David Greek, Hebrew and I think Arabic as well, and we all had Latin and some Greek, so we could actually make some sensible remarks about the subject."

After a few more steps, Frances said, "Christine hinted that David had been previously engaged to marry." I was silent a while, and then decided to answer. "He was. I met the girl two or three times." I hesitated, and then went on. "He was jilted. He went into the Army, saw her on leave, they were corresponding, all seemed well. Then, after he had been in France a month, he got a letter from her, informing him she had gotten married. I think the fellow owned a furniture store, but she must have been seeing him clandestinely at the time. She asked David to burn her letters, which he did, so," my voice had acquired an edge, "at least he got a bit of warmth from the relationship." Frances glanced at me as we walked on, but made no comment. I said, "After he came back maimed, he was very depressed. Eddie and I had him over for our *soirées*, as Eddie calls them, whenever I was on leave and I think that cheered him up. But Esther cheered him a great deal more. Again, I am very happy for them both."

We crossed a side street in silence. Then Frances said, "I have heard your landlady is very pretty." I was startled, but couldn't lie, so I said, "Yes, she is." "And a widow, I understand." I had the feeling the conversation was drifting rapidly onto shoals, so I decided to be as candid as I thought prudent. Glancing about, I saw no one near. "For God's sake Frances, keep this to yourself. Her husband is alive but he is mad. I found this out by accident from a fellow I knew at university who is now a doctor. He specializes in diseases of the mind. I don't remember the term…"

"Psychiatric" said Frances. I said, "He was talking about his patients, and one of them, a Guards Captain, basically just lies on his bed, except occasionally he weeps, never responds to anyone. His wife and their son visit him on Saturdays. They sit with him for two hours or so, then leave." "What a terrible story," said Frances. "Compared with all the happy ones?" I asked. More silence, then Frances asked, "And she has never talked about this with you?" I said, "Frances, the only conversation we had was when she interviewed me, to see if I wasn't too unsuitable, I guess, before I moved in. Since then, our entire conversation every morning is 'Good morning, Madam' followed by 'Good morning, Major'. At night, the place is dark." All true, but not the entire truth. Frances then said, "If the routine is so irksome, why do you stay? Your teaching is over." I was grasping at straws by now;

there was really only one reason I stayed but I couldn't tell Frances what it was. So I said, "It is possible I will be invited back," (possible but not likely) "otherwise, I suppose I am just used to the routine and have had other things on my mind" (one thing in particular).

We walked on. Then suddenly, Frances stopped and turned towards me. I had to stop and turn also. She said, "Then are you still in love with my sister?" There it was, out in the open. Then, Frances began to cry. I was shocked; I moved instinctively to shield her from passing gaze, put my arm around her shoulders, which were shaking, and reached for a handkerchief. "Here, Frances, it's clean, which is a minor miracle in itself." She took the handkerchief and dabbed at her face with it, wiped her face, and gave me the handkerchief back.

"Frances," I began, but she interrupted me: "It's all right, Matthew. You don't have to answer. I apologize for asking about such a sensitive matter." I said, "Frances, listen to me. You have asked a question that is important to you, so it is important to me. Let me answer it, please." She seemed to be about to protest, but I went on: "When your sister ended the engagement, for that is what it was, it was a bitter, although expected, blow. What happened after left me injured and limping, and I walked the 33 miles alongside the railway track more enraged than I have ever been. I swore that I would become so successful at whatever I did that no one, ever again, would be able to treat me as something disposable. And for months after, when I was tempted to lie abed, get more sleep, or postpone reading an assignment, I would recall your sister, sneering at me, and that would get me to work. I would also do this when I entered the Army to force me to pay more attention to my duties."

"However, I think I am basically too lazy to bear grudges or pursue vendettas. After I was wounded, I thought of your sister less and less; the last year or so of the war, I don't believe I thought about her at all. Then I met you. You seemed to be, well, I hate to use such a word, *nice*. And we met again and again, by chance, then on purpose, and it was sometimes hard for me to remember whose sister you were. As time went on and we saw each other more and more, the only times I thought about your sister were in relation to you, not the other way around; by now, your image has entirely displaced hers. So no, I am not still in love with your sister. The last words I spoke to her were I wished her happiness. I may have meant that then, I certainly do now. I hope she and her husband are perfectly happy with each other. I hope every couple is happy with each other; having lost my family, I consider such a relation the highest, finest form of existence, no doubt naively, but sincerely."

Frances said, "I don't mean to excuse my sister's behaviour to you, but, before you arrived, she was, well, nervous. I don't think she was sneering at you." "It doesn't matter now." I said. I reflected I hadn't considered diarrhoea as affecting the sister's behaviour.

Silence for a while. Then Frances began to talk again. "All my life, she has been the pretty one, the clever one. Try as I might, nothing I did or was could be good enough. If my marks were as good as hers had been, that was ignored. Otherwise, whatever I did was just more evidence of my second-place nature. Whatever good was available went to her. There was only enough money to give her some dancing lessons, there was none for me. When my mother dies, all her jewellery will go to my sister, nothing to me." Turning to me, "I love my parents and my sister, but I learned, over and over, that if I wanted something, I would have to get it on my own. I think that was one of the reasons I trained as a nurse – I would stand or fall on my own, I needn't fear any more comparisons. Do you understand?" she said. "Yes," I said, "Yes I do indeed."

She continued, "When she came back, engaged to marry you, my parents were livid. They hoped she would make a great match, with a man with a lot of money, perhaps a title or expectations of a title as well, and now she was attached to a" Frances paused, and I filled in, "lower class orphan in trade". "Yes," said Frances. "I am afraid I added my voice against the match, telling my sister that our family had certain expectations and she had a duty to meet them." Frances turned to me: "Of course, I hadn't met you, nor had Mother and Father. Not that my comments made any difference. I was ignored as was usual. I will say this for my sister: she resisted my parents' demands that the engagement be broken off at once. She genuinely liked you. Then Aunt Lydia wrote a letter, replying to one Mother had written, accusing my aunt of conspiracy and complicity in promoting the match. Mother left the letter out on the table when she went looking for Father and I read it."

"My aunt – she is Father's sister – denied any conspiracy or complicity, saying she was simply doing a favour for her niece. She went on to say she saw nothing untoward, though she thought you and my sister were very fond of each other. She reminded Mother and Father that, of the three of them, she was the only one who had actually met you, and had done so on four occasions. She said your dress was appropriate and your manners good, allowing for the fact you were left-handed, like my sister. She also said you were highly intelligent, very determined and hard-working, qualities she said any woman of sense would value highly, for you would do whatever was necessary to sustain your family. She added that you were imaginative, with an entrepreneurial streak, and had a marvellous sense of humour. She concluded that while my sister might well attract a man with money or property, a title or expectations of one, my sister would have to forego other qualities, qualities better suited for the long pull. You were a man for the long pull, she thought."

I was embarrassed by that woman's praise. It hadn't made any difference in the end to the older sister, but it probably made an impression on Frances, as she confirmed in her next sentence: "I remember reading that letter and thinking if my aunt thought so highly of you, there were likely good reasons for it. As it was, the letter strengthened my sister's reluctance to give you up, although Mother and Father were still very opposed. Then the war broke out. My sister is very patriotic, and wanted to help with the war, so she began serving tea and biscuits to convalescing officers. There she met Charles."

"I remember my parents thinking he was exactly the match they wanted. He was invited over to Millwood often and I could see he had the rest of my family captivated. He talked about his prospects – the next majority in his regiment, the property and money he expected to inherit from a great aunt and other relations. He paid no attention to me, like the rest of my family. I listened to him and thought him very full of himself. But my sister, Mother and Father believed him, believed in him, without reservation, which surprised me. As it was, he proposed to my sister by post, she accepted his proposal by post, and then realized she would have to do something about you. I thought she was not behaving very honourably, she shouldn't be allowing another man to court her while being engaged to you, but I said nothing, as no one would have paid any attention to me anyway."

"As things worked out, at the end of the war, Charles was still a captain, the great aunt hadn't left him anything and the other relations, I suspect, have little use for him as well. My sister had talked about training as a real nurse; Charles, Junior was my brother-in-law's answer to that ambition. Now he is at Millwood, talking about all the highly-paying jobs his friends are going to offer him. I fancy Mother and Father are beginning to see him as I have come to see him, as a self-promoter."

We had been walking as I listened to Frances. I struggled for a feeling of tolerance for Charles. "Well," I said, "Thank God he wasn't on staff. The only name we had for the cavalry that I can repeat to you was 'The Immortals'. We didn't have any names for staff that I would ever repeat to any woman."

Frances was silent for several steps, and then said, "Whenever Charles is annoyed with my sister, he reminds her of her 'barrow-boy romance', as he calls you." I kept my temper, and said, "Doesn't he realize that by ridiculing me and her, he is ridiculing himself as well, as she chose each of us in turn? Or is that too subtle a point?" Frances replied, "Charles is not a subtle man. He isn't stupid but he is, I think, mentally lazy. He has never had to use his brain. I think he has gotten into the habit of expecting whatever he wanted to be given him."

My tolerance for this Charles had vanished. I had the feeling that Charles and I, if we ever met, would not get on. "Well," I said, "he voluntarily assumed responsibility for a wife and a child. If he has any manhood, he will shift his arse – pardon me, Frances – and do whatever he can for his family."

We were getting close to the hospital. When we got there, we stopped, shielded partly by columns, facing each other. I thought Frances's face looked strained, and wanted to comfort her. She said, "That man I told you about, that I corresponded with. We were in love. He asked me to marry him and I accepted his proposal. On his last leave, instead of going home, he rented a room in the French town near our hospital. Things were quiet, so we were able to see each other every day. I went to bed with him. Are you shocked?"

"No," I replied, "If you loved a man it would be totally and without reserve. And although he is gone, I am sure your love for him enormously comforted and heartened him. I know such a love, if ever I had it, would have done that for me." The expression on her face changed, but in the flickering light cast by motor-car head lamps, I could not interpret it.

"After I heard of his death," she went on, "I couldn't continue. They sent me home. I stayed at Millwood two months, walking all day, every day." "Then you came back," I said. "They wouldn't send me overseas again, but kept me at home on a sort of sufferance." "And asked you to stay on," I noted, "so they must value you. What was your sister doing all this while?" Frances said, "Taking care of young Charles and writing patriotic pieces for the county newspaper."

"So," I said, "while she was exhorting the rest of us to greater efforts, you were dealing with bowel resections and cases of gas gangrene. I say nothing denigrating about your sister. Taking care of a small child is, God knows, extremely important. But there is no comparison between her service and yours. We weren't comrades in arms, our sex prevented that, but we were comrades in the cause. And your service ranks with that of anyone, including mine, and you can, and should, be proud of it."

We stood looking at each other a long moment. Then she said, "Matthew, I am thinking that perhaps we should not see each other again. I think that might be best." I said, "Frances..." She went on, "best for both of us." I panicked. "Frances, listen to me. For both our sakes. L-Listen. I-I have been thinking about you, more and more. Th-these past few weeks, I have missed you. I-I was going to tell you this, b-but was afraid I might seem too f-forward. This evening, when I c-called for you, you came down those stairs, t-turned towards me and smiled, and it was as though all the electric lights in the room were t-turned on at once, I was d-dazzled, you l-looked so l-lovely. I thought I would b-burst with p-pride at having so p-pretty a girl on my arm, and at the p-party tonight I saw you were easily the p-prettiest girl there – my dear."

Frances had thrown herself into my arms, we were embracing, we were kissing, I felt streaks of tears on my cheeks, perhaps from her, perhaps from me; it didn't matter. I kissed her on her mouth, her cheek, her throat; her scent was magnetic, and my God she felt good in my arms. At length, breathless, we separated somewhat, and she said, "But you haven't answered my question about whether we should part." I cursed, "What in Hell for? No! I w-want to see you again. Wh-when may I see you again?"

She looked at me, her mouth opening and closing, and then looked off to her right, and then our eyes met again. "My schedule is complex for the next few days, but I will be off for a while starting Thursday afternoon at six. If you call at seven, we can go out to eat, chips perhaps." "Seven Thursday evening," I repeated. "Frances, I have money. We can dine anywhere you want, anywhere in London." I gestured at the sky. "If we had means of getting there and back, on the moon. The bill of fare involves cheese, if I recall correctly." Frances smiled, leaned forward to kiss me again, and then said, "Chips will be all right." I held the door open for her. As she went inside, she said, "Goodnight Matthew." I said, "Goodnight, my dear." She turned a few steps in, raised her hand, I raised mine in reply and she was gone.

I stumbled down the steps, onto the street and began walking back to my room. I was astounded, overwhelmed. Frances was in love with me. I had never considered myself a loveable man. Hardworking? Definitely. Competent? Occasionally. But not loveable. Still, there it was. And how did I feel about her? There was no comparison with how I had felt about her sister, but that had been pure romance, and romance was fantasy and fantasy was brittle, it shattered on contact with reality. With Frances, my feelings were more confused, less developed. I had begun to feel protective towards her. I wanted to comfort her, shield her from hurt. But aside from that, I definitely did not want to part from her. I wanted to go on seeing her, and inevitably that meant marriage. How did I feel about that? Certainly I felt no reluctance. I was beginning to feel we were alike in many important attitudes; we understood each other much better now and sympathized with each other.

The house, as I approached it, was dark, well, it was getting late. I hoped my landlady would spare me this night, for I had begun to realize that the purely (or nearly) physical relationship I had with my landlady had seriously interfered with the developing emotional relationship with Frances, and that meant I would have to leave that house. I had no idea how this would affect my landlady. In a sense I felt very sorry for her and especially for her husband. However my continued sexual services were of doubtful benefit to my landlady's marriage, even if – oddly, I felt a stab of jealousy at the thought – I had had a predecessor or would have a successor. I finally understood that my landlady, for surely it was she I was rogering, was living two lives, and was making every effort to keep these separate.

It was not to be. She must have been waiting for me to come in. I had barely settled on the bed when she entered and, doffing her nightgown, climbed onto me. I responded, God help me, and, as she was leaving, I said: "I've got to get out of this house." I was startled. Had I spoken aloud? Had she heard me? It didn't matter, I told myself: I set the alarm for 5:30 as usual and went to sleep. I cleaned myself, my teeth, shaved, dressed and packed everything, and went out to the kitchen. Here my landlady forestalled me. She said she was taking a job and had invited an aunt to stay in my room and help take care of the child. She wanted me to leave right away. I nodded, fighting off another totally irrational spasm of jealousy, and said I would leave immediately. She insisted on returning the few shillings and odd pence I had paid beyond the time I had actually stayed, placing the coins on the table for me to reach. I took these, and said, "Goodbye, Madam." She said, "Goodbye, Major." I nodded to the maid, who ignored me, smiled at the boy, who was asleep, and left.

Outside, although light, there was no one about, so the land-lady's secret was perhaps safe, although it was possible the neighbours actually knew everything, at least of my existence. I walked quickly away, shaking my head to try to dispel irrational regrets. I was going to "a cleaner, neater maiden in a cleaner, greener land" or some such expression from Kipling. I bought newspapers, found a place that was open, that served something to eat and drink, and began searching for lodgings.

I wanted a flat. I felt I needed a place with a bathroom and a kitchen. At Eddie and Christine's party, I was solicited to prepare pasties for the group once again. I told them I had to have a kitchen. Well, now I would look for a place where I could entertain, Frances of course, and my friends. If I could get a flat without taking a long lease, for I had no idea where or when I might find a job, that would be ideal.

At length, I found a place I could rent for two months or so. The tenants were returning from Brazil September 1. The place had a slight odd smell to it, not unpleasant, just unexpected and unexplained, but otherwise fit the bill. I set my luggage down, and went over to Eddie and Christine's to begin moving my things, boxes of books and all. I told them what I had done, and would do, given hired assistance with the books. Christine especially was delighted, which I found a little odd as she had never objected before to the boxes I had been storing there. She asked me if I was seeing Frances again, and I said, "Yes, on Thursday evening." She then said, "And after?" I looked at her, then understood what she was saying, smiled and said, "And after." They invited me to dinner and naturally I accepted.

————

The boxes of books weighed 50-60 pounds each, and I simply was not going to be able to carry them by hand to my flat, so I hired some movers. In a sense, this was an irrational exercise, since everything would have to be moved again in two months or so, but I wanted to have all my possessions together for the first time since university days. While I was watching the men shift the boxes, Christine handed me an envelope. It was David's account. Even after their 20%, it was a gratifying sum, although I told myself Inland Revenue was going to take a swingeing cut in addition. Purchase of a property was in my reach, but that was a decision requiring a job and also Frances's ideas. It was oddly comforting to realize I had someone else in my life now, someone deeply interested in my doings and welfare. I very much wanted to see her again.

* * *

I had decided, as a concession to the fact I was to move again soon, not to unpack the books. I purchased towels, soap, bathroom things and told myself I needed to stock the larder, but that depended on several things, especially Frances. I had things washed and put away. In the end, I used all day Tuesday on trivial errands, and was oddly tired as a result. Getting used to not having to awake at 5:30 and being able to come and go as I chose was going to take time.

* * *

Wednesday I got the letter from the solicitor in Norwich, informing me that Mrs Paston had left me about £1100, which, added to the loot, made an even more impressive amount, even after Inland Revenue. I spent the day on financial errands, consolidating the money. I discussed matters with Eddie and Christine, and listened to their suggestions. I treated them to dinner – David and Esther were at their cottage – at our favourite restaurant. I wished Frances could be there but I was to see her tomorrow.

* * *

I decided to buy some ginger beer, and carrying several loose bottles, as I had no bag, was a bit exasperating. For some reason, after drinking one, I decided to see if there was any more mail for me, this week being notable for that. Indeed, there was a letter for me, from the editor of the historical journal. I steeled myself, opened it and found my article had been accepted, and in record time, I thought, barely two weeks. The editor and the reader were very kind in their comments. I was relieved, delighted, my tide was in flood. I would certainly have a great deal to tell Frances. Christine was out, so I celebrated with a sandwich at the usual place. I bought two bottles of pickles, left one at Eddie and Christine's with a note and took the other one to the flat. I then went back to the university to see if there was any job on offer for me. There wasn't: my good fortune had limits after all. I got my shoes polished, my clothes pressed, had a bath, re-shaved and swept out the flat, thinking I should have done the sweeping before bathing, but I was feeling very happy now, especially with what appeared to be a prosperous romance.

When I got to the hospital, I saw Frances talking to two or three nurses in the lobby. She noticed me, we smiled at each other, she had such a warm smile, she said goodbye to her friends and took my arm as we went out. I was very pleased we were back on such terms. As we walked, I told her of the move. She seemed pleased also but I somehow got the impression it was not news to her. I described the flat and commented on getting used to being able to come and go as I chose and having all my possessions at hand. Frances asked how my landlady had taken my leaving on such short notice. "Without noticeable emotion," I said, again uneasy at the resurrection of this topic. "She said she wanted the room for an aunt to take care of her son while she took a job." Frances nodded, and we neared the chips shop. I hated lying to Frances and resolved, if she pursued the subject, to tell her everything.

We got our orders, she with tea, I with a glass of milk. We sat down. Looking at Frances, I thought she was tired. When I asked, she confirmed she had had a long night of it, but was hungry. As she began eating, I pulled a sheaf of letters from my pocket and showed her the letter of acceptance for my paper. She understood its significance immediately, and asked if I had found any jobs on offer. This deflated me, and I said, "No. I had gotten papers yesterday and had looked though them also. Nothing, again. However, I got the solicitor's letter, with the cheque, today." I showed her this. She was eating chips steadily, but read the letter. She was delighted. I explained that the real value of the bequest was as camouflage.

"Let me explain," I said. "On three occasions I was sent across German lines, the last time to see where they were fortifying to meet our advance. I noted what I saw, and then had the lunatic idea of stopping a German staff motor and stealing the papers they were carrying. I did this. You may recall that shiny black valise I use for school papers?" Frances nodded. "A spoil of war," I said. "It was very heavy and the official I took it from was evidently of very high rank; at any event, it seemed a good part of the German Army was put in pursuit. I got away and opened it. On top was a sort of account book, under that was another book and under that were a great many gold coins, mostly Belgian, some French, one or two guineas, and a number of pieces of jewellery. I looked again at the account book: the fellow was selling clemency for various offenses. The amount, the offense and the name of the person, either the briber or the person being let off, all were recorded." I paused. Frances continued eating, watching me, very interested in my story. I leaned forward, "In some cases, payment was not made in money. I say no more. But I was very glad indeed I stole his gains."

Frances speared another chip, chewed it, swallowed and drank some tea. "I tore three pages out of the account book and put them, once I regained our lines, in a report, copy to the Foreign Office. I had buried the case with the loot where I could find it again. The Foreign Office was very interested and summoned me to London to identify the official. That was the day we met." We smiled at each other. "The Foreign Office official, when I asked, said I should just claim the loot as an inheritance. Provided Inland Revenue got its share, he thought nothing more would be said. This, mind, from a Government official. At any event, that is what I did: I asked David and Esther to flog the coins and jewellery – their fee was 20% – and this is what remains." I showed her the accounting from David.

Frances ate another chip and stared wide-eyed at the paper. "Adding the bequest from Mrs Paston – the camouflage – and subtracting about 25% for Inland Revenue leaves…" "Forty-seven hundred pounds," said Frances. "Just over," I corrected, then paused, impressed. The figures Frances had seen were quite new to her, yet she had immediately calculated the correct total. Evidently she was quick with figures, too. She chewed, swallowed, sipped her tea, and said, "Matthew, we can live some time on that but you still need to find a job." I nodded, said, "I am looking, as I told you. However, having this amount means it should be possible to buy a property, like David and Esther did with their commission, still have money to invest so as to have a bit of private income, and, best of all, I needn't be restricting myself to university jobs. A job teaching in a public school would bring in enough, so I need only try to find such a job in a good location, a nice place. I can cast my net over a much wider area."

Frances ate another chip, chewed, nodding, very excited about my news. I still had the sheaf of papers I was showing her in my hand. I drank some milk, dry because I had been talking so much, then folded the papers and put them in my pocket. I looked at Frances, who had a most peculiar expression on her face. I picked up my fork and looked down at my plate. It was empty, as was Frances's. I looked across at her, and then proceeded to ostentatiously look around my plate, lift it up and look underneath, look in the sugar bowl and salt cellar, search my pockets, look down the front of my coat, at the seat next to me, on the floor, while Frances shook with laughter.

Finally I planted my elbows on the table and looked across at Frances. "Let me hazard a guess," I said, "you had no breakfast." Frances shook her head. "Or lunch." Another shake, then Frances said, "You can get another serving, Matthew." I replied, "Yes, but I would have to eat it at another table or more likely in the Gents, and that would be awkward. Never mind. I had lunch late." We gazed at each other, and I reached across the table, took her hand and pressed it. We were smiling at each other. Then Frances assumed a demure expression, and I became uneasy. She said, "What happened to the book, Matthew?" "Book?" I replied, quite at sea. "Yes, you said the German official had an account book, another book and the coins and jewellery. I am asking about the other book. What sort of book was it?" I opened my mouth, and then closed it. Oh, yes, that book. I was sweating a little; I could feel this conversation heading not towards shoal water but over a falls. I struggled to temporize.

"Well," I said, "it had covers top and bottom, I think made of cardboard covered with calfskin, perhaps, and between them were a lot of rectangular pieces of paper, called pages, I believe." I wondered if I could offer to get her more tea, get another glass of milk for myself – anything.

"Did you open the book, Matthew, to look into it?" "Well, yes, just briefly, I was pressed for time…" "What sort of book was it?" "Well, you know, it had words printed on the pages…" "What language was it in?" I sighed. "French," I said. "And you don't read French." "No," I said. Not that sort of French, anyway, and I hoped Frances couldn't either. Frances was relentless: "Was the book illustrated?" "Illustrated?" I was really sweating now. "Yes," said Frances, "you know, drawings, photographs?" "Yes, it was." "With drawings or photographs?" My God, I thought, surely Frances wasn't interested in such things, was she? "Photographs, actually." "What were the photographs about?" "About?" I said weakly. "What did they illustrate?

There was nothing for it now. Frances was backing me into a corner, and from the look on her face, she was enjoying it. I looked around. No one near. "Frances," I sighed, "it was a b-book of p-p-porn-pornography." I faintly expected or hoped she would be repelled, affronted. No: she clapped her hands together with glee, she was grinning at me. "And of course you brought it back with you, spoils of war, that sort of thing." But there I had her. "No, I did not: I was pressed for space and anyway didn't think I needed a book like that about. I left it on the wardroom table, and the last thing I heard was one of the men, who was leafing through it while another looked over his shoulder, say, 'By Jove, I didn't think it could be done that way.'"

Frances was laughing uninhibitedly now, and I began to laugh, too. We quieted into smiles. I saw again how tired she was, and reached across the table to caress her cheek. "You are looking quite worn out. I had best escort you back." She did not demur. We got up. I left sixpence on the table for whoever cleared it and we went out onto the street. She took my arm, pulling me very close, which I liked. We had been a considerable time over our, well, her meal, and the sun was nearly set. We walked slowly back to the hospital.

When we got there, I was going to hold the door for her, but she pulled me into the shadows behind some pillars. She put her arms about my neck and drew me close for a kiss. I gathered her in my arms, our lips met. Then the kiss became passionate as her mouth opened and her tongue penetrated my lips. I had heard of such kisses, and opened my mouth to receive her tongue and used my own in the same way. I became aroused, very aroused, and attempted to draw my hips back, since I was embarrassed, but Frances pressed closer to me. My hands began to drift below her

268

waist, but this didn't persuade her to draw back either; rather the reverse, it seemed.

Eventually, we drew apart, both out of breath. Frances looked down at me, then up and gave me the wickedest smile I had ever seen. She took my lapel in her hand, drew close again and spoke. "Matthew, tomorrow morning I am going to resign my job here. I will have my things packed and down in the lobby by ten. If you come here then, we can take them over to your flat, then get married in a registry office." I nodded. "Tomorrow morning at ten." She then began kissing me again, in the same way with the same results, except my hands began fondling her hips and bottom.

Mutual breathlessness caused us to separate as before, and once again, Frances, inspecting me, was very pleased at what she saw, and I was embarrassed again, although not so much. Frances drew close once more and said, "After tomorrow, you won't need any more picture books." Then she kissed me again and I opened the door for her. "Goodnight, Matthew," she said and I replied, "Goodnight, my dear." She raised her hand in goodbye, I did the same, she walked a few steps into the lobby, turned once more and again waved goodbye. I did the same and she was gone.

I stepped back into the shadows, thinking, "What a saucy thing to say, Miss Millwood." I remained there until I had subsided, as I really didn't want to be arrested for Public Indecency on the eve of my wedding. Eventually I emerged in the dusking light and walked away towards the flat.

I had much to reflect upon. I was beginning to see that Frances and I had much more in common than might be supposed from our family backgrounds. We were both hard-working, determined people, aware that our part of the world could not be normally counted on to give us anything; we usually had to plan and work for whatever we wanted and that meant effort and sacrifice. But more importantly perhaps, we were each, in our different ways, wounded souls seeking comfort, reassurance, someone sympathetic on whom we could rely absolutely, someone who would always be available. I felt each of us was such a person for the other; I felt comfort in having Frances with me, beside me and thought she had come to rely on me for such comfort and understanding. So indeed we were a match and a good one.

But there was something else, something harder to pin down, something that also united us. Reflecting on the conversations we had had, I began to see a similar perspective in another sense: both of us had grown up on the outside of things, so to speak, so had independent outlooks.

I walked on. Frances had shown additional aspects, dimensions of her character this evening: her mischievous sense of humour, her sexual interest. I smiled at the memory of the evening. I also felt anticipation at being married to Frances: I strongly suspected she would prove extremely entertaining in bed.

My attention was suddenly taken by the realization that I had unconsciously made the turn down the street leading to my now former landlady's house. I immediately made an about-turn that even the brigadier would have approved and reversed course. I wondered how my former landlady would have reacted, felt again the entirely irrational jealousy at the thought she might have a replacement lover installed, shook my head and walked faster.

I suddenly remembered the odd dream I had the night after I met Frances. Elsie was gone, but I suddenly had a vision of my former landlady appearing to object to Frances and me marrying. Was she pregnant? I shook my head again, attempted to rationalize the situation: in the first place, my former landlady didn't appear pregnant and anyway was already married, and how could she know of our plans when these were just made and how would she know of which registry office we were to use? I didn't know that. It was a totally irrational fear, I told myself.

I gradually calmed down. However as I walked towards the flat, one thought kept recurring: during the evening at some point I must have asked Frances to marry me, and her answer was evidently Yes, but try as I might, I could not remember when I did this. Most puzzling and vexing.

I had set the alarm for 7 to have plenty of time. I bathed, cleaned my teeth, shaved carefully, and applied cologne sparingly to my face and a few other places, taking Eddie's advice of old. I dressed carefully: clean clothes, polished shoes and carefully knotted necktie. Clean handkerchief. Money – for a ring, taxis, fees. I was nervous. In fact, I was a bit frightened. Marriage was a big change in my life, a desired even a longed-for change, but I was venturing into a new life. Well, I told myself, most men marry and manage to adjust, so must I. And I had told Frances I would be there at ten; she was depending upon me to do so.

Outside, I realized I had no idea where the nearest registry office was. However, a constable came along, and I asked him. He gave me directions, it apparently wasn't too far away, and I thanked him, checked my watch, realized I needed to hurry and began walking fast towards the hospital. In fact I was nearly running by the time the place came in sight, and was somewhat breathless and sweaty. I passed the door at one minute past ten.

In the lobby were two suitcases, a larger and a normal-sized one. Towards the stairs was a group of women, mostly nurses in uniform, but Frances was easily distinguished by her height and hair colour. One of them alerted Frances to my appearance, she said goodbye to the others, turned to me and smiled. My nervousness and anxiety evaporated, I smiled back and basked in the warmth of her smile as she approached. She was very nicely turned out in a pale greenish blouse and brown skirt. I reached down and tried to pick up the larger suitcase with my right hand. It was very heavy and I felt a stab of pain in my shoulder and winced. Frances looked concerned, but I smiled reassuringly, switched hands and was able to lift both. Carrying hods in Egypt for the Millwood sisters, I told myself.

Frances opened the door for me and we went down the stairs. A taxi had just discharged some passengers and we booked it for the trip to the flat. Once inside, I asked Frances what in Hell was in that suitcase? She said books and some new recordings she

271

had purchased. Was my shoulder all right, she asked. I said it protested when too much weight was put on it, that was all. We sat, smiling at each other.

At the flat, we got out; I paid the driver and helped remove the luggage. Then Frances and I went in. "Up the stairs to the first floor, right along the landing, last door on the left," I said. I opened the door, set the suitcases on two book boxes and looked at Frances. We were still smiling at each other when I noticed she had no jewellery on and remembered what she had said about jewellery. I said, "Frances, you have no jewellery and don't expect to inherit any?" She said, "That's right." I went to a bookcase where Mrs Paston's jewellery box sat, brought it down, set it on a table next to the window and opened it. "Frances, I inherited these, and once we are married, they are yours." Frances stared at the contents, then picked up two brooches on top, looked at them, took them to the window where the light was better, held one then the other on her sleeve, and returned one to the box. She then pinned the other on, and looked again at the contents of the box. She seemed particularly interested in two of the pins I had given Elsie, which surprised me. Of course, they were solid metal, not plate, I didn't make presents of rubbish, but still.... I saw Frances's gaze sharpen and she reached into the box and brought out the ring I had given her sister so many years ago.

She held it up and our gazes met. "Are you sure?" I asked. She said, "Yes." So I took the ring, tucked it into my fob pocket, making sure there were no holes, and we were ready. On the street, I realized I had completely forgotten the directions the constable had given me, but here came the man himself, on his way back. I gestured to him; he interpreted the situation immediately and repeated the directions to the two of us.

It was a pleasant summer morning. We walked arm in arm to the registry office. It was empty inside save for the clerk and an elderly woman who presumably was the witness. We filled out the form. It was odd but satisfying to have my full name and correct birthdate; I felt, finally, as though I were a real, complete human being. And about to become more complete in a sense: Frances and I plighted our troth to each other, I put the ring on her finger – I knew it would fit – we embraced and kissed. I paid the woman a crown for her signature. I thought I could smell something I took, perhaps unfairly, to be gin on her breath. Then we walked out the door, husband and wife, a family.

When we got to the flat, I opened the door, swept Frances up in my arms and carried her across the threshold. Setting her down inside, I said, "Welcome home." "Home?" she asked. "Where you abide shall be our home," I replied. She gave me a very special smile, we embraced again and kissed. I realized I hadn't closed the door, did so, and then followed Frances into the bedroom. She wanted to remove the brooch and I volunteered to assist her, a gentleman to the core, but I was very clumsy, my hands kept wandering....

Frances was not buxom, but when she had taken off her blouse, I delved into her chemise top, caressing her breasts and bending over to kiss and gently suck upon her rosy coloured nipples. This was well received, but she suggested I begin taking off my clothes, too. I began to do so, complaining she was a distracting influence on me in this respect. I was having to ration my disrobing because I kept putting my hands on her, but she didn't seem too unhappy about this. Once her stockings were off – I again assisting – I caressed her drawers down, exposing her reddish-brown pubic bush. She kissed me again and began helping me get my remaining clothes off. Being naked and fully aroused before her was a little embarrassing, but once again, she seemed pleased at the effect she was having on me. She stood up next to me and reached down, and pushed my cock between her legs. I began moving it back and forth and she began moving her hips in time with my movements. She became increasingly moist, then slippery, and was clearly becoming very excited and this communicated itself to me.

She and I began to incline towards the bed, a bit awkwardly. Then I was on her and my cock entered her incredibly smooth, slippery tube and began sliding further into, then less into her and her legs seemed to spread more and more at each push as our excitement grew and grew. My cock seemed to grow in her as my satisfaction neared. My seed began to escape me, to spray, but she was gasping and groaning rhythmically, finally giving a groaning sigh, and I realized our marriage had been consummated. We held each other. We were as close as a man and woman can be and we kissed again. We were one, physically. I rolled onto my back and pulled Frances next to me. She slid her left arm under the pillows beneath our heads and we nestled.

We lay in each other's arms, both sweaty from our efforts, both still naked as it was a warm day. I thought Frances nestled superbly, and told her she was the pattern and model of nestlers. Frances answered, "That's not a word, Matthew." I had a feeling I had had a vaguely similar conversation before, and said, "In the privacy of our bedchamber, I think I can be as unabridged as I choose." Frances replied, "It's still not a word, but I'll accept the compliment."

We were silent a minute or so. Then Frances said, "That was a magnificent present of jewellery, Matthew. Thank you." I replied, "You are welcome. I seldom wear much jewellery myself, at least in the daytime." I waited for Frances to bite, but she only said, "I'm very glad to hear that, Matthew, for a number of reasons." We glanced at each other, both shaking a bit, laughing silently.

Then I remembered something, two things actually, and said, "I fear I have been remiss, dear. On two counts." She said, "In what way, Matthew?" I said, "I never asked you about a honeymoon. It didn't come up. We never discussed it. Where do you want to go? Paris? The Lakes?" Frances replied, "I've been to Paris. With some other nurses. The Lakes sounds nice, but I think we need to save our pennies, Matthew, to have as much private income as possible. Besides, the purpose of the honeymoon is for the man and wife to be alone together. This flat is perfect."

More silence. I looked at the clock: half past eleven. "I also undertook to see you missed no more meals. Did you have breakfast this morning?" "Yes," she said, "Also a large dinner last night." "I have some recollection of that," I said. Frances asked, "Did you have breakfast?" "No," I said, "and last night's dinner was on the sparse side." We were exchanging glances. I said, "What would you like for lunch?"

We had gotten up, used the loo, which embarrassed me but Frances took it in stride, the training as a nurse, I supposed, gotten dressed and checked the larder. Aside from the jar of pickles, there were two tins, both of which had swollen ends, which made us uneasy so they were tossed in a dustbin outside. There was also a sack of flour which had solidified, ditto. Frances said, "My God!" as she looked into a second sack of flour, which was crawling with insects. Also tossed. So we sat down with a sheet of paper from her smaller suitcase and began writing down a list of things to buy. Frances thought she would like corned beef sandwiches for lunch, so bread, tinned corned beef and mustard were listed. I volunteered to make a Spanish omelette for dinner, so more things were added. Frances said she definitely wanted pasties, but I said I would make those tomorrow as our list was getting a bit long. I asked her about drink. She rather liked wine for an evening meal, but said if I had religious or other scruples she would forego it.

I said, "If my lady wants wine, wine she shall have, but which wine? There seem to be a great many." Frances said she very much liked the wine served by Eddie and Christine, so I suggested we get things for lunch and dinner, then, after lunch, visit Eddie and Christine to get the name and vendor of the wine they served. I added that we would need some sort of shopping bag. Frances pulled one out of her smaller suitcase, and out we went to buy foodstuffs.

We had walked a hundred yards or so when I realized that since I had just moved into the neighbourhood, I had no idea where the shops were. Frances rationally suggested we ask passers-by, and eventually we found a grocery that had what we wanted, and even had garlic and olive oil, needed for pasties. Back at the flat, Frances sliced the bread using my very sharp knives while I sliced and dissected the corned beef. We set the table together, poured milks and sat down to our first meal as a married couple. I caught her eyes, raised my glass and extended it to hers.

She touched her glass of milk to mine. I said, "To us." "To us," she repeated.

* * *

Christine was in. On seeing us together, she threw her arms around Frances, kissed her, and then kissed me and stood beaming at the two of us. "You are engaged to marry?" she asked. "Married," Frances and I said together. "Wonderful," replied Christine, "I am so happy for you both. The three musketeers, now all married." She invited us to sit, and we explained our errand. She got up and brought a bottle of wine from the pantry, and insisted we take it as a present. We thanked her and asked where they bought it. Christine said Eddie bought it a case at a time from a vintner. The name meant nothing to me.

Christine invited us to dinner Sunday afternoon. I was about to accept when I glanced at Frances, who glanced at me and nodded slightly, at which I accepted for both of us. We talked about visiting David and Esther on Sunday week. A thought occurred to me: I asked if David and Esther also liked the wine. Christine said she was certain they did. I nodded and Frances and I said goodbye.

We took an omnibus back, as we had done going to Eddie and Christine's, since Frances felt we needed to economize. I had never been on one before, throughout the time I had been in London, but sitting on the top in the sun, with Frances sitting next me, was a delight. I told her that being with her was excursions and holidays in warm summer sunshine. She turned to me and said that being with me was concerts and dinners with friends, long walks and amusing conversations and love. I remembered something and said, "Music, laughter and love." She nodded, and repeated, "Music and laughter and love."

I said I agreed with economy in principle, but we needed to get a gramophone and perhaps more recordings. I noted that she was not the only member of this family that liked music. Frances smiled and said she would make that one exception.

* * *

276

Frances and I were lying in bed together. It was odd how that had happened: no words had been exchanged, just glances. Frances wondered why I had asked whether David and Esther had liked the wine; she said she was sure that they did. I said I was thinking that if she liked that wine sufficiently, we would arrange for Eddie to buy two cases, insisting on paying for ours and going halves for David and Esther's. I went on, that we would have to insist on paying for ours, because of the kind of people Eddie and Christine were, but that, if David and Esther were agreeable, we all four would take a case of the wine to them Sunday week.

We were silent for a while, just lying in each other's arms. Frances asked if it weren't too inconvenient for Esther and David to be traveling back and forth to the shop, especially now Esther was pregnant. I said, "I have a feeling that David – and Esther, for David would have thoroughly discussed the matter with her – was probably considering selling the London shop and opening a jewellery business, just retail and repair, near where they were living. When they could do this, I had no idea, for I imagined the London shop actually belonged to David's father, but I remember David telling us – Eddie was there – that the pawn business, besides occasional encounters with people attempting to pawn things to which they had no legal title, and consequent conversations with the police, was occasioned by loss, defeat, failure while the jewellery business was about hope, as well as pleasure and display."

Silence. Then Frances commented, "You three seem to have spent a great deal of time on intellectual topics. We nurses talked a great deal about men. So you never talked about girls?" "No," I said. "Really?" asked Frances. "No," I repeated, "we mostly talked about women." Frances burst into laughter, and then said I had made extravagant promises about Spanish omelettes and it was time I fulfilled these. So we got up, smiling.

* * *

I washed my hands in the sink and checked my fingernails. They were clean. The chopping board had been washed. I opened the tin of ham, cut off a reasonable-sized piece, and trimmed then minced it. I explained to Frances what I was doing, that I couldn't stand fat and gristle, these were either discarded or, in the case of beef, wrapped in muslin with the bones and tied with string and set in boiling water some hours to make soup stock. Frances was making toast, and while the toasting was going on, perched on a stool watching me.

An onion of appropriate size was peeled, sliced and chopped into small pieces – small pieces cook faster, I informed Frances – then a medium sized tomato and some cheese were similarly prepared. Then I asked Frances to get five eggs. I thought that appropriate for two hungry people. I lit the burner and set the fry pan on it to heat up while I broke the eggs into a bowl, and then poured some olive oil into the pan and beat the eggs with a fork. After a minute or two, I scooped the onion bits into the oil and cooked them, using a spatula to keep them from burning. By now Frances had buttered the first set of toast and was setting the table. The ham and tomato came next. I kept them stirring, then removed the fry pan to a cold burner and added the eggs. I mixed everything, turned down the burner and set the pan back on it, shovelled and turned the congealing mixture over and over. Then the cheese. I watched it melt, and then slid the omelette onto a plate while folding it – a lot of practice went into that manoeuvre I explained – and set the pan on a cold burner, turning off the lit one.

By now, Frances had accumulated six slices of toast. I suggested one more apiece. Looking at the remaining loaf, I remarked we would need to get another for tomorrow, if I was to make my patented toasted bread-melted cheese sandwich for breakfast.

Now came the hard part: opening the bottle of wine. That required a corkscrew. I had seen Eddie's butler-factotum use one, but was there one in the flat? I searched the drawers, eventually finding one. Frances had filled a glass of ginger beer for me and set out forks and napkins. I looked at the corkscrew. "Clockwise" I said, and began screwing it into the cork. Eventually it had bored deeply enough, I guessed, and pulled. Out it came. I smiled. Frances smiled. I looked for a wine glass. Only tumblers. I carefully poured the wine into one – I knew about lees – and set it next to Frances's plate. I corked the wine lightly, set the bottle down and set myself down, as Frances had divided the omelette.

About midway through the meal, Frances said it was by far the best omelette she had ever had, which pleased me, yet I realized I would be preparing them and other dishes for us for the rest of our lives. I in turn praised her toast-making skills, telling her she had even buttered the toast on the right side. "What side –" Frances began, and then stopped, but it was too late. "The uppermost side, of course," I said, adding, "Trying to butter the bottom side allows the butter to melt and drip onto the floor or into one's face, very distressing." "Matthew!" said Frances, but she was laughing, while looking about, I imagined, for something to throw at me.

We washed up everything. I was accustomed to doing everything myself, but Frances seemed able to anticipate what needed doing and do it, so we finished quickly. Frances said she needed to write to her aunt Lydia and her parents informing them of our marriage, and to some of her school and nurse friends who were distant. I said I would write to my grandfather and to a few other friends and former comrades, and we sat down at the table by the window. Frances set a pile of sheets of stationary, some envelopes and stamps on the table and we got to work.

After a few letters had been completed, Frances showed me the letter to her parents. She informed them we were married, where we were living, and that it was only temporary as I was looking for a teaching job, and signed it "Mrs Matthew E Dobbs". I looked at this, and then asked her how she normally signed letters to her parents. "Fanny" she said. I thought she should rewrite the letter, signing it in her usual way. The letter told them she was married to me, and signing it the way she did seemed defiant, throwing our marriage in their face, as it were. If they were opposed to our marriage, which seemed likely, there was no point in throwing fuel on the fire, but signing it the way she always had before would remind them she was still their daughter. After thinking this over, Frances redrafted the letter. By now it was getting dark. We washed ourselves up, cleaned our teeth, went to bed and made love. Not had sex, I thought afterwards, but made love. A very different thing.

We had gotten up a little early Saturday. I had a bath, tied a towel around my waist, cleaned my teeth, shaved and was splashing a bit of cologne here and there when Frances came in to get her comb. She sat down on the W. C. lid and looked at my right leg. "Matthew, these should have been stitched. Why weren't they?" I said, "Eddie offered to do that, but lectures were about to start, and they had stopped bleeding, or nearly, so I just let them heal. Eddie checked them every day and said they weren't infected. I must say, though, that I haven't been able to dance since that time." Frances bit: "Were you able to do so before?" I replied, "Well no, but I certainly haven't been able to since." Frances said, "Oh Matthew," and we put our arms around each other, kissed and laughed. And my towel fell off.

We went to buy ingredients for further meals, including a loaf of bread, some cheese, potatoes, flour, salt…and went to a butcher shop for a cut of meat. For pasties, I want as much clear meat as possible, so I am very particular about the cut. The butcher's display showed rather poor cuts on the top. I asked to see the ones underneath, which request was not well received. I insisted. The fellow didn't want to. I glared, clearly indicating we were going elsewhere if I wasn't able to choose what I wanted. Since no one else was in the shop, he grudgingly showed the buried cuts, which were clearly superior. After more demands from me to see the next one underneath, I eventually saw a piece that would do, and insisted on that one, no, the one to your left, yes that one…. He sullenly weighed the meat, I watching to be sure, as much as I could, that he wasn't altering the weight, and paid him. The transaction concluded to mutual dissatisfaction, Frances and I left.

Frances amused but clearly sympathetic, took my arm. I was still irritated. "I think in future we use a different butcher. I understand he is trying to move the inferior cuts first, but I never had this problem with the butcher I used while at university or with Eddie's butcher. It is just a peculiarity of taste of mine, but I

280

like my meat clear, as clear as possible. But tell me your taste in this matter." Frances said she would conform to my taste, since she didn't much care for gristle – did anyone? – and was indifferent to the fat.

We got newspapers and returned, put things away, and I prepared for the toasted sandwiches. Since it was now late in the morning, I prepared five. Frances brought out the bottle of pickles, cut two of them into quarters, and set up the table, wine for her, ginger beer for me. When the first sandwiches were ready, I set one each on the two plates and cut each in half before beginning the next pair. I warned Frances to let hers cool first.

The sandwiches were a clear hit. Frances asked how I had come to make them – usually rarebits were just cheese melted on one slice of bread. I said, "By accident. I had made a cheese sandwich, only the bread was soggy. So, after the fact, I decided to toast the bread. Well, that required a fry pan, and if the bread wasn't to burn, I had to butter it, each outside first. Anyway, the cheese melted while I was toasting it. After letting it cool, I tried it and decided I had discovered something. Serendipity is the term, I think."

We washed up, rather quickly. I commented she was quite efficient. Frances replied that we were becoming an efficient team. We smiled at each other, kissed and moved to the table. Frances had more letters to write and I would look at the jobs offered. I wasn't seeing much, and then noticed an advertisement, a public school in Dorset wanting a headmaster. I had seen this before, in fact, twice, at intervals of some weeks, I couldn't be sure exactly, but evidently they hadn't filled the job. I wondered why: the salary, £250/year, was not bad, and use of a house was included. Of course, I had very little actual teaching experience, only about five months, still.... Frances noticed my preoccupation and asked what I was looking at. I showed her, and commented on it. She suggested I apply – after all, what was the worst that could happen? I thought they might not merely reject me, but lay a curse on me for wasting their time, although, I noted, I was probably already under one from the butcher, so what was one more?

So I took a sheet of paper and wrote an application for the position. My qualifications in a formal academic sense were actually quite good but my experience risible. The history master at the university who had encouraged me to get my paper published and the man I had substituted for were listed as recommenders. I mentioned my military record and the fact that I had recently married. I showed her the letter. She said, "You were Mentioned in Dispatches four times, Matthew. You should say that." Recalling a remark I had made once, I said, "Favourably, I hope." Then I thought: I asked Frances how she knew this; I didn't know it. Frances acknowledged she had contacted a man at the War Office, a friend of her father, who had read my record to her. She said, "Your commanding officer said you were what he called a difficult subordinate, but that you were a first-class fighting officer and a lion on defence." I turned hot from this praise. It must have come from the brigadier. I really didn't know what to say, but pencilled in the Mentioned in Despatches (four times).

Frances went on. "I called the Registrar at university about you. He said you had taken a first." "But only by two marks," I protested, then something else occurred to me: the only person I had mentioned my landlady's name to was Eddie, but of course Eddie talked to Christine and I remembered Christine talking to Frances at the party and Christine or Eddie or both probably knew the woman or her family... I sighed, "My wife, the private enquiries agent." Frances said, "I was interested in you, Matthew, and you don't talk that much about yourself."

Frances added, "You should mention I worked as a nurse for three years and have an Efficiency Stripe." I said, "I am trying to flog my services, not yours." Frances replied, "But, it is, after all, true, and of course I would help if asked." So another pencilled insertion. Then Frances said, "And your letter should mention my maiden name, that I am the younger daughter of Lady Edith and Sir Edward Millwood, Bart., MP of Millwood, Berkshire." I looked at her, she looked back steadily and I bent to the letter with more emendations, telling myself that Frances knew what she was doing.

There was nothing for it but to rewrite the letter. I took another sheet of paper and began. In the end, it took two sheets, in my best hand. After signing it, I handed it to Frances, who read it while I addressed the envelope and attached a stamp. She read it twice, then nodded and handed it back to me. I folded it, put it in the envelope, sealed it and added it to two or three others, including a brief note from me to my grandfather telling him of my marriage. I turned to Frances and suggested we look for a player for our recordings. I really wanted to hear them. So we took the letters to the post and boarded an omnibus and rode to where the large stores that would be expected to sell such a thing could be found.

We found what we wanted very quickly and bought it. The price seemed a bit high, but then the prices of everything seemed a bit – or more than a bit – high. It was in a good-sized box, rather troublesome on the omnibus, but I was able to carry the thing back. Then we had to unpack it and assemble it, but together we managed, plugged it in – it was electric, not wind-up – and selected a recording, one of Brahms's Hungarian dances. Then we sat together on the couch, my arm about her shoulders, her left hand, with the sapphire ring, resting on my knee, occasionally tapping to the rhythms. After that, we listened to another, a Mozart opera overture on two sides.

By now it was late afternoon, and I began preparations for the pasties. Frances perched on her stool, while I explained what I was doing; again, I was not expecting her ever to prepare any, not that I really minded. I had the impression Frances was impressed by my efficiency, although I knew I was far off my between-terms university pace. Still, I put the tray in the oven set for the correct temperature, wrote down the time and added 25 minutes. "Ovens are different," I explained, "so I will look at these after 25 minutes rather than 30, in case this one is hotter than the setting." We looked at each other and reached for each other's hand, then walked to the bedroom. Twenty-five minutes should be plenty of time.

* * *

Only just. I opened the oven door at the 25 minute mark, looked carefully and decided 5 minutes more was about right. Frances, who had dressed quickly herself, began setting the table. I helped, and when the full 30 minutes was over, took out the pan and used the spatula to shift the browned pasties into a bowl, then onto our plates. I warned Frances to let hers cool; the liquid inside was essentially boiling, so breaking off pieces with her fork, then letting them cool should be done.

They were quite good as always. Frances, on her third pasty, told me she had never in her life eaten as well as she had these two days. I was very surprised. Didn't her family employ a cook at Millwood? Frances said of course, but the meals the woman turned out hovered around unappetizing, occasionally dipping into unpleasant. "Why keep her on?" I asked. "She is sort of an heirloom, and so the family is stuck with her. Actually, since we ate there most of the time, we, at least my mother, were probably unaware that better-tasting food was possible." "Amazing," I said. "I will use the bone and scraps to make soup stock. Aside from my vegetable-beef-barley soup, the only dish left in my repertoire is a walnut cake, for which, naturally, walnuts are helpful." "Naturally." said Frances.

Sunday morning we got up late. After dinner, we had drunk wine (Frances) or ginger beer (me) sitting together on the couch and listening to recordings. That night, Frances had had a nightmare. She was tossing, crying "Nolan, Nolan." I had put my arms around her, saying, "Frances, dearest, it's all right. It's only a nightmare. We're together, everything is all right." Eventually she woke up fully. I asked her if Nolan was her fiancé. She said, "Yes, Nolan Rutter." Silence. Then, "It's always the same. He is on the operating table. I am assisting, then he begins to haemorrhage, I can't stop it…." I said, "I had that reality at Passchendaele, men bleeding to death and I couldn't stop it." I asked her how often her nightmares were. She said when she was at Millwood, every night. After she returned to the hospital, perhaps every three or four days. She said, "This is the first one since we reached the understanding a week ago." Only a week ago? I thought. Frances asked, "How often are yours?" I thought and said, "Not very often now, perhaps twice a month." Frances asked what my nightmares were about. "Usually being buried alive," I said, "being trapped in a box or pipe so I can't move at all, can't free myself, goes back to the train wreck, I think." We were silent. I put my arms around her, and she did the same, nestling against me. I fell asleep, troubled that she still thought of her fiancé, had divided loyalties as it were.

* * *

I made toasted cheese sandwiches again, at Frances's request and we sat at the kitchen table eating. I noted how downcast Frances seemed, and finally I could bear it no longer. I wiped my mouth and hands on the napkin, got up and went round to Frances. I put my hands on her shoulders and said, "Frances, dearest, we are together and will stay together for as long as we are given. My duty, inclination and desire are to offer you whatever comfort, solace, and emotional sanctuary I can. For I do love you and want above everything to make you as happy as our circumstances permit." Frances had put one of her hands up on one of mine, and then she got up, turned and embraced me. I held her, thinking how

285

good she felt in my arms, and how she had become the centre of my life. She kissed me and said, "Thank you, Matthew. Thank you for that and thank you for being who you are and what you are." I smiled, and said, "You are welcome, although I want some time to think about that statement." She smiled in turn and we kissed again. Then I said, "And thank you for coming into my life, for joining your life to mine, indeed becoming the focus of my life." We stood together, embracing, as I reflected that, however it had happened, I did indeed love Frances.

* * *

We had done the washing up. The bones, etc., were being boiled for stock. We were sitting at the kitchen table, I was writing down things we would buy tomorrow, more bread, a good cut of beef for the soup, barley, more carrots as I was munching on the ones we had left over. Then Frances suggested cocoa mix for chocolate, which I wrote down, along with cream. Frances commented that the nurses made their chocolate up stronger than recommended, and that she had never had cream in her chocolate. I related my adventures with the Corps staff's supply, and said we would try her recipe with cream. After we had sipped at our drinks, Frances said, "Jam." I looked up and asked, "What kind?" She said raspberry and we thought about others, which I wrote down.

Frances also began washing the bed linens and other clothing, saying there were some domestic duties she could perform. I didn't mention I could do those sorts of things as well, just assisted her. She then thought we needed to get bed linens of our own, so the list got longer. She unpacked her smaller case, containing clothing, and then the larger. She did indeed have it nearly full of books, some of which I had, some new to me. Her recordings were beside the gramophone. We discussed how much unpacking should be done, and decided to leave the Paston books in their boxes, merely moving them out of the way. In this fashion, the day advanced until we decided we needed to start towards Eddie and Christine's.

I turned off the burner under the pot. Frances put on one of the necklaces from Mrs Paston and one of the pins, a small gold flower that I had given Elsie. She took her umbrella, as it threatened rain, and also took my arm, and we set forth.

It did rain, so we sat, rather crowded, on the lower level of the omnibus. Being crowded with Frances didn't bother me at all; eventually she wound up sitting on my knee, which I think we both liked.

* * *

After a prolonged, involved, amicable discussion, Frances and I and Eddie and Christine decided to descend on David and Esther in a week, assuming they were agreeable. Christine was sure they liked the same wine, so we agreed to take a case there. Eddie agreed to order two cases, one for us but he and Christine absolutely refused to take any money from us, calling our case a wedding present. All I could do was insist on paying for half the cost of David and Esther's case, which was two pounds ten shillings. We found that a case was twenty four bottles, tuppence over four shillings each – undoubtedly more sold as individual bottles – and agreed to meet at Eddie and Christine's and travel there together. Then we ate.

After dinner, I glanced at Frances, then proposed that we – glancing at Frances again – host a party at the flat, the same ten guests as were at the party at Eddie and Christine's, only a week and a day ago, with pasties and perhaps – I stressed the perhaps – a walnut cake for dessert. Glancing again at Frances, who nodded, I proposed Sunday week from the visit to David and Esther. Eddie looked to Christine, who looked to Eddie, and in one of those silent moments of communication that occur between married couples, both turned to us and accepted the invitation. After more discussion and music, Frances and I went back to the flat.

On the omnibus, we discussed the proposed party. Frances had no objection to being "*châtelaine*", in fact, she thought the party appropriate. I agreed: given the hospitality shown me over the years, it was little enough. Frances asked, "How many pasties will you prepare?" I said, "Three batches – fifty-one – should do it. My concern is the walnut cakes. I think two are necessary. The problem is I never made that many cakes and none in more than a year. With pasties, well, I once estimated I made about forty thousand in my time at university, so those I can prepare in my sleep, in fact, I thought I had done just that on occasion, but there were no complaints. But I really need come sort of recipe, at least to refresh my memory."

Frances said, "I have a book of recipes buried somewhere among my books." "Really?" I said. "But you never received any training in cooking?" "No," said Frances. A pause. Then, "At one point, my family wanted me to become a companion, presumably to some wealthy elderly lady, and it was thought I might have to cook something as part of my duties." Looking at her, I said, "That would have been a terrible waste." We were sitting together, turned towards each other on a seat. She smiled, "The idea was, I think, that some male relative would see me and marry me despite having no money. But, for me, the war offered other possibilities." "It certainly stirred things up." I remarked. "Were they that anxious to get rid of you?" Frances replied, "I think they were just trying to provide for me."

We were silent a while. Then I said, "I confess to feelings of disillusionment: I kept thinking you were all having a series of country-house weekends, with riding to hounds, shooting, fishing, exhibitions on the pianoforte and endless gourmet experiences." Frances said dryly, "It fell rather short of that. I mentioned our cook. When I became a nurse, I was surprised at how much the other nurses complained about the food. I thought it a considerable improvement. As far as the rest, I can remember gatherings at the house when I was young and Father was in Parliament. But in those days, the members weren't paid, and I think Father decided not to stand again because of the expense." "Did he enjoy being in Parliament?" "I can't say, as they never discussed such things, or anything much, before me, but I rather think so. Father certainly made many friends."

More silence. I asked, "What exactly is grown at Mill-wood?" Frances said, "Wheat and barley." I commented, "Barley, at least for human consumption, should bring in money, but I can't imagine wheat doing much." Frances said, "I remember comments to the effect that it didn't, so I don't know why it continues to be grown. You see, the estate was larger once, but there was a great uncle who liked to gamble, but unfortunately not successfully, so I fancy my family is just keeping afloat, financially, basically trying to keep something for Richard when Father dies."

We were at our stop. It had turned cool, so we put a blanket on the bed. Frances seemed unusually eager to make love that evening. I was happy to oblige but felt she was still upset about the nightmare.

Our agenda for today was to finish preparing the soup. After bathroom duties, we ate the remaining pasties from Saturday. Then we went to the bank where Frances had her account. She was closing it, explaining she had gotten married. The total she had saved over three years heroic service, which is how I viewed it, was £36 odd. She put some in her purse, gave me some – she had noted my notecase was getting a bit empty of banknotes – and we went in search of a butcher who was more accommodating. I commented, "An heiress after all; now I recall why I married you." Frances replied, "I thought it was because you wanted to take me to bed." I said, "Well, besides that." Frances swatted me.

We had a fairly extensive list of things to get, including a set of wine glasses. Frances didn't want to serve the wine in tumblers. And the butcher we were sent to by some passers-by was indeed willing to indulge my no doubt peculiar (to some) requirements in beef. More bread and butter, barley, carrots and items that should have occurred, at least to me, much earlier but didn't. Frances also called my attention to the tinned beef stew, a real favourite at the front, and, she said, with the nurses as well, yet equally scarce. We bought four tins, which filled up her shopping bag.

* * *

I had prepared the beef, essentially cutting the clear parts into small pieces and putting the rest into another muslin bag for prolonged boiling, to enrich the stock. I went out to see if there was any mail, leaving Frances to put the rest of our purchases away. I had just returned – there was nothing – when Frances opened a lower cabinet door, gasped, and said, "My God." I immediately went to her side, looked and saw what remained of a sack of potatoes, long since putrefied. It seemed to be moving. The source of the odd smell in the flat had been found. "Hell," I said, then told Frances not to disturb it, as it would smell much worse. We had to find something to wrap it in and eventually got a pair of sheets of newspaper. I scooped as much of it as possible into the newspaper and quickly carried it out to the dustbin.

By now, the smell was much worse, and we opened all the windows we could. We began trying to clean off the boards beneath the bag, using sponges and washcloths. Frances asked if the boards could be lifted out. I looked, tried them, and found they were loose. So we raised them out and took them to the bathtub and began washing them off, using hot water, soap and washcloths. Frances went back into the kitchen and began cleaning up what had seeped through the cracks between the boards. Soon I joined her.

The smell seemed to worsen, hard as we worked, at least for a while. Eventually we set the loose boards up to dry and rinsed out the sponges and washed the washcloths, each several times, until the cool air from outside began to displace the stinking air inside. At this point I began to laugh. Frances looked at me in surprise. "Here I am," I explained, "helping clean up this foul mess, and I am enjoying it, because I am doing it with you." Frances embraced me in response.

I said, "We should write a letter to the agent who rented this place, explaining what we found and did. Otherwise the owners will blame us." "A copy should go to the owners," said Frances. "If I can get their address from the agent," I replied. So we sat down at the table to draft the letters. Frances, feeling cold, put her coat on, the same one she had worn at all our meetings.

I drafted a letter to the agent and gave it to Frances. She suggested changes. I made these, then, after we each had reread the amended letter, wrote a fair copy and signed it. Frances also signed: "Mrs Frances M. Dobbs," now for the first time in a letter going out. We then wrote another letter for the owners. Because the letter would have to go by sea to Brazil, we made a second copy, a copy that Frances suggested be placed on the mantel. This was done. By now, the aroma of the soup had begun to overcome the stink of the rancid potatoes, which was a relief.

I noticed for the first time that Frances's coat was rather worn and threadbare. I asked her how old her coat was. She said, "I am not sure. It was given me after my sister got a new coat." I looked again at it, but could not recall seeing her sister wear it. I said, "Tomorrow morning we get you a new coat, one you shall select, one you shall wear with pleasure and pride for, well, I don't know how long. But I will not have my wife cold or uncomfortable in any way for any reason." Frances looked at me but did not object.

We were able to close the windows now, so the soup smell began to dominate. Frances asked when the rest of the ingredients were to be added. I said I would taste the stock until it was rich enough, then add the barley, the entire box, the chopped up onions and carrots and some potatoes as well. "Say an hour for the barley, then about a half hour for the rest. The idea," I explained, "is to prepare a soup in which a spoon, set vertically, remains vertical for at least a minute. By a watch," I added, smiling. We then sat down on the couch after setting a recording on the player. I put my arm, then both arms, around my wife, who nestled in response.

We were lying in bed together that night, when Frances said, "A very nice thing about marriage is being warm in bed at night." I kissed her gently on her forehead, which between us had come to be, among other things, interrogatory. "At Millwood," she went on, "my bedroom is in the northeast corner of the house, the window rattles in a northeast wind, it's as though there's no window at all." "I had a window like that at Earl's Cross. We were given only one thin blanket. I thought of bringing a blanket from the Paston's but realized it would almost certainly be stolen. So I went to bed fully dressed, except for shoes, including cap and coat. Good training for sleeping rough in the Army, but no other advantage I can think of, except of course to my character."

Silence. Then Frances said, "I wasn't allowed a second blanket. I don't know why, perhaps just to make sure I didn't lie abed in the morning. It wasn't much better as a nurse, it seemed. This is very nice."

* * *

We had breakfasted on rewarmed soup. I held it tasted better rewarmed, and Frances didn't argue. Noting how fast we were going through the bread, I added that to the list. Getting a coat for Frances took a very long time. Several shops were examined for coats. I told myself a husband's duty was to allow his wife whatever time she thought needful. I told myself that repeatedly, in fact. Eventually there was one she clearly liked but kept glancing at me; I guessed it was expensive, and I was right. However, I asked Frances if this was the one she wanted, and she nodded yes. So I told the clerk we would have it, and paid without comment.

I was rewarded by Frances's holding my arm very close as we went to shops for ingredients for a walnut cake. I had guessed at these, as Frances hadn't yet excavated her recipe book. The walnuts were last season's, so we would have to see if they had turned rancid.

* * *

I set the cake on the kitchen table. Both Frances and I considered it sceptically. I had used the recipe in Frances's book as it seemed similar to what I had used, although, confusingly, not identical. We had cracked the nuts together, Frances and I occasionally feeding each other bits of walnut to test. I poured milks as Frances set the table. Then I cut a medium-sized slice off for each of us, we took up our forks and tasted. It seemed all right. I had insisted on an extra half cup of walnuts – more flavour is better was my credo, I said – although the nuts, being old, would be expected to be strong- flavoured. I looked at Frances, who had already eaten half of hers. When I caught her eye, she smiled and nodded. No, I thought after my second, larger slice, not bad at all. "I think," I said to Frances, "we are ready to host our party."

* * *

Thursday we got the first mail at the flat: a note from Christine saying the wine had arrived. So Frances and I travelled to Eddie and Christine's. The case was a bit awkward, but just manageable, so we carried it off. Christine had heard from David and Esther accepting our proposed descent on them Sunday, so that was on. We had also written invitations for the party at the flat, Sunday week.

* * *

I must have had a nightmare that night, as I was sweating and shaking when I awoke. I could see Frances's face above me, and reached up and caressed her cheek. "You're real," I said. She said, "Yes, Matthew, I'm real. I think you had a nightmare. You were saying something but I couldn't make it out." I thought, but couldn't remember the nightmare. "Which is probably just as well," I remarked as she lay down in my arms again. Frances asked if her nestling was prompting any, since lying on me night recall the train wreck. I said no, since I could move both arms and both feet if it came to that.

* * *

Friday after breakfast – more soup, but that was the last of it – we got a letter from the school in Dorset. I glanced at Frances and opened it. Instead of a polite dismissal of my application, they invited Frances and me to visit on Monday. I showed Frances the letter. She was very pleased: "They're interested." A pause, then "Matthew, we need to get clothes for the visit. Today." I got up and together we went out to the clothing stores. We would have to buy ready-made as there was no time for a tailor. We would also have to reply by telegraph today, telling them when we would arrive. I commented to Frances that they seemed to be in a hurry. Frances thought there were problems at the school, and term was approaching.

We went to the biggest men's store we could find, and I tried on suit after suit. Frances evidently had something particular in mind, and I curbed my natural impatience, telling myself Frances knew what she was about. Eventually, there was a suit that she felt would do. In the mirror, looking at myself, I realized the suit made me look ... older, no, more authoritative, no, more headmaster-like, that was it. I paid and we went to get something for her.

She again had a particular look she wanted, and I waited patiently as she appeared in dress after dress. Finally, she chose one and appeared in it. Gazing at her, I decided she looked ... posh, was the only way I could put it, not frivolously, but more staid, more like ... a headmaster's upper class wife, yes. Again I paid and we went to the post office. There was a train schedule available. We would have to leave at seven, arriving about 11:30, so I composed a telegram and sent it to the head of the Governing Board. As it was nearly noon, we next went to a grocery for some more strongly flavoured cheese – Frances's suggestion – for future toasted cheese sandwiches.

For the evening meal, we had two tins of the beef stew, which Frances insisted on heating while I made the toast. I realized she wanted to contribute to the cooking in some fashion. She seemed willing to accept my instruction, so I told her to turn the flame down to a fairly low level: too hot a flame would burn the stew no matter how fast she stirred it. I pointed out that when I made soup, I kept the flame as low as possible consistent with a slow boil and stirred the barley, etc., often. I added that I had very extensive instruction in cooking from Mrs Christianson; otherwise, I had gotten a lot of experience and made many mistakes, all of which I had eaten. Then I made the toast and set out the plates and glasses and tableware. I encouraged Frances as she stirred the stew by holding her and kissing her neck. At least, that is what I told her my motive was.

Frances and I arrived at Eddie and Christine's in good time. Saturday we had bought jars of pickles for all of us, so we set out for the train station with the case of wine and a jar of pickles. We took two taxis, and once in the station, occupied much of a compartment. We talked about David and Esther's probable plans: Eddie felt our speculation about their moving their business was correct, although the time was uncertain.

David and Esther's cottage was fairly impressive, large enough for two or even three children, yet it seemed intimate, cosy. There were several large trees outside, two oaks, three walnuts. David was working on a garden, and Eddie and I talked with David about vegetables. I urged a hothouse, for winter vegetables, if only to improve Esther's diet. This got David's attention, and Eddie seconded my ideas in this respect.

The three women were talking together, I suspected pregnancies were a principal topic, and wondered if Frances would wind up in the same state as the other two. We had been taking no precautions whatsoever, hadn't discussed any, and I had the feeling that the matter had already been decided. Eventually the three musketeers drifted into the cottage for drinks and biscuits. Frances and I sat together as always, and I reflected how enjoyable this all was.

It turned out that David and Esther were well into the plans for relocation. There was a buyer for the pawn part of the London shop, and David and Esther had an eye on a location for their nearby place. I asked about jewellery repairs; it seemed there was a possibility of a partnership with a watch sales/repair shop owner, although those negotiations were complex and under way.

Frances mentioned our journey tomorrow and its purpose. Our friends were unanimous that the Board was interested and that there were problems. To my surprise everyone else seemed to think me capable of dealing with these. Esther asked me how much teaching I would have to do, and how much time it would take. I replied, "It can't be more than I was doing at that day school I was substituting in: the work was crushing and the pay half what the Dorset school promises." Frances added, "And that doesn't count the house." I nodded. I said, "If the problems are business problems, I think I can deal with those: I've essentially been in a business through university."

Everyone agreed. This brought up the party this Sunday week. The proposed menu was approved, although Eddie, seconded by Christine, thought biscuits should also be served. Frances and I asked for, and got, suggestions as to what biscuits in particular. We noted these. I asked, "Pickles?" No one objected but these, I judged, didn't really go with the rest of the bill of fare.

All the talk of food led to our being served at table. The meal, reminiscent of the food served at the wedding, was very well received. In fact, Eddie and I suggested visits on a weekly or even daily basis. David and Esther smiled and said we would all be welcome at any time. I said we were sure of that, and raised my glass of ginger beer in toast to our hosts.

Frances and I got up at 5, feeling very sleepy indeed. The fellowship had seduced us all: David and Esther had a new gramophone and some recordings none of the rest of us had heard, so naturally... and the conversation sparkled. Some of Eddie's anecdotes about travels on the Continent were related, all new to the rest of us, and eventually we agreed we all had, absolutely had, to leave, as all of us had jobs or journeys....

Frances and I bathed, cleaned our teeth, I shaved; we dressed in our new clothes and managed, just, to get to the station to catch our train. We nestled together, dozing at times until near the town. No express stop, this: we got off with a handful of others and looked about. A group of six, three women and three men, all in their middle years, advanced towards us.

"Mr and Mrs Dobbs?" asked one man. We acknowledged our identities. They each gave their names, which, in the case of the men, I tried very hard to get straight. We walked away from the station – the school and the house were less than a mile away, we were told – separating into two groups, Frances with the women. We were drawing apart when I heard one of the women mention "Sir Edward". I guessed the distaff side of the interview was in capable hands.

The four of us walked through the school buildings together. Everything looked run down, but then everything at Earl's Cross had looked run down too. I asked how many boarding students there were, and was told 353, that there was room for nearly 500, but enrolment was down. There was also, I noticed, and this was confirmed, some trouble with the roofs, so some rooms were uninhabitable. I got the impression that money for repairs was lacking. I asked about day school students, and was told there were none; the school had never admitted day school students. This was engraved on stone tablets handed down from on high at the dawn of time.

I began to put my oar in, as was my nature. I commented that day school students were among us at Earl's Cross and no one thought anything of it. I added that if enrolment was down, that admission of day school students this coming term, at, say, half tuition, would immediately ease the financial problem. I went on, saying I knew of no pedagogical problem this would cause, and it would also help improve relations between the school and the townspeople. I asked about these, and was not surprised to learn that some of the students were prone to getting into fights with town boys and there were acts of vandalism attributed to the students. The previous headmaster, I was told, had repeatedly lectured the students about this, without solving the problem.

I commented that having a large number of day school students in classes and in sports, and, I added, they should eat lunch with the boarding students, would do much more to ease if not solve those problems than any number of lectures at church parades. I asked if the school had a good reputation academically. My three companions looked a bit affronted but said it certainly had. "Then," said I, "there should be no trouble in getting local boys to enrol; I think at least forty or fifty should do to start."

We had reached a room with chairs round a table and sat down. One of the three – Willis, that was the name – asked if I had been married long. I smiled – I couldn't help that – and said, "One week and four days, eleven days." Another asked if the wedding had been at Millwood. Stourbridge, George Stourbridge, I thought. I replied, "No. We reached what you might call an understanding on a Saturday and married at a registry office the following Friday. We were both of full age and felt it was time we were together." I smiled again. "It has been holiday since for both of us, the first, I believe, in years for both of us."

Silence. The third man, who hadn't spoken before, cleared his throat and said, "We wanted a married man. We've had scandals." I blinked but said nothing. He was clearly referring to the previous headmaster, and I couldn't think of anything more destructive to his authority than becoming known for buggering some of the students. I forced a smile and assured them that I was about as married as it was possible to get.

The man I took to be the leader said their problems were otherwise financial. He said the masters were talking about taking positions at other schools, as the general cost of things had gone up. I nodded and said a reasonable increase should be offered – after all, experience was valuable, and the better masters would certainly have offers. The man said their supplier of foodstuffs was also asking for more money. I asked if I could see what was being charged and for how much. He pulled a sheaf of papers from his pocket and passed it to me, remarking that the school had been using the same supplier for years.

I immediately became alert – these arrangements might be common but were seldom cheap. I looked at the prices, so much a case for tinned peas, so much for milk, etc. The number of tins per case was listed and I made a calculation in my head of the price per tin. I blinked, recalculated and got the same answer. I looked at the prices of loaves of bread and quarts of milk, shook my head and remarked to the three, "My wife and I have been paying about this much at retail. And this fellow," – I checked the name – "wants to increase his prices?" I looked at the overall totals to be supplied over the two terms and said, "For this much business? I am sure there is a supplier in London or elsewhere who can and will offer much better prices." I checked the price for butter. "For that matter, aren't there dairy farms in the neighbourhood? I thought we passed some on the walk here."

The man I thought of as Number Two, Willis, said, "Yes there are. Unfortunately some of our boys apparently have been going out at night and frightening – I think the term is 'running' – the cows." I scowled: interfering with someone's livelihood was unconscionable. I said, "I was thinking we could buy at least butter. I don't know if Pasteurization of milk is done here, but if so, we could buy milk as well locally. Is any cheese made locally?" "Yes, some," Stourbridge answered. "Then cheese also. It should be possible to offer local dairymen somewhat more for a part of their production than they are getting from whomever they are supplying, probably at a lower price to us." I paused, and then went on, "When the students know where their butter, milk, and perhaps cheese are coming from, cutting down on the vandalism as well. As it is, I probably will have to personally apologize to some of the dairymen. Of course, if their sons are enrolled here, that will help as well."

Silence. Then the leader – Armitage, that was his name – said that one of the history masters had retired, leaving two. I said, "I could share with them. Three history masters sound about right for a school of this size. I think a course in Physical Sciences should be offered to the sixth formers, if a master can be found." I was thinking how useful that course had been to me, including saving my life. No one objected. Armitage suggested a tour round the kitchens and dining area, then the offices. I thought that a good idea and we went into part of the main building I hadn't seen before.

We went through the kitchens. I inspected these closely, surprising my escorts. They didn't realize how much experience I had had cooking. Things seemed somewhat dated but workable, storage looked adequate, but I would have liked to meet the cooks. With more day school students eating lunch – I thought this important in bringing them together with the boarding students – it would get a bit crowded. I asked if any of the masters ate at the evening meals and was told they did, turn about. I mentioned that I thought it a good idea, masters, perhaps with their wives, being present, at school expense of course. One of the Governors said the masters were charged for the meals they ate. I thought that, since attendance at meals was part of their duties, the school should pay.

We moved to the offices, which were unremarkable. Two or three women were there doing clerical things, also a middle-sized man who did not look very welcoming. He was introduced to me as the acting headmaster, which I grasped was the reason for his attitude. We moved off and I asked if he had wanted the headmaster position. He had, but was not seriously considered. He was a maths master, not well qualified, but well acquainted with school operations. I thought as we moved to meet the entire Board that an experienced, knowledgeable man was of value. Returned to the ranks, he was likely to become a pain in the arse if he didn't leave outright; otherwise, just no help to me.

The Board consisted of seven men, all middle aged or older, not welcoming to change. We were introduced and again I tried to fix their names in my head. Armitage told the others what I had proposed, and as I rather expected, received criticism. Admission of day school boys had never been thought necessary, why now? I pointed out the need for more revenue right away, this fall, and my own experience – here I was exaggerating, there weren't that many day school boys at Earl's Cross, since the town was so small – was that there were not only no problems but that better relations between town and gown were also worthwhile. I stressed that, aside from the policy being new here, it was nowhere else unusual, that I knew of.

One Board member, Foster, whom I (privately) dubbed The Fossil, asserted the current boarding students opposed such a policy. I asked how could this be known, if they were all ignorant of the proposed change. I added that the overwhelming majority of boys would be inclined to wait and see. I reiterated the need for more revenue, that it was too late to raise tuition for fall term, and, as politely as possible, asked The Fossil how he proposed dealing with the revenue problem, especially since repairs to the roof of the dormitory that were immediately needed would prevent admission of more boarding students even if applicants existed. The Fossil, after some harrumphing, suggested a circular letter to the Old Boys asking for donations.

I countered by saying that such a letter would be much better received, that is, more money sent, if it were for some specific project. I suggested a War Memorial Library and general study area be constructed. There was, I thought, a clear need for such, otherwise the boys had only their rooms to study and work. A library, in my opinion, promoted study by reducing distractions and increasing focus.

Noting that the rest of the Board seemed taken by my points, I asked The Fossil if he had previously prepared such a letter. He had, he said, several times, and these letters had been successful. I asked him if he would then be willing to prepare a letter, asking for donations for a War Memorial Library and study area. "Hall" said someone. I amended my proposal to "Study Hall". Everyone seemed favourable, and The Fossil asked if I wanted to sign the letter. I said no, I hadn't gotten the job yet and anyway no one would recognize my name. They would recognize his, so, if he were willing to prepare the letter, he should sign it. The question of admission of day school students appeared settled by default.

Armitage then brought up my proposal about asking food suppliers to bid for our business. Two or three members seemed to feel such a procedure disloyal. I weighed in, although very politely, with unwonted restraint, that the current supplier was, in my view, judging by the prices charged, I wouldn't say swindling the school, but was certainly taking undue advantage of the previous policy. I was certain a great deal of money could be saved, without any reduction in quality of goods. I added that if the current supplier really wanted to continue supplying us, let him reduce his prices. Loyalty, I said, should go both ways. I was not sure my point was well reasoned, but it was well received. Again, the new policy was approved.

I then mentioned using local farmers for some of our food. Advantages of greater freshness, almost certainly lower prices, and improved relations between the farmers and the boys, especially if some of the day school boys were the sons of the farmers, were, I said, compelling. When I asked, I found again that some cheese was produced locally and that the milk was pasteurized in some farms. There seemed general agreement.

I went on to say that the masters should receive a reasonable raise in pay, noting that experience in teaching was very valuable, and it made no sense to allow experienced, worthwhile men to leave to be replaced by inexperienced and possibly less able substitutes. I felt such an <u>investment</u> – I stressed the word – in proven competence was well worth while. The question of the acting headmaster was related to this point. I asked the Board to create a new position, Assistant Headmaster, for the man now discharging the duties, with a raise in pay to £200 per year and an office. I noted that, whomever they hired as headmaster, unless it was someone from within, the new headmaster would be completely unfamiliar with the people and procedures of the school, and this would cause a host of perhaps minor but certainly distracting problems. Keeping the man they had, the <u>experienced</u> – again, I stressed the word – man they had, would greatly help the new headmaster. This man would be the right hand of the new headmaster. The Board made no demur. There was silence. Then Armitage, glancing around, looked at me and invited me to lunch.

The lunch was, apparently, catered. The ladies, including Frances, who looked little short of spectacular in her posh togs and the necklace, bracelet and pin she was wearing, were already seated and eating. Frances seemed to be the centre of attention, graciousness and poise itself. We exchanged smiles.

There were sandwiches, made, I was told, of local cheese. I made a point of eating some. Not bad. Drink was, as always, a problem for me. I politely declined what looked to be, almost certainly was, port, also the scotch, and reluctantly sipped some tea. There were biscuits, also not bad, and some rolls. I wasn't able to sit near Frances.

One or two of the Board members called me Major, but I objected, saying Mister was formal enough, that although I thought I had given good service in the Army, I was a thorough civilian at heart. I said I wanted nothing more than to live with my wife – gesturing toward Frances – and do my teaching. Since we had by this time finished eating, although a few were still drinking, and not tea, Armitage suggested I go with Frances to look at the house. I guessed they wanted to discuss my application, but I was also curious, so thanked him, arose, collected Frances and left to see the house.

This was about half a mile from the school. We walked arm in arm. It was pleasant weather, "halcyon days" I said to Frances. I asked her how she liked the house. She said she liked it very much. Everything seemed in good repair, there was a gas line for the boiler, a chicken house and a hot house. No walnut trees though. I sighed. "They can be purchased, Matthew," said Frances. "It's not the same," I affected a pout.

To our right were low hills with some trees that looked inviting for a ramble. Frances read my mind, saying that one of the ladies said there were several footpaths, ideal for walks. I looked at Frances, commenting that rambles with her over hills would be wonderful. She smiled in reply as we reached the house.

It was of two stories. The lower had a good-sized kitchen, which I inspected. It looked very adequate. There was a dining room, a bit formal. I figured Frances and I would probably dine in the kitchen at a table there, but we would, always assuming I got the job, be giving formal dinners as well. There was a large room with a good-sized fireplace and many bookshelves, mostly empty. A bathroom completed the first floor. The second consisted of four bedrooms, each with beds, although no bedding, and two closets. The furnishings were worn but serviceable: we could move in and live there immediately.

Frances said there was a maid of all work who took care of the place, and a gardener-groundskeeper employed by the school who took care of the garden, hothouse and chicken house. At this, I moved outside to look at these. Miraculously for a hothouse near a school, all the panes were intact, but there was little inside. The garden also had few things growing, although I saw some carrots. The soil was unimpressive. I wondered what was done with the chicken dung. I mentioned this to Frances, saying that when well-rotted, it made the most marvellous fertilizer.

I saw no pile. Looking further, there was a ditch or ravine about fifty feet from the chicken house. I walked to it, Frances following. Looking down into it, I saw a patch of very rank vegetation, said "Aha" and pointed this out to Frances. "This is where it is dumped. Once it rots, it fertilizes any nearby plants. I will have to get a spade and bucket and haul the stuff back." Frances said, "I want to grow some flowers in pots." I said, "A mixture of one part of the rotted dung – it doesn't smell at that point – to two or three of the soil should grow anything." Frances nodded. We began walking back, arm in arm. A cat, an orange "tigger" as I called such creatures, perched on an upturned clay pot. I pointed my finger at it, and the cat cautiously touched its nose to the fingertip. I took advantage of this complaisance by rubbing the top of the animal's head and scratching its neck before it suddenly realized I was being, in its view, overfamiliar, and ran off.

Frances asked if I had had any pets. "No formal ones," I replied, "but 'no cat left unmolested' was my watchword and motto." Frances asked, "No dogs?" I said, "No. I am not sure why. Perhaps because of the chickens. There once was a puppy that came begging at the kitchen door. I fed it of course. It seemed very friendly but it died soon after, I don't know why. Mrs Christianson thought it had worms."

"What sort of dog was it?" asked Frances. "Just a stray. Like me," I replied. Frances said, "Well this stray has found a home." I said, "Does this mean I get fed regularly?" Frances said, "Provided you prepare the meals." I had no reply to that, and we finished the walk back, silent but together.

Everyone was sitting where we had left them. They all seemed genial and relaxed, which I took as a favourable sign. Sure enough, Armitage asked me how I liked the house and grounds. I said we both liked what we saw very much. Glancing about, he then turned to us and said, "The Board unanimously agreed to offer you the headmaster's position." I replied, after glancing at Frances, "Then I accept your offer. Understand I am not planning or foreseeing presiding over a failed school. With the measures we discussed, I am certain our finances will be on a sound basis, and that makes everything else possible. Be sure I will make every effort in my power to justify the trust you have placed in me. And I thank you all." Everyone, even The Fossil, seemed pleased. Frances and I sat down. She had some port. I had more tea. Oh, well.

Frances and I were pressed together in our compartment. Because of the season, our train was crowded, but neither of us was complaining. I had basically given the Board and the clerical staff their marching orders regarding admission of day school students and requests to suppliers of foodstuffs for bids for our business. I was assured many families in the town and farms about wanted to send their sons to a local school, so I hoped for at least 50 day students. I figured this would be enough; more, and we could get the roof of the dormitory repaired. The Acting Headmaster readily agreed to become Assistant Headmaster at the salary offered, so I would have a knowledgeable man in my corner.

Frances was very pleased I had gotten the job. I said, "We got the job." She had spent the afternoon talking to the nurse as well as the ladies of the Board, and, I was very sure, winning everyone's enthusiastic approval. We would return late but triumphant. Now we had to plan for departure: we were to return tomorrow week, so aside from the party Sunday, we had to pack and ship everything.

* * *

We got up, eventually, disgracefully late, as I had pointed out at 9:30, 11 and noon. We sat at the kitchen table, worn, happy, lethargic, and thinking as little as possible. Eventually, we decided on toasted sandwiches but with the somewhat tarter cheese than I usually used that Frances suggested. I prepared the sandwiches while Frances set the table, poured drinks, and, after dressing, getting the mail.

We ate the modified sandwiches in silence. Then I looked at Frances and said, "You first." She replied she liked the sandwiches and thought the different cheese an improvement, although she hoped I liked it, too. I stared at her, trying to be solemn, and then we both began to smile. I said I also thought the experiment a success, so we would use that cheese in future.

She handed me a note from her aunt, Mrs Lark. We were invited to call Wednesday, tomorrow. The aunt said she had been out of town and wanted to receive us earlier but hoped we could visit then. There was no time to reply by mail so we would just find a telephone to tell her we would appear at the time indicated. Frances told me her aunt had married a much older man, although the marriage was, she thought, a happy one. They had one child, Geoffrey, who lived in Australia, whom Frances had never met. Mrs Lark had been left with the house and some money which she had invested, apparently quite successfully. Frances proposed asking her for advice on investing our money, since we didn't have to consider buying a property now. I thought she was looking a bit apprehensively at me, perhaps thinking she was calling my financial acumen into question.

I sat thinking, and then leaned towards her. "I confess to having mixed feelings. On one hand, I have been in business – two businesses, actually – some years, and was successful, or successful enough. As a headmaster, I am apparently in the position of managing a business, I hope successfully. And I talked to Eddie and Christine about investing the money. They thought securities, shares in dividend-paying corporations, limited corporations, were the best strategy. I should say," looking at Frances, "I am not a gambler. I risked my life for that money, the larger part of it anyway, and will settle for a reasonable return provided it is from a safe, secure investment." Frances nodded.

"On the other," I continued, "they had no specific corporations to recommend. I think their money comes from trust funds; they make no such decisions themselves. And if your aunt was so successful, perhaps not surprising, given the level of ability in the women of your family I have met," smiling at Frances, "I would be very foolish not to listen to what she has to say. Besides, her advice would be, not self-serving or even disinterested, but designed to make us as successful as she has been, so I will listen very attentively indeed to her recommendations." Frances smiled and reached across the table to take my hand, which I in turn pressed.

"On a related topic," I said, "I need to make a new will. Right now, David and Eddie are my heirs, although were anything to happen to me, I daresay they would waive their claims. One more thing to remember to do." I thought some more. "You need to be part of any such discussion with your aunt, since, if anything does happen to me, you must be fully informed as to where the money is invested." Frances squeezed my hand and smiled. She had such a warm smile, I thought.

I said, "Once the new will is made, I will announce to Eddie and David I've cut them out, and will come up with some reasons, hopefully ones I can relate at the party." Frances began to laugh, and said, "I am not sure I want to hear what sort of excuse you will come up with, but am resigned to having to listen to something outrageous." "Would I do that?" I asked, "What a reputation to have." I looked at the table. "We need to do the washing up."

Frances lay nestled with me in our bed. We hadn't done the washing up or anything else we were supposed to do or could do. I reflected that, as newlyweds, we were expected, even required by iron social custom and usage to behave like animals in heat, and, as I had mentioned to Armitage and the other two Board members, we were on the first real holiday we each had probably ever had. And it was so delightful, being in bed with Frances.

She stirred. I gently kissed her forehead. She said, "Matthew, the wives of the Board members I talked to say your predecessor had to leave because of some scandal. Did you hear that?" "One of the Board said they wanted a married man because they had had scandals. I didn't ask for any details. I could guess enough. Did you enjoy talking to the ladies?" Remembering how her sister had objected to idle conversation, I wondered how Frances would deal with the wives. She would certainly be polite, as it was her duty to support me however she could, but I didn't want her bored or irritated by such a duty.

After a short silence, Frances replied, "Some of the women seemed a little awed by my pedigree, but I tried to set everyone at ease. The wife of one of the Board, Mrs Armitage, is a doctor." "Indeed?" I said. "Her husband is a magistrate." "He seemed to be in charge," I said. Frances continued, "We talked about her practice. I think, depending on our circumstances, perhaps someday I can work as her nurse." "If you wish, of course. I am sure you would be very helpful to her or to anyone."

Silence again. Then, "Another of the wives helps her husband run a nursery. That is what put the idea of flowers in my head." "Do they stock tomatoes?" I asked. "I'm sure they do. Matthew, what happens to the eggs those chickens produce?" I said, "I think I can guess. However, judging from the number, we should be able to have omelettes when we choose and perhaps hard-boil a few to take with us when we go on rambles."

"That would be nice. I look forward to that." "So do I." More silence, and then I said, "Frances, I am apprehensive about asking you this, but how much if any entertaining are you willing to help with? I suspect we may be expected to do a significant amount, but I won't burden you with any tasks you find uncongenial." Frances stirred. "We are a team, Matthew. I am prepared to hold a party or dinner every week if you think it necessary. Why do you ask? I don't mind parties, not at all." I said, "I remember your sister, in her letters to me, complaining about having to go on country house weekends, especially having to talk to people about commonplace things." Silence. Then Frances said, "I don't recall her ever objecting to going to any such places. Perhaps she was trying to reassure you. I don't care for idle, pointless chatter myself, but I enjoyed talking to the Board wives. I doubt any of the women we will be having over will be that empty-headed." Silence. Then I said, "How many should we have at a time? I never looked that closely at the dining table." Frances said, "While we could probably have ten guests over, I think six or eight makes for better conversation."

Frances continued, "It was a bit embarrassing, being treated as an aristocrat, as someone special, because growing up I never had such a sense." "You are very special indeed to me." Frances kissed me, snuggled closer – if that were possible – and we dozed off. The past two or three days had been enjoyable, interesting but taxing.

We were to take the Underground to Aunt Lydia's. In all the time I had been in London, I had never taken the Underground. Frances asked why, and I said I supposed I simply didn't want to be in a tunnel. However, I said I was sure I would be all right: it was simply a new experience with her. So we went.

Aunt Lydia's house looked much the same, since – when was it? – five years ago: everything well kept up. Mrs Lark came to the door herself and received us in person – hadn't there been a maid? I reminded her that "a satisfied customer always comes back." She laughed, seemed very pleased to see us together, and Frances and I sat down together on the couch. We sat as we always did, close together, my right arm behind her, her left hand with the sapphire ring on my right knee.

A maid came in with a tray of biscuits and cups of tea – there was indeed a maid – and we ate a biscuit or two and had some tea, although I managed to pour a fair amount of cream in and add sugar as well before I had to drink it.

Frances told her aunt about my job. Mrs Lark was im-pressed: the position, the salary and use of a house together made her nod in approval. Frances cautioned that there were problems, but that I had proposed solutions to these. Mrs Lark looked at me and I explained what these were. Again, nods of approval. "And you will be teaching, also," she said. "Yes," I said, "upper form history."

"Did you always want to be a teacher, Matthew?" Mrs Lark asked. She, and no doubt Frances, was expecting a conventional reply, but madness seized me. "A pirate, actually," I said. Frances's head swivelled towards me. I had to continue, "Or a gigolo. I am not sure what a gigolo is or does, but when I heard the term as a child, I knew that was my goal. And if anyone can tell me how one goes about ... becoming ..." Here I had to stop, as Frances was hitting me with a cushion. This provoked a brief wrestling match in which I secured the cushion, leaving us face to face, so we kissed and embraced, laughing – but I kept hold of the cushion.

Mrs Lark was reduced to hysterics, but eventually was able to ask Frances if I was always this outrageous. "Certainly not," I objected, as Frances said, "It's usually after making love." This caused me to turn sharply towards her, then to look desperately about the room, searching for something to say. Eventually I suggested weakly that there was a cobweb on the ceiling, no, just a shadow of a branch....

We eventually all calmed down, although Frances would occasionally move her hand towards the cushion, prompting me to jerk it farther away, which made Aunt Lydia, as I was beginning to call her, helpless with laughter each time. Frances finally broached the question of investments, asking Aunt Lydia for her advice. I told aunt Lydia the approximate total we expected to have to invest, about £4500.

At this, we adjourned to the dining table. (I left the cushion on the couch but sat between it and Frances.) Aunt Lydia began by saying that money was, after all, merely a means to an end, to enable one to do or get what one wants. Frances and I nodded. Aunt Lydia went on to say her investments were ones that she didn't want to worry about or even think about. Nods from both of us. She then produced a sheet of paper with a list of firms on it, three marked with X's – a steel mill, a coal company and a railway. She said she found those three unsatisfactory – she didn't think they had much of a future. The others were large, many made things people ate or drank, often worldwide; several did business and were traded internationally – mostly tea, beer, scotch, and chocolate, all well-known firms. Two were American. There were nine of them. Frances and I again nodded. Aunt Lydia said she thought investing in as many good firms as possible was the safest course. I glanced at Frances: her aunt was making, I thought, good sound sense. I commented we could buy about £500 of each if divided evenly. Mrs Lark then produced a card with a broker's name on it. She recommended the man because he would sell us the shares we requested without trying to promote others. "I had to train him," she said dryly, "so be sure you mention my name." Frances and I nodded once more.

Aunt Lydia then produced a newspaper with share prices and dividends, etc., printed on it in type so small Frances and I had to squint to see the numbers. Aunt Lydia explained what each number meant. Frances and I did some calculations, how many shares of each we could buy and how much in dividends we could expect. We looked at each other, then at Aunt Lydia. "These should bring in a private income about equal to the one the school pays," I said. Frances nodded. Aunt Lydia reminded us that the dividends and share prices would tend to go up with the general cost of things, so we wouldn't have to worry about that either. Frances and I sat back, pleased. Frances, after exchanging glances with me, said, "We will buy these then, as soon as possible." I nodded: no reason to hang about. We thanked her for her advice, said it would be followed. Mrs Lark cautioned that all investments were gambles, the future could not be precisely or sometimes generally foretold, but these were as safe and reasonable as any she knew. We rose and went to the door.

There Mrs Lark beamed at Frances and I, arm in arm. "I am glad one of my nieces managed to secure you, Matthew." I was taken aback, but said, pressing Frances's hand, "I am very firmly and happily secured." We exchanged smiles and Frances and I walked away.

"Gigolo, indeed," she said. "It was just a childhood ambition," I protested. Frances shook her head and we both began laughing.

I had gotten up to empty my bladder and was returning to our bedroom when I heard Frances crying out, "Nolan. Nolan. Matthew, please help. Please, Matthew." I quickly moved to the bedside, took Frances in my arms and said, "Frances, dear, I am with you. It's me, it's Matthew. We're together. It's only a bad dream, a nightmare." Frances's eyes opened and she grabbed me, shaking. Eventually, I asked, "The same dream?" Frances said, "Yes, but I thought you could help, so I called for you." "And here I am. And shall remain."

Frances curled up beside me and I held her tightly. Gradually she relaxed and began to sleep. I lay thinking. I wasn't jealous – how could I be jealous of a dead man? Yet her feelings for him remained, naturally enough. They must have gone deep, and while I was sure she loved me, and was slightly encouraged by the fact that she called for me this time, I wondered about the depth of her feeling for me. I felt slightly ashamed at wanting to displace Rutter's memory, it really was selfish of me, yet the feeling was there.

The rest of the day after leaving Aunt Lydia's had gone very quickly: a trip to warn our banker of our plans, then a call on the broker. It was amazing how quickly the transaction went: £4,500 spent in less than half an hour. As I remarked later to Frances, we spent four times as long getting a few shillings' worth of meat for pasties (her request for the evening meal).

* * *

Thursday we scurried about: looking for a lawyer, a firm to move the boxes of books – for our party, we wanted to clear the floor as much as possible – and consulting with Christine on what sorts of things to provide. I felt Frances was busying herself in these errands to distract us both from her latest nightmare. I kept putting my arm about her, trying to comfort and reassure her. I could not be sure how successful I was.

Christine mentioned that scotch would probably be appreci-ated by some guests, besides the wine. We got her recommendation and went to a spirits store. On the way, I remembered the name she gave us as the brand the tank commander was drinking. I told Frances the story, to divert her. She was quite amused, but wondered if the man was actually going to drink the entire case. I shook my head, explaining that the ways of tank men were beyond the comprehension of ordinary mortals, or even me.

In the store, I discovered that the stuff did indeed retail at a guinea a bottle, actually a little more. I bought one, then Frances and I got some appropriate glasses and decanters, very decorative but pricey. We told each other we would need them, entertaining at the school. We needed some other things for that purpose and spent much of the rest of the day buying them.

* * *

Saturday we began preparations for the party. We got more meat and walnuts and a few other things, then, after lunch, began cracking the nuts, feeding bits to each other to ensure they were of good quality, or so we assured each other.

The boxes had been taken and were on their way. We had telegraphed Armitage, warning him – he had volunteered to be our contact with the school. And we had a new will, although Eddie and David had only been demoted, not cut out. If Frances and I both died without issue, Frances's brother Richard, Eddie and David would divide our estate. A bit grim but realistic perhaps.

Sunday we began the cooking. Frances did the measuring, I the mixing for the cakes, and we were able to bake both at one time. Despite having two people working on the cakes, we actually got through rather efficiently, I thought. Then the pasties: I began preparing the bits of meat and onions and mashing the garlic, working as fast as I could to cook them up quickly. I set the cooked meat and onions aside and began cutting up the carrots and potatoes. What measuring was needed, Frances did. In fact she began mixing the dough for the shells while I was doing the cutting.

When the first batch of pasties went into the oven, Frances and I collapsed together on the couch, each with a drink. "Two more," I said. Frances nodded, and then rested her head on my shoulder. I smiled and kissed her. She smiled back. We were a good team after all, I thought.

With the second batch in the oven, Frances and I began setting the table, putting out the wine and scotch, decanters, glasses and all, biscuits in two bowls, all on our new tablecloth with our new napkins and tablewear.

The third batch allowed Frances to bathe and dress. She chose the bluish dress she wore the night of Eddie and Christine's party, a bracelet and a brooch. On removing the third batch, I bathed, shaved again, cologned myself into social tolerability and dressed. Our guests would arrive at four, and it was now a quarter of. Close, but we had made it.

* * *

I proposed the now customary toast as we all sat around the table, drinks in hand: "To absent comrades." Then I asked David to propose the toast he had described to Eddie and me years ago: "*Lachaim.*" Both were drunk with feeling. I began serving the pasties, but Frances insisted on helping, bringing plates over to me so it was done quickly. We served two each initially, figuring more would be desired shortly. So it proved.

I had figured that a few pasties would be left over, but had to give the last to the Regular and his wife, dividing it between them. Frances and I then served the cake, with more wine, although I saw three or four of the guests with the scotch. With David's help, I got Eddie to give his hilarious account of his encounter with one of Wagner's operas at Bayreuth. Since Eddie tends to modify his stories each time he relates them, I was anticipating amusement, although David and, I assumed, Christine would have heard the basic story before, as had I. Christine, however, had apparently never heard the story before, and Eddie's improvements had all of us laughing. When Eddie finished, I solemnly assured everyone that I was certain there were elements of truth in Eddie's story.

At this, Eddie suggested I tell the infamous story of the Place With A Golden Loo Seat, with David's enthusiastic seconding. I glared at them both, but Christine, who must have heard Eddie speak of the story, also insisted I tell it. I protested that it was an indecent story and that there were ladies present and also women, which got everyone laughing, at which I realized what a foolish thing I had said. I became lofty, saying I declined to contribute to the degeneracy of the times, to the further erosion of moral standards, but Frances fixed me with her gaze. "Matthew," she said. I looked at her and crossed myself. I heard the Regular ask if I was Catholic, at which David said, "On occasion." Frances, struggling to maintain a stern expression, said, "Matthew, we all insist on hearing this story, without further persiflage."

"Oh, very well. You have all been warned." No one seemed deterred by this, so I pushed back my chair to free my hands – I like to gesture when telling this story – and told it. I gave the last line, got up and poured myself a ginger beer and sat down again. Everyone, including David and Eddie, who had heard it before, was laughing without reserve, so I concluded I hadn't significantly lowered moral standards after all.

I then proceeded to tell Eddie and David they had been demoted from primary heirs to secondary, on account (here I looked pointedly at Christine and Esther) of their animalistic behaviour – which, I went on to say, were an inspiration to the rest of us. More laughter; Eddie, Christine, David and Esther no less than the rest.

* * *

Frances and I collected plates, glasses and tableware for the washing up. The party had gone into Monday, which indicated it was successful. All the pasties, nearly all of both cakes and the biscuits, and, most surprising to me, all but about an inch of the scotch were consumed. I asked Frances who was drinking the scotch – I thought people would mostly drink the wine. Frances said everyone save us. I wondered if we were going to have to stock the stuff at the school. At better than a guinea a bottle, it would make us very popular and significantly poorer. Frances agreed on both counts.

We stood together doing the washing up. The napkins and tablecloth required washing and I was beginning to feel the weight of our early Tuesday departure. We began discussing what needed to be done. We decided to contact the estate agent to be sure the business of the potatoes didn't return to haunt us and to inform her of our departure more than a month early. I didn't expect to get any money back – I had paid two months in advance – but we needed to arrange to get the keys to the flat back.

We needed to wash some clothes as well. And pack. And decide what could be shipped and what had to be carried with us. And, once the washing up was done, we were tired. It had been enormously enjoyable, seeing our friends once more, but it had made for a very long day.

The estate agent was pleasantly sympathetic. She said to leave the keys on the table; she would pick them up tomorrow morning, and, I guessed, check on the condition we left the flat in. She said our efforts to contact the owners were sufficient. More, she offered to refund one month's rent. We were surprised but agreeable and I gave her the address of the school and my name: "Matthew Dobbs," I said. "Matthew E. Dobbs," corrected Frances, and the agent wrote "Matthew E. Dobbs, Esquire, Headmaster" on the envelope.

* * *

We got up at 5 AM again. "The last time," I promised Frances (and myself). We had re-boxed the wine, packed the table things, new bed linens, etc., in a box recovered from behind a spirits store and shipped it all. This left the re-boxed gramophone, Frances's shopping bag with our remaining groceries, and four pieces of luggage. We had contracted with a taxi firm to pick us and our goods and chattels up at 6:30. It was just short of that and we stood in the flat facing each other. I said, "I am very sorry to cut our honeymoon short, dearest." Frances said, "I rather think our honeymoon will go on for the rest of our lives together." I smiled. "My wife, the incorrigible romantic." Frances replied, "Who is married to another." We embraced and kissed and I said, "True. Quite true." Then we began moving everything outside to wait for the taxi.

* * *

We had gotten to the station with enough time to fee a porter to help us move everything to an empty compartment on the train. We settled in. Despite the season, no one else joined us. We sat together in silence a minute, and then Frances turned to me and said, "Matthew, the man I told you about: if he had been spared, we would have married and, I daresay, been happy together. But I want you to understand that the man of my dreams, the love of my life, is here: it is you." I couldn't speak but held her and kissed her. After this, she added, "And I don't ever want you to feel you had to settle for second-best." I swallowed, and said, "On the contrary, my darling. Quite the contrary." And we embraced and kissed again as the train began to move.

Our love does us call

To venture together.

Our path yet untrod,

The music, the journey are all.

Lightning Source UK Ltd.
Milton Keynes UK
UKOW05f0625291117
313553UK00012B/615/P